This Thing of Ours

This Thing of Ours

FREDERICK JOSEPH

CANDLEWICK PRESS

First edition 2025

Library of Congress Control Number: pending
ISBN 978-1-5362-3346-9

SHD 30 29 28 27 26 25
10 9 8 7 6 5 4 3 2 1

Printed in Chelsea, MI, USA

This book was typeset in Arno, Avenir, and Gerbera.

Candlewick Press
99 Dover Street
Somerville, Massachusetts 02144

www.candlewick.com

EU Authorized Representative: HackettFlynn Ltd.,
36 Cloch Choirneal, Balrothery, Co. Dublin, K32 C942, Ireland.
EU@walkerpublishinggroup.com

For the children of Yonkers,
who dream in the language of steel and sky,
who turn sidewalks into symphonies
and find the rhythm in every shadow.
This is for you—
the poets of playgrounds,
the architects of hope.
May your stories rise like the sun,
sharp and glorious,
cutting through the fog of any doubt.
You are the future,
and the future is a song.

It All Happens So Fast

"Of course I'm angry! Look what they're doing! Why *wouldn't* I be angry?"

My words fill the sweat-laced air of our cramped shoulder-to-shoulder huddle, an open question to Coach Ryan, who's looking at me like he's examining some sort of knot he can't untie. It's one of those tense time-outs when every second seems to vanish like smoke in the wind.

I sit down in a chair to give my legs a moment of rest as Coach Ryan's answer rolls in on the heavy breath of late-game exhaustion. "You can be mad, Ossie," he says, his voice echoing with the hard clang of missed shots and offensive fouls. "But stop trying to get even—get ahead. Let's win the damn game!"

"I hear you, Coach! But look at these scratches on my arm!" My voice is thick with frustration. "These white boys are trying to hurt me, and the refs are either blind or racist, 'cause they haven't been calling anything!"

Coach Ryan frowns at me. "You know I support most of the Black Lives Matter stuff, Ossie. But not everything is about race. You've been acting like a hothead out there, swinging your elbows around like you're trying to start some shit."

"If those white boys weren't playing dirty and trying to hurt me, I wouldn't have to swing my elbows—" I begin, snapping with the irritation of someone who was nearly clotheslined on multiple layups. But my bench-warming teammate Patrick decides to jump into the conversation.

"The problem isn't about them being white. It's about you shooting four for fifteen while everyone swears you're the next Kevin Durant or something," Patrick says snidely.

Patrick always knows how to push my buttons. How many times have I imagined shutting his pasty redheaded ass up? Too many to count. And yet I've always held back. Until now.

"Why are you speaking, Patrick? You barely even play. If your daddy didn't work for Nike, you wouldn't even be on the team!" I glare at him, years of suppressed dislike rising to the surface. "You should be thanking me for carrying your bum ass to the state championship!"

The blunt honesty of my words bounces off everyone in the huddle, exposing more than just a disagreement. Patrick jumps in my face as if he'll hit me if I say anything else. His six-nine frame is significantly bigger than mine, at six five, but I'm not afraid of him. I spring from my chair to meet him where he stands.

"Enough!" Coach Ryan's eyes dart between Patrick and me, then to the court, where Milwood High is locked in for the final three minutes of the game. "We're down seven, and we only have a few minutes to turn this thing around. So cut the shit and focus on what matters—winning this game and going to State!"

As he speaks, his gaze sweeps over everyone on the team, but when it reaches me, it lingers for a few extra seconds. We both know he's talking to me. I'm the one who needs to get us to where we're trying to go. The only reason Coach Ryan recruited me. The only reason Braxton Academy gave me a full ride. The state championship.

As the gravity of Coach Ryan's words settles around us, the silence that follows is a beast in and of itself. Each second is a striking clock hand, a testament to the moments that are about to live forever. Patrick and I exchange reluctant nods, silently acknowledging that our issues can wait, there's a more important battle to win.

"All right, everyone, bring it in," Coach says. We huddle together, each hand falling over the other, forming a tower of unity and solidarity.

"Remember the game plan! Be smart—don't let them get in your heads! I want to see you hustling on every possession! Play Braxton basketball! If you hear me, give me a 'Bears' on three!" he bellows, a general leading his troops into war. "One, two, three!"

In unison, we roar, "Bears!"

When our voices die down, the others seem left with a sense of urgency and renewed focus. But when the game starts again, my head still isn't in it. It's like I'm stuck in a whirlpool of anger and frustration over how they've been fouling me while no one cares.

On our first few plays after the time-out, I know if I try driving for a layup, they're just going to foul me, so I settle for jumpers like I have since the first quarter. My teammates are doing their best, feeding me good looks, but I'm missing shots I normally make in my sleep. Brick after brick, like I'm trying to build a house, while Milwood extends their lead. As they lay up another two points, the score is 69 to 78, with a little over two minutes left in the game.

Looking around, I see everyone's hope of a state championship appearance fading away. My hope of honoring my father's legacy disappearing right along with it.

Our home crowd's collective sigh, heavy with disappointment, washes over me. The murmurs carry the sound of people giving up—including my girlfriend, Laura, who is wearing the look of someone who doesn't believe. Along with my blue-and-white letterman jacket. Everyone is writing us off.

Well, everyone except Grandma Alice—who has never missed one of my games and probably knows more about the sport than most NBA fans.

Her voice, usually soft with a comforting southern tinge, cuts through the tense gym. "Enough jumpers! If they want to get physical, give them something they can't handle!" As her shouts reach me, I look her way. She's at most five foot two but somehow always towers over everyone around her.

When our eyes meet, she says one last thing. This time she isn't yelling. She speaks softly, but she knows I can read her lips.

"Stop playing. Go bust their ass, baby."

A small smile curls at the corners of my mouth as I nod at her. She returns my gesture, an understanding passing between us. Her words ignite a spark within me, reminding me who the hell I am.

It's time to show them why I'm the third-ranked high school player in the country.

When we get back on offense, I gesture for Tommy, our point guard, to give me the ball. He seems hesitant to trust me, his eyes searching around, considering other teammates to pass to. But I'm not about to let this moment slip away.

"Trust me, I got this!" I yell, my voice carrying an assurance that eases him.

Tommy tosses the ball to me. Taking control, I wave my team-mates away, making space for an isolation play. The audience in the gym holds its breath as I square off against my defender. If I miss this and they score, the game is probably over.

As I dribble, my mind starts plotting, calculating the perfect moment to strike. Anticipation builds as I wait for the defender to commit. I can tell from his stance that he's bracing for me to shoot, believing I'm hoping to avoid another harsh foul. Little does he know that's exactly what I want.

With a swift head fake, I trick my defender into believing I'm about to launch a three. The moment he takes the bait, I drive hard into the paint. As my defender recovers, he barrels into me from behind. But I'm already exploding into the air. Their center, trying to stop me, jumps with me and delivers a direct hit to my mouth. But it doesn't faze me.

This is the kind of explosive, gritty, relentless basketball I learned playing on the cracked courts of South Yonkers, where I matched up against men who didn't hesitate to knock a twelve-year-old on his ass. Grandma Alice was right: this is something these rich suburban kids can't handle.

As I continue to rise, the ball is cocked back for a one-handed dunk that lands with resounding authority, dropping their center flat on his ass and sending our home crowd into a thunderous roar. Even the referees can't deny me this time as the whistle signals my march to the free-throw line.

"Y'all thought that shit was sweet, huh?"

My words aren't about ego; they're about affirmation. I'm here.

My chest heaves with the thrill of the fight as the blood from my busted lip stains my jersey. Our assistant coach, Jerry, runs over, his face tight with worry. But when he notices I'm fine, he sighs with relief and dabs away at the fresh streak of blood with his towel. Then he's back off to the sideline.

A deep breath, and the shot. The ball sails through the air and slips through the hoop as if it were destined to do just that. Their lead, once seeming impossible to overcome, now feels more like an obstacle that will inevitably be out of our way soon. Just six more points to go.

Milwood, obviously flustered and eager to regain control of the game, gets careless with the ball. Tommy comes alive and steals it right from their point guard's hands. Without hesitation, he sends a bullet pass my way. I look at the rim, and something has changed. It no longer seems like a small target at the end of a long tunnel but more like an ocean, vast and welcoming. I set my feet and release a three-pointer. The sweet sound of a swish fills the gym as the ball cuts through the net, slicing their lead to just three.

Frustration hangs over the Milwood team like a dark cloud as they try to gather themselves. They hand the moment over to their small forward, who has been leading them the entire game. I can see that he's confident, his eyes burning with determination. I pick him up on a defensive switch. He sees me and smiles, thinking he can dance past me, likely score an easy layup, save his team's lead.

Nah.

I've been studying him, anticipating his moves. As he drives, I shadow him, letting him believe he's shaken me off. Then, as he goes in for his layup, I block him. My palm meets the warm leather of the ball and pins it to the backboard.

"Gimme that!" I yell, swagger pouring out of me.

With the block acting as a shot of adrenaline, our team races back down the court. Tommy feeds the ball to me, and I push hard, the rim in my sights. But this time, I choose not to go solo. I flick the ball out to the three-point line, where my teammate Zack is waiting, locked in and ready. His shot takes flight, and it's a thing of beauty that ends with a swish. The game is tied.

The crowd erupts. Booming cheers shake the walls of the gym.

With the clock ticking away, now at a nerve-racking twenty-two seconds, Milwood is visibly shaken. They scramble, taking a rushed, bad shot that barely touches the rim. We get the rebound, and Coach Ryan calls a time-out. He pulls out his whiteboard and starts mapping out our next move. He decides to go with an isolation play for me.

I can feel the weight of what's about to happen. I've wanted this my whole life. The type of moment I wish my father was still around to see.

Across the court, Milwood is huddled, their coach whispering, their eyes cutting in my direction.

As we break from our time-out, Tommy gets the ball and instantly passes it to me. I hold it, allowing a few precious seconds to bleed from the clock. I dribble and tease my defender with a head fake, but he doesn't fall for it again. So I decide to try something else. I hesitate to my right and cross back left. He reaches to steal the ball and is momentarily off balance. I take the split-second opportunity to blow past him.

I'm a freight train bound for my destiny.

I push off the ground with all the athleticism I can muster, not sure if I'm aiming for a dunk or a layup. I just know I need to score. The world around me slows. My body feels completely free for maybe the first time in my life. The clamor of the crowd dims to a muffled hum, my focus on a solitary thing—the rim.

Suddenly, a forceful shove from the defender I blew by sends me tumbling from the sky. I crash into the camera crew standing on the baseline, toppling equipment, my flight ending in a brutal landing on the cold, unforgiving floor.

My left knee is in unbearable pain. The noise of the crowd overloads all my senses. I can barely understand what's happening.

The last things I hear as the world blurs into darkness are the sharp sound of the referee's whistle and a stampede of footsteps running toward me.

PHENOM OSSIE BROWN DERAILED BY INJURY

AFTER BROWN INJURY, SYRACUSE LOOKS ELSEWHERE FOR NEXT STAR

FROM THE NEXT LEBRON TO WHAT COULD HAVE BEEN

Chapter One

The sun dips low, casting a burnt-orange hue across my bedroom walls. Tomorrow morning is the start of senior year, and the weight of it presses on my chest, like a bag filled with bricks and bad news.

I've spent the entire summer hidden alone in the pages of a story nobody really wanted to read, but now I'm about to be thrust back in front of everyone, open to their scrutiny. My gaze is settled on my father's jersey, preserved in a frame on my wall next to all the trophies and medals I earned trying to be like him.

My dad was more than a man; he was a legend. On the courts of Philly and under the banners at Alderbridge University, he danced with the ball; people say he was like Michael Jackson with the rock. And he was. As a kid, I watched videos of his games almost every day on DVD. I loved hearing the crowd chant his name: "August! August! August!"

Sometimes I'd gather my action figures and stuffed animals, seating them beside me, imagining we were all immersed in the roar of the stadium, our voices melding with the rest. I was supposed to continue his legacy, but now I feel more like a speck faded in his shadow.

The buzz of my phone on the nightstand draws me out of my thoughts.

I squint against the brightness of the screen. It's Tommy again. That makes it eight texts in the past few weeks. Despite everything, I can't help but appreciate his persistence. Out of all the guys on the team, guys who claimed to be my brothers, Tommy's the only one still reaching out. And me? I keep ghosting him.

But I just can't bring myself to talk to anyone.

It's been six months since that game, and the court feels like a distant memory. Five months and twenty-eight days since the doctors told me I'd never play again. Since everything was stolen from me.

After the injury, the media wouldn't stop harassing me at school, so I was allowed to attend classes remotely, which turned out to be a blessing in disguise. Without it, I would've probably been Braxton's daily spectacle, a constant target. But even in the sanctuary of our apartment, there was no escaping the whispers on Zoom, the pitying looks, the questions that felt like a thousand tiny cuts.

Especially after Laura broke up with me.

I roll onto my back, staring at the ceiling as memories of our time together flood in. The way her laughter filled a room, how her eyes sparkled when she talked about her favorite music. But as quickly as the happy memories come, they're overshadowed by the pain of her leaving. The hurt is still raw, the wound still fresh.

I've spent so much time over the summer wondering if everyone feels like I do after their heart is broken. Like, at a certain point, the only things I really wanted back were the pieces of myself I came in with. Like my favorite hoodie, the one that's all soft and worn in, now just a memory of Laura's perfume. And that playlist I made of my favorite songs, but none of them sound the same now that she and I aren't listening to them together. Or how I used to laugh at all sorts of things but haven't even smiled in months. All these things that were mine, now tangled up in the shadow cast by my ex.

I sigh deeply, tracing an invisible outline over the deep groove in the skin of my left knee. It feels rough and uneven, the mark of a wound that runs deeper than just the surface. A five-inch-long, sixteen-stitch memorial of my deceased basketball career.

Every time I run my fingers over it, I'm reminded of that night: the lights, the crowd, the gasp as I went down. That moment, suspended in time, like a frame taken out of a movie.

Outside, the rhythm of South Yonkers carries on, the sound of car engines, the occasional shouts of kids playing, life moving at its usual pace. Even though the streetlights are about to come on, I can still hear people playing on the court where I made a name for myself, right outside my window.

Whenever Grandma Alice would see me after a long day of being out there, bruised and battered, she'd shake her head, a mix of concern and exasperation in her eyes. "Another story to tell," she'd say, dabbing at the fresh wounds with a wet cloth. She always made it sound poetic, as if each scrape and scratch was a badge of honor, a testament to my tenacity and passion for the game.

She said something similar after the doctors gave me the news about how bad my knee was. "Not every scar has to remain a blemish."

Grandma Alice is usually right. But this scar? This one's different. It's a gnawing reminder of everything I've lost. My dreams, my ambitions, the hours of sweat and effort I poured into perfecting my craft, trying to be like my father.

The thick humidity of summer's last night clings to me like my sadness. But if I'm going to let this sadness swallow me whole, I might as well do it with the right soundtrack. With deliberate motions, I place my earbuds in my ears and press play on a Frank Ocean playlist. His voice, like aloe on a wound, fills the room, drowning out everything but the emotions. Each lyric fills the empty spaces in my heart, and I find myself sinking deeper into the bed, the ceiling above becoming a blank canvas for my thoughts.

The moment is interrupted by the insistent buzz of my phone.

A flutter of anxiety grips me as I see the notification. SportsTalk USA, one of the biggest sports sites in the country. A part of me screams to ignore it, to keep the protective walls up. But the other part, the part that makes decisions I shouldn't make, can't help but look.

I tap on the notification, and there it is, a digital slap in the face. A post detailing Braxton's downward spiral in the high school basketball rankings, all because of my injury. It's like they've dragged me into the spotlight. There was no need to tag me, no need to remind people that I still exist. Yet they did.

And if the post was a slap, the comments below are punches. Each one aimed at my most vulnerable spots, landing with precision.

If it wasn't for Kareem Matthews and Tyler Patis missing games because of covid @OssieBrown woulda never been ranked as high as he was in the first place.

@OssieBrown is good, better than his father, but I don't think he has the same work ethic. He's shown a lot of great things. But I still think he's overrated and can be a bit thug-like on the court.

I hope @OssieBrown comes back. But I heard Coach Ryan is already planning on running a new offense that focuses more on team play like it's supposed to be. Instead of that Yonkers Southside basketball OB plays. Let's go, Braxton! #BraxtonBears

I groan and hurl my phone across the room. But I aim it to land on a pile of clothes on my bed, knowing damn well I can't afford a new one.

I must've groaned louder than I realized, because my mom's at my door, banging away. "Everything okay in there?"

"I'm good! I just dropped something!" I shout back, praying she won't barge in. She'd have my head if she saw the mess and got a whiff of the subway-station-in-a-heatwave odor that's started to permeate the space, especially after she asked me to clean it days ago.

"All right. By the way, you need to call your grandmother. She texted me saying she's been trying to reach you and hasn't heard anything back," she says.

"Yeah, sure!" I answer, eager to get back to my self-loathing.

"Excuse me?" she responds, her tone sharp as a knife.

"Sorry. I meant yes, ma'am."

"That's more like it. I'm heading to my shift at the store. Don't forget to call your grandmother. Or better yet, go see her. The walk will be good for you." Her voice fades down the hallway.

When I hear the front door close, a deep sigh leaves my body. It's not that I don't want to talk to Grandma Alice, not at all. It's the words she'll be packing that I don't want to hear. It's the truth punches she's always swinging at me, trying to knock down the walls I've built these past months.

And as much as I know they're punches of love, they're punches all the same.

But I can't hide from her forever. I retrieve my phone from the bed and slide my finger across the screen, lighting up her name, feeling the inevitability of our conversation pressing on my chest. The phone starts to ring, a single chime that somehow sounds both ominous and comforting. She picks up almost instantly, her voice curling around me like the lyrics of a favorite song.

"Hey, baby!"

"Hey, Grandma," I return, my voice scratchy, like I've been

swallowing sandpaper instead of ignoring her calls. "I'm sorry I didn't call you back sooner."

"Oh, don't you worry about that. I'm just so happy to hear from you."

From there, we wade into easy waters. She tells me about the book she's been reading, a movie she thinks we'd both love, and a brownie recipe she found that she wants the two of us to try soon.

But I'm not fooled. I know what she's doing. She's skirting around the elephant in the room, biding her time until she can lead the conversation in the direction I've been dreading. So I decide to pull off the Band-Aid.

"Grandma, it's cool," I start. "You can ask me about school tomorrow."

Her response is laughter, warm and genuine. "Well, damn. You know me well. Fine. So, how are you feeling about it all?"

"I'm okay with it," I lie.

She catches it, the way I'm sure she's caught every lie I've ever tried to sneak past her. "Baby," she scolds gently, "you don't have to lie to me. It's okay not to be okay."

Her words, wrapped in such understanding and tenderness, sting the backs of my eyes. I bite my lip, wrestling with the lump in my throat, desperate to keep my emotions settled.

She softly continues. "It's okay. I know how much tomorrow has to be sitting on your spirit."

I suspect she *does* know. She's the one person in my life who truly considers me. I stare at the ceiling, counting the small cracks in the plaster, trying to hold back the tidal wave of thoughts relentlessly crashing onto the shore of my mind.

Every slow step toward those school doors, every murmur and whisper, will be a cruel reminder of the dreams I've lost. The thought of seeing Laura arm in arm with Matthew—his mocking eyes and cocky stride—feels like a stone in my stomach.

But the hardest loss to confront is the loss of basketball. The halls will be filled with mementos, from the faces of my former teammates to the trophies behind glass and the banners hanging from the rafters—trophies and banners that I helped us win.

The ghost of the life I should still have feels like it's wrapping around me, choking me slowly.

Grandma Alice's words pierce the heavy fog of my thoughts: "You still with me, baby?"

I can't respond. My voice feels like it's been stolen, stuck somewhere inside the hurt in my chest.

"I know how much you love basketball and wanted to make your father proud," Grandma Alice tells me. "Trust me, if August was still with us, he would be so proud of who you are. Basketball doesn't define Ossie Brown."

Grandma Alice has this way of seeing to the heart of a problem and finding just the right words to soothe you. It's a trait I desperately wish my mother had inherited.

My relationship with my mother, once a strong bond when I was much younger, has been strained over the years, cracking under the weight of my growing resemblance to my father. Though it's still often her that the world sees in my dark-brown complexion and high cheekbones, as I grew tall and lanky, and gravitated toward basketball, the distance between my mother and me started to widen.

Grandma Alice often tries to help me understand why my mom made herself so distant. "Healing can take a lifetime," she'd say, explaining my mother's absence and her seeming indifference. "Your mother loves you, Ossie. One day, she'll find the pieces of herself she thinks were buried with your father."

But that day didn't come, and as we drifted further apart, I continued to find my peace away from her and on the court.

Basketball became my refuge from everything, and a chance to feel connected to my dad. It consumed my free time, my thoughts, my existence. I chose it over the simple pleasures of childhood—playing in open fire hydrants during the summer or engaging in snowball fights during winters. Even when COVID hit and the park's rims were removed to enforce social distancing, I would spend my time on the court practicing my handle.

As the weight of my past collides with the uncertainty of my future, tears begin to fall, each one carrying a profoundly lingering pain.

Grandma Alice's voice pulls me back. "Child, I know it feels like the whole world's against you. And I know it don't feel like it now, but you're gonna be fine."

My breathing is ragged, every inhale a struggle. "But, Grandma, they're all just gonna see me and think *There he goes—he had it all and lost it*. They'll just see a failure."

She sighs softly, a sound filled with the wisdom of age. "And who are they to you, Ossie? Them fancy kids with their silver spoons? Or that Coach Ryan, with his slick talk and that blond mop on his head trying to pass for hair? I never did trust that man. Sending you flowers after what happened. He couldn't even show his face at the hospital! Remember how he sweet-talked you, promising you'd be part of the 'Braxton family'? Pfft. If that's family, I don't want it."

Grandma Alice was always very vocal about my all-consuming commitment to basketball. She'd share her concerns with me and my mother, emphasizing the importance of a balanced life—urging me to prioritize my academics and to explore what she thought was a talent for writing. But the allure of basketball, the legacy of my father, was too important. I saw in it not only a reflection of him but also a path forward, a bridge to a brighter future for all of us.

Braxton Academy, despite its glaring whiteness and the constant microaggressions, represented an opportunity. They have a nationally known basketball program, and Coach Ryan, with his time in the NBA, seemed the perfect mentor to guide me toward my dreams. The offer of a full scholarship was the clincher. It was, however, a double-edged sword. On one side was the promise of recognition and success, and on the other, the discomfort of being in an environment where my very presence was constantly questioned.

"Sorry, baby," Grandma Alice says softly. "I got carried away cursing that damn coach and that godforsaken school."

I manage a faint "It's okay—I understand." A hint of the city's nighttime hustle reaches my ear. "Where you at, Grandma?"

"Just taking a lil' evening walk, baby. Not venturing too far."

"You be safe, okay?"

"Always am, sweetheart."

She breathes deeply and says, "Look, Ossie, the truth is when you walk through those school doors tomorrow, you won't be the six-five basketball star anymore. To everyone there, you'll just be another Black kid. Someone they can ignore, someone they can throw away without a second thought. But remember: you're Ossie Brown, and you've been bigger than a ball and rim from the moment you took your first breath."

I can't help the grin that tugs at my lips. "Thank you, Grandma. I hear you."

"Good."

Just then, there's a knock at the front door.

"I better let you answer that," Grandma Alice says. "You take care, baby. I love you."

"I love you too, Grandma," I mumble as I gingerly approach the door, each careful step a reminder of my still-healing ACL.

"Who is it?" I call out.

A voice, muffled and unnaturally low, grumbles, "It's me."

There's a familiar tinge beneath the distorted tone. I squint through the peephole, spotting Grandma Alice, her eyes sparkling mischievously. She's holding up a DVD of our favorite movie, *Dreamgirls*. I chuckle and fling open the door.

"I couldn't let your last night of summer end with you feeling all down." She stretches her arms out, and I cling to her, feeling the warmth of her body seep into mine. A tear, the kind that only springs from pure joy, slides down my face, making a wet trail on my cheek.

She pulls back, her expression serious. "Now, I didn't mention this over the phone, but let that ex-girlfriend of yours act up this year, and I'll march right down and give her a piece of my mind."

A laugh, deep and heartfelt, erupts from me. I can't remember the last time I laughed, but I've missed it.

Chapter Two

The next morning comes at me too fast. My alarm clock sounds like the beginning of a funeral procession, forcing me to face the inevitable. It's a fight to slowly swing myself off the side of the bed, a war to stand up on my one good leg. I sigh as I look down at the scar on my knee.

My Jordans lie at the foot of my bed, looking as skeptical about the day as I am. The sleek design of the Space Jam 11s looks out of place next to my school uniform. The blazer, a shade of royal blue that manages to be both dull and glaringly bright, is stiff and unyielding. The plaid pants are no better, with intersecting lines of blue and gray that make me think of old television static, a pattern that's neither modern nor charmingly vintage, just—ugly.

After putting on my uniform, I slide on my brace. Balancing on one leg, I begin fumbling with my shoelaces, the other leg awkwardly extended, still not quite healed. Each tug feels like I'm tightening the knot of anxiety in my gut.

The walk from the projects to the bus that'll take me to Braxton used to take me fifteen minutes. But with my leg all jacked up, it's closer to thirty-five. Every hobbled step I take feels like it's under a magnifying glass. The neighborhood's eyes, some filled with pity, others with shade, seem to be tailing me like shadows.

Just as I'm passing the corner bodega, I bump into Big Teak and his squad. Teak isn't your average street kingpin. Sure, he's got the city on lock, but there's more depth to him than most give him credit for. Grandma Alice used to babysit Teak when he was a kid, and ever since then, he's had our backs. He even became cool with my dad. When my dad would make those trips from Philly to Yonkers during his college breaks, chasing after my mom, Teak would be right there, balling with him, learning moves, soaking up game.

Teak's always fresh, always clean — one of those smooth, light-skin dudes with a sharp fade. Women around the hood are all about him.

He sizes me up, his eyes lingering on my leg, and he lets out a low whistle. "Damn, them Milwood boys still got you messed up, champ," he murmurs, his voice a mix of sadness and genuine concern for my banged-up state.

"Yeah," I respond, my own voice barely more than a whisper.

Teak's eyes soften, and he offers a gentle nod. "I heard about you losing them college scholarships. I know Ms. Alice would kill you and me if you got involved with my work, but if you ever need anything — you already know."

"Appreciate it, Teak," I answer, spotting my bus approaching in the distance. "I'm good, though. I gotta dip."

Teak flashes a smile. "Hit them books, superstar." Then we dap each other up, and I limp on.

As nervous as I am about heading back to Braxton, I'm just as nervous about going to the bus stop to get there. This isn't just a place where I catch my bus to Braxton; it's an emotional war zone. Because this stop is also where all the kids from my neighborhood who go to Woodcrest catch *their* bus.

When I reach the crowded bus stop, a murmur ripples through the crowd of people I used to play with growing up, used to know, before Braxton. The voice of Monica, from two buildings down, breaks free, loud and unapologetic: "Good for his ass. We wouldn't have let them white boys do him like that if he played for Woodcrest."

I try to blend into the scenery, but of course that ain't happening. From the back of the crowd, Jamel, whose sister used to braid my hair, cuts through the chatter, sharp as a knife. "Word, and peep this traitor nigga's stupid-ass uniform. Homie lookin' like he headin' to help massa out at the plantation or somethin'."

A ripple of laughter bursts from the crowd. I can feel heat rising to my cheeks, my ugly uniform suddenly feeling ten times too tight.

Maybe I am a traitor—and for what?

The arrival of the bus interrupts my thoughts—and the whispers. The driver, Mr. Sanders, who went to high school with my mom, greets me with a broad smile. "Ayyy, Ossie! How you doing there?" His good-natured cheer feels like a grating contrast to the tension at the bus stop.

"I'm okay," I reply, but the fatigue in my voice betrays my real feelings.

He looks at me for a moment before switching to a more serious tone. "You're gonna need to use the wheelchair ramp, Ossie."

"I can make it up the steps; just give me a second," I protest, but Mr. Sanders shakes his head.

"Sorry, Ossie. It's policy."

"You deadass, Mr. Sanders?"

"Deadass as can be, champ." His voice is soft, empathetic, but it does nothing to alleviate my humiliation.

The back of the bus begins beeping to signal the ramp slowly descending, the cherry on top of my public embarrassment. The Woodcrest kids are laughing harder than ever.

"Nah! Look at that!" one of them hollers, pointing at me.

I keep my head down as I begin my walk of shame.

A few phones flash in my direction, capturing the moment.

"Really?" I ask, the humiliation burning.

"Yeah, this might go viral!" Tiffany, who was my elementary school valentine, replies with delight. Our past obviously doesn't mean anything now that she has a chance to gain social media clout.

As I step onto the bus, the doors shut behind me, blocking out the laughter. I find a seat, my heart pounding and my forehead soaked in sweat. I'm drained before even getting to the worst part of the day.

The hour-long bus ride from Yonkers to Scarsdale feels like slipping from one world into another. From the lively energy of where I live to the manicured landscapes of Scarsdale, with its white picket fences and suspicious eyes.

As the bodegas and familiar corners of my world fade in the rearview, I pull out my earbuds, hoping some Childish Gambino will be a refuge from the tsunami of thoughts in my head. But instead of the beats grounding me, they rip me further apart. Gambino is Laura's favorite artist. Her memory hijacks my thoughts, and against my better judgment, I find my fingers pulling up our old text conversations. I read through a digital trail of laughs, dreams, and late-night heart-to-hearts before I get to the part where our relationship was shattered.

It's that kind of self-sabotage we all do when heartbreak has us in a choke hold. Like picking at a scab, knowing it'll bleed but doing it anyway.

June 6

BOO BEAR: What did the doctor say babe??? Did your mom go?

ME: Yea. Her and Gma Alice came

BOO BEAR: ???

BOO BEAR: So are you gonna tell me what happened?

ME: Can you come over?

BOO BEAR: You're making me nervous Poo Bear. Just tell me what the doctor said

ME: It's not good. They don't think I can play again at the level I did before. I need to see you

BOO BEAR: Why would you wait to tell me that!?

ME: I'm sorry. I've been dealing with a lot. Please can I just see you?

BOO BEAR: You are so selfish Ossie! This isn't just your life its mine too. I need to think. I can't see you right now. I need space

June 9

BOO BEAR: I saw Coach Ryan on the news confirming you aren't playing this season

ME: Yeah. Have you had enough space?

BOO BEAR: I wanted to talk to you about that. You're going to be going through so much right now with rehab and figuring out your life. I dont want to get in the way of anything. So I think its best if we dont see each other over the summer

ME: The whole summer??!! Laura please. I need you right now

ME: Are we still together tho?

ME: Boo Bear . . . ?

ME: Please

August 29

LAURA: Hey Ossie. I hope you've been well. I wanted
to let you know that over the summer my family
went to the Hamptons with Matt's family. He was
so different there. One thing led to another and
we started dating. I just thought I should tell you
myself instead of you hearing from someone else

I stare at that last message, sent only five days ago. Funny, she said she wanted me to hear it from her, but I'd known about her and Matthew for almost a month by then. Social media has no regard for feelings. Some friend of Matthew's posted a pic of them kissing on a beach in the Hamptons, and just about as soon as it was online, everyone and their moms started tagging me in the comments.

They even had a hashtag, #Maura, which added insult to injury, because we had one too before that—#Laussie. Which was always obviously corny.

I sigh and put away my phone. It's just how breakups work, I guess. Instead of being mad, you wind up wallowing, digging up old texts and photos, feeling sorry for yourself. And here I am, missing Laura instead of being pissed at her not only for stabbing me in the back but also for picking Matthew Astor, of all people, to replace me.

"You must be our new shooting guard, Uzi."

It was our first week of ninth grade when Matthew said that. Matthew Astor. Walking like the world owed him something, probably because it had already given him so much. Blond hair shining a bit too bright, skin baked a bit too bronze, moving with all the confidence of an entitled brat. And his friends? Each one looked like a clone of him. The air around them was thick with the scent of Axe body spray and prejudice.

I found out quickly that unlike the other students at Braxton, Matthew wasn't born with a silver spoon in his mouth. His spoon was pure gold, encrusted with diamonds, and probably pried from the dead hands of somebody in Africa. He was the grandson of Yonkers's former mayor as well as the nephew of a US senator—and he made sure everyone knew it.

Kids like him are Braxton's royalty.

Even though I didn't know all the ins and outs of Braxton when I arrived, I wasn't going to let anyone there disrespect me.

"It's Ossie," I told him.

"Huh?"

"My name. It's not Uzi. It's Ossie."

"Well, I heard you're the shooter our basketball team has been missing. Which makes sense, coming from Yonkers." He snickered, flashing a grin at his minions. "So I think Uzi's a perfect nickname."

Grandma Alice always told me, most of us only have two things— our family and our name. You don't let anyone disrespect either.

"This is the last time I'm gonna say it—my name is Ossie," I responded, the sound of my locker slamming shut ringing in the air. The shock on Matthew's face told me he wasn't used to people challenging him.

In the silence that followed, tension boiled just beneath the surface, ready to erupt. Then Matthew shrugged.

"Whatever you say . . . my nigga."

His words hung in the air, a grenade lobbed, before exploding in my soul. At that moment, I was tempted to throw away my opportunity to be at Braxton just to wipe the smug smile off his face.

I leaned in close, my voice low and furious. "Say it again—I dare you," I whispered, letting him feel the heat of my words, feel the promise of a fist about to meet his face.

But just when the air got thickest, just when it felt like everyone in the hallway was holding their breath, Laura Wong-Stanton slid between us like a breeze cutting through the tension. Tall and commanding, she stood like a tower. Her brown eyes sparked with fire.

"NEPHEW OF SENATOR ASTOR HURLS SLUR AT BLACK ATHLETE—I can see the CNN headline now," she said, staring down Matthew.

"I said *nigga*, not *nig*—" Matthew attempted to argue, but Laura silenced him.

"Just stop before you make this even worse than it already is."

Matthew tried to play it cool. "Come on, it was just a joke. You know how I—"

Laura cut him off again, throwing her hands in the air. "Just go, Matt!"

With a final glare in my direction, Matthew backed down and left, his friends following like a villain's loyal henchmen. The atmosphere settled, and the hallway cleared until it was just Laura and me standing in the calm after the storm.

She sighed. "Don't mind him, okay? He's not as bad as he wants people to think he is. He just listens to the nonsense his parents say." She ran a hand through her hair, which was brown and wavy. "I've known him since elementary school, and our families go way back. My mother and my aunt went to Braxton with both of his parents. Anyway, I'm sure he's just jealous because everyone has been talking about you being here instead of him. Even my aunt, who's a huge basketball fan, was saying how important it is that Braxton has you here."

I figured her aunt meant I was important to the *team*, but Laura continued: "She said that Braxton desperately needs more Black and brown students, and she's right about that. We could use more Asian kids, too, but there have still always been way more of us than all of you."

I blinked, not knowing what to say, then muttered, "I appreciate you stepping in."

She tilted her head, a sly smile dancing on her lips. "If you wanna show appreciation, how about you walk me to class?"

I raised an eyebrow. "Uh, sure. Yeah. I can do that. Definitely."

And that's how it started. From that first walk together down the hallway to late-night phone calls, from goofy texts that made my sides hurt from laughing to her cheering louder than anyone else in the bleachers at my games. She wasn't just the girl I was with; Laura was my anchor, my compass, my rock.

We became an "it" couple at school and on social media, which is where our ridiculous #Laussie hashtag came from. Laura was excited by the fame and attention. And with over five million followers at the time on my various socials, there definitely wasn't a lack of either. Though I lost a big chunk of that after my injury. Probably also because I never post anything, since I've never really liked social media.

Having a massive platform on social media is its own trauma. I remember telling Laura about how when I first gained a large following, every time I posted about my family or issues that were important to me, people would comment things like "Shut up and dribble" or "No one cares about your father, get to work on your jumper." Which is why I stopped using social media altogether and just focused on hooping and Laura. But she and her parents always had a different tune. "Ossie, you need to focus on your brand," they'd say, mapping out starry dreams and flashing lights for me. They saw a stage; I just wanted to ball.

Laura and I agreed the plan was for me to get drafted, then get married. A blueprint her parents were on board with. I had developed a close relationship with both of them; they came to nearly as many games as Laura and Grandma Alice, and always offered advice on my future finances and direction. My mother and Grandma Alice didn't like that. Their shared disapproval of not only Laura but her parents trying to help me with business things was a rare agreement between them.

When I defended Laura and her parents, Grandma Alice would say, "Sometimes the only reason people listen to us is to better understand what song they need to play to make us dance for them."

Turns out she was right. Because it wasn't just Laura who dropped me after my accident; I haven't heard from her parents—people who said they'd be my future in-laws—since the doctors told me my career was over.

Before I realize it, the bus grinds to a halt blocks away from the school. Classic Braxton. They don't let peasant things such as public buses come too close.

As I slowly make my way to the school's doors, I'm readying myself for what will undoubtedly be a storm of stares and whispers. But maybe, just maybe, I'm buggin'. I mean, these are my Braxton Bears. The same ones who were hyping me up last season. They've gotta be better than those faceless trolls online, right?

Nope.

It's immediately clear that I got it right the first time: these people suck.

The staring, whispering, even giggling, is fine. But when I arrive at my locker, it turns out that someone filled it with hundreds of Band-Aids and wrote on a large sticky note, "For your boo-boo, LeBron."

By the time afternoon rolls around, I've spent most of the day with my head low, trying to ignore the remarks and dodging those pity-filled glances. It feels like I've been stuck in a hell, and I'm just tryna make it out in one piece.

As I round the corner to my final class, I stop as abruptly as if I hit a brick wall. There's Coach Ryan, with Kyle and Porter, two of my former teammates.

They look like they've seen a ghost. Maybe they thought Braxton wouldn't still be allowing me to get an education if I can't dunk. (In their defense, I assumed the same until I got the email from Dean Blackburn telling me that based on school policy, I still had my scholarship and was able to come back for my senior year if I wanted.)

"Ayy, Ossie!" Porter hollers, way too chipper for someone who hasn't reached out since I got hurt.

I lift my chin. "Sup."

"Just gearing up for the new season," he says, eyes flitting to my leg. "Looks like you're healing up nice."

Kyle just shakes his head as Porter mentions my leg. Porter, as always, missing the memo.

There's an awkward silence for a moment until Coach Ryan tries to fill the void. "How's it hanging, Forty-Five?"

Man, if I had one of them smoke bombs Batman uses, I'd throw it down and bounce. But I'm never that lucky. So I muster up a half-hearted "I'm good."

"Glad to hear it," Coach Ryan says, but the air between us is tense. Like everyone's holding their breath, waiting for the next move in a chess game.

I decide to bail us all out of this awkward moment. "Good to see y'all. But y'all know how Ms. Carrigan gets about people being late to class," I say, tossing in a half grin to play nice.

Coach Ryan, trying to mirror my casual vibe, nods slowly. "Yeah, yeah, for sure."

But as I start to make my exit, with every step a reminder of that day on the court, his voice pierces the air again. "Ossie! You know where to find me if you ever need . . . anything, okay?"

The hair on the back of my neck stands up. I want to turn around and tell him about himself. We both know he doesn't actually care. I haven't heard from him in months. But instead, I toss back, "Will do, Coach. Will do." And keep it pushing.

When the last bell rings, I'm already mentally mapping out the quickest route home. All I need is to make it to the special-access elevator, zip down to the first floor, and head straight for the bus. The elevator is a godsend, really. It's exclusively for those with injuries or disabilities, which has helped me dodge some unwanted encounters today.

I limp to the elevator and wait for it to arrive, thinking about how good my bed is going to feel soon. Suddenly, I hear a familiar chuckle traveling down the hallway in my direction.

No. No. No! No! No! Come on!

I desperately jam at the elevator button, willing the doors to hurry and open.

But luck isn't on my side today. Laura turns the corner, and our eyes lock instantly. It's like time freezes, and we're two statues, caught in a moment of shared surprise. And then, as if things couldn't get any worse, Matthew Astor trails right behind her.

Chapter Three

Laura swallows hard, tucking her hair behind one ear, a nervous habit. "Ossie," she starts, her voice timid, like she's approaching a wounded animal, "I didn't think I'd see you this year." Her gaze flicks to my knee brace and then quickly away.

I lift an eyebrow. "Why not? I told you before that my scholarship was still good even if I got hurt. Guess you were pretending to care about that, too?" The bitterness sneaks into my voice. Not what I intended, but it's there now. No taking it back.

The truth is, I don't want to be at Braxton at all, but what choice do I have? If I go to Woodcrest, I'm in hell with people who think I'm a race traitor. If I stay here, I'm in hell with people who think I don't belong. The devil you know is better than the devil you don't.

Before she can respond, Matthew slides up next to her, his smirk as sharp as a blade. "Ahh," he drawls. "Looks like you've hurt more than just your knee."

Laura's jaw tightens. "Matt, stop it."

I chuckle, a forced sound, pushing the anger down. "Good one, Astor. Makes sense that y'all are together—you've been wishing you were me for years."

Laura's face turns a shade redder. "C'mon, Matt, let's just go—"

But Matthew steps in front of me. "Why would I want to be you? You're just a welfare baby from the ghetto whose mommy works at a department store and whose daddy died because he was a junkie."

I step to Matthew, my fingers curling into fists. Heat swells inside me, each word Matthew spat a coal stoking the fire. My breaths quicken, and the hallway seems to shrink, everything else fading into insignificance. Just me and Matthew. Just me and a place to put all my pent-up rage.

But before I can bridge the gap, before my knuckles can meet that smug face at last, a familiar broad frame crashes between us. Tommy.

"Yo, Ossie!" With an arm that feels like a steel beam, he shoves me back, forcing distance between me and my goal. "This ain't it, man. This ain't the move."

I try to push past him, but even though he's shorter than me, Tommy's built like a wall. A brolic, stubborn wall.

"Nah, he deserves it, Tommy," I growl.

Tommy's eyes, usually so calm and collected, now blaze with intensity. "And you giving it to him is what he wants. Don't play his game."

Over Tommy's shoulder, I see Laura gripping Matthew's arm, her fingers digging into his flesh as she tries to pull him away. "Matthew, let's go. *Now*."

Matthew, high off the confrontation, locks eyes with me. "Looks like your boy saved you today." He sneers.

Laura's frustration bubbles over. *"Enough!"* she yells, her voice echoing through the hallway. With surprising force, she yanks Matthew back, sending him stumbling. "Come on."

Matthew finally complies. They disappear down the hallway, leaving behind a silent tension that seems to choke us.

Tommy releases me. "I see you're feeling better than the last time I saw you," he murmurs, his breath shaky.

I nod, trying to catch my breath, trying to process everything. "You should have let me show him what's up."

Tommy rolls his eyes. "Well, that's one way to thank someone for stopping you from turning Matthew Astor into a punching bag. And, you know, saving you from getting kicked out of Braxton. Oh, and let's not forget his family probably ruining your life with their connections."

I let out a sigh. The weight of the day, of the past months, hangs heavy on me. "Yeah, sure," I mutter, the words tasting bitter. "Sorry, man. Thanks."

The elevator arrives, and I walk on, trying to disappear. But Tommy isn't having it—he steps on with me.

"What's your problem?" he asks me. "I've been blowing up your phone for months. Radio silence. What's up with that?"

"I've been . . . busy."

Tommy arches an eyebrow. "Yeah, you must have been *real* busy training to throw hands with Matthew when school started up."

I grimace, looking down at my now-scuffed Jordans. "It's not like that, man."

"Then what's it like, Ossie?" Tommy presses, his voice softer now, filled with genuine concern. "Talk to me, man. I'm your friend."

The elevator hums, the vibrations traveling up my legs as Tommy and I stand there, simmering in a silence that's thick enough to cut. Each second stretches on, feeling longer than the last, before I finally reply. "We aren't friends, Tommy."

His head snaps toward me, eyes wide. "What are you talking about?"

"We were teammates. But now that's done. We don't have to pretend to be friends."

"That's messed up, man," Tommy says, shaking his head. "We *are* friends. You were the only one on the team I really got along with outside of ball."

I scoff, a bitter taste in my mouth. "You'll be fine. None of y'all have to worry 'bout making the Black kid feel comfortable anymore." He looks confused, so I decide to clarify things for him: "I heard the way Patrick and the rest would talk when they thought I wasn't around."

His face hardens, frustration evident. "I'm not like those idiots, Ossie. I'm your boy."

"That's what they all say when they want something," I shoot back coldly. "So, what do you want? The ghetto kid doesn't have anything left to give."

He stares at me, his face a mask of hurt and anger. "You know what, man? Whatever." The elevator door slides open, and Tommy hurries out, leaving a chill in the air.

The door closes, and I'm left with nothing but the hum of the elevator and the ache of loneliness.

The next few days are a parade of hours spent limping—physically, academically, and emotionally—through the halls of Braxton. I knew that with basketball gone, I would be treated differently at school, but the sting is sharper than I thought possible.

Classmates who once cheered me on now hiss, "He doesn't belong here," "Overrated anyway," "No more handouts for him," as I pass by. Even most of my teachers treat me as if I've been a bad student, despite the A- average I maintained before going remote.

When the first Friday of the school year rolls around, the morning bell's tone is still ringing in my ears when the PA system starts up, drowning out the soft mutterings of my classmates.

"Ossie Brown," the voice booms, and I can feel every eye in the room on me, "please report to Mrs. Wright's office."

I blink, thinking, *Mrs. Wright? Why would the guidance counselor wanna see me?* The last time I met her was when I was a new student here. Fresh meat in the Braxton jungle. I slowly gather my things, ignoring the murmurs that ripple across the room. Limping out, I can't help but feel like I'm walking to my doom.

And when I finally push the door to Mrs. Wright's office open, my feet almost stop in their tracks. Grandma Alice? And Ms. Hunt, my English teacher from last year? Together? This can't be good.

Grandma Alice sits with her back straight. Ms. Hunt stands next to Mrs. Wright's desk, her sharp pixie cut glistening under the overhead lights. And Mrs. Wright? She's behind her desk, her dreadlocks pulled back today in a tight bun. The presence of three Black women fills the room, an energy that makes me straighten my shoulders a bit more.

"Hi, Ossie," Mrs. Wright greets me, a friendly smile on her face. "Why don't you take a seat? We were just catching up with Ms. Alice before you came in."

I sit in the chair next to Grandma Alice, my knee brace making the movement stiffer than I'd like. "What are you doing here?" I ask her.

Grandma Alice blows out a heavy sigh, like she's tired of singing the same old song. "Well, they called your mother first—"

"But she had to work, huh?" I jump in, finishing her sentence. The routine has become all too familiar—missed games, empty chairs at school events, milestones she wasn't there to see. I get it.

She gives me a stern look. "She's doing the best she can, Ossie." I wish Grandma Alice would be honest and say *Your mother doesn't really mess with you.*

It's something I've known since I was much younger, and honesty would make it easier on everyone.

Across the room, Ms. Hunt and Mrs. Wright shoot each other a look. A silent *Who's gonna tackle this one?* After a moment, Mrs. Wright takes a deep breath.

"Look, Ossie," she starts gently, "I'm truly sorry for all you've been carrying. Life's thrown some curveballs at you." She pauses, hoping her words might provide some relief.

Ms. Hunt and Mrs. Wright are two of the only bright spots in the difficult space of Braxton. Ms. Hunt is the main reason I enjoy English. I had her as a junior, and the books she assigned were always interesting and made me feel seen. And Mrs. Wright is everything someone could want in a guidance counselor, always checking in, always trying to put students in positions to be successful. They are also the only two people who seem even remotely willing to show up for any students who aren't rich or white.

Despite the two of them being stark contrasts in style, they radiate a similar energy. Ms. Hunt, with her ever-changing wardrobe that always seems straight off the runways of New York Fashion Week, and Mrs. Wright, with her clothing that tells tales of her African roots and pride, often adorned with kente patterns or beaded jewelry. Their vibes are different, but their essence is the same: powerful Black women standing tall in a place that often feels like it was built to make them feel small.

Mrs. Wright continues: "The thing is, you've always been an excellent student. But, of course, basketball is what gave you the golden ticket to attend just about any college you wanted. However, with your grades slipping while you were remote learning, and basketball now out of the picture . . ."

The pause is longer this time, as if the next thing Mrs. Wright is going to say carries special significance.

"Look, I'll just be direct here," Mrs. Wright says, staring me straight in the eyes as if she's trying to find something lost inside me. "Do you still want to go to college, Ossie?"

"Of course he does!" Grandma Alice interjects before I can even open my mouth. "My baby's more than just that damn ball and hoop!"

"All right, Ms. Alice." Mrs. Wright nods, her eyes never leaving mine. "But I need to hear it from your grandson. Ossie, can you still see yourself in college?"

Honestly, ever since the injury and my athletic scholarships were rescinded, I haven't really given college much thought. But when you don't have a clear answer, sometimes the best play is to give them what they want to hear.

"Yeah—I guess," I say with about as much energy as a deflated balloon.

"Great. Since that's the case, let's get real about where you are and what Ms. Hunt thinks you can do to still make college a reality," Mrs. Wright says.

"Sure," I mumble, my mind already wishing it was back home, rewatching *Love & Basketball* for the hundredth time since Laura and I split. Every time I press play, I feel pathetic. Wondering if she's sharing all the songs, all the movies, I put her onto with Matthew.

"You've still got a respectable 3.4 GPA," Mrs. Wright says, "despite your academic performance at the end of your junior year. That GPA will get you into decent schools, but it won't get you the kind of financial support you and your family need."

"But there's good news!" Ms. Hunt jumps in. "With your talent, I think there just might be a chance for you to get the sort of recognition you deserve *and* the scholarship money you need."

"I can't play anymore," I remind her.

"I know, Ossie," Ms. Hunt replies gently. "I'm not talking about basketball. I'm talking about your writing."

"My writing?" I ask, my eyebrows rising in surprise.

"You're a very gifted writer. I noticed it the first time I read one of your essays last year. Your writing is rough, but it's got a voice, a rhythm to it. That's something even many professional writers don't have," she says, sounding deeply proud. "I think you should apply to Braxton's Mark Twain Creative Writing Program."

For the next few minutes, Ms. Hunt and Mrs. Wright run me through the program. They tell me that if I get accepted—and if I pick up my grades—it could open the door to academic scholarships, maybe even a full ride, depending on the school.

The program's competitive, Ms. Hunt explains, with only twelve spots a year and over 150 applicants. Every applicant has to write an essay to go along with their application. The essay can be on any topic but has to display a standout ability to write. Ms. Hunt is running the program this year, but the judges for acceptance are an anonymous seven alums who were former students in the program.

"I can't make any promises about you getting in, Ossie. But if you open yourself up on the page like I've seen you do before, there's a great chance," Ms. Hunt says before she leaves for her next class.

Mrs. Wright tells me the application's due Monday morning. So I've only got three days to get it done, while others have been working on their essays for weeks or even months. It doesn't just sound like a long shot—it sounds like a waste of my time.

"I appreciate the offer, but I'm good," I say, getting up from my seat.

"Boy, ain't no request being made here," Grandma Alice says in that tone of voice she reserves for when things get real.

She rises from her chair and stands in front of me. "I love you, baby.

More than words can tell. I want more for you than what I've had. So if writing can get you into a good school, then you better believe you're gonna write. You write from the deepest part of you and snatch up one of those spots."

Grandma Alice gives me one of those long, hard stares, the ones that make you feel like she's looking right into your soul. Then she reaches out, pulling me into a tight hug. The scent of her shea butter lotion fills my nostrils. It's familiar. Comforting.

"You've got more in you than you think," she whispers close to my ear. "Don't you forget that."

I nod against her shoulder, finding it harder to pull away than I thought it would be. But eventually I do. "I hear you, Grandma."

She smiles, a warm, wrinkled smile that feels like home. "Go on, now, back to class. Get them grades up."

The classroom feels even colder than when I left. Every giggle, every whispered conversation, seems like it's about me. It's suffocating. I can't focus on what the teacher is saying; my mind is stuck on Grandma Alice's words, on the pressure of that application essay, and the weight of expectation.

I spend the rest of the day scribbling half-hearted notes about what my teachers are saying, but my mind keeps wandering. The memories of the past months, the injury, the breakup with Laura, and now this new opportunity with the writing program. It's all too much.

When the bell rings, signaling the end of the day, I leave school as fast as possible. I need a break. A moment to breathe.

The weekend can't come soon enough.

I spend the next two days in my room, struggling to figure out what I want to write. The night before the essay is due, I'm still in a deadlock with these damn words. I'm not used to this. Assign me a topic, and I can spit out an essay with no sweat. But when you tell me to flex my so-called gifted-writer muscles by writing an essay on anything that comes to mind? I don't even know what that looks like.

Each sentence I type is worse than the one before.

"In this essay I plan to . . ." Trash.

"Barack Obama once said . . ." Yuck.

"Throughout history . . ." Yawn.

I'm starting to question Ms. Hunt's judgment.

Before I know it, it's 11:00 p.m. on Sunday. The 7:30 a.m essay deadline is breathing down my neck. But I know how badly Grandma Alice wants this for me—she even let me skip Sunday family dinner at her place, which she never allows. Just so I can sit here, slumped in defeat, as my words crumble to dust.

The room feels smaller than usual, the walls inching in with every failed attempt to string together a decent sentence. My laptop screen glows mockingly, the blank document staring back with that blinking cursor—like it's waiting for me to impress it.

I glance over at the stack of books on my desk, books that are supposed to inspire, guide, and help me write a strong essay. Some lady named Joan Didion, and my mom's favorite writer, James Baldwin. Grandma Alice lent them to me with such hope in her eyes. "These'll help, baby. Just you see."

But right now, all they're doing is reminding me of how far I am from the greatness they represent.

My chest tightens, frustration bubbling, rising, threatening to spill over. "I can do this shit," I mutter, trying to convince myself more than anyone else. But the words sound hollow, empty.

In a sudden burst of anger, I swipe my arm across the desk, sending the books crashing to the floor. They land with thuds, pages flapping, covers splayed. The noise reverberates in the silent room, echoing the chaos in my mind.

The room's dim, lit only by my computer screen and the soft, orangey glow from the streetlights outside seeping through the blinds. I crawl into bed, but the covers feel like quicksand, pulling me down, down, down, until I'm all but swallowed whole. I toss them aside and snatch my phone from my nightstand, thumb through playlists. I'm not in the mood for anything hype. I need something relaxing.

R&B it is.

The first song comes on, and it's like Solange is in the room, serenading my broken spirit. The melody is soothing. Each lyric seems to be about my own silent screams.

My gaze drifts up to the wall, and there it is, always watching— Dad's jersey. Faded, a little frayed around the edges, but always there. A lump forms in my throat, thick and stubborn. With a shaky breath, I whisper, "I'm sorry, Dad."

The music continues to play, wrapping around me like a blanket. My eyelids grow heavy. The room blurs. The weight of the day, the weight of life, sinks me. And before I know it, I begin to drift off.

I failed—again.

Chapter Four

My eyes snap open, heart pounding like it's trying to escape from my chest. Sweat clings to my skin, and my mouth's dry, like it's been stuffed with cotton.

My father's voice still lingers in my mind. That disappointment in his eyes, the hurt in his voice when he said, "So you're just giving up on college? You're not my son—I wouldn't have raised a quitter." That dream—no, that nightmare—felt too real. As though I was there, standing in front of him, the gravity of his disappointment pulling me in like a black hole.

I sit up, clutching the sheets, trying to slow my heavy breathing. Every nerve in my body is on fire, reminding me of the challenge I left unfinished. Looking around the dim room, my eyes find my open laptop, its screen dark, as though it's given up on me. The clock on my nightstand glows a soft blue, reading 3:07 a.m. The world outside is silent, but inside my head, a storm is raging.

Maybe I can't change what happened to my leg. Maybe I can't rewrite the story of my broken hoop dream. But this? This essay? This is something I can control.

I'm not going to disappoint you again, Dad.

Swinging my legs over the bed, I plant my feet on the cold floor, drawing strength from the chill. I approach my desk, reaching down to pick up the scattered papers and books, victims of my earlier frustration. I enter my password on my laptop, the screen's brightness temporarily too much to bear. As my eyes adjust, that blinking cursor returns, taunting me, daring me to impress it. This time, though, it feels different. I feel different.

I take a deep breath, my fingers hovering over the keys. Instead of thinking about the pressure, the expectations, the looming deadline, I think about my father. His hard work, his sacrifices, his death. And I begin to type.

The words burst out of me like water breaking through a dam. Every sentence, every paragraph, is a piece of me. Raw, unfiltered, unapologetic. I write about the highs, the lows, the heartbreaks, and the triumphs. I write about how it feels to be me, about the shadows of giants I've always felt I had to measure up to.

Hours fly by, and the first light of dawn starts to creep in. And there it is, staring back at me—my essay. My truth.

TO: Ms. Tasha Hunt

SUBJECT: Mark Twain Essay

Ms. Hunt,

To be honest, I'm not even sure what I'm supposed to write. But here's all I've got. I hope it's what you're looking for.

Is There Anything More for Me?

Two oceans' worth: the amount of tears that flowed from me over the summer.

One wrong move: what it took for all the work I'd put in since I was four years old to mean nothing.

Two and a half hours: how long the doctors tried to repair our only chance at something better.

Fifteen seconds: a stretch of time that felt like it lasted forever. Filled with words as clear as day, that felt as dark as night:

"I'm afraid that due to the severity of the injury, it's unlikely you'll be able to play at your former high level again."

One dream, forever shattered.

"What do you mean?" My mother's words were loaded with years of work and a lineage of unfulfilled aspirations. "How is that possible? Before the surgery, y'all said—"

"The tear was worse than we had thought," the doctor explained gently. I could tell it hurt him to give us that news. Maybe he cared more because he was a Black doctor, the only Black doctor I had ever met, actually. So maybe he understood the stakes: I didn't just want basketball; I needed basketball.

"We did the best we could," he finished.

I felt as though I was about to vomit. "What about this season? I just committed to Syracuse!"

"I'm so sorry," the doctor said, sounding like he really meant it. Not that that changed a damn thing.

Basketball was the way my family was going to break the cycle of spending three generations in the projects after escaping the toil of sharecropping in Georgia. Those brick buildings have a way of killing all parts of you, and I knew my family was dying slowly.

My grandmother's neighbor once told me, "America has always been another name for the Grim Reaper." I was four, and that was the last time I saw him. The Reaper came to claim his body in the form of a drug addiction. But his words stayed with me, like a warning that the Reaper would claim my family if I didn't get them out of our neighborhood. My dad had been trying to get my mother out. And now there was no one left to save us.

Because this broken body can't jump, it can't run, and they tell me that's the only way boys like me can rescue my family from a slow death.

Uncountable: the number of lies they all told me, back when they cared enough to lie to me.

"Even if you don't go to the NBA, it won't matter. It's you and me against the world, Ossie. Always."

"You have more in you! Give me more!" His roars echoed through the gym as we practiced beyond exhaustion. When no one else could find anything left to give him—I did. I gave him everything I had because unlike my teammates, what I didn't have was other options.

They acted like they cared when I told them why I needed basketball. When I told them about the Reaper, about my dying family, about my dad's legacy. They acted like I was more than a vessel for them to reach their skies.

Sometimes when I look at the sky, I wonder if there's anything more for me up there than the rain that seems to always be falling. A star. A cloud for me to rest on. An angel who goes by the name of my father.

Is there anything more for me? For my mom? For Grandma Alice? For my father's legacy?

Boys like me aren't given the sky and whatever is beyond it. Boys like me are told that we're too dark to fly any closer to the sun. But I want to know what it feels like to be warmed by happiness. My mother and father were sun-kissed, and it was magic. Even if only for a moment. But Black mothers and Black fathers aren't supposed to fly. Not in a world built for them to crash if they dare to try their chance in the clouds.

But when the courts have become dilapidated and withered away into a memory, and there are no more balls to shoot because they've all sunk to the bottom of the ocean, and the backboards have shattered and become sand in the wind, boys like me will still exist, and the sky won't be enough. Not for us, or the parents who brought us into this world.

Infinite: the potential that lives inside every Black soul. We are more than what they've decided to let us become, more than vessels for others' visions and dreams. And there will be a day, inevitable as the sunrise, when each of us will fly, unshackled and unburdened, into the boundless skies of our fullest selves.

Today is my day.

The morning sun has illuminated my entire room by the time I click send. My heart does this weird little dance. You'd think after what feels like a lifetime of last-second shots and crossing defenders, I'd be immune to this kinda anxiety. But this ain't a game. This is my truth, digitally inked out on a page, and now Ms. Hunt and a bunch of faceless people have a front-row seat to it.

I grab my blazer and choose a pair of sneakers, then head into the bathroom and splash some cold water on my face. My reflection, all tired eyes and hair needing to be braided, stares back at me, challenging. *You've got this*, it seems to whisper.

The trek to school feels even longer today. Each step's a little heavier, a little slower. Maybe it's the gravity of the essay, maybe it's starting a fresh week of jokes from the Woodcrest kids, or maybe it's just Monday doing its thing. But when Braxton Academy's brick walls come into view, I straighten up. Doing my best impression of someone who is ready for another week of darts being thrown at me.

When the bell rings later in the morning, signaling the beginning of the third period, I bump into Ms. Hunt on my way to class.

"Ossie," she starts. I smile nervously, hoping, praying for some hint of what she thought of my essay. But all she says is "Tell your grandmother I said hello."

I nod, muttering a quick "Got it, Ms. Hunt," before continuing to class.

Ms. Hunt's silence had volume. Loud enough to drown out every word I spilled onto that page, every tear I dropped when no one was looking. But I remember the plan: keep my head down, do the work, get the grades. My essay was a shot in the dark. But it's clear as day what I need to do in the rest of my classes.

Days slither by, each more silent than the last. I'm obsessively checking my email, but it's nothing but spam and the occasional interview request from someone wanting to write about my derailed career. It's like waiting for rain in a drought, each cloud that passes by bringing hope, then drifting away with nothing to show.

When Wednesday evening comes, I'm deep into my social studies homework, scribbling notes about some old slave owner the textbook praises for some reason, when my mom knocks on my open door.

She leans against the door frame, her eyes scanning the room before settling on me. "Your grandmother told me you applied for some writing program," she says, her voice a mix of curiosity and awkwardness.

I look up, surprised. "Yeah, I did," I reply, trying to gauge her reaction. There's a tightness in the air, like we're dancing around a thousand things unsaid.

She nods slowly, her eyes searching mine. "Well, good luck with that," she says, and then, as if she's shared too much, my mom turns and heads back the way she came.

Although it was just a brief exchange, it feels like she crossed a bridge over to my small island. It's the first time in what feels like forever that she's acknowledged something I'm doing, something I'm trying to grab for myself, for us.

That night, I lie in bed, staring up at the ceiling, thinking about that interaction. About the writing program. About how good it felt to write what I did. About the fact that my mom wants this for me, too. I need to know already.

The wanting, the yearning for this acceptance, snuck up on me. One moment it was all about making someone else happy, and the next, I was the one with my heart in my throat.

Just as I'm slipping between the sheets, preparing to start this awful waiting all over again in the morning, my phone dings with a new message alert. I fumble to open my email. It's from Ms. Hunt. My heart's racing, sounding like a beat J. Cole would rap on. I run my fingers through my hair, my palms sweaty. Maybe I'm not ready for whatever's inside that message. Maybe I should just tuck my phone under the pillow, try to get some sleep, and deal with it in the morning.

But who am I kidding? I'm not sleeping until I know.

I start pacing, my room feeling smaller than ever. Back and forth, back and forth, like I'm trying to burn a path into the carpet. My reflection in the window shows a face that's all tense lines and furrowed brows. I pause, take a deep breath, and finally tap the notification.

The email loads, the white screen lighting up the dark room.

TO: Ossie Brown
SUBJECT: Your Application to the Mark Twain Creative Writing Program

Dear Ossie,
I hope this email finds you well. First, I wanted to express my gratitude to you for sharing such a powerful and deeply personal essay with us.

Your words resonated with all of us on the voting committee who read them, and the narrative you wove was both poignant and captivating. As I said, you possess a natural talent for writing, one that is rare and deserving of nurturing.

Having said that, I regret to inform you that you have not been accepted into the Mark Twain Creative Writing Program this year. Please know that this decision was incredibly difficult, given the fierce competition and the limited number of spots available. Your essay was among many exceptional submissions, and the selection process was challenging.

While I understand that this news may be disappointing, I genuinely hope that you won't let this decision deter you from your writing journey. Your voice is strong, unique, and essential. The world needs to hear more from individuals like you who can shed light on experiences that often go untold.

I welcome the opportunity to discuss this further in person and to answer any questions you may have. To that end, please come to the English Lab tomorrow morning at 8:00. I very much hope you'll find the time.

Warm regards,
Ms. Tasha Hunt
English Department
Braxton Academy

Ms. Hunt's email nearly breaks me in half. It feels like déjà vu, a cruel reminder of that doctor letting me know I had spent my entire life dedicated to basketball for nothing. Now here I am again, staring at another closed door.

I feel the tears before I realize they're falling. I let them flow, surrendering to the grief of another loss.

The pain of everything—the injury, the end of my basketball career, the breakup with Laura, and now this rejection—feels like too much to bear. I pull the covers over my head, trying to shut out the world, to find some semblance of peace in the darkness.

What Grandma Alice said sits in my mind: "You've got more in you than you think." But right now, all I feel is empty, hollow, like there isn't anything left inside.

Chapter Five

I blink, groggy and weighted down, feeling like I've been trying to push a boulder up a hill all night. The remnants of yesterday's disappointment still cloud my mind.

Even though I set my alarm for earlier, I still haven't decided if I should go see Ms. Hunt. What's she gonna say that her email didn't? Maybe she'll tell me how I missed the cut by just a bit, how my story was close to making it. Or maybe she'll say it was miles away, that I have a long road ahead if I wanna write something that matters.

Staring at my reflection, I realize I have to know. I owe it to myself. And maybe, just maybe, she sees something in me that I can't right now.

By the time I reach Braxton, it feels like I've run a marathon. My heart's racing, and I keep wiping my palms on my plaid slacks. I head straight to the English Lab. The door's cracked slightly open, allowing me to hear the murmur of voices. One of them is Ms. Hunt's and the other is high-pitched and nasally, like the speaker *wants* everything she says to be annoying. Dean Blackburn.

I don't mean to eavesdrop, but as their conversation grows more heated, their murmurs transform into clear words.

"It's not just unfair, Dean Blackburn. It's unethical." Ms. Hunt's voice, laced with frustration, rises. "You know as well as I do that Ossie's essay was light-years ahead of some of the others. The committee voted him in fair and square."

Dean Blackburn sighs. When she speaks, her voice is dripping with condescension. "Ms. Hunt, I understand your passion, but you need to see the bigger picture. Some of these students come from families who've made significant donations to Braxton. Others are legacies, carrying a name that's been associated with our school for generations. We can't afford to reject them."

My heart thuds in my chest, its rhythm syncing with the sharp inhales and exhales I try to muffle. Every word they exchange is another slap to the face, another revelation of how the system works against kids like me. It ain't about talent or hard work. It's about connections, about money, about legacy.

I've heard enough. Just as I start to walk away, though, Ms. Hunt glances at the door, her gaze catching mine through the narrow opening.

There's this moment, this electric pause, when our eyes lock. Then she continues, her voice louder, more deliberate, as if she's speaking for an audience. Which I guess she is. "I can't believe you used your power as dean to override the unanimous decision of the acceptance committee. How is it in 'Braxton's best interest' to accept someone who isn't as deserving?"

Dean Blackburn's reply is cold. "We clearly have different definitions of 'deserving,' Tasha. But no matter; what's done is done."

Ms. Hunt sighs. "Fine, then. I guess there's nothing left to be said."

With that, I hear the familiar *click-clack* of Dean Blackburn's heels approaching the door. My mind races, debating whether to confront her or let the moment pass. But before I can decide, the door swings open, and there she stands, looking up at me with a mix of surprise and dread.

Ms. Hunt tilts her head. "Oh, Ossie, is it eight o'clock already?" she asks, but her surprise seems like an act.

She knows. She knows I heard every word.

Dean Blackburn, her eyes darting from me to Ms. Hunt and back, clears her throat. "Mr. Brown," she starts, her voice honey-sweet, a distinct difference from the ice in her eyes. "Just how much of our conversation did you hear?"

"I think," I begin slowly, deliberately, "I should go call my mom before saying anything."

A flicker of panic dances across Dean Blackburn's eyes. "There's no reason to do that," she says quickly. "As you may have overheard, the program received a record number of outstanding entries this year—so many so that we were forced to make some very tough decisions about who should receive a coveted spot. However, my conversation with Tasha—Ms. Hunt—got me thinking: if we can find a way to give everyone a spot who deserves one, we should. Wouldn't you agree, Tasha?"

Ms. Hunt's lips press into a thin line. She holds Dean Blackburn's gaze, a silent battle of wills taking place. After what feels like an eternity, she finally murmurs, "Mm-hmm."

Satisfied, Dean Blackburn nods, her posture straightening, confidence returning. "And in that spirit," she continues with forced cheerfulness, "I would like to be the first person to congratulate you, Mr. Brown, on your acceptance into the Mark Twain Creative Writing Program." She breaks into a wide, teeth-baring smile. "I know you and the others are going to do wonderful work with Ms. Hunt."

I force my expression to remain calm. But inside, a storm rages, a mix of anger, relief, and a hint of satisfaction. While I know that Dean

Blackburn is only letting me into the program because I overheard her confessing to interfering with the admissions, I also heard Ms. Hunt say that the committee's decision to give me a spot was unanimous. I earned my spot fair and square.

The boulder in my chest seems to shift a little, like a bird that's decided to rest its wings for a while.

Ms. Hunt's eyes, so stern in her earlier conversation with the dean, soften. "Congratulations, Ossie," she says, that familiar warmth seeping back into her voice. "We meet here, in the English Lab, every Friday at 3:15. Meetings last two hours, all right?"

I nod, still reeling from the absurdity of everything that just went down. "Thank you, Ms. Hunt," I say.

"No need to thank us, Ossie," Ms. Hunt says quickly. "You earned your spot in the program. *Never* doubt that."

Dean Blackburn, with her stiff posture and painted smile, gives a frustrated nod. As she strides away, heels clicking assertively against the linoleum, I can feel Ms. Hunt's eyes on me. When I turn to her, she winks. The world may not always play fair, but in this moment, it feels like we've just scored a point against it.

With a newfound bounce in my step, I head toward my first class. The day might have started with clouds, but right now, it feels like the sun's breaking through, promising clearer skies ahead.

On Friday when the final bell rings, I feel like I've got this electric current running through my veins, the kind that makes your fingers tingle and your heart beat a little bit faster. Though I only agreed to apply for the program because Grandma Alice wanted me to, it feels good to be doing something that isn't about basketball or Laura. It's about me. Just me. Ossie.

As I step into the English Lab, it's like plunging into a pool of ice water. I can almost hear everyone thinking, *What's he doing here? They must have thrown him a bone because they felt sorry for him.*

Looking around the room, I recognize a few of the faces. But my focus is on Luis and Naima, as the only other students of color in the program. We've never really spoken, but I've noticed them around before. They both have eye-catching style, especially for Braxton. Their kicks, their hair, the way they accessorize—they stand out. Somehow they even make our ugly school uniforms look fly. If my pockets weren't so empty, I'd try to do the same.

Everyone is either silent or having low conversations with people they already know, until suddenly the moment is broken by a familiar voice entering the room.

"Looks like they lied about this program being exclusive."

It's Matthew. Along with Morgan Henley and Sydney Danvers. The three of them are part of a friend group that I'm pretty sure is a youth chapter of one of the groups that stormed the United States Capitol, but I can't prove it.

Matthew sneers. "How many jerseys did you sign for Ms. Hunt to get in here?" Sydney and Morgan laugh. "Doesn't she know your signature is worthless these days?"

I can feel my jaw tightening. But Tommy was right; it's what he wants. I take a deep breath and calm myself. He's not worth it.

But Matthew has more to say. "Anyway, when you need some help from someone who *earned* their spot, don't feel too shy to ask. I got you—if I'm not too busy with Laura, that is." He smiles smugly, then heads to a desk.

My blood boils, and I consider walking out. I don't need this shit. But just as I'm considering getting up from the desk, Ms. Hunt walks through the door.

"Good afternoon, everyone! Congratulations on your acceptance to this program," she begins. "Receiving such an opportunity means you have some talent. But talent isn't everything. It takes dedication, passion, and, above all, hard work to succeed in this program, just as it does in life. This isn't going to be easy."

A mix of fear and anticipation settles in my stomach.

Ms. Hunt kicks things off with one of those "Let's get to know each other" moments. Ugh. Icebreakers. Why? Every kid starts rambling about their summer, flexing their fancy vacations. After hearing stories about the South of France and safaris in Africa for what feels like an eternity, it's Luis's turn.

"For those who don't know me, I'm Luis Martinez. I'm here because I love writing in general, but I've been writing poetry and taking photos since I was a kid. I want to figure out creative ways to combine those things," he announces, his voice filled with confidence.

Luis is about six feet tall and has this athletic build that makes me wonder why he isn't on one of the sports teams. His skin has an olive glow, the type that many Braxton kids spend way too much time in tanning beds trying to get.

His hair's long, falling just right, like he rolled outta bed with that movie star vibe. Between his build, his hair, and his killer jawline, I'd be surprised if modeling scouts haven't hit him up yet. It's wild that there aren't rumors about him and a bunch of Braxton girls. Maybe he's the rare rich kid who doesn't like to parade his relationships across social media.

As Luis sits back down, Ms. Hunt calls out another name. Naima.

She steps up, voice smooth as silk. "What's up. I'm Naima Johnson. I'm here because I want to have a career as a novelist and journalist. Telling stories of people who are usually ignored."

Naima's about five and a half feet of straight bohemian vibes. Her skin's that deep, Lauryn Hill kinda brown—pure and radiant. And her hair. Man. It's wrapped up in these dope crochet faux locs, shining with gold beads and all sorts of fly accessories. But what really gets me? Her smile. It's the kind that lights up a room, full of pearly whites and sunshine. She flashes it at the entire class, and for real, I'm wondering how the walls are still standing.

I'm so caught up in her whole aura that Ms. Hunt's gotta holler my name, not once, not twice, but three times to pull me out of my daze.

"Mr. Brown . . . Mr. Brown . . . Ossie, are you in this dimension or what?"

I fumble to my feet so fast I slam my bad knee against the desk. "Shit!" I hiss, feeling that familiar sting race up my leg.

Balancing awkwardly on my good foot, I shoot off a quick intro: "I'm Ossie Brown. I'm here to become a better writer. Umm. Yeah." Then, with an awkward slight limp, I slide back into my chair.

After the final few students introduce themselves, Ms. Hunt stands in front of her desk and addresses us.

"Thank you all for introducing yourselves, and congratulations again on being here. It's no small feat. This program is more than just a badge to add to your college applications. It's a commitment. A journey. An opportunity to grow not just as a writer but as a person.

"The program has always been anchored in actual creative writing, and there will be a fair amount of that, of course. But I want to focus this year on what makes a great creative writer."

She leans back against her desk, hands folded in front. "Here's the thing: creative writing is beautiful. It's the soul laid bare on paper. But we're living in times when the truth is getting twisted every which way. Fake news. Alternative facts. Echo chambers. So for the first half of the academic year, we're gonna dive deep into the world of nonfiction essays and personal reflections."

A few murmurs ripple through the room. I can tell some students are thrown off, probably had their hearts set on writing the next Great American Novel or something.

Ms. Hunt raises a hand, silencing the whispers. "The best creative writing," she begins, "is true writing. It's about exploring and confronting the very essence of the human experience. What better way to master the art of truth-telling than to start with the literal truth? By delving into nonfiction, we lay the groundwork for understanding and conveying the realities of life, not just for ourselves but for everyone who engages with our words."

She moves away from the desk, pacing slowly, her shoes tapping softly on the floor. "And you know what else we're going to do? Become well-read. You wanna write? Great. But first, you've gotta read. And not just the stuff you like. Everything. The good, the bad, the in-between. Understanding different voices, perspectives, narratives . . . that's how you hone your own voice. That will make you a great creative writer."

She stops pacing and fixes a sharp gaze on us. "My expectations are simple. Commitment. Open-mindedness. Willingness to learn, to push beyond your comfort zones. If you're here just to coast, this ain't the place for you."

As Ms. Hunt's words hang in the air, crisp and clear, I catch a glimpse of Matthew leaning in toward Morgan and Sydney. *Ain't?* he mouths, like he's tasting something sour, something off. Morgan and Sydney both raise their eyebrows, judgment written all over their faces, as if *ain't* is a crime against the dictionary or something. But to me, it sounds like the truth. It sounds like someone's not just teaching from a book but speaking from the heart.

"But if you're willing? If you're ready? This program can open doors. Not just to colleges but to life. To understanding. To empathy. To connection."

And just like that, Ms. Hunt's got me hooked. This ain't just about words on paper anymore. This is about life. About growth. About finding my place in this wild, messed-up world. And I'm all in. Ready for whatever she throws at us.

"For your first assignment, I want you to choose a film, any film. But it has to be one that moves you, even if just a little. From that film, find one quote that speaks to you. Once you've got that quote, write a short essay about it—why it speaks to you, what it says in the context of the film, and what it says to you personally. Essays should be at least fifteen hundred words. Submit it to me by next Wednesday."

There's a buzz in the room, like a beehive that's just been shaken. Some look excited, others nervous. A hand shoots up. It's Morgan Henley. "Can more than one of us choose the same movie?"

Ms. Hunt nods. "Absolutely. As a matter of fact, you can watch it together if you want. Make a movie night out of it. But remember, the essays are solo. Your own thoughts, your own feelings. No piggybacking off someone else's insights."

The tension eases a bit with a few chuckles around the room. Ms. Hunt concludes, "All right, that's it for today. Have a good weekend, everyone. I'm excited to see what you come up with."

With that, the room bursts into motion. It's like when the bell rings at the New York Stock Exchange, everyone racing, negotiating, forming groups.

And then there's me. Ossie. The island. I sling my bag over my shoulder and limp toward the exit.

Except for the laughter and chatter from the English Lab, the after-school hallways of Braxton are quiet. I put in my earbuds and let Kendrick Lamar bring me somewhere other than where I am.

As I'm making slow progress down the hall to the elevator, I hear someone calling my name. "Hey, Ossie! Wait up!"

I turn to see Luis and Naima walking toward me. What could they want? An explanation of why I'm in the same program as them and all the other talented writers of Braxton?

"Luis, Naima," I greet them, trying to keep the nervousness out of my voice. "What's up?"

Luis's dark eyebrows rise in surprise. "You remember our names."

Naima rolls her eyes and shakes her head. "Calm down, thirsty," she teases Luis. "We just introduced ourselves a little while ago."

"Yeah, and I've seen you both around," I say. "Plus I like to keep a mental list of all the Black and brown folks at Braxton. Just so I know who's available to draft in case the race war breaks out here."

Naima laughs. "So we're talking about ten of us against a thousand? Sounds like typical odds for Black folks." All three of us chuckle.

"Anyway," Luis begins, "it seems like everyone decided to make a group to watch movies, so we thought you might want to make one with us two. Naima's coming over to my place tomorrow—you should pull up, too!"

I squint, wondering what these rich kids want with me: What's the catch? So I go with my gut. "Nah, I'm good. But thanks."

Luis shrugs. "All right, maybe next time."

"Too bad," Naima says. "One of the movies we're watching has your namesake in it."

Hold up. "What movie is that?"

"*Do the Right Thing*," she says, all casual-like. "Aren't you named after Ossie Davis?"

She catches me off guard. Most people don't know who I'm named after and why. My parents held a deep love for Spike Lee's movies, with *Do the Right Thing* being a particular favorite. Grandma Alice told me they would reenact scenes between the characters Mother Sister and Da Mayor, played by Ruby Dee and Ossie Davis, regardless of the setting or audience. The two of them admired Ruby and Ossie not only for their Hollywood status but also for their social justice activism. They also loved the fact that Ruby and Ossie were married in real life.

A small voice inside nudges me: *Maybe you're trippin'. They seem cool. And do you really want Matthew commenting on you being the only one in the program without friends?*

I clear my throat. "Matter fact, you know what, I'm down. Y'all seem to know a thing or two about good movies. What's your math and addy, Luis?"

We exchange numbers, and Luis and Naima stride off toward the student parking lot. I make my way to the bus stop, feeling an unfamiliar thrill. I can't remember the last time I hung out with new people.

Chapter Six

I shuffle onto the bus, my limping rhythm matching the old vehicle's chugging engine. The journey to Luis's place in Irvington is like riding through a slideshow of privilege. Every house I pass, each grander than the last, screams of money and tradition, things that feel light-years away from my own zip code.

As I'm finally hopping off the bus, the driver shoots me a look of concern like: *You ain't from here. Don't get too comfortable.*

Finally, after feeling as though I've walked Moses's forty years through the desert, I set my eyes on Luis's crib. Damn. Behind an imposing gate sits a massive mansion overlooking the Hudson River. The property could comfortably host the Olympics. I figured they'd have coins. But this? This is some Monopoly-millionaire stuff.

Doubts creep in, whispering maybe this was a bad idea. But just as I'm about to spin on my heel and dip, the gate stirs to life, an intercom voice, thick with a Latin American accent, calling me inside. As I walk through the gate and head toward the house, I'm taking it all in. Suddenly, a golf cart with a large Afro-Latino dude in a crisp uniform rolls up. He offers a ride with a nod. My pride's telling me to pass, but my aching leg has a louder voice today. So I hop on.

When we reach the front door, I'm greeted by Luis's parents. His father has the same handsome olive-toned features as Luis. With a large diamond-crusted ring glinting on his finger, he cheerfully waves me inside.

"The famous Ossie Brown!" he exclaims with a hint of the same accent I heard on the intercom. "You're even bigger than on TV! Come in, come in!"

Luis's mother is much lighter in complexion, with sparkling blue eyes and blond hair framing her beautiful face. Her accent's a bit thicker, and her tone is even warmer. "Oh, we've heard so much about you! Welcome!"

They are both so good-looking that I can't help but stare. It's like I've stepped through a portal into some alternate universe where everything is just a little too perfect. What did I get myself into?

Walking through their door, I feel like I've entered the lobby of one of those fancy hotels I used to go to with the team for basketball tournaments. You know, the kind that makes you want to tiptoe because you're scared of leaving dirt on the floors. The air's different in here, thick with the scent of deep pockets.

I spent a lot of time with Laura's family at their place over the years and thought that was something special—but this is next level.

Every corner of the entryway has a sculpture, some piece that looks like it belongs in a museum. A painting on the wall grabs my full attention. It's of a woman holding up the Dominican Republic's flag. The brushstrokes, the colors, the raw emotion in her eyes—it's like she's telling a story.

The living room is also like a page ripped out of a luxury magazine. Luis's parents guide me to a chair that's so plush, I feel like I'm sinking into a marshmallow. As they have a seat across from me, a parade of staff walks in. They're holding trays of food that looks like it came straight from a five-star restaurant.

It's clear to me that Luis's parents are more than just pleased by my visit; they're genuinely excited. Their smiles are broad and frequent, their glances between each other and me full of barely contained anticipation. I can't help but feel like I'm in the sequel to *Get Out*.

With obvious pride in his voice, Mr. Martinez breaks the ice. "We're so happy that Luis has a friend like you. A *real* young man." I'm puzzled by what he means, but before I can think it over, he continues: "I'm sure you know that the two of us have a lot in common—though it's been a while since I played in the NFL. But five Pro Bowls and two Super Bowl rings don't just disappear."

He laughs and I laugh along. I have no clue who Mr. Martinez is. But I keep nodding and smiling, letting him think I'm impressed by his achievements, which he enumerates for what feels like an hour, though it's probably only a few minutes.

Eventually, Mrs. Martinez takes the baton in the conversation. "While Hector is focused on his scouting work for the Giants, I run his nonprofit, Jerseys for Change." She smiles, white teeth gleaming. "I'm sure you've heard of it. We've done a lot of work in neighborhoods like yours."

It's no secret that I'm from Yonkers; the media loved to make a big point about my "humble" origins when they were highlighting my achievements on the court at Braxton. But the way Luis's mom alludes to "neighborhoods like mine" makes me even more uncomfortable, as though every Black kid comes from the exact same place—and that place is one that needs saving by people like Luis's parents and nonprofits like this Jerseys for Change.

As they keep talking, a cloud starts to form over my head. Here I was thinking maybe Luis and Naima were different, but they're just like all the other Braxton kids. I mean, sure, they're not white, but it's clear as day where they come from. Where they stand. And it's not next to people like me.

Every word out of Mrs. Martinez's mouth feels like a polite pat on the head, a "Good job for surviving in the hood" kinda vibe. There's an ache in my gut as a realization dawns on me—the scholarship I got to Braxton? It probably comes from folks just like this. People who think I'm charity.

Suddenly, Mr. Martinez leans in close. "You know, Ossie," he begins, his tone rich with expectations, "I really hope you influence that son of mine. Don't get me wrong; I think it's important not to be too tough all the time. But the boy, he's like Charmin. You know, soft tissue."

Just as I'm figuring out what to say to Mr. Martinez, Luis slides into the scene.

"Okay, Papi! We get it! You wished for a son who spends all of his time throwing touchdowns and hitting home runs, not writing poetry and taking pictures." Luis's words are filled with sarcasm and hurt. "Can Ossie go now?"

"Ah, mijo, you know your dad didn't mean anything by what he said," Mrs. Martinez says to Luis.

"Whatever, Mami." Luis extends a hand and hoists me to my feet, guiding us out of that stuffy living room.

"Naima's hanging out in the home theater. We were tryna figure out what to eat."

I stop in the middle of a hallway that's like another wing of the Martinez family art gallery. "Look, man, I don't know about all this," I say, my voice low, eyes searching his. "Maybe I should just dip."

Luis's eyes are full of apology. "I'm sorry about my parents.

They're . . . Well, you saw. They're a lot. More than a lot. Like, a whole universe of too much. I would've rolled up to save you sooner, but I didn't see your car outside, so I didn't know you were here."

"Oh, um, I took the bus. My car's in the shop," I say, trying to sound casual. I don't want to feel any poorer by comparison than I already do. "Hit a pothole the other day. Messed up the axle."

"Damn, that sucks! Why didn't you tell me? I would've come pick you up. No one needs to be on public transportation if they don't have to be."

The comment stings and reminds me how much I don't belong here.

"Listen, Luis—" I start to say, my thoughts on my escape.

But he stops me. "Look, man, about my parents . . ." He runs a hand through his hair, frustration evident. "They've got this way of making everyone feel terrible about themselves. But don't let them be the reason we don't hang out. Please."

I should probably leave, but there's something honest in his eyes. Something real. Something that says he isn't like his parents.

"All right," I finally mutter, rolling my shoulders back. I nod toward the direction of the door to the home movie theater. "But these snacks better be fire."

Luis's face lights up. "Don't worry, I got you. I'll have the chef whip up some dim sum."

Hold up. *Chef*? Ain't no way I'm ever letting him see where I live.

The door to the Martinez's movie theater swings open, welcoming us into a space that can only be described as jaw-dropping. It's less of a home theater and more of a mini Madison Square Garden, rows upon rows of cushioned seating, and a screen that covers an entire wall.

Naima is standing in the center of the room, looking like she stepped out of a revolution and into a fashion magazine. The stark white of her YOU'RE ON STOLEN LAND sweater pops against her brown skin. And her fresh Jordan 1s match perfectly. No doubt she's making a statement, and I'm here for it.

"You down for some dim sum?" Luis asks her.

Her eyes light up. "Always down for dim sum. You know me."

"Hey, Ossie." She smiles, and just like at yesterday's writing program meeting, I don't know if anything could convince me this isn't the best smile I've ever seen.

We settle into the plush seats, and it's not long before an assortment of bamboo steamers floods the small tables in front of us, the aroma of dumplings and buns filling the air. As we eat, we talk, and I'm relieved to find out that it feels . . . easy and comfortable. Like slipping into an old pair of shoes.

Time seems to blur, and before we know it, an hour's flown by. Naima glances at her watch. "We better start these movies unless you're about to host a sleepover, too, Luis."

Luis nods, reaching for the remote. "All right, all right. Well, Naima should know what I'm picking. . . ." He grins, a twinkle in his eye.

"He's been obsessed with *The Lord of the Rings: The Return of the King* since we were like six," Naima says, rolling her eyes but smiling all the same.

"Yup! It's one of the greatest stories ever told, and it has everything. Action, friendship, romance . . ."

"And nary a Black or brown person to be found! Unless you counteth the orcs, of course," Naima interjects with a mock–Old English accent. We all burst into laughter.

"True, true," Luis responds, leaning back into the cushioned seat. "And you're still locked on *Do the Right Thing*?" he asks Naima.

"Nah, I changed my mind," Naima says. "I want to watch *Ma Rainey's Black Bottom*. I love all of August Wilson's writing, and it was Chadwick's last performance. Plus it's just good as hell. My essay is going to be about how Black pain is appropriated, used as entertainment, and sometimes even considered, but you never really understand it unless you're Black."

Luis says, in what seems to be his typical joking way, "So something light and inconsequential, as usual."

Naima laughs. "You know it. Ossie, what about you? What movie are you going to choose?"

"I'm gonna go with . . . *Moonlight*. Have y'all seen it? It's stacked with lines and moments that stick in your mind. They're deep. I'm thinking of writing about what it's like to feel like an outsider in a world that doesn't want you to be true to yourself."

Naima nods slowly, her eyes sliding to Luis and then back to me. "That's a really good choice. We can probably all relate to that feeling, especially at school."

I shrug. "Maybe it's a good thing we don't fit in at a place like Braxton."

"That's facts," she says, her gaze lingering on me as if she's pleasantly surprised. Then she grabs the remote. "We should probably get to it."

We start with *Return of the King*, which is already epically long but is made even longer since we keep pausing to discuss specific parts— or, in Naima's case, to call out Tolkien's racism.

"So you're telling me Tolkien couldn't make a single wizard or hobbit a nigga? But we have these hulking monsters with dreadlocks? Come on, that's an obvious allegory for Black and brown people!"

Eventually the credits roll on *Moonlight*, the last of the three films, signaling time for our deep dive into the lines that hit us hardest. Luis steps up first, plucking a gem from Gandalf's wisdom: "'I will not say: do not weep; for not all tears are an evil.'" His reasoning is like poetry: "You know, we rarely talk about the beauty of tears. The reality that some tears remind us that we're human. Some cool us down from the pain that burned us."

The depth of his analysis is unexpected. I didn't think anyone could think so deeply about hobbits, elves, and dragons.

"What about you, Nai?" he asks. "Which quote are you going to write about?"

Naima's fingers glide over the glass surface of her phone before she starts to recite lines from the film. "'White folk don't understand about the blues. They hear it come out, but they don't know how it got there. They don't understand that's life's way of talking. You don't sing to feel better. You sing 'cause that's a way of understanding life.' I don't think I could've asked for a better quote to support what I want to write about."

Luis and I nod, sitting with what Naima read.

Then the spotlight's on me.

"All right, Ossie, whatcha got for us?" Luis asks, all anticipation.

No lie, after Luis's and Naima's profound dives, I'm feeling the heat. I mean, *Moonlight* is like a treasure chest, with so many jewels. But I have to lock in on one. Ms. Hunt's faith in me echoes in my mind. Am I the real deal? Or just a project she took pity on?

I look at the quotes I typed in my notes app, then drop a line that resonated deep: "'Let your head rest in my hand. Relax. I got you.'"

The room falls silent as Luis tosses a "Why?" my way. I shuffle my thoughts around, stringing together a coherent response. "I'm not sure. It just . . . It was painful and beautiful, in a real way. I'm not gay or bi, so most of the movie is a learning experience for me. But that line. Chiron swimming, trusting Juan—maybe the first man who ever invested in him . . . I felt that. I've imagined my father holding my head above water. There to make sure I never drown."

Luis and Naima nod slowly.

"That's some deep shit," Luis says.

I feel a flush of pride, a spark of validation.

A short while after, I glance at my phone, and my eyes nearly pop out my skull. "It's almost midnight!"

Both Naima and Luis gaze at their phones, their eyes widening in shared surprise.

"Damn, we've really been hanging out for that long?" Luis chuckles, scratching the back of his head.

Naima nods, stretching her arms. "Time flies when you're calling out racism in your best friend's favorite movie." She laughs.

A slight sadness fills the room, the kind that comes when you know it's time to end something special. Something real. I reluctantly grab my bag. "I'm going to call an Uber. I had a good time; I appreciate y'all inviting me."

Luis quickly jumps in. "Nah, man, you don't have to do that. I got you. Let me drop you off."

Before I can protest, Naima cuts in. "Actually, I'll take him. I kind of have to drive toward Yonkers anyway to get home. Plus don't you have that call to make?" She arches an eyebrow at Luis.

I wonder who he's calling at this hour? But I'm more concerned about them seeing where I live, the side of Yonkers they probably ain't familiar with. "Nah, it's all good. It's too far," I argue, hoping they'll leave it at that.

"It's really not that far, Ossie. And it's on my way," Naima says. Her tone has this soft determination that's hard to argue with. And I can't deny a tiny, sneaky part of me wants to spend more time with her. Not to say I haven't had a good time with Luis, too. But Naima just has a certain . . . thing.

Sensing my hesitation, she adds, "How about I just drop you at the Metro-North station? It's a few miles closer, at least. Easier for you to get an Uber from there, too."

Feeling the pressure and not wanting to keep arguing, I give in. "Yeah, okay. The Metro-North works. I appreciate it."

She grins. "Great."

Luis gives Naima a hug, then daps me up. "Take care, y'all. This isn't the last movie night, all right, Ossie? We're doing this again."

Feeling a genuine smile creep onto my face, I nod. "Sounds good. 'Night, man."

Chapter Seven

I feel way different walking out of the Martinez mansion than I did walking in — calmer, more relaxed. The driveway stretches out like a ribbon, leading us to Naima's car. The moonlight glints off the blue of her Mercedes, its shine mocking my earlier bus journey. It sits there looking like a sleek beast from a zoo I can't afford to visit.

She clicks a button on the key fob, and the lights flash briefly. I can't help but think the price of that car could probably pay five years' worth of rent for my mom's and Grandma Alice's apartments combined.

"I hate this car; it's too flashy," she says, and I wonder if she somehow guessed what I'm thinking. "I wanted something more . . . subtle. A Smart car or something, but my dad wanted to spoil me."

"It's a nice car. Perfect for those days when you're driving around flexin' on 'em. Top down, diamonds shining, bumping Lil Baby," I respond, trying to make light of the expensive vehicle.

"Shut up," she says, taking a playful swing at my arm. "I'm serious," she continues, her tone more thoughtful. "This whole sports car thing isn't my vibe. The only thing I really splurge on is kicks, which is a habit I'm also trying to break."

I glance down, my eyes landing on the Jordan 1s hugging her feet. Out-the-box fresh. "Yeah, I peeped your Js. Let me find out y'all dripping out in the suburbs," I comment, the teasing flowing easily.

She grins as we get into the car. "I don't know about the others in my neighborhood dripping, but my family is originally from Harlem," she says with pride in her voice. "And if I was bumping something with a top down, it wouldn't be Lil Baby."

The Mercedes's engine purrs as we pull out of the front gate. I can't deny the comfort of the leather seats, the kind that seem to mold to your body.

"All right, if not Lil Baby, who you got on your playlist, then?" I ask, genuinely curious.

She shrugs, fingers lightly tapping on the steering wheel as the car glides effortlessly down the road. "It's not that I don't like Lil Baby. He's cool and all. But that sort of rap just isn't my go-to, you know?"

I raise an eyebrow, intrigued. "So what is your go-to?"

"R&B, hands down. I grew up on soul music, so I like things that are an extension of that, I guess."

I chuckle, trying to picture this rich girl listening to the same kind of music my mom does. "Oh, word? Like who? Give me a few artists."

She thinks for a moment, then lists off, "Snoh Aalegra, H.E.R., the Internet, Frank Ocean, Mary J. . . ."

I nod, impressed. "Okay, okay. Not bad. I see you know a little something."

She casts a sly glance my way, the streetlights catching the gleam in her eyes. "Oh? And what do you know about R&B?"

"Please. I'm an R&B expert. If I hadn't spent so much time on basketball, I probably could have had my own radio show or something with my R&B knowledge."

Naima's eyebrows shoot up. "Really? Expert, huh? Prove it."

I blink, thrown off guard. "Deadass?"

She nods, her expression serious. "Yeah. Connect to the Bluetooth. Show me what you got, Mr. R&B Expert."

I hesitate for a moment, but then think, why not? "All right, hold on," I say, pulling out my phone and searching for a track that'll seal my status as an R&B expert. "Okay. I've got something."

Naima chuckles, her laughter blending seamlessly with the hum of the car engine. "All right, let's hear it."

With a sly grin, I hit play on my pick: "Dragonball Durag" by Thundercat. As the funky bass riff starts to hum through the car's sound system, Naima's eyes widen in delight.

"Okay!" she exclaims, bobbing her head to the beat. "This is my jam! I didn't expect you to play this."

The groove's infectious, and it doesn't take long before we're both immersed. Our voices, a little off-key but filled with passion, join Thundercat, harmonizing and belting out the chorus. There's an electric energy that builds with every note.

As the song fades, Naima shoots me a teasing look. "All right, that was impressive. But one-hit wonder or can you keep it going?"

Feeling emboldened by her response to my first selection, I lean back and let my fingers dance over my phone's screen, settling on a track I'm sure she'll appreciate: "Whipped Cream" by Ari Lennox. As the smooth neo-soul sound and Ari's velvety voice fill the space, Naima starts swaying in her seat, humming along, completely lost in the music.

Watching her, I can't help but chuckle. She is a sight to behold — singing her heart out to Ari Lennox in the middle of the night.

"Well," I say as the song winds down, "seems like the R&B expert strikes again."

She laughs, a deep, gorgeous sound that fills the quiet car. "All right, all right, I'll give you that one," she admits with a good-natured roll of her eyes.

The drive continues, but she soon breaks the musical spell, glancing at the fuel gauge with a frown. "Do you mind if I grab some gas before dropping you off?"

I nod, appreciating her thoughtfulness. "No worries. Do your thing."

"Cool," she replies, her smug look returning, "that gives me more time to test your music expertise. Show me what else you got."

I let the calm ambience set the stage for my next pick. There's a certain warmth, a vibration, I want to capture, so I scroll until I find "Gonna Love Me" by Teyana Taylor. As the opening chords flow through the car's speakers, both of us instantly tune in, nodding in unison to the song's smooth rhythm.

Naima floats a glance my way. "I love this song," she murmurs softly, almost as if she's sharing a secret.

"Yeah, me too," I reply, matching her subdued tone.

Her smile widens, and I can't help but mirror it, feeling a subtle energy that's been foreign to me for a while. The kind of energy you feel when you're fully in sync with someone. It doesn't have to be romantic. Just . . . comforting.

As the chorus flows, I realize this is probably the first time I've ever been alone in a car with a girl other than Laura. It feels good not to be weighed down by the baggage of a shared history. Even with Luis earlier, I realized how much I enjoy getting to have my own thing. Start from scratch.

The music feels like it has its own gravity, pulling in all other sounds. So we are silent—and it's golden. No need for words when the music speaks volumes.

The song starts to wind down as Naima signals and pulls into a gas station. The bright fluorescent lights break our little bubble, and as she turns the car off, the sudden absence of music makes the world outside seem louder.

I glance over at Naima, the gas station's lights painting her face in sharp contrasts. "You want me to pump the gas for you?" I offer.

She chuckles. "Why would I want you to do that?"

I scratch the back of my head, feeling a little embarrassed. "I dunno," I mumble. "It's just . . . my grandmother always said it's something a gentleman should offer. And Laura, my ex, she always had me do it whenever we were out driving."

Naima laughs, the sound light and airy. "Look, Ossie, I appreciate the sentiment, I really do. But not everyone expects or needs that sort of stuff."

I nod slowly, processing her words. Feeling embarrassed—I'm sure she can tell.

"But I appreciate you," she adds, her tone sincere. Some of my embarrassment fades.

With a graceful movement, she opens the car door and steps out. She swipes her card and begins pumping the gas. I watch her for a moment, admiring her independence, her confidence. Naima's words echo in my mind: "Not everyone expects or needs that sort of stuff." Maybe I should think about the fact that a lot of my understanding of what people need and want from me comes from people who were using me. What do expectations look like when people might not need anything from me other than to be—me?

Naima grips the nozzle tightly, the numbers on the display climbing higher and higher. As she does, three police officers emerge from the gas station's convenience store, coffee cups in hand, their uniforms crisply defining who they are. Two of them are white, one Black.

Whenever I see cops, I can feel the tension rising in me, a tingling in my fingertips, a tightness in my chest. It's a learned response, built from years of experiences, stories, and warnings.

Naima seems to be in her own world, unbothered, but I can't help but watch their every move, monitoring them for a change in their demeanor, a sudden approach.

They glance our way, their eyes resting on Naima's Mercedes, then shifting to her. There's an unspoken question in their gaze, a subtle skepticism. I catch the Black officer's eye for a second, searching for some sort of acknowledgment, maybe reassurance. But he's unreadable, his gaze as inscrutable as his colleagues'. Then, as quickly as they appeared, they move on, climbing into their patrol cars.

The sound of the gas pump clicking off shakes me from my focus on them. Naima replaces the nozzle, her face calm, her movements deliberate. I wonder if she even noticed them. As she slips back into the car, she picks up our earlier conversation.

"The train station is only about four minutes away," she says, starting the car, "so you've got like one song left. Impress me."

I flash a smile, taking the bait. "All right, one song to seal the deal."

My fingers scroll through my library, searching for the perfect track, something with depth, with soul, something that'll echo the emotions of the night. The car's engine hums, filling the silence as I think. I find the perfect song as Naima pulls away from the pump.

But before I can hit play, blue and white lights from one of the patrol cars splatter against the rearview mirror, chasing away the calm of the night. The sharp sound of the siren is like a slap, jolting, demanding. "Driver, pull over! Now," booms a voice from the car's speaker.

I feel my heart speed up, my hands curling into fists. Naima's face tightens, but she eases the Mercedes to the side of the road.

"Stay calm," I say under my breath, not sure if I'm talking to Naima or myself. The air grows heavy.

I hear the sound of boots on the asphalt as one of the white officers approaches the car. The glow from the streetlamp elongates his shadow on the ground, and I swallow the boulder in my throat, feeling a mixture of frustration and fear.

He taps on Naima's window, and she rolls it down. "Whose vehicle is this?" he asks, his voice full of suspicion, eyes scanning Naima and me.

Naima, clearly annoyed, responds, "It's mine."

The officer's gaze doesn't waver. "This is a pretty expensive car for you, isn't it?" The insinuation is clear, and it hangs in the air between us, thick and dirty.

Naima's eyes flash, and for a moment, I worry she might say something we'll both regret. But she takes a deep breath, her voice steady even as her hands grip the steering wheel. "Yeah, that's why my parents paid for it."

There's a pause, the officer clearly taken aback by her confidence. I try to keep my breathing even, but it's hard. My every instinct is screaming at me that this isn't right. That it's not about the car, not really.

The cop's flashlight flicks on, a beam of aggressive white light cutting through the dark, making me flinch. It zips around inside the car, bouncing off the leather, the gleam of the dashboard, the sheen of the rearview mirror. And then, like a searchlight locking onto its target, it settles on our faces. The sudden brightness stings, and I squint, trying to shield my eyes without making any sudden moves.

Naima throws up a hand to block the light, her voice sharp but controlled. "Look, can you just tell me what you want me to do so we can get home?"

The officer's response is cold, filled with abusive authority. "You can *shut up*, is what you can do. *I'm* in charge here, and I need to make sure this car isn't stolen."

I can feel Naima's anger rising. When she responds, her voice is tinged with disbelief. "Why would I steal an expensive car and casually pump gas in front of police officers? Come on. Does this make you feel big, picking on a Black girl because she drives a car you can't afford?"

His face reddens with anger and embarrassment. "You know what, wiseass? You can get out of the car."

Naima's hesitant. "For what?"

"Get out of the car NOW!"

From the corner of my eye, I see the other white officer, the backup, making his way over. The situation's escalating fast, and every fiber in my body screams with fear. "Come on, Naima," I whisper, my voice barely audible. "Let's just do what he says."

She hesitates for a split second, her eyes searching mine. I give a slight nod, my message clear: It's not about pride right now. It's about safety.

Naima's door creaks open, and she steps out, her shoes finding their place on the asphalt. The cop stares at her for a moment and then peers inside the car at me. His gaze feels like chains. The chill of the evening wraps around me, but it's not the cold that has my hands shaking.

"Face the car!" the officer barks at Naima, and before I can even process what's happening, he's patting her down, rough hands grazing places they have no right to touch. The violation is clear. She clenches her teeth, refusing to give him the satisfaction of a reaction.

And then he pushes. The harshness of it presses Naima's face against the cold metal of her car. Every muscle in my body tightens as my hand, a coil ready to spring out of the car, reaches for the door handle.

"Hey!" I shout, my voice louder than I expected. "You don't have to do that!"

His eyes, icy and defiant, meet mine. He aims his flashlight beam at me again. "Say another word, boy," he snarls, "and you'll end up just another name scribbled on cardboard signs."

His words hit like a gut punch. A reminder of the world we live in. I can barely breathe.

Suddenly, the second officer, the backup who's been silently watching from a distance, steps forward, his eyes widening in recognition. "Holy shit! This is Ossie Brown!"

The first officer, still gripping Naima, looks up, confusion clouding his features. "What are you talking about?"

"This kid . . . He's a famous ballplayer up at that Braxton school. Hell, he's in the papers all the time."

The grip on Naima loosens ever so slightly. The realization dawning that maybe, just maybe, they've made a grave mistake tonight. Even as I feel slight relief, anger claws at me. It shouldn't matter who I am. Shouldn't matter if I'm a famous ballplayer or just another kid from Yonkers. This—what's happening right now—it shouldn't be happening to *anyone*.

The second officer looks at his colleague, a silent warning in his gaze. It's a look that tells the first officer that these aren't the kids he wants to mess with tonight. A moment of tense silence presses down on all of us.

Reluctantly, the first officer lets go of Naima. "You watch that mouth of yours, little girl," he hisses at her, his face twisted with a mix of frustration and anger. Without another word, he turns and makes his way back to their patrol car.

As they pull away, I can't help but glance at the officers in the second car, which remained parked a few feet away throughout the ordeal. I spot the Black officer in the front passenger seat. His face is stone, as if he wouldn't have cared if Naima and I ended up in body bags tonight. Blue over Black, I guess.

The chilliness of the night enters the car when Naima does. We sit in silence for a moment, Naima's fingers gripping the steering wheel so tightly they turn white. With a scream of frustration, she slams her hand against the wheel, the movement nearly shaking the small space.

"It's going to be all right," I try to reassure her, but the words feel hollow even to me.

She looks at me, her eyes glistening with unshed tears. "You don't get it, Ossie. You can't possibly understand how that felt."

"I do, though," I respond, my voice laden with a lifetime of similar experiences. "That's exactly why I wanted you to stay calm. He was looking for a reason, any reason."

Naima's voice rises. "So we should just let them do whatever they want to us? We have a right to stand up for ourselves."

"I get that," I reply, my own emotions bubbling to the surface. "But in that moment, it's also about staying alive. It's about choosing your battles."

She scoffs, her gaze sharp. "You sound like a coward."

My pulse quickens. "And you sound like someone who's never had to deal with the police breathing down your neck every single day. Cop cars sitting in front of your building sunup to sundown. Where I'm from, it doesn't matter whether you're eight or eighty; they're waiting for *any* excuse. I've seen what they can do right in front of my eyes. If being quiet means I might make it home to my family . . . I'll be a coward."

Naima stares ahead blankly. She says nothing.

Taking a shaky breath, I say, "I'm gonna call an Uber home." I open the car door, the cold night air hitting my face. I start walking away, and I don't look back.

Chapter Eight

Thinking about what happened last night, what the cops did, what Naima said, it all feels like sandpaper rubbing against my insides. The sun's up, but everything feels shrouded. Naima's words play on loop in my head, each time cutting deeper than the last. Rich kids, even the Black ones. They think they know it all, but they've never really known the struggle. She's just another one of them. She doesn't get it.

Pushing the thoughts from my mind, I prep myself for the highlight of my week: Sunday dinner at Grandma Alice's. She might not have much in terms of money, but when it comes to food, man, you would think she's rich. I swear, her kitchen is some sort of magic portal, producing more dishes than seems possible. And it's not just the quantity; it's the love. Each dish is like a warm hug, a reminder that you're cherished.

As I walk into her apartment, the rich aroma of collard greens and yams mixed with the savory scents of meatloaf and chicken fills the air. My stomach rumbles in appreciation. But the food isn't the only reason people flock to Grandma Alice's on Sundays. It's her. She's got this open-door policy—everybody's welcome. And I mean everybody.

There's Ms. Jenkins from 3B, a single mother of three who works two jobs just to keep the lights on. And then there's Ahmad, who recently came home from doing fifteen, trying to find his footing in a world that's changed so much since he went inside. Mr. Green, who recently lost his job and is struggling to make ends meet, and Miss Loretta, living in her memories since her family moved away. All these faces, all these stories, they find peace at Grandma Alice's table. And if they don't come to her, she sends me to them, plates of love in hand.

But the beauty of her apartment isn't just in the food or the people; it's in the atmosphere. Walking into Grandma Alice's apartment is like stepping into a world where Black culture is celebrated in its purest form. The walls are covered with Afrocentric art—vibrant paintings of Black women, photographs from the civil rights movement, African sculptures. The living room is blanketed in African-print throws and the comforting scent of lavender incense. It's like a temple, a space where you're reminded of the beauty and strength of our people.

Yet even in this haven, the weight of last night lingers, the sting of Naima's words, the coldness of her gaze casting a shadow over everything. I'm pulled from my thoughts when Grandma Alice sets a heaping plate in front of me, her eyes searching mine.

"You okay, baby?"

I try to smile, to assure her, but the simple act feels like a large task. "Just . . . thinking, Grandma."

She places a hand on my arm. "You know you can always talk to me, right?"

I nod. I appreciate the offer, but I'm not sure I'm ready to unpack it all. Not yet. For now, I just want to try to lose myself in the comfort of dinner.

The moment Grandma Alice begins standing from the table, though, my mother's voice slices through the air, sharp as a knife. "You know the boy has hands and feet. He can make his own plate next time."

I look up, catching her eyes—those intense, always-expecting-more kind of eyes. It's like she's constantly waiting for me to mess up, to give her a reason to criticize me.

Grandma Alice, always the peacekeeper, chuckles. "Oh, Denise, hush. He's still nursing that leg; he doesn't need to be walking around when he doesn't have to."

"He's fine," Mom snaps back, eyeing me with that familiar look of disappointment. "He should've been in here cleaning those vegetables earlier or doing something else to help out. He's not a little kid."

The room suddenly seems a little smaller, a little tighter. It feels like all she ever does is either ignore me or criticize me. She hasn't asked once how I'm coping with losing ball. She doesn't care. The other day, when she checked in on the writing program, I thought maybe, just maybe, she was changing because I wasn't doing something connected to my dad. But I guess it was one of those full-moon moments.

Grandma Alice lets out a soft sigh. "Denise, let the boy eat. We're all here to enjoy each other's company."

Mom's lips tighten into a thin line, but she doesn't say anything more, just turns and walks away. The conversations around me pick up again, the cheerful chatter slowly filling the void left by the brief back-and-forth.

The thing about Sundays is as much as I love them, I've always thought about them as my mom's day. A day when she can put on a smile, even if it doesn't quite reach her eyes. Sundays at Grandma Alice's, with the sizzle of frying chicken and the sweet aroma of baked pies in the air, are one of the few constants my mom has had. Grandma Alice told me stories about my mom's younger days—about how she'd been right by Grandma's side, learning the secrets to her recipes. How she'd take those lessons to college, whipping up Sunday feasts in her dorm kitchen for my dad and their crew.

I've never really known that version of my mom. But when I watch her stirring pots and seasoning meats, she's got a certain rhythm, a kind of joy she doesn't have at other times. I've caught glimpses of her lost in thought, a distant smile on her face, probably reminiscing about Dad. About their Sundays together.

She's never really spoken to me about it, about how cooking might be her lifeline to him. Maybe it's too raw, too close to the heart. But I see it. I see her. The way her hands move with extra care when she's kneading dough, a soft hum escaping her lips when she's stirring batter. It's like she's holding on to something precious, something that, if she lets go, might just slip away forever.

I wish she treated me like a lifeline to him, too. Not like just what's left over from the nightmare of losing him. I can't help but wonder if she wishes I wasn't here sometimes. Or if, just for a day, she could have her Sunday without the reminder of me, of us, of the family we never got to become.

The door to Grandma Alice's apartment swings open, letting in the vibrant energy of Ms. Peters and Mrs. Collins, Grandma Alice's oldest friends. As always, they come bearing their signature additions to dinner. Ms. Peters has her legendary caramel-drizzled apple pie. Its aroma immediately competes with the existing fragrances in the room, turning heads and widening eyes. Mrs. Collins, always the life of the party, holds her typical bottle of cognac in one hand and a worn-out deck of cards in the other. They both stride in, their years of friendship evident in the way their laughter harmonizes and their steps sync.

Them and Grandma Alice have been close for almost forty years. In many ways, they're more like sisters than friends. Argue like sisters, complain about each other like sisters, and protect each other like sisters. Which is why they've basically always been like my great-aunts.

"Ossie, sweetheart." Mrs. Collins beams at me, her voice filled with years of stories. She leans down, her perfume a comforting blend of vanilla and flowers, and plants a soft kiss on my cheek. "Every time I see you, you're a little more handsome."

Ms. Peters, not one to be left out, chuckles and follows suit. "I'm sure them white girls are chasing you down at that rich school. Love them a chocolate man. Ol' model-looking self . . ." She trails off with a kiss on my other cheek, making me blush (even though I hate being referred to as food).

This Sunday-evening ritual—the rest of the neighborhood filtering in, each bringing their unique flavor to the mix, while my mom and Grandma Alice mastermind the feast. It's the one time of the week when everything feels right, when the weight of the world is momentarily lifted off our shoulders. The only time that was able to bring a sliver of joy after my injury, when I was ducking away from the world outside. Away from the media, the team, Laura.

As the hours melt away, the ritual works its magic on me yet again. As it always does, the centerpiece of the evening inevitably becomes the card table. It's been the arena of countless legendary showdowns, most of them featuring Ms. Peters and Mrs. Collins as the main antagonists.

"You think you've got me this time, Sandra?" Mrs. Collins challenges Ms. Peters, her fingers nimbly shuffling the cards, the deck dancing between her hands.

Ms. Peters, never one to back down, smirks over her glass. "Girl, I've been running tables since before you knew what spades was. Tonight won't be any different."

The beauty of these evenings lies in the fact that everyone can just be themselves. Here, in the heart of Grandma Alice's sanctuary, there's no need to wear masks or play roles. The burdens of the outside world, with its judgments and expectations, is left at the door. The freedom to be unabashedly Black, to revel in our shared culture, history, and spirit, fills the room. There's no code-switching, no silent policing of behaviors or words. Only the authentic pulse of life, undiluted and unapologetic.

The food coma sets in as the last hand of spades gets played. Ms. Peters throws down her card, triumphant. Mrs. Collins just rolls her eyes, muttering something about a rematch next week. Slowly, the room begins to empty. The laughs fade into the hallway, the memories carried out into the night.

I push myself up, my belly full but my heart still heavy. I figure I should help Grandma Alice and my mom clean up, especially considering everything that was said earlier. As I enter the kitchen, I see both of them, sleeves rolled up, hands deep in soapy water.

"Y'all need a hand?" I ask, grabbing a towel from the drawer.

Grandma Alice looks up, her eyes crinkling with a smile that says she knows I'm also trying to make a point to my mom. "That would be great, baby," she says warmly.

The clinking of dishes and the gush of running water are the only sounds accompanying us for a while. Grandma Alice's hands, old but strong, scrub a pan with gentle determination. My mom is busy stacking plates, her actions precise, like everything she does. Eventually Grandma Alice breaks the silence.

"You know, I didn't have a single doubt you would get into that writing program," she starts. "I told Ms. Hunt and Mrs. Wright, with all these books around here and how you used to fill that journal up, you definitely know a thing or two about writing."

I can't help the small smile that tugs at my lips. "Yeah," I admit, wiping a plate dry, "but it wasn't easy to get in."

I toy with the idea of telling her about Dean Blackburn trying to snatch away my spot. But that would only make a mess. Because knowing Grandma Alice, she'd be up at Braxton tomorrow, raising hell. I don't have the energy for all of that.

She eyes me, probably sensing there's more to the story, but she doesn't push. Instead, she goes another route. "Made any new friends in the program?" she inquires, her eyes twinkling with curiosity.

I shrug, thinking of last night. "Nah, not really." I choose my words carefully. "I hung out with these two kids yesterday, Luis and Naima. But it was whatever, I guess. I probably won't hang out with them again."

Grandma Alice studies me. "Why's that?" she presses gently.

I hesitate, torn between the desire to share and the instinct to shield her from the drama. "Just . . . didn't vibe well," I mumble, focusing on the glass I'm wiping.

"Well, that's too bad," Grandma Alice says. "I always did love the name Naima. Just like the Coltrane song; such a lovely tune. Maybe you should try to get to know them some more. Give it another day. You never know."

I shake my head, the image of Naima at the gas station flashing in my mind. "Nah," I reply firmly. "I don't think so."

Mom, never one to pass up an opportunity to cut me down, smirks and says, "Ma, you trying to create trouble between him and that little girlfriend of his? I'm sure she wouldn't appreciate him having a female friend. Especially not a *Black one*."

Grandma Alice's brow creases in confusion. "What girlfriend?"

Mom rolls her eyes. "What do you mean, Ma? You know the one. The Asian girl he's been sprung on for years. You feeling all right?"

Grandma Alice's eyes grow wide, and she looks at me for confirmation. "Ossie, you're back with Laura?"

Frustration boils up within me. How did Mom not know that Laura and I broke up months ago? I was heartbroken, and the signs were all there. Has she really been that oblivious to my pain?

"No, we aren't back together," I reply, trying to keep my voice steady. "How do you not know we broke up, Ma?"

Mom throws her hands up in defense, a hint of genuine shock in her eyes. "How was I supposed to know? You don't ever tell me anything, and I can't be expected to keep up with every single detail of a teenager's life."

"It's not about every single detail. You never pay any attention to me! And I don't just mean about breaking up with Laura. I'm talking about everything. My basketball games, my school stuff—all of it!"

She glares, her features tight with anger. "You're acting like a brat, Ossie. I'm sorry I can't notice every single thing you're doing. I'm sorry I'm not perfect."

A frustrated laugh escapes me. "It's not about being perfect! I'm just asking you to pay attention! Grandma Alice, she notices. She sees me. Even Laura's parents paid more attention to me than you do."

She scoffs. "Laura's parents? Are you that naive? They never cared about you. All they saw was a potential NBA star, a way to add to the money they already have. You were a meal ticket, nothing more. How long did Laura wait till she dumped you after you got hurt, huh? Wake up!"

Grandma Alice tries to cut in and soothe the moment. "You two, that's enough." But she's too late. The train has already left the station and is heading toward my mom and me saying all of the things we've been holding back for years.

"At least they pretended like they cared, then! They asked about my day, asked about my dreams, wanted to know how I was doing. They came to my games! I'd rather that than someone who doesn't even bother to pretend!"

My mom takes a step closer, her voice rising. "Do Laura's parents work constantly to put a roof over your head? Clothes on your back? Food on your damn plate? I do everything I can to make sure you have everything you need to chase your dreams, even if mine were stolen."

My eyes narrow, frustration simmering. "So that gives you the right to treat me like I'm a burden? You should have just put me up for adoption after Dad died, since you're so miserable being my mother."

She jabs a finger toward me, her voice shaking with emotion. "You have some damn nerve. You walk around here with that chip on your shoulder, thinking you know everything, but you don't know shit. I have sacrificed *everything* for you. If that's not enough, then I don't know what is."

I shake my head in disbelief. "You've sacrificed everything? You probably only kept me to prove to Dad's family that you weren't a gold digger just like Laura. But maybe you were. Maybe you were only with him because you thought he was going to the NBA."

The words come fast, too fast, like bullets leaving a chamber, and as soon as they hit the air, I wish I could snatch them back, swallow them whole. But it's too late, and in a heartbeat, I feel a sting across my face, a sharp echo of the harshness of what I said. It's not my mom who's slapped me, though; it's Grandma Alice.

The slap stings, but it's Grandma Alice's eyes that hurt most. They're like coals, burning with an intensity I've never seen before. "How dare you, Ossie!" she thunders. "Don't you *ever* speak that way to your mother!"

I turn to my mom, expecting more fury. But instead, her eyes are pools of sorrow and anger, caught between tears and rage. The weight of it all—the years, the struggles, the sacrifices—seems to be sitting on her shoulders. And I realize I've added to that weight.

"I—I'm sorry," I stammer, the regret thick in my throat.

And then I bolt, the power of my own guilt propelling me to move faster than I have since the accident. I rush out of the apartment, the door slamming behind me, the sound of the storm I've left behind.

The hallway is cold, and I can feel the sting on my face, both from the slap and the tears that now flow freely. Why did I say it? Was it the pent-up anger from the night before with the police? The hurt over Laura? Or the years of feeling like I was invisible to my own mother? Maybe it's a twisted mix of all those things. But right now, all I know is the feeling of regret eating at me.

I need to escape, to find a place to hide. But where do you go when the pain you're running from is inside you?

Chapter Nine

The ghost of the argument with my mom at Grandma Alice's apartment still haunts me days later. I sent Grandma Alice a text apologizing again, but she said I need to be apologizing again to my mother and also to myself for being less than the person she knows me to be. I want to say something to my mother, but for some reason I can't bring myself to do it. I was wrong for what I said, but so much of it was how I really feel. So the two of us just say nothing. Acting like we're both invisible when we're at home together. After turning in my movie quote essay, I spend my time in my room chipping away at my homework.

But home isn't the only battleground. Braxton's hallways also feel like a personal hell. Every corner turned could lead to a run-in with Luis or Naima, or my old teammates, or Laura and Matthew. All of which happens, of course.

The first time I see Luis, he flashes his easy grin and tries to say hello, but I turn away, dodging him like he's a land mine. After what happened with the cops and the things Naima said, I realize that the time I enjoyed with them—the laughter, the conversations—was just them putting on a front. Playing a role.

I've had enough people play me.

Each day, I also have to dodge Laura and Matthew. Laura's eyes, once warm and inviting, now look at me like I'm a wounded bird. Matthew, meanwhile, tries to pour salt in the wound, making sure to do some public display of affection whenever he knows I can see.

And to add to my pile, I've seen Tommy a few times and wondered whether I should apologize to him for saying we weren't friends. But he doesn't even bother to look my way long enough for me to feel as though there's even a slight opportunity to do so.

So I walk the school campus with my head down and my music up. But even my earbuds can't drown out the world entirely. Murmurs still reach my ears. About the upcoming basketball season. About Laura. About everything.

It feels like I'm dragging around the past, the present, and a questionable future. Then, before I know it, Friday arrives.

Fridays always have a bittersweet feeling. You know, the taste of almost freedom but not quite there yet. Except this Friday feels more bitter than sweet. The last thing I need after a week of playing dodgeball with my own emotions is to be stuck in a room with Matthew, Luis, and Naima.

Matthew's voice, loud and proud, hits me when I walk into the English Lab: "*Apocalypse Now* is obviously a brilliant piece of art, and I could've chosen any number of lines to write about. But I've always found a specific line to be most striking: 'I wanted a mission, and for my sins, they gave me one. Brought it up to me like room service.'"

The students gathered around him ooh and aah as he finishes stroking his own ego.

"Writing about that line allowed me to deeply reflect on the many privileges we have in the US and how little we understand the horrors of the third world. It's one of my better pieces."

I want to vomit in my mouth. It takes a special sort of person to sound this obnoxious at only seventeen years old.

I slide into a seat at the back, hoping to be invisible. But along the way I make eye contact with Luis, then Naima, and finally Matthew. And of course Matthew is more than happy to take a moment away from crowning himself the next great American writer to try and lob a few emotional grenades my way.

His voice rises, making sure I can hear: "Honestly, you guys wouldn't believe the dinner Laura's mom put together for me this past weekend," he brags, each word glazed with a smugness that makes my skin crawl. "I mean, it was something out of a five-star restaurant. Full of East Asian dishes I've never even heard of. They really went all out."

He pauses for dramatic effect, sweeping the room with his eyes to ensure he has my attention. "Mrs. Wong-Stanton said that she's never cooked such a big meal for any of her kids' partners before. It's almost like they see me as part of the family." Each word is a calculated missile designed to hit its mark. I shrink a bit in my chair, wishing I could disappear.

Naima whips around to face Matthew. "Do you ever give it a rest, Matthew? Like, shut up for once. Some of us are actually here to write."

I hold back a smile. Matthew is momentarily stunned. His mouth moves, searching for the right comeback, ready to unleash his next assault.

But fate is on our side, as just at that moment, Ms. Hunt walks in. With her sharp gaze and even sharper fashion sense, she commands the attention of every student in the room. The atmosphere tenses, the previous conversations fading into an expectant silence.

Naima leans slightly back, shooting me a sympathetic half smile. Maybe an olive branch.

"Good morning, Ms. Hunt. I was just talking about how much I enjoyed writing my essay on *Apocalypse Now*. I can't wait to hear what your favorite parts were," Matthew says, kissing ass. Though I'm not sure if it's Ms. Hunt's or his own.

"Mr. Astor, I'm happy to know you think so highly of your essay . . . I only wish I could share your enthusiasm," Ms. Hunt says.

I catch Luis's and Naima's reactions as they share a snicker. But the moment is short-lived, as Ms. Hunt redirects her attention to them. "I'm not sure what anyone finds amusing. Matthew's essay wasn't the exception. Only a few of you turned in anything remotely close to the level I'm looking for."

Matthew's friend Morgan speaks up, a touch of resentment in her voice: "What was wrong with what we turned in? My father is an English professor at Columbia, and he thought my essay was 'stellar.'"

"Well, I'm happy you ask, Morgan. Though I do want to point out that your father's perspective holds no weight in this program," Ms. Hunt says, letting everyone know that their power and privilege aren't going to help them shine in her eyes.

She continues: "That said, the issue with the writing is not that it isn't technically sound. Indeed, in some cases the prose was almost lyrical at times. The issue is that by and large, the essays weren't honest or vulnerable. The best writers leave pieces of themselves in their writing. Pieces that profoundly reflect how they fit into the world around them."

"I'm pretty sure I did that, Ms. Hunt," Matthew says in frustration.

Ms. Hunt sighs. "I'm pretty sure you *believe* that—and I'm *absolutely sure you didn't.*"

Matthew's eyes widen; clearly he can't believe his teacher has the audacity to think he isn't perfect.

"You wrote strongly about the kinds of afflictions and horrors that happen in places like Vietnam: civil unrest, broken educational systems, children dying from a lack of basic resources. But you failed to acknowledge that these issues are also realities in your own country. For instance, in many inner-city neighborhoods across America, civil unrest erupts in response to systemic injustices and police brutality, echoing the kinds of societal turbulence seen in some so-called developing countries. Furthermore, the educational systems in numerous rural and urban areas in the United States are plagued by a lack of funding and resources, leading to a disparity in educational opportunities akin to those in overexploited nations. You treat these issues as though they are solely existing in 'third world' countries—an extremely offensive term, by the way—and ignore the history of your own nation. You might consider whether your privilege is causing you to overlook the truths that are just miles from your front door."

Ms. Hunt barely finishes before Matthew jumps in: "Sure . . . I guess. But America is still far superior to most of the world."

When Ms. Hunt replies, her voice is calm but firm. "Actually, Matthew, a multitude of countries rank higher than the United States in education, quality of life, and many other aspects. Your perception of this country's greatness might benefit from a bit more research," she suggests.

Matthew's face shows a mix of surprise and frustration. He takes a second to find a response, but all he can land on is a reluctant "If you say so."

Ms. Hunt turns to the rest of the class. "I know it feels like I'm pushing you hard, but that's because I believe that what you're doing in this program is immensely valuable. Your essays aren't random stones being thrown into a river. They're the bricks that can help you build the foundation of something towering—something great to be remembered for."

She also drops a bomb on us, saying while our work won't be

graded, she has the power to drop anyone from the program if she feels they aren't giving the work their all. The other students here might be able to give up the badge this program would be on their college applications, but I'm not one of them. The way things are going at home, I need to get a scholarship now more than ever.

"Honest and vulnerable writers," Ms. Hunt declares. "That's what you need to become." And in pursuit of those goals, she gives us our next assignment. An exploration of *Beloved* by Toni Morrison, a book that's unknown territory for me, though copies lurk in both my mother's and Grandma Alice's collections.

We have two weeks to read the book and write up a reflection on the direction for our response essay, then another week to write the final essay.

Morgan raises her hand. "Are we going to have to read books like this all year?"

Morgan's got a track record for being that type of person. The one who always brags about her pricey new car, rambles about her parents' investment that helped build Braxton's new science wing, or says something cringey about anyone who isn't a straight white person.

"Books like what?" Ms. Hunt asks.

"You know—by minorities or whatever. I know it probably means a lot to you, but—"

"'Marginalized people' or 'people of color,'" Ms. Hunt cuts her off, her voice treading out each syllable with patient clarity.

"Huh?" Morgan responds.

Ms. Hunt's smile is firm, resolute. "Most of the people whom you refer to as *minorities* are actually part of the global majority. Therefore, there is nothing 'minor' about them. Let's use terms that reflect that, please."

Morgan grumbles a half-hearted "Sure," looking as if she just sucked on a lemon.

Ms. Hunt perches on her desk. Behind her, posters and photos of famous white writers line the walls. "But to answer your question, Morgan, yes, we will be reading 'books like this' all year. Broadening your horizons with different perspectives will help you to hone your own perspective—and, as I've said before, perspective is an essential part of successful writing. This isn't confined to race; it extends to other identities and experiences, too."

Matthew, Morgan, and Sydney begin whispering to one another, but Ms. Hunt ignores them.

We spend the rest of the meeting doing this free-writing exercise, the kind where you're supposed to let your thoughts spill out onto the page. "Just write about whatever's on your mind," Ms. Hunt said. But I've got too much on my mind, thoughts bumping into one another like they're trying to get out but don't know how. So, instead of diving into all that, I focus on something simple. I stare out the window on the other side of the classroom. There's this tree, tall and quiet, just standing there like it's got all the time in the world. The perfect thing to write about.

When class is over, Ms. Hunt has to clap her hands gently to break the spell. "Have a good weekend, everyone."

As I trail toward the exit, she beckons me over. When we're alone, she pierces me with honesty: "Ossie, your essay was a letdown. It feels like you phoned this one in. In fact, it was the most disappointing of all of them."

My heart sinks. "I—I'm sorry, I just—" I stammer, but she cuts me off.

"No need to justify. I know your potential, and this isn't it. Step it up."

I knew I was distracted while writing the essay, but I didn't know it was *that* bad. I stumble out of the room, Ms. Hunt's words bouncing around in my head, and don't even notice Naima and Luis standing by my locker until it's too late.

"Hey, Ossie," Luis says.

I shuffle my feet, looking for an escape route. "Hey. I can't really talk now; I got stuff to do."

Luis inches in, his eyes pleading. "Look, I know what the cops did to you and Naima last week. That shit was horrible . . . and I'm sorry. I really can't imagine what you're going through. But listen—I think you've got us wrong. I know people haven't been what they claimed to be, but me and Nai are different. Give us a second chance."

"I really gotta go." I'm about to push past them, but then I see him shoot Naima a look that's loaded with so much frustration, so much hurt, it stops me.

"Naima, you need to fix this," he tells her. "Ossie, please, just hear her out. I'm gonna head to my car and let you two talk."

He turns and walks away, leaving a lengthy silence in his wake.

Naima breaks the silence: "The police put my father in the hospital for months." Her eyes are full of sorrow.

"What are you talking about?" I ask, confused.

"My father is a professor at Fordham University. He teaches Afro-Latino studies," she starts. There's a hint of pride in her voice, mixed with a raw pain that's impossible to mask. "When I was in middle school, some of his students were holding a peaceful protest in the city after the murders of George Floyd, Ahmaud Arbery, and Breonna Taylor. I begged him to take me, so he did."

She swallows hard, her voice catching in her throat. "The protest *was* peaceful, just like it was supposed to be, until the police began attacking everyone for no reason. They even started pepper-spraying kids." A tear rolls down her cheek, but she wipes it away quickly, determined to get through the story. "I was just twelve years old, and one of them tried to pepper-spray me, too."

I feel a cold chill run down my spine, imagining young Naima in the midst of that chaos. My jaw clenches involuntarily.

"My father knocked the pepper spray out of the officer's hand before he could spray me. That's when they started to beat on him. Over and over." Naima's voice breaks. "I tried to help him, but one of his students held me back so they didn't hit me, too." She takes a shaky breath, her eyes haunted. "I screamed for them to stop until I didn't have a voice anymore. But they kept hitting him, Ossie. It was like they didn't even see him as human."

"That's . . . horrible," I say, my heart heavy. "I'm so sorry."

"My father ended up needing multiple surgeries. He recovered, but he's not the same person he was before. Not fully. Even beyond the physical scars, you can tell it still haunts him—it haunts all of us." The dark gravity of the moment somehow feels as though it's pulling me in as well. I'm mortified and furious for her, her father, and all of us. "No news outlets even covered it because the police lied and said he attacked them first, unprovoked."

Her voice has become distant, like she's traveling back in time to that exact moment. The pain, the anger, the injustice of it all. She takes a moment, swallowing hard, pushing through the anguish.

"So I decided two things that day," she says, her voice now filled with a fierce determination. "That I was going to become a journalist and help the truth get out there even when no one else is talking about it. And that I would never let the police take as much from me again as they did that day."

The hallway is quiet as we stand there, consumed by the darkness of her past. The air is stagnant. Time is a myth.

She breaks the silence. "Look, it's not an excuse for what I said to you, but I'm really sorry. I didn't mean it. I was just so caught up in all this stuff inside me. I took it out on you. You weren't the coward the other night. I was."

The power of her apology sinks deep, its impact finding a way to parts of me few other people have reached. It's the kind of apology I've been yearning for, the kind I never got from Coach Ryan, my mom, my teammates, or Laura. The recognition, the acknowledgment. The simple act of saying "I see you, and I'm sorry for the pain I caused."

And I understand her better now, understand what was going on in her mind that night. Not fully, because how could I ever? But I get the magnitude of her pain and the reason behind her harsh words. We're both just trying to navigate a world that seems to want to break us.

"I can't pretend to understand everything you've been through," I say, "but I appreciate you sharing that with me. And for what it's worth, I don't think you were a coward. I think you were put in an impossible position and did what you had to do."

Naima brushes away the last of her tears. "Thanks, Ossie. And thanks for listening. Like I said, I'm really sorry." She starts to walk away, her Jordans squeaking softly against the hallway's polished floor.

For a moment I just watch her, knowing that we're at a crossroads and it's up to me to decide which way we'll go.

"Hey!"

Naima turns to face me, her eyes questioning.

"So am I ever gonna get a chance to play that song I was about to put on the other night? I still need to prove I'm the R&B god."

She smiles, bright and genuine. "Oh, you went from R&B expert to R&B god? That's a big jump. But, yeah, I think we can make that happen." Then she adds, "But just so you know, Luis swears he's the actual R&B expert. So you've got some competition."

I laugh, shaking my head. "Challenge accepted."

Chapter Ten

The next few days are a blur of late-night reading sessions, music-filled debates, and growing friendship. After Naima's honesty with me, I decide to be honest with them in return. When I told them that I don't actually have a car and that part of the reason I lied was because of how uncomfortable Luis's parents made me feel the first time I was at his house, they both got it. "I'm nothing like them," Luis said. "I don't care about stuff like that—Nai, either." And I knew it was true.

Thankfully, Luis's parents are vacationing around Europe for a month, as they apparently do every year, so he's got the house to himself. We've been able to hang out there without any of their nonsense—but with full access to their dope-ass chef.

Every time we hang out, one of them drops me off at the Metro-North station, where I usually catch the bus if it's still running, but an Uber if it's not. Though Naima and Luis keep offering to drop me home, I always politely decline. Getting a car home a couple nights a week is making my wallet cry, but I'm not ready for them to see the grit and grind of my neighborhood. It's not shame, not really. It's just that . . . where I live is different from what they know. Their world is paved-gold roads and picket fences; mine is potholes and bodegas.

Luis's house without his parents there becomes the most chill place on earth. It's like we have our own universe, one where there's no judgment, no expectations. Just us, our conversations, our laughter, our writing, and the music and movies we love. Day after day, we plop down in Luis's living room, surrounded by stacks of books, notebooks, and Luis's and Naima's laptops. (I don't feel like carrying my ancient laptop around.) Together we work our way through *Beloved*, dissecting every paragraph, every word. The book is about the legacy of slavery told through the life of the main character, Sethe, in post–Civil War Ohio. It's a deep reflection on trauma, memory, and family bonds. There are times when the book is so haunting that I have to put it down. I've never read anyone who makes words come to life like Toni Morrison.

When we're not dissecting a powerful passage from *Beloved*, we're in the middle of back-and-forths about things like whether Kendrick Lamar is a top-five rapper of all time.

"Naima, you're wildin'! Kendrick ain't top five," I argue, defending my lineup: Jay-Z, Lupe Fiasco, Biggie, Nas, André 3000.

Naima raises an eyebrow, clearly amused. "You're buggin', Ossie. Kendrick has dropped some of the most influential albums of all time! *To Pimp a Butterfly*? That's artistry. That's poetry. You can't even compare!"

Luis, trying to play instigator, interjects, "I'm with Naima on this one. I actually think he's the GOAT."

"Nah. You can't be deadass, Luis!" I scoff, and even Naima is laughing at that one.

The room is alive with energy, the kind that only comes from passionate debates between friends. There's an easy flow to our conversations, like we're performing a spoken-word piece, each of us dropping lines, making our case, waiting for the applause or the boos.

Our talks about *Beloved* are just as intense. There's something about the way Toni Morrison writes that digs deep, uncovers emotions and memories we didn't even know we had. Luis, with his photographer's eye, often points out the visuals in the prose, the imagery that makes the scenes come alive. Naima, with her journalist's instinct, always dives into the deeper meanings, the societal reflections, the truths that hide between the lines.

I guess I'm somewhere in the middle, thinking about the world of words and the world of emotion, trying to make sense of it all. Every discussion feels like a puzzle, each of us holding a piece, trying to see where it fits. And when it all comes together, the satisfaction is unmatched.

And the music in the background provides the perfect backdrop to our discussions. Every so often, we take a break, nodding to the beat, getting lost in the melodies and lyrics. Luis sometimes puts on some bachata, the lively beats sending us to the streets of Santo Domingo. Naima, always with her love for R&B, introduces us to some old-school jams that make us feel like we're in the nineties.

In these moments, when the music is just right and the conversation is perfect, it feels like nothing can touch us. Even with Ms. Hunt's looming expectations, I find myself looking forward to working on my essay. Sitting in my Word document has become my safe place, my escape. I feel like I'm writing in my journal again, like when I was a kid.

As amazing as the Martinez's home theater is, the dopest place in Luis's home is his bedroom. From the doorway, it looks like any other room, but step inside, and you're transported. His walls aren't painted with bright colors or plastered with posters of music idols or sports legends. Instead, they're alive with moments. Moments Luis captured with his camera. Every inch of the space is covered with beautiful black-and-white photos that make you feel something deep down.

There's a candid shot of an old man sitting on a park bench, feeding pigeons, his eyes telling a lifetime of stories. Another one shows a child, no older than five, laughing, all teeth and unabashed joy. Each photograph is a portal to another moment, another story. Luis doesn't just take pictures; he captures souls.

I can't help but think of those trips with my mom to Gordon Parks exhibits. Those images, powerful and unfiltered, telling stories of a time and place that felt both distant and intimately familiar. I see the same depth, the same truth, in Luis's photos. It's like he's channeling Parks's spirit, seeing the world through a lens that catches the magic in the ordinary.

But the tragedy is, his parents don't see it. To them, the photos are just snapshots. They don't see the art. They don't see the genius. They just see a boy they wish was more like his father. Macho. Toxic. Every time Luis talks about his photos, there's this distant look in his eyes, a mix of longing and resignation. I get it. I really do. When the people who are supposed to be your biggest cheerleaders don't even show up for the game, it leaves a mark.

What impresses me most about Luis and Naima isn't their encyclopedic knowledge of music or the depth of their interests; it's the depth of their perspectives. Naima's thoughts on the "daily wars and tragedies that Black folks, especially Black women, have endured since slavery" are something special.

According to Naima, Morrison portrays these struggles better than most authors, and after hearing her talk about it, it's impossible not to agree. The truth is, Naima usually initiates our deepest discussions.

Just like what she's saying to us right now: "You know, homelessness and hunger . . . they only exist because people with the *real* power and resources don't care."

I nod. "Yeah, I feel you. It's like how corporations are the ones most responsible for climate change, and yet they act like we're the ones who are supposed to fix the problem."

Luis leans in. "The systems are designed in a way that those at the top stay at the top and everyone else is left to deal with the consequences."

Naima's eyes flash with passion. "That's why Luis and I decided to stop code-switching at Braxton, to show that intelligent people don't all have to look or sound the same. It's like, by changing the way we talk to fit into their narrative, we're just reinforcing the shit we're trying to fight against."

"Exactly," Luis jumps in. "We have to move the needle when we can, challenge their perceptions."

I sigh, running a hand through my hair. "Real talk. It's like we're constantly trying to walk this tightrope, trying to balance between who we truly are and who the world wants us to be."

Naima smiles at Luis. "And sometimes you've got to just say 'Screw the tightrope!' and be unapologetically you."

Talking to them is energizing. Every word, every sentence, feels like something powerful. And Naima? Man, she's a force. The kind of person who makes you feel like you should be changing things, shaking some shit up.

Her passion for fixing, well, just about everything wrong with the world is partly what inspired the idea for my book essay: "When America Loves Black Women."

I decided to find data, historical references, and center the women in *Beloved* to make the argument that for America to ever actually be the great nation it claims to be, it would first have to stop being a grave-yard for the hopes, dreams, and health of Black women.

Luis's essay focuses on the generational horrors of slavery. And Naima has taken inspiration from the quote "Me and you, we got more yesterday than anybody. We need some kind of tomorrow." She's writing about how the book teaches us the importance of exploring what the future holds for Black people.

We spend the next week working on our essays, trying our best to write from the place of hope, truth, and struggle we found in the book. Luis and Naima are both amazing writers. Naima's prose is sophisticated yet authentic, while Luis's sentences are always beautifully melodic, and I'm picking up so much from them.

After what Ms. Hunt said about my *Moonlight* essay, though, I know I need more; I need to go harder. Need to make sure I don't disappoint the people who want this for me: Ms. Hunt, Grandma Alice, Mrs. Wright—and myself.

It's late, the kind of late where the world's noises dim to a hush. I'm working on my essay, and every idea, every sentence I type, feels basic, not enough. Not the standard I've set for myself.

Glancing over, I see my father's jersey hanging on the wall. The fabric seems to shimmer in the low light, a reminder of the legacy he left. I can hear his voice, deep and profound: "You want to be great? You have to become a student of your craft. Dive deep. Obsess over it."

I remember watching an interview where he said that. He was talking about basketball, about his drive, his hunger to be the best. But I know his words also apply to me, to this essay.

I hear you, Dad.

Opening a new tab, I start searching for "best essays ever written." The lists on most sites primarily feature white guys. But I find one that has Ellison, Baldwin, Didion. I start reading, diving into their worlds, their minds. The flow of their words, the depth of their thoughts, it's art. Pure, amazing art.

Hours go by, my screen filled with tabs of essays, critiques, and analyses. I see patterns, styles, techniques. How the authors play with sentences, how they weave in emotions, how they make the reader feel.

The more I read, the more I realize: this is how I studied ball. Breaking down moves, analyzing players, understanding the game inside out. Now I'm doing the same with words, with essays.

I pull up my document, the cursor blinking, waiting. And I begin to write. Not just words but emotions, thoughts, a piece of my soul. Every sentence, every paragraph, crafted with purpose, with passion.

The sun starts to rise, the first light of dawn pouring through my window. I lean back, tired but satisfied. The essay, my essay, is done. And it's good. *Damn good.*

After working our asses off on our essays and handing them in on Wednesday, there's an excited nervousness heading into the writing program that Friday. My heart's pounding as if I've just finished a full-court press, adrenaline still pumping. But the moment I step into the room, Ms. Hunt stops me, eyes filled with a kind of pride I've seldom seen. "That's what I'm talking about," she says simply, and gives me a subtle fist bump.

It's the sort of affirmation you don't know you need until you get it. Matthew notices. He glares at me as I take my seat.

Once we're all settled in, Ms. Hunt doesn't waste time. She begins the meeting by complimenting us all on our essays, saying they were a "definite step up" from the last round. "However," she goes on, "too many of you are still holding back. Only three of you truly captured the depth and power of *Beloved*: Ossie, Naima, and Luis. Congratulations, you three. The rest of you, keep pushing yourselves. You'll get there."

The three of us share a glance, humbled and surprised by her praise.

When Ms. Hunt announces that the next book will be *The Prophets* by Robert Jones Jr., the room is silent at first as a few people begin stealthily searching for more information about the book online. And then they erupt. A Black queer love story set during enslavement? Yeah, most of them aren't happy.

Morgan, never one to hold back, is the first to object. "Another woke book," she says, her voice dripping with disdain.

Ms. Hunt locks eyes with Morgan. "Another book with valuable perspectives and stunning writing. You can do the assignments," she says slowly, "or drop the program."

The room feels electric, charged with tension. But for me, Luis, and Naima, there's nothing but joy. First we're called out by Ms. Hunt for having the best essays, and then she assigns another powerful-sounding book from a Black author. Matthew shoots me a look as if he's blaming me for all of this, but I just return it with a smile.

After the meeting is over, Luis says we should celebrate. "You guys wanna grab dinner and go to the movies tomorrow night?" Me and Naima are down, so we each head home, promising to text restaurant and movie options for the group to vote on. We eventually settle on a Jamaican restaurant a few towns over and an eight p.m. showing of the latest A24 movie.

Naima is waiting outside when my Uber pulls up. The restaurant is buzzing, a low hum of conversation, the clinking of glasses and silverware. The smell of grilled chicken and spices wafts through the air, making my stomach rumble. We snag a booth by the window, a cozy corner spot where the evening light casts a golden hue over everything.

She pulls out her phone, dialing Luis. It goes to voicemail. "Luis, it's Naima. We're at the spot, waiting for you. Hit me up when you get this."

We order some appetizers while we wait. As we're munching on some crispy calamari, the strangeness of his absence settles in.

"You think he's okay?" I ask.

Naima shrugs. "Probably just got distracted. You know how he is with his camera. Might've seen a perfect shot on the way and got sidetracked."

She suggests we go ahead and order our entrées, so we do. But as the time comes up on an hour, the gnawing feeling in my gut won't go away. This isn't like Luis. He's usually really communicative.

"Maybe I should hit him up?" I suggest. "Just in case your phone isn't getting his calls or something?"

Naima raises her eyebrows, then shrugs. "Yeah, why not? But if he answers your call and not mine, tell him we're fighting on sight."

I call Luis's number, but it rings through to voicemail, just like it did for Naima. I leave a short message and then hang up, feeling slightly panicky.

As we wait for the bill, both our phones buzz.

"Is it Luis?" I ask, fumbling for my phone.

Group Chat - The Dope Writers Society (Naima, Luis, and Ossie)

LUIS: Don't hate me! But something came up. I owe you both, enjoy the movie.

I text him back right away.

ME: You good?

LUIS: Yeah, don't worry!

NAIMA: Be safe

"You know what he's up to?" I ask Naima, thumbing out of the text thread. She shrugs, but her eyes are bright with a slight mischief.

"I know he wouldn't bail if it wasn't important," she says. "But you still wanna catch that movie? I'm down if you are."

Chapter Eleven

The city's Saturday-night hum is a backdrop, cars honking, people shouting, laughter erupting from a nearby bar. But all I can hear is Naima's question ringing in the air. Is it just wishful thinking or is there something more to the invitation than simple friendship?

"You sure you're down for this?" I ask, trying not to let my eagerness show.

Naima seems to consider for a moment before she replies, a playful tone in her voice, "Yeah, I'm sure. You're not too bad when Luis is around. But, you know, you really find out who someone is when it's one-on-one."

I can't help but laugh at her honesty. "Okay," I say, feeling a bit of excitement at the prospect. "Let's do it, then."

As we're walking, a flickering neon sign catches our eyes. It's an arcade, just as bright and loud as I remember from my childhood.

Naima's face lights up. "Yo, my father used to bring me here all the time when I was a kid! I would spend my entire allowance playing air hockey," she says.

"Small world." I laugh. "My mom used to bring me here, too. I would hit the Pop-A-Shot mostly, but I was nice at air hockey, too. Her and I would play constantly; I remember she used to go hard, like it was the Olympics or something."

Naima looks over, eyes twinkling with a challenge. "I probably would have smoked you in air hockey."

My chuckle echoes down the street. "Nah, doubt that."

Her eyebrows shoot up. "So what's up? Let's find out. We don't have to go to the movies."

"Say less." I grin, and we make our way into the arcade.

We quickly spot the air hockey table, its surface gleaming under the flashing lights of the arcade, and head to our opposite sides.

"You sure you're gonna be fine playing on that leg?" she asks. "Because I'm not about to go easy on you."

I let out a laugh. "Yeah, don't worry about me. Trust me: my leg is more than ready to hand you a few Ls."

The blue-and-green glow from the lights, highlighting the excitement in her eyes, somehow makes Naima even more beautiful than she normally is. "All right, then, Ossie. Let's do this."

The game begins, the puck gliding effortlessly across the slick surface. I score first, the electronic scoreboard beeping in triumph.

"You sure you want this smoke? We can go play a fighting game or something instead." I grin, swiftly bending my hurt leg she asked about.

Laughing, Naima shakes her head. "Not yet. I was just seeing what you got. Get ready for me to play for real."

She places the puck on my side of the table since I just scored, then grips her paddle. Her fingers move lightly on it as her stance readies, and her eyes sharpen.

"You ready?" she asks.

"Yeah," I respond, not knowing yet that the last thing I am is ready.

I start us up again, hitting the puck toward Naima, and it begins darting from one side of the table to the other with reckless abandon. After this happens for a few seconds, something changes in Naima's face. She has a look I recognize well. It reminds me of what I used to look like when I was in attack mode on the court.

Naima's paddle strikes the puck with a measured force, sending it whirling toward my goal. There's something almost otherworldly about the look in her eyes as she scores her first point, the way her face beams in celebration, and the light song of laughter that escapes the depths of her body. It's like watching a flower lean toward the sun, a sight that makes me smile, too—even though she just scored on me.

"You were saying?" she teases as the scoreboard beeps to indicate her point.

"Okay, okay. Let's see if you can do it again," I challenge, striking the puck back to her side of the table.

We launch deeper into our duel, the sounds of the arcade drowned out by our laughter and playful ribbing. Naima sends the puck skating across the table, her actions swift and calculated, as I attempt to block, matching her move for move. But she's relentless, an unstoppable force. She scores on me, once, twice, and then three times.

Losing usually hits my pride, but with Naima, it's easy to shrug off. As I watch her across the table, her expression glowing with competitive fire, I find myself not caring about the game's outcome. She makes it easy to like seeing her win—even when it comes at my expense.

Maybe it's the sweet glances, the lighthearted jabs, and the shared laughs. Maybe it's the tiny sparks of connection I feel when our fingers brush as we go to grab the puck, or how when our eyes meet, it's like a silent conversation held over the low hum of the table's music and sounds. I try to dismiss it as just static. But deep down, I think it might be more.

After about an hour, she's beaten me in more games than I can count—though I'm sure she is counting them just fine.

"Want to try to get some wins back with Pop-A-Shot?" she asks, gesturing toward the familiar basketball arcade game on the other side of the room. "Or are you scared I'll beat the great Ossie Brown at his own game, too?"

She means it as a gentle dig, but her words linger in the air. My gaze drifts over to the Pop-A-Shot machine. I haven't touched a basketball since the injury. The very thought brings an ache to my chest, a bitter nostalgia. "Nah, I'm good," I respond, trying to keep my tone light.

I see a change in Naima, her playful demeanor softening as she senses something going on with me. She quickly changes the topic. "You like sweet potato pie?"

"Yeah, of course."

Naima flashes her keys at me. "Great! I know a place that has dessert fit for an air hockey champion." She giggles, a wide smile taking up her entire face. "It's a drive, though. You down?"

I'm not gonna lie—the idea of continuing our night of adventure excites me. "Yeah, I'm with it. Maybe on the way, we can get you a trophy."

The drive with Naima takes longer than I expected, but I'm not mad at all about it. We're cocooned in her car, our conversation bouncing between the various songs she's playing. It's like there's an invisible thread connecting our shared interests. From music to books to sports, the two of us talking is just easy.

Before I know it, we're about forty minutes from Westchester, where the arcade was, in the heart of Harlem. After she tucks the vehicle into a parking lot, she tells me we're about to hit up a soul food spot her parents used to bring her to that has great desserts.

I figure it's going to be some high-end imitation of a soul food spot—the kind made for tourists or rich people looking to capture "authentic" experiences for their social feeds. But she leads me to a humble hole-in-the-wall place. It's the type of spot that seems not only *authentic*-authentic but also like it won't cost an arm and a leg, which is a relief, because after spending so much on Ubers to get home from Luis's place, I can barely afford a peanut butter and jelly right now.

We step inside, the door squeaking behind us, and the staff greets Naima like she's the heir to this small kingdom. I can't help but be surprised by how excited and warm her reception is.

"You and your fam come here a lot, I'm guessing?" I ask.

"We used to, all the time," she says. "It's been a minute, though. But I still try to pull up at least once a month. There ain't no food like this up where I live. I like being home."

While all the food smells amazing, since we already ate, we each just get a slice of pie, then find a spot at one of the bare wooden tables. For the past few weeks, I've used Luis and Naima as a reason to opt out of Sunday dinners, hoping to avoid my mom. But after one bite of sweet potato pie, I realize how much I've been missing the food at Grandma Alice's.

"How's the pie?" Naima asks, laughing; I've nearly eaten my entire piece already.

I chuckle, my mouth half full. "It's *real* good; I can't lie. But it isn't touching my grandmother's."

"Really? Well, I'll have to put that to the test sometime."

"Yeah, you should. My grandmother's a beast in the kitchen," I toss back, grinning. "And she taught me everything she knows, too."

She laughs in disbelief. "Oh, word, is that right?"

"Well—not everything," I admit, laughing along. "But I know a little something."

"Okay, if you say so, Ossie," she teases.

"I'm for real!" I reply, unable to keep my grin from stretching wider.

Our back-and-forth is interrupted when two young Black boys, clearly brothers, nervously shuffle our way. Their wide eyes are fixated on me, excitement sparking off them like a live wire. Behind them is a man who appears to be their dad.

"You're Ossie Brown, right?" he asks.

"That depends on whether I did something wrong," I joke.

The man chuckles, as the younger of the boys nudges his older brother. "See, I told you it was him!"

"My boys love you, man. They've watched all your games. They play ball, too," the man says, clearly tickled by their enthusiasm. "Mind if we get an autograph?"

"Of course," I agree, signing the napkin their dad hands me. When I offer to pose for a few selfies with the boys, their delighted squeals vibrate off the walls in the restaurant, making heads turn.

The dad snaps some pictures, then the younger one says, "On TV they said you won't ever play again, but I don't believe 'em. I hope you feel better soon, Ossie."

His words stun me, leaving me grappling for a suitable response. And then I remember the kind of boundless hope Grandma Alice always offered me when I was around his age. The sort of hope I want all Black kids to feel.

"Thanks a lot," I reply, forcing a smile. "I'll work as hard as I can to get back on the court. 'Cause maybe I'll have to guard you two one day."

The boys' faces light up with thrilled anticipation, then they run off, their dad trailing behind. He gives me a thankful nod on the way out.

In the quiet of their departure, Naima lifts her eyes from her plate to meet mine. "You were really good with those boys."

I shrug, feeling warmth crawl up my neck to my cheeks. "It's nothin'," I reply, my voice muffled by my last bite of pie. "They were cute kids."

"Yeah," she says. Then she asks softly, almost carefully, "You okay, Ossie?"

"What do you mean?" I ask, stalling for time, pretending I don't know.

"Well," she starts, her fingers nervously twirling the straw of her drink. "Them asking about basketball. Saying they don't believe the reports . . . That's gotta be hard."

I'm silent for a second, words fumbling around on my tongue. "Some days it's hard," I admit, and then I smile. "But today? Today's an okay day."

She smiles, but her gaze is still searching, like she knows there's more I need to say. And so I say it: "The hardest part is feeling like I'm losing my connection with my father. He was an amazing player, and he died when I was a baby, so I don't have any real memories of him— just what I've seen in videos of his games. I always felt closest to him when I was on the court."

Her eyes rest on mine; the look she's giving me feels like she's drawing soothing circles around my heart. "I'm so sorry, Ossie."

I nod and shrug, not wanting to dwell on such dark feelings while we're having a good time. "I guess it's hard, too, feeling like I lost the only thing almost no one could deny I was really good at."

I say it almost as an afterthought, just trying to wrap up the conversation so we can move on to happier topics, but Naima leans across the table.

"Ossie," she says to me, her voice firm, "basketball isn't the only thing you're really good at. You're an amazing writer."

"Eh," I deflect, looking away. "I don't know about all that. You and Luis are the amazing writers. I'm just some dude who's happy to be here." I think about the conversation I overheard outside Ms. Hunt's office; I may have gotten a unanimous vote from the committee, but I know for a fact that I'm lucky to have wound up in the program.

Her scoff punctures my self-deprecating bubble. "You're buggin'. Me, Luis, and almost everyone at Braxton have had writing tutors or been in after-school arts programs since we were kids. All that work, and you're just as good, if not better, than the rest of us."

"If you say so."

"I'm serious, Ossie. How hard did you have to work to be as good as you were at basketball?"

My mind reels back to all those days and nights on the court, all those endless hours running, jumping, sprinting, and drilling until my legs felt like jelly. "I spent almost every day on the court. More hours than I can count, since I was a little kid."

"See!" Her finger jabs the air as if she's scored a point. "You grinded and pushed yourself to get there. But your writing, Ossie—it's just as good as ours, even though we've been practicing for years. And you haven't even really broken a sweat to do it. Honestly, you might be more of a natural writer than basketball player."

I've never thought of it that way. I haven't put in nearly the type of work with writing as I did with basketball, yet it feels so second nature.

"I appreciate you saying that," I finally respond with a slight smile. "But we've spent more than enough time on me. Can I ask *you* something?"

"Sure," she says, looking a little wary.

"You have a luxury car, go to one of the most expensive high schools in the country, live in a great neighborhood—so why do you care so much about issues in the world that don't really affect you?"

"That's . . . a loaded question. I mean, things do affect me, like climate, social justice, women's rights . . ."

"True, but you care about, like . . . everything," I respond.

"There are lots of things that don't really affect me directly. But if I had to give a reason for why I care, I guess it would be . . . because someone has to."

I nod. "I feel that. It's like . . . people with a lot of privilege, they usually box up all the world's problems and pass them to someone else. That's why there's so much wrong."

"Damn," she says. "That's real. That's exactly what I mean."

We pay for the pie, then head back to the car.

"It's late. You should let me actually drive you home," she says.

For some reason, I'm suddenly comfortable with the idea of her seeing my neighborhood.

"Sure. Why not?"

But nervousness bubbles in my stomach as the buildings of Harlem whiz by, replaced by the buildings of my neighborhood. I imagine her taking in the sight of my world, comparing it to her world of luxury. Yet as we pull up to my apartment building, what she says is, "This looks kind of like where my mom and dad grew up."

I laugh. "Oh, they grew up in the hood, too?"

"I guess you can say that," she responds, her eyes fixed on the playground down the block illuminated by the night's bright moon. "But what I meant was a neighborhood where Black and brown people can be themselves. Where folks are out on the block kickin' it, listening to music, walking to the bodega at all times of night. A place where people aren't tone-policing each other and don't have to pretend to be something they're not to make their neighbors feel comfortable."

The magnitude of her seeing the beauty of my neighborhood hits me like a gust of fresh air. "I guess being in it, I don't always see it that way."

We're silent for another moment, neither of us wanting to be the one to end the night. Eventually, though, I break the spell. "It's late. I should go. Thanks for the ride, Air Hockey God," I say playfully, and open my door.

"We should do this again sometime," she says.

I smile in agreement. "Yeah, we should. Luis is gonna be jealous when he hears what he missed out on; he definitely won't bail on us next time."

Her eyes search mine for a second, then she nods. "Yeah. For sure."

As soon as she finishes speaking, I feel like I missed some sort of opportunity or said the wrong thing. But I don't know how to fix it, so I just thank her again for a fun night and get out of the car. She pulls away, leaving me in the glow of streetlamps.

Hours later, as I lie in bed, thoughts about my night with Naima floating through my mind like clouds, my phone lights up like a tiny firework. It's a video call from Luis. At two a.m.?

I swipe to answer, hoping everything is okay.

"Hey, Ossie!" Luis greets me, and it's immediately obvious he's at a party in a dorm room packed with people holding red cups. I can barely hear him over the noise. "Heard you and Naima had a good time tonight!"

"Yeah, it was chill. Everything good with you?" I ask, my voice laced with worry.

"I'm fine! Listen, I need a solid. If my parents ever ask, I was at your place tonight, okay?"

I squint at him. "Uh. Where are you, really?"

"I'm at NYU. But can you do that for me?"

"Yeah, yeah, sure, but—"

A strange voice breaks in. "I wanna say hi to Ossie! It isn't every day you get to talk to a celebrity!"

Luis groans something in Spanish, and then my screen's filled up with a guy in an NYU hoodie, dark skin glowing, curls wild.

"Hey, Ossie!" He beams. "I'm such a big fan of yours! I used to watch all your games!"

Before I can respond, Luis snatches back the phone, and the guy is gone as quick as he came.

Luis's face pops back up. "Gotta go, Ossie. But I owe you one!"

"Wait!" I'm not about to lie for him without knowing what's up. "Who was that guy? Is everything really okay with you?"

"That was Mateo. My boyfriend. It's all good, I promise! But I gotta go! Let's catch up tomorrow!" And with that, he hangs up, leaving me in a mess of thoughts.

Boyfriend?

Chapter Twelve

I wake up Sunday morning, still wearing the confusion of my video call with Luis. But before I can unpack my thoughts, he calls me.

"Guess we should talk about what I said last night?" Luis mutters, skipping the hellos.

"You mean asking me to lie for you about where you were?" I ask.

"I expect any good friend of mine to lie to my parents about me at some point," Luis says, not entirely being sarcastic. "I'm talking about me being gay."

What's largely been floating in my head since learning about Luis's boyfriend is how his parents would react. Knowing they're always trying to shove him into their standards for a guy. That must be even harder for him than I thought.

"You don't have to talk about it if you don't want to," I say quickly. "You seemed happy last night. That's all that matters."

"Good," Luis says, his voice tinged with relief. "'Cause I don't have the energy for the Luis-in-the-closet drama right now. Remind me to never play drinking games with college kids again, okay?"

"Sure." I chuckle. "But just so you know, whenever you do want to talk . . . I'm here."

There's a pause on the line, a breath held and then released. Like Luis is realizing that our friendship is a place where he might be able to set down some of the weight he feels.

"You're kind of okay, Ossie," he finally says. Then he clears his throat and shifts gears. "But enough about me . . . Let's talk about you and Naima while I find some aspirin."

"What about me and Naima?"

"She sounded like she had a great time last night," Luis probes. "Think you might do it again?"

"Yeah, for sure," I answer honestly. "We had a good time. You definitely missed out."

"O-*kay*," he says slowly. "But what about hanging out with just Naima again? Would you be up for that?"

"I mean, yeah, I guess, if you're busy with Mateo or whatever," I respond guardedly.

A soft chuckle, weary but amused, slips through the speaker. "Ossie, you're really fitting into the whole clueless-but-beautiful-athlete stereotype right now. Let me be blunt: I think Naima wants to do what you two did again, but this time on an actual date."

I laugh nervously, not wanting him to know how much the idea thrills me. "I think you might be off about this one."

"Trust me: I'm not. I've seen the way she looks at you. And we've known each other since preschool. I think I've got a good read on her. She's into you."

My heart begins drumming. "Looks at me? How?"

Luis lets out a heavy sigh. "Like you're a jigsaw puzzle she's trying to figure out. The same way you look at her. Like she's a piece you need. Like she's something you've been searching for, even if you didn't know it."

I'm caught off guard, and words are stumbling over themselves in my head, "I don't—"

"Which is exactly why I parent-trapped you two yesterday," Luis interrupts.

"You what?"

"Parent-trapped you. I set you two up. I texted Naima yesterday afternoon to tell her I couldn't make it 'cause I had plans with Mateo. I wanted to give you two a night without a third wheel."

My mind races, piecing together the events of last night. Naima's secretive look when he texted—it suddenly makes sense. She was hiding the fact that he had set us up, and that he was with his boyfriend.

"So . . ." Luis begins, "what are you going to do about you and her?"

The question hangs in the air like a star waiting to be caught by the night. It's exciting to think that Naima might be feeling me. But still . . .

I draw in a deep breath. "Nothing."

"Nothing?"

"She's amazing," I admit. "But last night reminded me how important our friendship is. I don't want to risk that. Besides, I'm still figuring out who I am outside of my ex and basketball. I'm not ready for my identity to be tied to someone else again."

He's quiet for a minute. "I respect that," he says eventually. "I won't bring it up again. And I'm sure Naima isn't going to say anything if she hasn't yet. So let's just move on."

"Cool," I respond, relief washing over me—along with disappointment, not gonna lie.

After we're off the phone, I plop onto my bed and reach for the copy of Octavia Butler's *Parable of the Sower* that I took out from the school library. I read online that fans of Toni Morrison will enjoy Octavia Butler—I'm hoping so. After reading *Beloved* and researching my essay, I've been excited to find more novels by Black women.

But as I'm trying to read, my mind wanders back to my time with Naima. I can still taste the pie, hear her laughter, and see the beauty of her smile.

Every time I close my eyes, all I can see is Naima. Like she's been painted onto my eyelids with watercolors, blending in with every blink. Maybe Luis is right about the way she looks at me—and the way I look at her. My head's a storm, swirling with thoughts of her, and I'm standing right in the eye of it.

I grab my phone, thinking of texting her, then hesitate. What would I even say? "Hey, can't stop thinking about you and that pie"? I put my phone down, trying to shake off the feelings. But it's like trying to shake off a tattoo.

I'm not ready for all this. I'm not ready for the butterfly flutters in my stomach, the way my heart feels like it's got a subwoofer every time I think of her. I need some space, some distance. Need to get my head straight.

That's why, when Grandma Alice calls, asking me if I'm coming to dinner tonight, I immediately say yes. Suddenly the awkwardness of seeing my mom doesn't feel as daunting as a night spent thinking of Naima.

But when evening comes, my mom's missing from the scene. Turns out she's been pulling extra shifts at the department store and hasn't had a chance to make it to Sunday dinner for the past few weeks, either. I'm oddly disappointed.

As I look around, I realize something else is off. Dinner feels different, like someone's turned the volume down on the event.

Grandma Alice is usually the life of the party, her voice echoing through the house like a jazz singer's leading her band—all while being a tornado in the kitchen, her hands easily maneuvering through chunks of cheddar for her famous baked mac and cheese, whisking the batter for her signature sweet potato pies, and monitoring the collard greens with the precision of a seasoned chef.

But today she's different. Slower. Her steps seem unsure, her hands fumbling. The food is still being cooked hours later than usual. She keeps forgetting where she placed her seasonings, her magic potions she's been using since I can remember. A twinge of worry knots in my chest.

"It's just the flu, sweetheart. The changing weather's been giving me the chills," she explains when I ask her if everything is okay. Her voice is weak, weary, not the booming, confident sound I'm used to. "Guess your mom helps more with Sundays than I give her credit for."

I offer to help, to do what my mom usually does. But Grandma Alice just laughs, a weak version of her hearty chuckle.

"Boy, you can't handle this kitchen like me and your momma," she teases, with some of her usual spark. "You might know how to clean some vegetables and stir up some cornbread mix, but that ain't cooking. You gotta know how to put your foot in it." She holds out a forkful of collard greens for me to taste, her way of driving home her point.

I taste the greens, their flavor bursting on my tongue. I have to agree that I'm nowhere near her league. "Okay, okay, I can't cook like this," I concede, laughing. "But I do pay attention and I can do a little something."

Her laughter bounces through the kitchen, a familiar sound that lightens my heart. "Maybe one day, you and your momma can host a Sunday dinner. Lord knows you two could use some quality time."

Thankfully, Mrs. Collins and Ms. Peters end up coming in and helping Grandma Alice finish everything so we can serve the guests and get the night on track.

When dinner is over, after we've washed the dishes, I'm about to leave for the night. I can't help but ask Grandma Alice one more time about how she's feeling. Her usual vibrant self seems so dulled down.

She waves me off with a gentle swat of her hand, a thin smile perched on her lips. "It's just a cold, baby," she says, her voice raspy and worn. "No need to worry."

Despite her reassurances, a layer of concern covers my heart. Still, I hold on to the warm feelings from dinner. It wasn't the typical grand feast that Grandma Alice usually throws down, but the food was still amazing. She could probably make a dish out of cardboard that would have me licking my fingers. The company was great, too. Between the Sunday dinner and my time with Naima, I'm full with a kind of joy that feels like it seeps into every part of my body. It's a fullness I haven't felt in a while—not since I had basketball and Laura to fill my days.

Fast-forward to the next morning, and I'm standing at the foot of the massive iron gates of Braxton after walking from my bus. I'm greeted by an unexpected sight: Luis and Naima.

"What are y'all doing here?" I ask, surprised. I'm one of the few students who walks through these gates, because almost everyone else, including them, has a car they park in the student parking lot about a ten-minute walk from here.

They exchange glances. "We just thought you might want some backup today," Luis says, as if it's the most obvious thing in the world.

"Backup?" The word rolls off my tongue, wrapped in a thick layer of confusion. "Why would I need backup? Did the race war start and nobody told me?" I wait for them to chuckle, but neither even cracks a smile. "Oh, wait—is this because of homecoming?" Even with everything that's been going on, I still know that this is homecoming week, which means the halls will be filled with athletes, cheerleaders, photos . . . all the usual mayhem that I used to be a key part of. "I appreciate y'all caring, but it's cool."

Naima takes a step forward. "There's something else, something apparently you didn't hear about."

The two of them share another one of those looks, a silent conversation happening that I'm not privy to.

"Can one of you just tell me?" I ask, my anxiety rising.

Luis swallows, looks me in the eyes, and says, "Matthew and Laura . . . They got picked as homecoming king and queen."

Hearing that hits me like a sucker punch to the gut, a deep ache spreading through me. But I push it down, put on my best poker face. "Oh, cool," I say, shrugging like it doesn't matter. "Is that all?"

Naima studies me. "You sure you're okay?"

"Yeah, it is what it is." I force a smile, trying to make it reach my eyes. "Good for them."

But as we walk through the towering gates of Braxton, the universe seems to be in cahoots to remind me of my pain. Not only are the school's walls plastered with homecoming posters featuring a photo of Laura and Matthew, but in the center of the main hallway is a massive poster celebrating the sports teams. The players in the basketball team's photo stare back at me. My team. Only, I'm not in it.

Each step I take feels heavier, like I'm dragging my past with me. My pride, my identity, my heart, all wrapped up in these things that have been taken away from me.

Luis and Naima seem to sense my struggle. They close in on either side of me, forming a protective barrier. But even with them beside me, the void feels vast. The voices of classmates fill the air around us, their excitement obvious, but it all feels distant, muted.

Naima tries to lighten the mood. "Don't let these posters get to you," she says, nudging me playfully. "Remember, it's just a bunch of overpriced decorations that'll be in the trash by next week."

Luis, seeing on my face how painful it all actually is, suggests we skip our first classes and chill in his car instead. Away from the noise for a bit. But just as we pass the guidance counselor's office on our way out, the universe decides to play one of its cruel "Gotcha, Ossie" jokes.

Mrs. Wright steps out of her office, her face all business. Right behind her is Laura, clutching a stack of glossy brochures—each one screaming of bright futures and collegiate dreams. For a split second, it's like the world narrows down to just me and Laura. It's as if we're caught in a silent conversation, with our eyes saying everything our mouths don't. Just when the silence feels unbearable, Mrs. Wright's voice breaks through: "Congratulations again, Laura. Why don't you head to the festivities?"

Laura mumbles a quick "Yeah, okay." She pulls her gaze from mine and, with a hurried pace, disappears down the hallway.

Mrs. Wright looks at us. "And where might you three be off to? This isn't the way to any of your first-period classes."

Luis stammers, trying to string together an excuse. But Mrs. Wright, always perceptive, takes in the posters, the atmosphere, and then my face. Understanding seems to dawn on her. With a knowing look, she simply says, "I didn't see any of you—just make sure each of you stops by soon so we can check in on your college applications."

We nod gratefully, then continue our trek toward the student parking lot. But Laura's eyes and unsaid words linger, pulling at the edges of my thoughts. *She seems happy. She's with Matthew Astor, and she seems happy.*

The basketball team seems happy too. Coach Ryan is probably happy. Everyone is happy. They don't need you. They never needed you.

You don't matter.

By the time we reach the door leading to the parking lot, I feel like my body is begging to breathe, and oxygen is telling it no. My pulse is racing, and Naima's worried voice breaks through the fog of anxiety, asking if I'm okay.

Words elude me, and I can only shake my head to let her know I'm not okay at all.

I hear Luis say, "I think he's having a panic attack, Nai."

"Let's hurry up and get him to your car."

Luis places my right arm over his shoulder while Naima wraps her arm around the left side of my waist. They carefully walk me to Luis's car, and as soon as I'm safely in the passenger seat, they begin guiding me through breathing exercises, their voices soothing, their presence like a lighthouse calmly helping me through a storm of emotions.

As my frantic heart falls into more gentle beats and my breaths lengthen into a normal pattern, Naima says to Luis, "Throw on the Bali playlist."

"What's the Bali playlist?" I ask, eager to latch on to anything that will distract me from the turbulence I was just going through.

Luis grins. "It's our little life-saving secret," he explains. "Naima and I started adding songs to this playlist back when we were freshmen."

"Me and Luis have dealt with anxiety and panic attacks, too," Naima admits, her words resonating through my slowly calming body. "I started getting them after what happened with my dad and the police. I felt helpless all the time, overwhelmed."

Luis nods. "For me, the attacks started back in middle school, right around the time I realized I'm gay. Let's just say, in my house, being someone like me wasn't exactly a walk in the park." He glances at Naima before continuing. "I started the playlist after Naima told me about her anxiety. We asked each other where we'd rather be in the world in our bad moments. We agreed on Bali. So the Bali playlist was born."

Naima then chips in. "We use it along with breathing techniques I learned in therapy. It helps us both calm down, and it reminds us that we're not alone, even when we can't physically be there for each other."

The end of her sentence merges with the opening notes of a classical song flowing from the speakers of Luis's SUV. The melody fills the air like it's wrapping me in a hug.

"Close your eyes," Luis suggests gently. "Let the music do its thing."

So I do as he suggests.

In the stillness, with my eyes closed and the music washing over me, a sense of familiarity tugs at my consciousness. I recognize the song.

"This is from an anime," I murmur.

"You watch anime?" Naima asks.

I nod. "Yeah, this one's from Studio Ghibli's . . . um, *Howl's Moving Castle*, right?" I open my eyes.

Naima beams at me, her expression nearly as delighted as when she was beating me in air hockey. "Yeah, the song is 'Merry-Go-Round of Life'!"

"Oh, yeah! That's my shit. I'm a huge Ghibli fan! *Spirited Away, Princess Mononoke*—they're all amazing," I respond, excited that Naima is a fan, too.

Luis shoots a glance at Naima. "All the anime music on our playlist was added by Naima. You should join the playlist! See what you can bring to the mix—or how much you might have in common."

Naima teases, "He doesn't need to be part of our 'emotionally messed-up people' playlist, Luis."

I can't help but laugh, the sound mingling with the lingering notes of the music. "Nah, I'd like that. Seems like this 'emotionally messed-up people' playlist is exactly what I need these days."

"Good," Luis says, already scrolling through his phone to add me. "We don't just use it for panic attacks. It's also there for those days when you need to unwind or get your mind off things. We're always finding new music to add. Can't wait to see what you put on there."

"Thanks," I say, warmth spreading through me. "For everything today—and the past few weeks. Y'all have really helped me so much. I'll have to think of a way to return the favor."

Naima's voice is as soothing as the music when she replies. "You don't owe us anything. That's what friends do."

"Speak for yourself, Nai. I'm sure I'll think of something," Luis jokes, sending us all into laughter. We sit there in the car, the music continuing to play, the three of us free, if only for a moment, of the harsh realities of everything outside.

Chapter Thirteen

Over the next few days, homecoming week at Braxton swings into full gear, but it doesn't hit as hard as before. Not even when Coach Ryan gives a huge speech about how the team is going to be better than ever because they'll be a "real unit" this year, as if I was some sort of toxic force. Thankfully, Luis and Naima are like my human shields. Without me asking them to, they meet me every morning at the front gate and escort me to class to make sure my day starts off okay. It's a silent pact, one forged in the fires of friendship and understanding. Something I've never really had.

On my way to school, I've been listening to the Bali playlist, letting it drown out the world around me. And I've been reading the book Ms. Hunt assigned us, *The Prophets*. I've been sucked into it, reading almost the entire book in just a few days. The complexity of the characters, the depth of the narrative, it's got me hooked. It's like I've been transported to another time, lost in the beauty of the prose and the intricacies of the story.

The playlist is the perfect thing to complement the reading. It's not just music; it's like a refuge. Each song carries a message, emotions, and memories that Naima and Luis have invited me to share.

The songs on the playlist have a gentle back-and-forth between nostalgia and discovery. But what's most captivating about it is learning how much of a music connection there is between me and Naima. I mean, Luis and I, we share many of the same tastes, but with Naima, it's different. It's more profound, more intertwined.

Her music choices seem to constantly reflect mine — soundtracks from my favorite movies and shows, songs from rappers buried so deep underground that I thought I was their only listener, and the rhythm of jazz and soul songs that I associate with my mom cleaning the house or dinner at Grandma Alice's.

I start contributing to the Bali playlist, trying to add tracks that echo both Naima's and Luis's style, but without consciously doing it, I'm mainly adding things I know will speak to Naima. Songs that feel like extensions of her interests. Almost as soon as I add a song, she shoots me a text, surprised when she knows a song, excited about a new song she's discovered because of me.

But our growing closeness, for me, reaffirms the importance of a friendship I don't want to ruin. A chance at being hurt I don't want to take.

I decide to visit Grandma Alice after school on Thursday, to check in on her after she wasn't feeling well this past Sunday. As I step into her apartment and take my earbuds out, Al Green's mellow tones spill into her living room.

Grandma Alice's ears pick up the tune. "What you know about that song, baby?" she asks, surprised. She closes her eyes for a moment and listens along as I switch the song from my headphones to my phone speaker. "Mmm-mmm. Feels like it's been years since I last heard this."

I raise my phone to her. "It's on a playlist. Naima added it," I explain with a touch of pride.

Grandma Alice leans back in her chair, a joyful look on her face as she listens to the end of the song. "Well, that Naima sure seems like she has good taste in music."

As we settle in her living room, I study Grandma Alice with a careful eye. She looks somewhat better than before, but the hoarseness in her usually vibrant voice and lingering raspy cough make it hard for me to not be concerned.

"How are you really feeling, Grandma?" I ask.

She attempts a dismissive wave, an action that's contradicted by the cough that grips her. "I told you, it's just a little cold, sweetheart," she says when she's recovered. "I've been taking my meds, don't you worry," she reassures me, but I'm not entirely convinced.

"Grandma, you probably need to see a doctor."

"Listen here." She leans forward, her chair creaking in protest. Grandma Alice's eyes lock onto mine. Her presence is firm and unmoving, like an old tree standing tall against the winds of my concern. "I've lived on this earth for over seventy-six *long* years. I know a cold when I feel one. Ain't no need for you to be fussing like this."

"But, Grandma—"

"But nothing, boy," she interrupts, then sighs, softening her tone. "Look, I know you think I'm supposed to be around forever. But I'm getting older. These are the sort of things that happen when you get older."

"I get it," I say, my voice light, not wanting to consider what she's saying. "But you have a lot of time left, Grandma."

A smile crinkles the corners of her eyes. "That's not necessarily true, baby. I mean, I hope so. But nobody has forever. And that's why I want you and your mother to fix what's going on between you. Because one day you'll wake up and realize you don't have the time to mend things anymore."

I swallow hard, the lump in my throat growing bigger with each word she says.

"Trust me, I know," she continues. Her face seems to be filled with regrets and what-ifs. "That's what happened with your mother and me. We were distant, just like the two of you are now, when she was your age. I was dealing with all sorts of things after her father left us and started another family. Just like her, I was so focused on my own pain that I missed out on being there for my child. And then one day, she was a mother, and I realized I had missed so much that I can never get back."

I look down, my fingers playing with the hem of my shirt. "But y'all have an okay relationship now," I mumble, trying to find a silver lining.

"Yeah, it's okay on some days. But you know how we are. We still butt heads, can hardly agree on anything." She chuckles, the sound both bitter and sweet. "But I'll never forgive myself for all the times and moments we could've had and didn't. It's not on you to fix, but I don't want that for you two."

I take a deep breath. It's a lot to process, but it's a reality I can't ignore.

Feeling heartache swallow the room, she swiftly changes the subject. "Anyway, enough about that. Tell me more about school, the writing program, your new friends . . ."

I spend the next hour or so filling her in. About the way the books are speaking to me, how they're sparking something new in my mind. How Ms. Hunt is pushing us to be better. How Luis and Naima have been like two homes for someone feeling lost.

"I'm glad you've found so much joy in books . . . and in writing again," she says, her hand reaching out to squeeze mine. "And I'm especially happy you've found someone new."

"What . . . what do you mean by 'someone new'?" I ask, trying to keep my voice steady.

"Naima," she states simply.

"Naima? Nah, we're just friends, Grandma."

"No, sweetheart. You and Luis are friends. Heck, you might even be on your way to becoming brothers," she says, her tone matter-of-fact. "But when you talk about Naima . . . there's a way your face lights up that I haven't seen in a long time. Maybe not since you were a child begging me to come down to the court to see that you finally had enough strength to get the ball over the rim.

"'I'm going to be just like my dad, Grandma!'" She chuckles as she mimics the childhood version of me.

I can feel the heat creeping up my neck, setting my cheeks on fire. I'm not sure if I'm blushing because of what she's saying or because deep down, I know she's right—I'm catching feelings for Naima.

"Boy, your face is redder than that time I walked in on you on that website with the—"

"Okay, okay, Grandma! Enough," I say, feeling my cheeks hurt as I try to stop myself from cheesing too hard. "You're right. I . . . I guess I do like her."

"So, why haven't you asked her out?" she nudges, leaning back in her chair.

My eyes drop to the carpet. "I don't know, Grandma," I admit.

"Is it about her coming from money, like your ex?" Grandma Alice asks.

I shake my head. "No, she's nothing like Laura in that way. At least not from what I've seen. She doesn't really care about material things, so I don't think too often anymore about her family having more than we do."

Grandma Alice nods, seeming pleasantly surprised. "Okay. So what is it, then?"

I let out a long sigh. "I'm just not ready to lose myself in someone again, not after what happened with Laura. I can't go through that type of heartbreak again. It just hurts too much." The confession floats in the space between us, a quiet truth I'm still trying to accept.

I've lost too much of myself to people who are gone. Laura, my dad—my mom.

The air thickens with silence for a few moments, until Grandma Alice begins to speak, her words flowing like a river, deliberate and slow. "Baby," she says, her eyes capturing mine intensely, "when you care for someone, it isn't about losing yourself in them, it's about them adding more layers to your story—and you to theirs."

She shakes her head then, like she knows something I don't but is going to share her wisdom. "Your mother," she begins, tracing an invisible pattern on the armrest of her chair. "You get that trait from her. She poured so much of herself into your father after they met, she started forgetting who she was without him. What it was like to see the beauty of the sky if she wasn't looking at it with him. That's why now, even seventeen years after his death, she's still figuring out how to be a whole person without him."

She falls into a thoughtful silence for a moment, a distant look in her eyes, as if she's watching footage of old memories. Then she continues. "When you lose someone, like how you and her each lost your fathers . . . it shatters something in you. Makes you start searching for glimpses of who you lost in other people, and when you think you've found it, the rest of the world doesn't matter. Even the face you see in the mirror starts losing significance."

I sit, absorbing what she's saying. I know she's speaking the truth—and it cuts deep.

"Baby, people always leave," she resumes after a breath, her tone soft like a feather but her words landing like an anvil. "Death, distance, time—they make sure of it. But the fear of loss shouldn't keep you from growing close to people. When it comes to people we care about, we should only fear not creating the kind of memories that make us ache when they're gone. This thing of ours—life, you see—is only as beautiful as the bonds we make as we journey through it."

I know she's right. I feel it, that deep honesty, in my bones. But knowing something and acting on it are two entirely different arenas. And right now, my feet are cemented in fear, heavy and immovable.

The next day, as we're all huddled up in the writing lab, Ms. Hunt breezes in. There's an excited bounce in her step, like she's been injected with pure sunlight. As she does, Naima leans in, her words a low murmur, just loud enough for me and Luis to catch.

"I'm surprised to see her so happy," Naima begins. "Did y'all hear about the complaints against her?"

Luis's eyebrows knit together. "What complaints?"

Naima rolls her eyes, but there's a seriousness underlying her tone. "Apparently, some students and their parents have been running their mouths about her teaching style and her approach to the writing program. My parents told me about it last night. Said there was an email sent out to everyone on the school advisory board."

I blink, taken aback. "Already? We *just* started the year. And the writing program has been great so far . . ."

Luis nods. "Exactly. Everything we've been doing feels real. Fresh. Like we're doing work that will matter."

Naima sighs. "Yeah, I know. But apparently some students are saying the books we're reading aren't 'interesting' and don't 'resonate' with them."

I shake my head. "Of course they would say they aren't 'interesting.' It wouldn't matter if they were the best books ever written; they weren't going to like them anyway. Because the books aren't about *them*. They don't care about other real human experiences."

"Exactly," Luis says again. "They don't like that these stories challenge their white-centric, heteronormative bubble. They're used to reading books that validate their experiences, their perspective. Now they're being asked to step into someone else's shoes, and it's uncomfortable."

Ms. Hunt stands in front of the room. Oddly, she's not only cheerful; she's almost euphoric.

"Good afternoon, everyone!" she exclaims, laying her bag on the desk and connecting her laptop to the overhead projector. "I have some exciting news for you!"

The projector hums to life, casting an image of a blank book cover against the whiteboard. We're all buzzing, curiosity sparking, theories spinning.

"I'm sure you're all wondering what this is," Ms. Hunt teases.

"A book!" Matthew calls out from the back of the room, playing the unnecessary role of class clown. Inciting a few others to chuckle along.

"Wonderful powers of observation you have there, Mr. Astor," Ms. Hunt responds. "I would love to see you begin applying this skill to your writing."

Matthew's face flames red. I can't help but wish I was recording this. The perfect content for when I need a good laugh.

"This," she says, gesturing toward the screen, "is a golden opportunity.

"Michelle Barton, my dear friend and a top editor at Vision Press, one of the most prestigious publishing houses in the world, is currently working on an anthology. Yes, Sydney?" Ms. Hunt asks with admirable patience.

Sydney lowers her hand. "Are we going to get free copies or something? Because that's cool and all, but . . ." She trails off, her tone making it pretty clear that for someone like her, a free book isn't actually "cool" at all.

"Something much better," Ms. Hunt responds, her excitement barely contained. "The anthology is called *The Art of Tomorrow: The Coming Voices*. It's a collection of pieces from talented writers who have not been published yet. You all are going to submit your own essays. The most insightful, powerful piece will be chosen by Michelle and her team and earn a spot in the anthology. Published, recognized, and . . . awarded a three-thousand-dollar prize."

The room comes alive with excitement and chatter. This isn't just an interesting opportunity; it's a potential life changer. "Published while in high school by a major publishing house" is the type of thing that could set a person apart for college applications, internships, jobs, even careers.

"There is one catch for this opportunity," Ms. Hunt says, beckoning everyone's attention. "You will all be writing about something of my choosing."

Excitement morphs into confusion, and for some disappointment—the power to choose, to control our narrative, suddenly yanked from our hands.

"What are we writing about?" asks Sydney nervously.

I don't know much about Sydney, other than the fact that she is friends with Matthew and Morgan and laughs whenever they say something inappropriate, trying to be witty or rude. Well, that and the rumors that her parents are secretly funding the entire campaign of a politician who openly stated that he wants to end immigration from countries where people happen to be Black or brown.

Ms. Hunt smiles. "You'll each be tasked with writing about some area in which you would like to see the world progress. It can be any-thing from climate change to protecting endangered animals to social justice. It's up to you. Because it's also *about* you. I want you using the skills we've talked about in this program to put yourself on the page. I want your essays to explore progress in a way that resonates with you, deeply and personally, and to explore why."

"That's not fair." Sydney's voice vibrates through the room, high and whiny like a child's.

Ms. Hunt doesn't skip a beat. "What exactly is unfair about it, Sydney?"

"Well, that sort of essay is easier for someone who is—" Morgan gives her a sharp elbow, and Sydney swallows the rest of her words. "Nothing, Ms. Hunt."

With the Sydney moment out of the way, Ms. Hunt gets back to discussing the opportunity. She explains that our writing will have to be more vulnerable and honest than ever before. To help us begin tapping into that, Ms. Hunt says everyone should be about done with our most recent assigned book, *The Prophets*, and next she wants us to read James Baldwin's essay "A Letter to My Nephew." She tells us how Baldwin wrote this essay in the form of a letter addressed to his young nephew. In it, he unravels the threads of racism, his words filled with hopes and prayers that his nephew's journey into manhood might be less burdened by the same hardships Black and brown people faced at the time. Ms. Hunt explains that the letter's format makes the essay especially heartfelt and intimate.

"You won't be writing about the letter. I want each of you to read it and reflect on it before the next meeting. Then, next Friday, we will spend our time discussing *The Prophets*—which you all will surely have finished by then"—a few nervous chuckles are scattered throughout the room—"and Baldwin's essay. The week after, you'll write your own letter to someone close to you, inspired by Baldwin's letter. We'll talk more about what form, exactly, that letter should take at our next meeting. But that essay will be turned in the following Wednesday before our program meeting. That is the day *before* Halloween, so that should give you time to get it done right before whatever mayhem you all have planned."

I'm excited about the project, especially because I know my mom and Grandma Alice love James Baldwin's work. This is just the excuse I need to prioritize reading something by him.

When the meeting is over, the usual suspects—Matthew, Morgan, Sydney, and a few others—form a huddle in the hallway. They started doing this a couple weeks ago—gathering to gripe about the writing program. I never really paid their whining much attention, thinking it was just petty venting. But knowing they've taken their issues outside their circle and that they're complaining about Ms. Hunt specifically fills me with frustration.

As Naima and I walk past, I can feel their eyes on us, but we don't give them the satisfaction of acknowledging their presence. We've got weekend plans to discuss, distractions to dream up, and no time for their negativity.

Luis mutters something about needing to use the restroom and disappears around the corner, leaving Naima and me waiting. We lean against the lockers, the cool metal pressing into our backs, grounding us. We chat about possible hangout spots, movies to go see, and whether we should visit the park Luis keeps talking about taking photos at.

In the middle of our chatter, my phone vibrates.

LUIS: #ParentTrap

ME: Huh?

Then, a few seconds later, both our phones vibrate almost simultaneously. We exchange a glance, then each check our devices.

Group Chat - The Dope Writers Society (Naima, Luis, and Ossie)
LUIS: You two are taking too long for me. Naima do you want to go on a date with Ossie?

As I read the second message, I look up at Naima, wondering if she's going to be staring at me as if I have three heads. But she isn't; she's just smiling at her phone and typing something. My phone vibrates a second later.

Group Chat - The Dope Writers Society (Naima, Luis, and Ossie)
NAIMA: If Ossie is done avoiding me . . . I'm free Sunday

My eyes scan the message more times than I can count before I fully comprehend what it means, and I lift my head to find Naima smiling at me. That smile that could melt an entire world—and with it, all of my fears about expressing my feelings for her.

Chapter Fourteen

Planning my date with Naima, I'm glad movies like *Love Jones, Love & Basketball,* and *Before Sunrise* used to be my religion. They aren't about the big grand gestures; they're about those little, intimate moments. The stolen glances, the soft touches, the whispered confessions in the middle of the night. That's where the magic lived. That's where the real love stories unfolded.

Which is good, because those are all things you don't need a lot of money for—and I'm popped.

But while I might not have cash to flex, I do have a plan. All I need is for Naima to agree to meet me at eight a.m. on Sunday at the 1 train on 242nd Street in the Bronx. The perfect time to go to my spot before it's filled with tourists. Which she does—reluctantly.

NAIMA: Damn. That's early as hell for a Sunday . . .
but sure I guess

That part is done, but there's another ingredient to this love recipe—Grandma Alice. I need her cooking magic, her expertise.

I call Grandma Alice on Friday evening and ask whether I can come over the next day, if she'd be willing to show me some of her skills. While I'm there, I can also help her get a head start on prepping the food for Sunday dinner so she isn't left doing everything by herself, since my mother is still working extra shifts.

The next day, I head to Grandma Alice's apartment armed with Tupperware containers and a small menu for my date with Naima. She laughs a bit at my plan but is more than happy to guide me as we prepare the meal for Sunday dinner and the dishes for my date. I'm happy to find that while she still has a slight cough, her health seems much better.

When Sunday morning rolls around, Naima shows up to join me for the ride to Manhattan on the 1 train. Because of the cool autumn air, I'm wearing a peacoat over an athleisure sweat suit, which makes it look like I've upped my fashion game. Which I'm thankful for, because Naima looks great. Her oversize sweater, leather coat, and green combat boots, topped off by a beanie that barely contains her locs, paint a picture of urban chic. She's stunning, to say the least.

Summoning up my courage as she walks closer, what I manage to blurt out is: "Glad to have you here."

WHY WOULD I SAY THAT?

"Thanks for having me, sir," Naima jokes, holding out her hand to shake mine as if she is at a job interview. Her laughter mingles with the crisp morning wind.

As we enter the subway station, the familiar scent of the underground wafts up to meet us.

Naima pauses at the top of the stairs, looking down at the tracks, a small smile on her face. "You know," she starts, "since I was a kid, I've loved the subway. There's something about it that just . . . feels like the heartbeat of the city."

I glance at her. "Really? Most people I know just complain about it."

She laughs, and it's like a song. "Oh, don't get me wrong. Delays, crowded cars, occasional weird smells—they're all part of the package. But there's also something beautiful about it. The way it connects people, the stories it holds. Every time I step onto a train, I feel like I'm stepping into a new chapter of a book."

I nod, leaning against the railing. "I get that. It's like for a moment everyone's on the same path. Different destinations, different stories, but all of us moving together."

"Exactly!" Her face lights up with excitement. "It's like this living, breathing thing. Every station, every line, it tells a different story. And just think about all the people you pass by—each one of them with their own world, their own thing going on."

I can't help but chuckle. "You're making me see the subway in a whole new light now."

She grins, nudging me playfully. "Good. It's about time someone joined me."

The ease of our conversation calms my nerves. With Naima, things just flow. It's like we've known each other for years, like every time we talk, we're picking up a conversation we started a lifetime ago.

As we get on the train and take our seats, Naima looks at me with feigned suspicion.

"You know, I have no clue where we're going," she says as she looks at what I brought with me. "The least you can do is tell me what's in the basket. I'm just trusting that you aren't trying to take me somewhere to harvest my brain for research."

"Don't worry—you'll find out soon," I reply. "Plus, if anyone's brain would be worth harvesting, it would be mine."

"Oh, hold up!" she protests, laughing. "You're the one who was afraid to ask *me* out, which was obviously because I'm the one with the genius brain that intimidated you."

This launches us both into a fit of laughter. For the rest of the train ride, we debate whose brain would outprice the other's in a hypothetical black market auction.

When we arrive at the Seventy-Ninth Street subway station, I let Naima know it's our stop, and we walk over to Central Park. I lead her to a hidden gem of a spot—a quaint gazebo, tucked in the lush trees of the park and brushing against the calm morning water of the Central Park lake. The beauty of fall is unfolding all around us, as if an artist's brush was stroked across the trees, painting the scene in browns, oranges, and yellows reflecting perfectly off the lake.

Naima gasps. "This place is gorgeous, Ossie! I don't think I've ever been to this part of the park."

The morning chill gives me an excuse to reach into the basket for some of the comforts I've brought. I hand Naima one of the cozy blankets I had the foresight to bring from home. As she wraps it around her shoulders, I pour her a mug of hot cider from a flask. The way her eyes light up makes me grin.

"You must come here often," Naima guesses, curling her fingers around the mug, the steam warming her face.

"It was a favorite spot when I was younger. Haven't been here much recently, though," I admit, fumbling a bit with the picnic basket, taking care to avoid messing up the moment as Naima watches.

"I would have never thought you would be so shy," she observes as she takes a careful sip of her cider.

"Sorry," I mumble, finally daring to meet her gaze.

"There's nothing to be sorry about. It's cute," she assures me.

My heart stutters a beat. *Oh, shit. She thinks I'm cute.*

"I get it," Naima says. "I'm nervous, too. I've only been on a few dates—which weren't that great. How about we just talk how we normally do—as if we're not on a date?"

"That's a good plan," I agree, feeling a wave of relief wash over me.

Naima glances around, taking in the serenity of the gazebo and the shimmering lake. "So how'd you find this place, anyway?"

"My mom used to bring me here when I was a kid. It was our little hideout from the world."

She smiles. "You two must be pretty close."

I hesitate for a moment, then shake my head. "Nah, not really. Not anymore."

There's a pause, a moment of contemplation, before Naima ventures, "Do you mind me asking why?"

"Nah, it's all good." I take a deep breath, then let it out slowly, gathering my thoughts. "Things started to change once I got seriously into ball—once I reminded her too much of my dad. She never really went to my games or showed much interest in what I was doing. Meanwhile, my grandmother never missed a single game—home or away."

"I'm sorry," she murmurs. "That sounds really tough. But it's nice that your grandma was so supportive." Her eyes crinkle as she smiles. "And from what I recall, she wasn't your only die-hard fan."

I laugh and duck my head, my heart fluttering a little at her awareness of my past with Laura. "You mean Laura and her folks?"

"Um, *yeah.* Didn't they have, like, custom jerseys made with your name on them? They were pretty hard to miss."

I shrug. "Yeah, well, they're nowhere to be seen now. Turns out they were more interested in Ossie the basketball star than they were in *me*."

"That really sucks. I'm sorry."

I shrug again, trying to keep the mood light. "It's all good. Just as long as you know who you're dealing with here—a broke-as-hell former athlete who doesn't want to boost you on social media—then we're good."

Naima sets down her cider and pretends to start running away while staying in place. We both laugh as she sits back down.

"So I guess becoming your next big hashtag relationship is out of the question? Damn," she teases, her smile infectious. "I figured we would be 'Naissie' or 'Ossima'—a girl can dream."

I laugh. "That's a low blow."

"Sorry, couldn't resist. Luis told me about the whole 'Laussie' thing, and it's hilarious," she says, still grinning. "But don't worry: I don't really use social media, so I haven't had time to follow you and find any other embarrassing things from your past."

I jokingly roll my eyes. "Thankfully you wouldn't find anything else, since I don't really post much."

She takes a sip of her cider, and I turn the questions around on her.

"What about you? We've only talked a little bit about your family. What are they like?"

Naima searches the horizon as if she's plucking the right words from the morning sun. "So," she begins, "my dad, he's . . . brilliant. Like, literally brilliant." There's a shadow of pride in her tone, but it trembles with something else, something heavier. "He's actually the head of his department at Fordham now. But—he's so different these days. He used to be fearless. He'd stand up, speak out about anything and everything." She pauses, the memories pressing down. "But ever since the police . . . since that day, it's like they snatched something from him. He isn't the same anymore. Now he's just . . . He seems scared, all the time." Her eyes cloud over, reflecting a storm of unspoken pain. "I guess I can't blame him. It's like they took his fire, left him choking on the ashes." She looks away. "He's still brilliant and sweet, but that's all he is. Brilliant and sweet and scared."

"That's awful . . . I'm sorry."

"It is," she admits. "And then there's my mom. She's an orthopedic surgeon, and it's so fascinating watching her work. She has this gift with people. The kind where she can turn any frown into a genuine smile, both literally and figuratively."

I chuckle. "Seems like they're both dope."

"They are." Naima nods. "They've both worked so hard to build a life for my brother and me, to give us more than they ever had. But, you know, sometimes . . ." She trails off, her gaze dropping to her hands.

"Sometimes?" I prod gently.

She looks up, her eyes meeting mine, vulnerability shining through. "Sometimes their dreams for us feel like . . . like they're more about them than us. Like they're trying to fill in the gaps of their own pasts, their own regrets, through our futures."

I nod slowly, absorbing her words. "That sounds . . . like a lot."

Naima lets out a shaky laugh. "It is. And don't get me wrong, I love them, and I appreciate everything they've done for us. But it's hard when they don't see, or maybe just don't want to see, what my brother and I truly want. What we need."

I reach out, placing a hand on her shoulder. "It's okay to want something different. It's your life."

She nods. "Yeah, for sure."

The moment stretches between us, comfortable and understanding. It feels like we've crossed a threshold, moved into a deeper understanding of each other.

"What's your brother like?" I ask, breaking the silence. "Are you two similar?"

Naima laughs gently. "Well, Jamal is only eleven. So we aren't super similar, since that's a little young for him to be idolizing Malcolm X like I do," she says, her mouth turning into a half smile. "And Jamal has Down syndrome and a lot of trouble with his verbal skills, while I have *no* trouble talking, as you know." She's making light of it, of how vulnerable she's just made herself, but I catch how she's watching me, as if waiting for me to hurt her. And I wonder what's happened to make her expect to be hurt.

"Tell me more about him," I say.

A huge smile lights up her face—and somehow I know I've managed to say the right thing. "Jamal is my whole heart. He's super shy at first. Partly because he struggles with his speech but also because he's learned to be nervous around new people. I think he gets some of that from my dad—but once you get to know him, once he opens up around you, he's the absolute sweetest kid ever. He's a total goofball, and his laugh is just . . . There's no better sound in the world. Oh! And he's a big basketball fan," she adds with unmistakable pride.

"Yeah?"

"Yeah. The school he's at has a basketball program, and they play on Saturdays. That's why I wasn't free yesterday." Naima is a beautiful surprise around every corner.

She tells me more about Jamal as we sip our cider and enjoy the morning. Eventually, though, she nods to the picnic basket.

"So, you ever gonna tell me what's in there?"

"Oh, right!" I respond. I can't believe I forgot!

One by one, I start to pull out plates, silverware, and condiments, all carefully arranged. As I open the Tupperware containers, the scents of a homemade feast coat the morning air: salmon cakes, grits, biscuits, bacon, and scrambled eggs, all carefully prepared and neatly packed.

Naima's eyes widen as she surveys the food. "You made all of this?"

"Yeah. Well, with a little help from my grandmother," I admit. "I told you I can do a little something in the kitchen, so . . ."

"Wow, Ossie. Just . . . wow. This is amazing. A soul food breakfast picnic is possibly the Blackest thing anyone has ever done."

Our laughter spills into the air, harmonizing with the birdsong that hangs in the background.

As I begin serving up the food, my stomach drops. The food's cold! I heated it up before I left my apartment, but I didn't account for the journey to Manhattan or for the fact that we might not eat it right away.

Caught off guard, I stammer an apology and begin to close the containers, planning to pack everything back into the basket. But Naima stops me, her laughter filling the air again.

"What are you doing, Ossie? A little cold food won't kill us. If the food is good, the flavors will still do their thing. Pass me those salmon cakes or we're going to fight."

I'm grinning so hard I can feel my cheeks beginning to ache. We dive into our plates of cold soul food, appreciating the flavors that linger despite the temperature. Thankfully, even cold, Grandma Alice's recipes still taste incredible.

"You good?" I ask as Naima has a mouthful of food, eager for her feedback.

"You did a little something here," she admits, reaching for a second salmon cake after polishing off the first. "The flavors are hitting— I can't lie."

As we eat, I ask Naima something that's been on my mind since she dropped me off at my apartment the other night and said that thing about Black and brown people just being themselves. "What's it like being Black where you live?"

She doesn't respond immediately, as if she's trying to come to terms with her experiences.

"Well, it's not so different from being Black at Braxton, you know—like constantly being invisible but also always being the most visible thing around. And it's interesting because my parents do well for themselves, but it's not generational money. So there's always this unsaid thing, like if there are a few bad years for some reason, we'll be right back in Harlem."

"I hear you," I respond. "A lot of Black families that come into new money still don't have the safety net that white families have."

"Exactly," Naima replies, as if she's excited someone gets it. "But sometimes I wish we could just go back to Harlem. We lived a few blocks from the Apollo until I was about eight. We left after my dad got his PhD and my mom finished her medical residency and they got better jobs."

"But why would you want to go back? You're driving a Benz and probably living in a house straight out of a magazine," I argue, genuinely baffled by her longing.

"True, but the grass isn't always greener. Yes, it's nice to have material things, but they're not everything. There's something comforting about being around people who share your culture, your interests, your skin color. Even though I was a kid when I lived there, Harlem is the only place that's ever truly felt like home."

"I hear you, but like you said—the grass ain't always greener," I respond, the warm truth of our conversation lingering around us.

Her eyes rest on me, like she's trying to sketch a moment in time. There's a silence that settles between us. Not awkward. Just thoughtful. Like we're both digesting the things we've been talking about. Slowly, she breaks eye contact and looks out onto the lake.

There's something amazing about being so comfortable with another person that you don't have to fill all of your time together with words. It's enough to just be together.

After a few minutes, Naima says, "I guess I wonder where the grass actually is green for Black people. I have to believe there is somewhere, because if not—what's the point?"

I nod slowly. "I feel you. I've been thinking about things like that a lot with the books and stuff Ms. Hunt has been assigning."

Naima's fingers play with the edge of her mug. "Can I ask you another question?"

I nod, my heart rate picking up a bit. "Yeah, sure. What's up?"

She takes a deep breath. "There's a lot of rumors," she starts, her voice quivering just slightly, "and I never wanted to ask, but since we're having these deep conversations . . ."

I can tell she's uneasy. "It's all good," I assure her. "Ask your question."

She swallows hard. "What happened with your dad? I've heard so many things about how he passed, but it just seems like there are a lot of different stories."

A lump forms in my throat. The memories, the pain, the lies—they all come rushing back. I take a moment to collect myself, then reply: "A lot of people say my dad died from a drug overdose. That's what his college told the media, and it's true—but it's not the whole story. Everyone assumed that because he was Black, he was popping pills or something worse."

Naima's face is a mix of confusion and sympathy. "So what really happened?"

I take a deep breath, trying to steady the tremor in my voice. "He died from a pain pill overdose. But they weren't street drugs or anything. They were pills prescribed by the basketball team's medical staff. My father got hurt pretty bad in a game, but the team needed him.

According to my mom, they kept telling him to 'suck it up' and take the pills so he could play. They had a big game coming up, and when the usual dose wasn't working anymore, the staff told him to take more. A lot more. And . . . he did." My voice breaks. "Before the game, he collapsed. And that was it."

Naima's eyes are wide, shock painted on her face. "Oh, my God," she whispers. "How do more people not know about this?"

I let out a bitter laugh. "The only person who knew what was going on was my mom. But who's going to believe a basketball player's poor Black twenty-year-old girlfriend, who happened to have a baby at nineteen, over a massive, well-respected university?"

She looks down, her fingers still fidgeting. "I'm so sorry, Ossie. That's . . . that's just not fair."

"Yeah, that's why I didn't even consider committing to Alderbridge University. I jumped at the chance to play for Syracuse because they're in the same division. I was gonna destroy them," I say, feeling the old fire and pain bubbling up. "You know the worst part, though? My dad's family settled with the school for millions and didn't help my mother or me with any of it. She's had to struggle her whole life to keep a roof over our heads and food on our table, and meanwhile they turned their backs on her. On us."

Naima's hands clenched into fists. "Oh, my God. Couldn't your mother have sued them or something? You're his blood!"

"Yeah, sure," I reply, my voice thick with emotion. "But she didn't want anything from them after that. They tried to claim she was a gold digger, told her she'd need to provide a paternity test to prove that I was really my dad's son. She knew the truth, and that's all that mattered. My mom and dad, they were in love. In fact, I was planned. They were young when they had me, but they already knew they wanted a life together—a family together—and didn't want to wait. That's part of why I started hooping. I wasn't just going to make it to the NBA for my dad—I was going to give my mother the things she deserved. Show the world that they were wrong about her, too."

Naima's eyes are soft, filled with sympathy. "Wow," she whispers.

Suddenly, I become aware of just how cold it is—and right on cue, my entire body starts shivering.

Naima bursts out laughing. "Why on earth didn't you bring a blanket for yourself? You're big as hell, Ossie, but you're not immune to the weather."

I laugh, too, the sound a bit shaky from the cold. "Yeah, I realize that now. I'll definitely remember for next time."

She shakes her head. Without a word, she scoots right up next to me, adjusting her blanket to cover me with some of it as well. The warmth from her body and the blanket drives the cold away. She leans her head on my shoulder, and I can smell the sweet scent of her shampoo and feel the gentle weight of her locs against me.

I turn my head slightly, looking down at her. She tilts her face upward, our eyes locking. Time seems to slow; the park blurs, leaving just the two of us in sharp focus. And in that split second of electric life, I lean down and our lips meet.

It's soft, hesitant at first, a gentle exploration. And then it deepens, becomes more insistent. The taste of cider still lingers on her lips, mixing with the natural sweetness of her. My heart races, and I feel her fingers lightly gripping my arm. It's as if I've never kissed someone before this moment.

It's intimate, warm. *Right.*

Chapter Fifteen

After our date ends and Naima drives home, I'm on cloud nine. It's like my feet aren't even touching the ground. That kiss has me walking down the street with a bounce in my step, wearing a grin that feels like it's been superglued to my face. I'm heading to Grandma Alice's for dinner, happier than I've been in forever.

Big Teak is parked in his car, treating it like his personal office while bumping 21 Savage at a volume the entire neighborhood can hear. But as soon as he spots me walking by, he lowers the music to say what's up.

"What's good, superstar! What got you looking all cheesed up?" Teak calls out, his voice carrying down the block, a grin spreading across his face like he's in on a private joke.

I can't help but chuckle as I walk over and dap him up, trying to play it cool. "Nothing, man. Just a good day, you know?"

Teak squints, his grin widening. "Nah, I know that look. You ain't fooling me, youngun'."

I laugh, still feeling the lightness of Naima's laughter, the warmth of her lips. "Whatever, I gotta dip. Trying to make it to my grandmother's for dinner. Not tryna have everyone kill all the food before I get there."

He nods and daps me up as I begin to walk away.

"Oh, wait, hold up," Teak calls out. I spin around to face him again. "You see that viral video? That joint with the homie from your school?"

"Huh? What you talking about?"

Teak's already fishing his phone out of his pocket, his large fingers swiping across the screen. "Man, it's this white kid from your school, going off on some rant. Talking all kinds of shit about his 'woke' teacher. It's blowing up. I wasn't sure it was the same school at first, but then I peeped that ugly-ass uniform you be wearing."

I frown, the lightness of my mood starting to evaporate, replaced by a toxic feeling bubbling in my stomach. "Let me see."

He hands me the phone, the screen already glowing with a social media video. It's Matthew, looking smug as ever. I turn up the volume, leaning in, my heart starting to race.

He's going off about how his Black teacher is trying to indoctrinate students, make them "woke," how she supposedly hates white people and refuses to teach about them. Though he doesn't name her, it's clear he's talking about Ms. Hunt. The same Ms. Hunt who's done nothing but try to help us—help me.

The video was posted Friday, right after our writing program meeting. It's already racking up views, hitting a million, and the comments . . . Man, the comments are like a cesspool, a frenzy of hate and ignorance. It's like watching a wildfire, the kind that starts small but grows, consuming everything in its path.

I feel my chest tighten, my mood plummeting from the high skies to the gutter. I hand the phone back to Teak, my mind racing, my heart pounding a troubled rhythm. This ain't right. This ain't right at all. Ms. Hunt, she doesn't deserve this. "Thanks, Teak. I gotta go."

Teak nods, a serious look replacing his usual calm demeanor.

"Aight. Be careful with those white folks up there. If they try to do you filthy, hit me up."

I nod, feeling the gravity of the situation.

When I walk into Grandma Alice's apartment, the place is buzzing with the usual Sunday-dinner energy. I greet everyone, but my mind's distracted, trapped in thoughts of that damn video, that venom. Then I hear Ms. Peters call out from the kitchen, her voice slicing through my thoughts like a warm knife through butter. "Hey, Ossie!"

I walk into the kitchen, trying to mask the storm inside me. As I approach her, Ms. Peters turns, her hands busy with some kitchen magic. She leans in and presses her lips on my cheek, her kiss seasoned with a hint of fried chicken and the warmth of her affection.

"That grandmother of yours wasn't lookin' too hot. We gave her a COVID test, and it was negative. But we still made her go put up her feet while we handle the rest of dinner."

Mrs. Collins struts by like a diva, holding a large pot of collard greens like it's a fashion statement. "Alice needs to learn to take a break every now and then. Lucky for her, you two got the food prep done earlier. She sure as hell wasn't up to cooking tonight." She lands a kiss on my other cheek, balancing out Ms. Peters's.

I say hello to a few other guests, then head into Grandma Alice's room, where she's tucked in bed, fighting the pull of rest. I ease down onto the bed beside her, the creak of the mattress springs breaking the silence. She's propped up on her pillows, a weary smile on her face. My anger over Matthew's video fades, replaced by a fog of worry for her.

"You were right," she admits, her voice softer than usual. "I guess I did need some rest."

"I'm glad you're getting it," I say, trying to keep my voice even.

She chuckles, a weak but genuine sound. "Yeah, I'll take a few days off. Get back to it next week."

I shoot her a look of caution. "Don't rush it, Grandma. Take all the time you need."

She waves a hand dismissively. "Your mother said she's going to finally be back at dinner next week. Ain't no way I'm missing out on that."

"Oh, okay," I reply, a mix of emotions swirling inside me.

Then, with a sly grin, she asks, "So, tell me about your date. Was it as amazing as you hoped?"

I can't help but smile, the memory flooding back. "Yeah, it was incredible. We talked a lot, about everything. She's . . . she's really something, Grandma."

As I'm telling her all about the date, Mrs. Collins slips into the room, balancing a plate piled high with food and a steaming mug of tea. "Everyone out in the living room's drunk and making noise," she declares, handing me the plate and setting the tea on the nightstand for Grandma Alice. "You two should just stay in here and enjoy each other tonight."

I thank her, and she leaves with a knowing smile.

So that's what we do. I tell Grandma Alice more about Naima, about the picnic, even about the kiss. She listens, her eyes bright with interest and affection, until she eventually falls asleep. I tuck her in, give her a kiss on the forehead—it doesn't feel feverish, I'm relieved to notice—and head home.

I'll visit her this week to make sure she's still resting. A few days of that and hopefully she'll be fine.

Later, when I'm back in my room, my phone buzzes with a text from Luis. He's asking about the date. But I can't respond. Not right now. Since the moment I came home and finished my essay on *The*

Prophets, I've been glued to my screen, replaying Matthew's video, feeling my blood boil with each rewatch. At one point he mentions that Ms. Hunt prefers the "minority students" in our program and that she "favors them for half the effort." I know he's talking about me, Luis, and Naima. It's probably mostly about me, though.

Rage washes over me, consuming every bit of my attention. Even when Naima texts, saying she had a great time, all I can muster is a "Me too." My mind is trapped in that video, fixated on Matthew, on what I plan to say to him tomorrow. I'm done letting him be a piece of shit.

The next morning, I'm like a ghost at the bus stop. The Woodcrest kids are making their usual jokes, throwing comments around like they're nothing. But I don't hear them. During my bus ride, my earbuds are in, but no music plays. Just the sound of my own thoughts, churning, plotting.

The hallways at Braxton are buzzing with the usual Monday-morning energy, but none of that matters to me. I'm like a missile, locked on target, every step fueled by a burning rage. If my knee disagrees with the pace, I'm not hearing it. I push through the crowds, my eyes scanning for Matthew. When I finally spot him, my jaw clenches. He's standing by his locker, his arm casually wrapped around Laura's waist, laughing as if he hasn't got a care in the world.

I march right up to him, my feet pounding against the floor. Students around us stop and stare, sensing the storm brewing.

He turns to face me, his smug grin widening. "What do you want? Can't you see I'm busy?" He emphasizes his point by tightening his grip around Laura's waist, pulling her closer to his side.

His jab is irrelevant. "Delete that video about Ms. Hunt," I snap. "Or I'll *make* you delete it."

Laura steps forward, attempting to defuse the situation. "I know how his comments might've seemed, but Matthew is just coming from a different perspective, Ossie—"

My words slice through the air like a sword: "If you want to be with this dude, that's fine, Laura. I don't care. But stop pretending he's some decent guy. He's trash, and you're just as bad for choosing to be with him."

Matthew's face contorts with rage. "Watch your mouth!" he snarls. And then, without warning, he shoves me with all his might.

I stumble backward, my feet scrambling to regain balance. In a flash of fury, I'm lunging forward, shoving him back with even more force. He stumbles, then quickly recovers. Our eyes lock, both of us burning with anger, the air around us crackling with tension.

The hallway erupts into pandemonium. Students hoot and shout, most egging us on, others calling for us to stop. A circle quickly forms around us, trapping us. Some of my old teammates are in the crowd, cheering on Matthew. I wonder if they would support me if I was still playing with them—or if whiteness is the only team that matters.

Before we can escalate things further, two security guards cut through the ring of onlookers. They head straight for me. Their grip is iron, their faces set in determination. I struggle against them, trying to break free, but they're too strong, too many.

"Stop! Let him go!" Laura's trying to reach me, her face twisted in fear and concern.

But Matthew is already pulling her away, his hand gripping her arm. "Come on," he barks.

Laura's face is a portrait of conflict, her eyes staring back at me, filled with something that looks like regret. But she doesn't resist. She goes with him.

The security guards slam me to the ground with unnecessary force.

My face presses against the cold, hard floor, my heart pounding, my mind reeling.

Around me, the noise of the crowd fades into a distant roar. I'm pinned down, my dignity stripped away in front of everyone. Anger and frustration boil inside me, but they're slowly replaced by a deep, aching sense of fear.

"Enough! Enough!" Dean Blackburn's voice booms through the chaos. Her presence commands everyone's attention. "Everyone clear out! Now!"

The students start to disperse, their muffled jeers and chatter filling the air as they reluctantly obey her command. The security guards finally loosen their grip on me, allowing me to stand, but they keep their hands firmly on my shoulders.

"Bring him to my office," Dean Blackburn orders, her tone inviting no argument.

The walk to her office feels like a march of shame. Anger and humiliation battle within me, each vying for dominance.

Once we're inside her office, Dean Blackburn dismisses the security guards. The door clicks shut behind them. Dean Blackburn looks at me, her expression stern. "Do you understand the gravity of what just happened? I could expel you for this."

"Matthew put hands on me first. Why isn't he here?"

She ignores my question. "Look, I'll skip over the pleasantries and get to the point. I know a few weeks ago we had a little misunderstanding about who was and wasn't accepted into the creative writing program. I also know you're a bright kid who deserves a shot at a better future. So here's what I'm going to offer you: going forward, you permanently forget about that little conversation you overheard between Ms. Hunt and me, and I'll forget about what just happened with Matthew. Water under the bridge for both of us."

I'm silent. It feels like a trap, a deal with the devil.

"Or," she continues coldly, "you can be expelled right now and derail any chance you have of going to college."

The room feels smaller, the air thicker. I can feel my future slipping through my fingers. I have to make a choice, and I have to make it now.

I swallow hard, my pride fighting against the practicality of the situation. "Okay," I finally say, the word wrenched from my throat. "Fine."

Dean Blackburn nods in satisfaction. "Good. Now leave my office."

I stand up, my legs feeling like jelly and my knee hot with pain. When I step out of Dean Blackburn's office, the hallway is empty, like a ghost town, but I can't shake the feeling that everyone's eyes are still on me.

Then I see Naima and Luis rushing toward me, their faces etched with concern.

"Ossie, we heard what happened," Luis says, scanning me like he's looking for bruises or something. "You good?"

I nod, trying to muster a smile that probably looks more like a grimace. "Yeah, I'm all right."

They both let out a sigh of relief, but it's short-lived. Now comes the scolding.

"Dude, why didn't you tell us you were gonna confront Matthew?" Luis says.

Naima nods. "Yeah, we could've had your back."

I look down, feeling a twinge of guilt. "I'm sorry, y'all. I just . . . I saw that video and lost it. Wasn't thinking straight."

They both shake their heads, but I can tell they're just relieved I'm not in handcuffs or something.

Then, because I don't care about keeping my word to someone like Dean Blackburn, I tell them about the deal I struck with her and the conversation I overheard between her and Ms. Hunt. It feels like I'm admitting to some crime. "I had to agree to let it go. In exchange, she won't expel me."

Luis frowns. "Man, that's messed up."

Naima's hand finds mine, giving it a gentle and surprising squeeze. "We'll figure it out. Together."

My heart flutters in excitement.

Luis notices our hands. Always the one to try and lighten the mood, he flashes a crooked grin. "Hey, before you two lovebirds decide to go fight another racist at school, can you at least update me on how the date went?"

I can't help but chuckle, and Naima laughs, too, a sound like sunshine breaking through clouds. For a moment, things feel a little lighter.

But I know that won't last long.

The week ends up feeling like stepping into a hurricane, the winds of drama and chaos swirling around me, threatening to toss me around like a rag doll. Matthew's video is everywhere, sweeping through the internet like a tornado. And just when I think it can't get any worse, another video surfaces—the one of me and Matthew nearly coming to blows.

The media pounces on it. "FORMER BASKETBALL STAR ASSAULTS CLASSMATE," the headlines scream. They're trying to paint me as some kind of monster, a fallen hero turned violent. The accounts of what happened are all twisted and wrong, but that doesn't seem to matter. The truth rarely does when it comes to people like me.

Everywhere I go, even outside of school, it seems like everyone is watching me. It's suffocating. I try to keep my head down, but it's like I'm wearing a sign that says, *Look at me! I'm the guy from that video!*

The only places of refuge in this storm are reading James Baldwin's "A Letter to My Nephew," becoming closer with Naima, and visiting Grandma Alice—who is still resting, thankfully, and looking a bit better every time I see her. We talk about everything and nothing, and for a little while, I can forget about the chaos outside.

Chapter Sixteen

Friday comes, the day of our first creative writing meeting since Matthew's video dropped. It's also the day of my second date with Naima, though it's been hard for either of us to concentrate on tonight with everything that's been going on.

The moment we walk into the English Lab, I can feel the tension in the air. Ms. Hunt is obviously trying to act like things are normal, but it's like trying to pretend you don't see a volcano erupting.

Impossible . . .

Ms. Hunt stands at the front of the room, her usual energy dimmed but not out. Though anyone with half an eye can see she's off—like a record with a scratch, skipping beats, missing rhythms. She starts by talking about *The Prophets*, saying she hopes we enjoyed it, that it's the kind of honesty in storytelling that any of us could be capable of writing one day if we continue to apply ourselves. She shifts gears to Baldwin's letter to his nephew.

"So," she says, "I'm going to open the floor to whoever wants to start us off with thoughts on Baldwin's letter."

Three hands shoot up. Naima's is one of them. But just as Ms. Hunt's about to call on someone, Matthew cuts in: "It sucked."

The room freezes. You could hear a pin drop, a heart stop. Ms. Hunt keeps her cool, though. "Please raise your hand so I can call on you next time, Matthew. But—since you've kicked things off today, why don't you expound on your critique that it 'sucked'?"

Matthew leans back in his chair, smugness radiating off him like heat from a fire. "It's just more woke nonsense from a Black person who has a victim complex."

Ms. Hunt doesn't flinch. "Interesting," she says calmly. "Please, tell me more about this victim complex, Matthew."

Matthew sits upright again, clearly eager to enlighten us all. "If Black people like James Baldwin spent less time complaining about white people, they could be picking themselves up by the bootstraps like the rest of us and actually become something."

Before Ms. Hunt can respond, Luis cuts in, his tone sharp, like he's trying to slice through Matthew's ignorance: "Did you just say James Baldwin could have become something if only he'd pulled himself up by his bootstraps? You mean, something other than one of the greatest writers in American history?" Luis begins to laugh. "And what bootstraps are you picking yourself up with exactly, Matthew? The ones attached to your white privilege?"

Morgan sneers at Luis. "No, the ones attached to the boots that your illegal cousins shine."

The room erupts into gasps and mutters. Ms. Hunt steps in before Luis can say anything back, but there's fire in his eyes, a burning anger that I relate to.

"Enough of this." Ms. Hunt's voice parts the noise like the Red Sea. "Your comment is inexcusable, Morgan. You need to leave."

Matthew scoffs. "This is a joke. You obviously favor minorities and hate white people."

Ms. Hunt's eyes narrow the slightest bit. "Matthew, that is the furthest thing from true. I will simply not tolerate bigoted comments. If you're aligned with the sort of comment Ms. Henley just made, you can leave with her."

The fog of tension in the room is so thick, you could get lost in it.

"You shouldn't even be the head of the program. You only got the job because you're—" Matthew begins his attack, but his words are cut short. A resounding thud echoes through the room as Ms. Hunt slams a book on her desk, her action as commanding as her words.

"Get out, Matthew! Don't come back until you're ready to show some respect." Her demand shakes the entire room.

Matthew gathers his things and strides toward the door. Morgan grabs her belongings and trails after him like storm clouds following a tornado. Predictably, Sydney does the same.

At the door, he turns, and the look he directs at Ms. Hunt reminds me of the way that police officer looked at Naima and me weeks ago— a familiar mix of hatred and rage.

"I don't need you or this program; I'm going to get into Harvard either way. And I don't need to pretend to respect you—you don't deserve it."

The door closes behind him, Morgan, and Sydney, leaving a silence that's loaded with words unsaid, feelings unexpressed. Ms. Hunt takes a deep breath, the kind that's more like a sigh, and looks around the room, her eyes landing on each of us like she's trying to find something. Or maybe trying to give us something.

"Look, everyone," she starts, her voice softer now but still with that edge of steel, "I'm sorry you had to witness that. I don't want this space to be one where anyone feels attacked. We're here to learn, to grow, and sometimes that means having tough conversations. But there's a line, and it was crossed today."

Nods ripple through the room, like we're all feeling the same thing but don't quite know how to put anything into words.

Ms. Hunt clears her throat, shifting the energy. "Now, let's try to refocus. James Baldwin's letter is a powerful piece of writing. It's vulnerable, it's honest, and that's what makes it impactful. As writers, that's something we can learn from. How to be raw, how to be real. It's not just about words on a page. It's about what those words carry."

We spend the rest of the meeting diving into Baldwin's letter, peeling back layers, digging deep. It's intense but in a good way. Like we're mining for something precious.

"Take everything we discussed today and pour it into the letters you're going to be writing over the next few days. Don't forget to lead with vulnerability," Ms. Hunt says as we're exiting the room at the end of the meeting.

Luis, Naima, and I walk together to the student parking lot, since I'm leaving with Naima for our second date while Luis is headed to the city to see Mateo.

"That was wild in there," Naima says, her eyes still wide from the drama that unfolded in the meeting.

"Yeah, but Matthew got what he deserved," I add, feeling a mix of satisfaction and unease.

"So did Morgan and Sydney," Naima chimes in. "It's good they won't be around anymore."

Luis looks pensive. "Yeah, but something tells me this is going to be a mess for everyone." He shakes his head as if to clear it, then turns to us with a forced smile. "But anyway, on a lighter note, what do you two have planned for tonight?"

Naima seems excited. "Well, since Ossie planned our first date, the second one is all me. We're going to a drive-in I found online that's showing *Hereditary*, which is my favorite scary movie."

I can't help but grimace. "I haven't seen it yet, but I hate scary movies."

Naima grins and nudges my arm. "Awww, I'll protect you."

Luis lets out a laugh. "You two are adorable. Hurry up and become official so Mateo and I can double-date with you."

Naima and I share an awkward laugh, both of us blushing a bit.

Then Luis's expression shifts, and I can tell he's about to drop something on us. "So, my folks are finally back from their never-ending Europe trip."

Naima raises an eyebrow. "That's good, right? They must have enjoyed themselves."

Luis shrugs. "Yeah, I guess. They do their thing. Anyway, they're throwing their annual Halloween costume party next Thursday night. I kinda have to go, so . . . you guys should come, too."

I feel a twinge of reluctance, remembering my last encounter with Luis's parents.

Luis gives a half smile. "It's in your neck of the woods, Ossie, if that sweetens the deal at all. At Untermyer Gardens in Yonkers."

The mention of Untermyer Gardens brings back memories of gruesome stories from my childhood, the horror of hearing about the infamous cult activities, including the mutilations of dogs, that took place there in the seventies.

I raise an eyebrow. "The dog-murder park? Seriously? Do your parents know about the history of that place?"

Luis laughs humorlessly. "*Oh, they know.* And so do their rich, bored friends. They find all that stuff thrilling."

"But won't it be cold, having a party outside this time of year?"

Naima jumps in, shaking her head. "I went last year; they go all out—heaters, tents, the works. You'll barely notice the cold. Plus, it's always fun to people-watch."

"Yeah," Luis adds, grinning cheekily, "and you'll finally get to meet Mateo."

"Wait, Mateo will be there? Did you tell your parents about the two of you?"

Luis erupts into laughter. "Hell, no! Mateo's tall like you, so I'm just going to tell them he's one of your old teammates."

"So you're *using* me?" I respond, pretending to be outraged.

Luis shrugs. "Think of it as being a good LGBTQ ally. Plus I'm letting you steal my best friend from me, so it's the least you can do."

"Good point," I say, grinning. "All right, man. I'm in—but only because I'm an ally."

Luis chuckles, a load clearly lifted off his shoulders. "Thanks, Ossie. It'll be fun, I promise."

Naima gives my hand a reassuring squeeze. "We'll make the best of it," she says, her smile as warm as a summer night.

I keep hold of Naima's hand as we walk toward her car, a wave of excitement washing over me. The night air is crisp, the kind of cool that lets you know fall is really here, but it's not the biting cold yet. Just a teaser.

We pull into the drive-in, and it's like entering another world. The big screen stands tall against the night sky. Naima's got this whole setup planned out. She pops the trunk, reminding me of a magician's hat in there, endless surprises. Blankets, pillows, snacks, the works. We make ourselves a cozy nest in the back seat of her car, the stars overhead shining through the sunroof.

"Damn, Naima," I say in genuine excitement. "You really went all out."

"Oh, you thought you were the only one who could pack a picnic?" she says, passing me a mug and pouring still-hot cocoa in it from a thermos.

I laugh. "I see you picked up a thing or two from me."

The movie starts, and I'm trying real hard not to jump at every little thing. Naima's loving it, her eyes wide, glued to the screen. Every now and then she squeezes my hand, and I can't tell if it's because she's scared or because she knows I am. But it's cool. It's more than cool; it's perfect.

The movie ends, and we're both a little jittery from the adrenaline. But it's a good kind of jittery, the kind that makes you feel alive.

Saturday comes, and I'm sitting at my desk, staring at a blank screen as I try to start my letter for the writing program. My mind is a whirlwind of thoughts, hopes, and fears. I spend half the day drafting something to Naima about our first date but then delete the file; it's way too cheesy for this assignment. I know Ms. Hunt wants us to dig deeper than that, to make ourselves vulnerable the way Baldwin does in his letter. I start a new document, this time writing to my dad. But the words that come don't feel as honest as they should, and I know I'm still far from the mark.

The weekend slips by, the hours blending into each other, and I'm stuck in the muddiness of writer's block and mounting frustration. Before I know it, Sunday evening is here, and it's time to go to Grandma Alice's apartment. Which means it's time to face my mom. I haven't talked to her since our blowup a few weeks back; our schedules mean we're not often in the apartment at the same time, and when we are, we manage to avoid each other without it seeming like that's what we're doing.

I brace myself as I get ready to leave. It's like gearing up for a heavyweight fight, but the opponent is my own mother. My insides are a jumble of nerves. I keep telling myself, "You got this, Ossie. You can handle it." But the person I see in the mirror knows I'm lying.

Finally, I'm walking over to Grandma Alice's, my feet dragging like they're made of lead. Each step feels heavier than the last. When I get there, the place is buzzing with the usual crowd, the familiar faces from all the buildings in our projects and people around the neighborhood. But Grandma Alice and my mom are MIA. I scan the room; no sign of them.

"Hey, Mr. Edwards," I say, nodding at the old man from a few buildings down who has had a crush on Grandma Alice for years. "You seen my grandmother around?"

He looks at me, pushing his glasses up the bridge of his nose. "I think she's in her bedroom, talking with your mom." He's barely finished speaking when Grandma Alice walks out, her face lit up with a smile. She's got more pep in her step than the last time I saw her, like she's been charged with some new energy.

She sees me and her smile grows wider, if that's even possible. She comes over and wraps me in this big, warm hug. My mom walks out of the bedroom a few seconds after Grandma Alice. She looks the exact opposite of Grandma Alice—sad and deflated, like someone let the air out of her. And she's wiping her eyes, like she's been crying or something. I'm confused. What's going on? What did I walk into?

Before I can ask any questions, Grandma Alice and Mom disappear into the kitchen. I decide not to follow them; my mom's energy is weird, but maybe some time with Grandma Alice will improve her spirits. My apology can wait.

As the night wears on, the guests start to thin out, and the energy begins to settle. While Mom's not exactly *happy*, she at least seems better than when I walked in, chatting with the guests, making sure everybody has enough food on their plates and drinks in their glasses. I feel like it's now or never. I take a deep breath, like I'm about to dive into the ocean, and head over to her.

"Ma," I start, my voice shaky, like a bike on a cobblestone road. "I . . . I just wanted to say I'm sorry. For what I said a few weeks ago. After dinner."

She looks up, her eyes tired, like they've been carrying too much for too long. I feel a stab of guilt, knowing I've been part of that burden lately. "I appreciate you saying that, Ossie." I wait for her to say more—to apologize for her own role in our argument, maybe, or even tell me about myself for speaking to her the way I did. But she seems fine with leaving it there. I know if we do, though, this thing will still sit between us.

So I push forward. "I was hoping we could talk. About how I've been feeling, you know?"

She shakes her head. "Now's not a good time."

I frown. "When *is* a good time? I know you're busy, but I really think we should talk about—"

"I said not now, Ossie."

It's like a door slamming shut in my face. I feel this rush of disappointment, like a wave crashing over me, leaving me wet and cold. I nod, trying to hide the hurt. "Okay, no problem."

I find Grandma Alice and kiss her good night, tell her I'm heading home. She looks concerned, but I just say I need to work on my essay—which is true but is definitely not why I'm hightailing it out of there.

As I push open the door to my room, the familiar creak of the hinges sounds louder than usual, like the universe is emphasizing that I'm back in my own space. But tonight it feels more like a cell. A place to hold all the things sticking to me I can't seem to shake off.

I slump onto my bed, the mattress taking the weight of my body but not the weight in my chest. My mind's racing, thoughts bouncing around like they're in a pinball machine. And the thought that keeps flashing bright, like the high score on the screen, is that maybe my mom just doesn't care. Not about me, not about what I go through, not about what I want for myself. And that thought, it's like a sucker punch to the gut.

I'm not even mad. Anger is like a fire, and right now I don't even have the spark. No, it's just this deep, hollow sadness. Like maybe she never wanted to be my mom without my dad being around. Maybe she never wanted this, any of this. Me.

The room is silent, but it's loud in my head with memories, words, all the times I looked for her approval, her love. It's like a highlight reel of letdowns. And just like that, it hits me. The assignment. The letter.

I reach for my laptop, and the device feels heavier than usual in my hand, as if it has hardened for the pain I'm about to bear.

Little Pieces of Heaven

Ma,

I've been assigned the task of writing an honest letter to someone important to me, similar to how James Baldwin wrote a powerful letter to his nephew. Obviously, I'm nowhere near James Baldwin's talent, but I hope I've learned enough to find the words that will reflect the pieces of me.

I've been thinking about time a lot lately. How its unforgiving ways have formed a crater between us, transforming the beauty of our bond into a battlefield of disconnection and misunderstanding, until the very air around us, once full of shared laughter and loving embraces, has become a vacuum. Something pulling in our past selves, turning what's left of us into something ugly.

There was a time when you were the softest place I could land. That era feels like a bedtime story now, whispered through the night to soothe a restless child. How can one reconcile it with our now, the delicate strands of our relationship barely holding, our love a treacherous terrain, each step filled with doubt and longing?

Each day, I wonder if you also hear the song of our shared silence. Its melody is bleak, a sad tune with notes in the familiar rhythm of our lives. It's the sound between our few conversations, the unfinished thoughts that sit on our tongues, the smiles that don't reach our eyes. We live under the same ceiling, within the same walls, but it feels as though we're miles apart, isolated on either end of a bridge that once connected our hearts—a bridge that has long since been demolished.

There was a time when my world revolved around you, and I know for a fact that I was at least a moon to yours. I remember the times we'd lie on your bed at night and you'd read me stories or introduce me to old anime movies you like. Despite all the pain and sadness that surrounded us, it felt like we were carrying the weight of what we had lost together. Lifting each other.

Do you remember those days?

You once told me I have my father's eyes. At the time, that made me happy. But I have come to realize that anything of mine that reminds you of him is actually a curse, serving only to remind you of what is gone. You have spent so much time avoiding eyes you believe are his that I fear you are unable to see that they are also yours.

Why can't you hear my laugh, which Grandma Alice says is your laugh? Why can't you recognize my toes as larger versions of your toes? Why can't you see that my tears flow from the same broken dam as yours?

We both lost him—but when did I lose you? Because for years now, it feels that you are nowhere to be found. You've raised me, kept the lights on, fed me, and maintained a roof over my head. But there is a difference between building a house and building a home.

I know some of what this world has done to you, and how narrowly you have survived it. You've been through so much, and you're still here. I consider myself blessed for that. But I miss you, Ma. I miss when we had a connection that pierced through all of the pain and sadness that has lingered since Dad was stolen from us.

Maybe there's still hope for us. We don't have to live in a place between loved and unlovable. We can sit down with each other, talk about our experiences, share our stories, laugh and cry together until his void is filled up with the comfort of knowing that we are here for each other. I'm willing to do whatever it takes. Are you?

I don't write any of this to accuse. I'm only here to plead, a desperate son on his knees begging for his mother. Come back to me, Ma. Come back while we still have time.

Your son,

Ossie

I decide to submit my letter as soon as I'm finished instead of waiting until Wednesday, when it's due. Afraid I may lose my nerve otherwise. Once I do, a sudden emptiness washes over me. The kind that isn't necessarily bad.

Whether I ever say any of that to my mom or not, I feel better for having gotten it out.

Chapter Seventeen

After Naima, Luis, and I turn in our letters, we're all about getting ready for the Halloween party.

It feels like I've been holding my breath since getting the invite. I'm nervous about being around Luis's parents and their rich friends. This isn't a world I'm used to — at least not outside of Braxton.

Naima swings by my place to pick me up. As we pull up to the venue, my jaw drops. Naima and Luis weren't playing when they said this event was going to be something else. It's a spectacle, for real. Untermyer Gardens, the same old stretch of green I've seen countless times, has morphed into something straight out of a fairy tale. It's like a five-star hotel crashed into a botanical garden wedding, and they decided to throw a party together.

Folks are walking around wearing costumes that scream money. I'm talking about outfits that probably cost more than a month of my mom's salary. Everything's shimmering, glittering under the moonlight and the strategically placed lights. Even the valet, who's dressed up as a werewolf, looks like she just walked off a high-budget horror movie set. The costume is so detailed, so lifelike, I almost expect her to howl at the moon.

Naima's looking at me, her eyes twinkling with excitement. "Told you," she says.

I can only nod, feeling like I've been teleported to another planet. This isn't the Halloween I know. This is Halloween on steroids, Halloween with a trust fund.

"Ready?" Naima asks, her hand finding mine.

I squeeze her hand. "I guess I don't have a choice but to be." I smile nervously.

Just as we enter the party, Luis walks toward us, Mr. and Mrs. Martinez beside him. They're dressed in coordinating costumes, all from *Game of Thrones*. Luis is wearing an amazing dragon costume, scales shimmering under the party lights, while his parents are perfectly costumed as Jon Snow and Daenerys Targaryen.

"It's good to see you both; thank you for coming!" Mrs. Martinez says before scanning me and Naima. "But what are you two dressed as?"

Naima, her outfit covered in fake knives, points to herself. "A killer." Then she points to me, covered in an assortment of cereal boxes. "And he's cereal."

Luis, who wears his camera around his neck, takes a few pictures of us. "Amazing!" he says.

Mr. Martinez squints at us. "I . . . I don't get it."

"We're a serial killer. Kind of like the Son of Sam, who hung out right here in this park," Naima answers. "It's a nod to the venue."

Mr. Martinez's brows furrow. "A couple's costume? But I thought you and Luis—"

Before he can finish, Luis's face lights up like a spotlight. "Ossie, look! Your friend Mateo is here!"

He raises his camera to snap a pic, then rushes toward Mateo, whose arms are open wide, expecting a hug. But Luis reaches out for a fist bump instead. Mateo quickly adapts and fist-bumps him in return. Naima nudges me, a silent reminder that Luis's parents are supposed to think Mateo is *my* friend.

I stride over, putting on my best performance.

"What's good, my G!" I say to Mateo, trying to initiate some nonexistent intricate handshake. After a moment of clumsy fumbling, we settle for a simple one-armed hug. Then I guide him over to Luis's parents to introduce him.

Mr. and Mrs. Martinez take a step back, examining Mateo's costume, a glamorous gold-and-purple butterfly outfit that could fit right in at a fashion show.

Mr. Martinez purses his lips but says nothing. Mrs. Martinez, managing to recover her composure, says, "Nice to meet you, Mateo. We need to mingle with some other guests. Enjoy your evening, everyone." With that, they quickly slip away into the crowd, leaving us standing in the buzz of the party.

Luis exhales, a gust of relief, then turns to me with a grateful look. "Thanks, Ossie," he says, sounding like he's trying to navigate a maze of tension. "For real, Mateo couldn't be here without supposedly being friends with you."

I shrug, feeling frustrated by the way Luis's parents looked at Mateo. "No problem, man," I reply. "I got you."

He turns to Mateo, reaching out to touch his arm gently. "Sorry about that, babe," he murmurs. His voice is barely above a whisper, but it carries the weight of a hundred apologies.

Mateo smiles, the kind of smile that's trying to smooth the moment's roughness. "It's fine; I get it. I know how your parents are," he says, subtly squeezing Luis's hand.

He then looks at me, and there's a warmth in his eyes. "I appreciate you pretending, Ossie."

"All good," I respond, smiling. "But we are going to have to work on our handshake." We both laugh.

The four of us hit up the buffet and pile our plates high with food, because, hey, if it's free and fancy, why not? And then we find a cozy corner away from the rich eyes that seem to size up the world like it's for sale. Away from the wealthy tongues that speak in currencies and stocks.

It's hard not to be stunned watching these rich folks. They're like characters out of a comedy. Drowning in their cocktails, they're trying to dance, but it's like their bodies just can't find the rhythm. Like they're robots trying to understand human fun. It's hilariously tragic, honestly.

But if the party itself is kind of a bust, I really enjoy getting to know Mateo, at least. The guy's a walking encyclopedia, able to dive deep into subjects as far apart as politics and the upcoming NBA season. From the way he talks so passionately and knowledgeably about everything, you'd think he's lived many lives. So it's not surprising to learn that he's currently the president of the NYU undergraduate student government, as just a sophomore. And next year he's going to play soccer there. As I listen to him talk, I can see the spark in Luis's eyes.

Naima's nodding along as Mateo speaks with fire about politics. She obviously likes him a lot, and her opinion is probably the most important of anyone's in Luis's life. "The next president of this country needs to be all about climate change," Mateo says. "No ifs, ands, or buts about it. It's like, how many more warnings do we need? How many more hurricanes, wildfires, and floods—how many more lives lost, especially of Black and brown folks? It's real, it's now, and it's hitting us right in the face."

"Exactly!" Naima exclaims. "It's like we're living in a house that's on fire, and instead of trying to put it out, we're arguing about who started it. It's ridiculous! The planet's heating up, and some folks are still playing with matches."

Mateo's hands slice through the air, like he's trying to cut his point right into our brains. "*Right!* That's why we need someone in charge who's not just going to talk about change but will actually make it happen! Not in the future, not in a decade, but right now!"

Naima's eyes spark as she agrees. "Yeah! We need policies, not promises! *Real* action!"

The two of them are a match made in heaven. As Luis and I watch them, we can't help but laugh with each other.

At some point Luis wanders off to snap photos of the event. I enjoy seeing him in his element. But the best part of the night is seeing just how much he and Mateo care about each other. The way they look at each other is nothing short of magical.

As the night starts to become late, Naima offers to drive Mateo to the Metro-North station so he doesn't miss the last train back into Manhattan. I opt to stay behind with Luis, who can't leave the party.

"Where are your parents?" Mateo asks Luis. "I want to say good-bye and thank them for including me," he says with a deep kindness in his voice.

Luis shoots him a nervous look. "I don't know if that's a good idea. My parents are—"

But before he can finish, Mateo interrupts. "Babe. I know who your parents are, but that doesn't mean I'm going to be less of the person I am."

As Mateo heads over to say good night to Luis's parents, I can feel the tension thickening. He's all grace and smiles, but Mr. and Mrs. Martinez? They're like statues, their faces carved out of stone.

"Thank you for having me," Mateo says, his voice warm, his energy open and friendly. He's reaching out, trying to bridge a gap that's wider than the Grand Canyon.

But Mr. and Mrs. Martinez are unmoving—and unmoved. Their eyes dart around, scanning the crowd as if they're worried someone might catch them talking to Mateo. He's dressed as a butterfly, all colors and beauty, but to them? He might as well be a moth drawn to a flame they don't want burning.

Naima's by his side in a flash, her hand on his arm. "Let's go," she says, her voice low but firm. It's a rescue mission, and she's the hero. They turn, walking away, and it's like watching two pieces of the night peel off and disappear.

As soon as they're gone, Mr. and Mrs. Martinez come alive again. They stroll over to me and Luis, all smiles and warmth, like they just switched on a light.

"Ossie, thank you for coming," Mrs. Martinez says, her voice dripping with something that sounds like honey but tastes like vinegar. "Did you have a good time?"

I nod, because what else am I gonna do? "Yes," I say, forcing out the word. "Thank you for having me."

They nod, pleased, and I feel like I'm on stage, playing a part in a play I never auditioned for.

"Good, I'm glad," Mrs. Martinez replies with a gracious smile. But then her expression turns serious. "But, Ossie, could you just make sure if you bring a friend next time, they are more . . . fitting with our views."

I squint at her, pretending to be puzzled. "I'm sorry—what do you mean?"

Mr. Martinez chuckles. "Your friend Mateo, he seems like a good kid. And it's admirable that you're so . . . accepting. But his costume tonight, the way he prances around, it was a bit much."

Mrs. Martinez laughs in agreement. "Right. You already snatched Naima from our Luis. The least you can do is bring along a potential girl for him, not just a boy who dresses like one."

Their joint laughter sounds like nails on a chalkboard. I look at Luis, not knowing what to say.

And then . . . Luis begins laughing. He laughs right along with them. I feel like I've gone to another dimension, leaving me dazed and confused.

"Yeah, Ossie. I didn't realize you hung out with fairies." As Luis speaks to his parents, the look on his face says he feels as though he has stabbed himself in the back. "Anyway, we should get going," he says to his parents. "We have school tomorrow. Te veo en casa."

He gives both of his parents a hug and then steers us toward the park entrance, where Naima will meet us once she's back from dropping off Mateo. I glance at Luis, his face half-lit by the glow of the party lights, half-swallowed by the shadow of his and his parents' words. He's looking off into the night, his eyes distant, like he's seeing something far beyond the glitz and glamor of this manicured garden.

I want to say something, anything. But my throat's all tied up, like it's been laced with barbed wire. Eventually I muster an "I'm sorry, man."

Luis turns to me, his eyes meeting mine. There's a sadness there, a deep, oceanic sorrow that seems to go on forever. "It is what it is," he says, his voice hollow, like he's speaking from the bottom of a well.

I nod, even though it feels like agreeing to something that shouldn't be agreed to. This isn't how it's supposed to be. Luis and I stand there, side by side, lost in thought. The silence stretches on, but it's not awkward. It's like we're both taking a moment to mourn something. Maybe it's the loss of the idea that the world is an accepting place. Maybe we're mourning the fact that Luis has to hide who he is, to tuck away his love like it's something to be ashamed of.

A few minutes later, Naima's car rolls up. The glow from the streetlamps bounces off her windshield, and it feels like she's pulling up to the saddest scene in a movie. As soon as her eyes meet ours, I can see the question forming.

"What happened?" she asks, concern hovering over every syllable.

The silence wraps around our bodies like a straitjacket. Luis looks like the definition of sorrow, with his eyes glued to the street.

Naima tries again, her voice a little shaky this time. "Guys, talk to me. What happened?"

A tear begins tracing a path down Luis's face. It glistens in the dim light, like a drop of joy leaving his body.

"I appreciate you two coming," he says, his voice barely a whisper. "I'm going to go for a walk."

"You want me to walk with you?" I ask, my voice shaking. "You want to talk about it?"

Luis shakes his head, giving me a slight smile. "No, Ossie," he says. "Nothing happened tonight that I'm not used to." Each word is a stab to my heart.

Then he walks away, disappearing into the night. And all I can do is watch, wanting to pull my heart out my chest and exchange it for the one that I know is breaking in his.

I fill Naima in on what went down, and though we both reach out to Luis over text, checking in to make sure he's okay, he doesn't respond.

But the next day, when we step into the bustling school hallway, there Luis is, walking like he's on a beach, not a worry in sight. Flashing a grin that could rival the morning sun.

As if everything isn't just fine, but better than fine.

Naima slides up to him. "Are you okay, Luis?"

He just smiles, bigger, brighter. "I'm all good, Nai. I promise." So we back off, Naima and I, let him bury his feelings if that's what he needs. We'll be here when he's ready to talk.

Later in the afternoon, we have the first writing program meeting without Matthew, Sydney, and Morgan. It's amazing. The atmosphere is so much more peaceful. I hadn't fully grasped how much Matthew's presence was like a dark cloud hanging over me, suffocating me in anxiety and anger. Even Ms. Hunt seems transformed without them being there. Her whole demeanor is lighter.

But the best part of the meeting comes when we learn that Ms. Hunt was thoroughly impressed by everyone's letters. Her words of praise feel like a gentle, encouraging breeze, lifting our spirits. She tells us that we're all moving in the right direction. Then she says she's going to switch things up a bit. Instead of assigning us something to read and write about, she's going to let us choose a novel by an author who is someone outside of our own identity, whether that means a person of color or someone who is disabled, queer, or belonging to some other marginalized group. "The idea is to expose yourself to perspectives that are different from your own—maybe a little bit different or maybe hugely different. Expand your view of the world, challenge your assumptions—and become a better writer and a fuller person for it."

And then, she says, we are going to spend the next few months writing and editing a 7,500-word short story about one of the characters from the novel we chose.

Everyone's buzzing with excitement, ideas already bouncing around the room like Ping-Pong balls. This is what many of us have been waiting for—the opportunity to flex our creative-writing muscles.

After the session wraps up, Naima and I approach Luis. Trying to sound nonchalant, I ask, "Hey, you wanna hang out this weekend or are you planning to see Mateo?"

He shakes his head. "Neither. Mateo's tied up, and I'm just gonna chill alone this weekend."

Naima and I share a concerned look. The last thing Luis needs is to be home alone with his parents all weekend.

But I've got a better plan, something that might bring him out of his shell. "Nah, man, I have a better idea. Let's meet up tomorrow afternoon, all three of us."

He looks at me with a mix of curiosity and reluctance. "What's the plan?"

"I want to show y'all a place that means a lot to me. Don't say no."

Naima's face lights up. "I'm with it."

Luis hesitates for a moment, his gaze shifting away as if he's weighing saying no. But then he meets our eyes again, and he can see our expressions begging.

"All right," he agrees. "Where should we meet you?"

Chapter Eighteen

I've asked Naima and Luis to meet me at an old warehouse in Yonkers, right near the Hudson River. It's a spot that's got more memories for me than a family photo album—though when they finally arrive, I can tell they're both thrown off.

Luis, with his brows knitted, asks, "Is this the right place? It looks like an abandoned warehouse."

I can't help but laugh. "Close. It's an old sugar factory. But it's a lot cooler than it looks. Just come on—you'll see," I say, waving them forward. They follow me, a bit hesitant, as I lead them through a broken door on the side of the building, the metal creaking like it's got a story to tell.

Inside, the vastness of the space hits us immediately. It's like stepping into a forgotten world. Sunlight streams through the broken windows, shooting slanted beams that cut through the dust-filled air. The ground is littered with remnants of its sweet past—scattered pieces of machinery, rusted conveyor belts, and large empty vats that once housed molten sugar. The walls, peeling and covered in graffiti, hold stories from a time when this place was alive with the hum of productivity.

We start climbing up an old metal staircase, each step groaning under our weight like it's complaining about having to work again after all these years. To my surprise, my knee doesn't hurt as much as I expect it to.

"Is this even safe?" Luis asks.

I grin. "Yeah, you're fine. Don't worry." My voice bounces off the walls, filling the hollow space.

We keep climbing, step by step, the air around us filled with the scent of old things, lost yesterdays. I can feel their curiosity, almost like it's another person climbing with us. But I know what's waiting at the top, and that keeps me moving, keeps my smile in place. Because up there, above all this rust and ruin, there's something special. Something worth every creaky step.

Finally, I push open the rusty, screeching door, and we're there— the roof. Then we're out in the open, and the world hits all three of us at once.

"Wow," Naima breathes out, her voice soft, like she's afraid to break the magic of the moment.

Luis just stands there, his eyes wide, taking it all in. The Hudson River stretches before us, a glittering ribbon winding through the landscape. To the south, Manhattan's skyline cuts into the clouds like some kind of concrete-and-glass mountain range. And to the north, the suburbs sprawl, little boxes of life lined up one after the other.

The wind up here is a gentle whisper, and the sun's high, illuminating all the goodness of the world. It's like we're standing on the edge of everything, and for a moment, just a moment, all the noise, all the hurt, it just fades away.

Luis turns to me, his eyes still wide with wonder. "Ossie, man, how did you find this place?"

I shove my hands in my pockets, feeling a smile pull my mouth sideways. "My mom told me about it. Said when my dad used to come from Philly to see her during school breaks, she'd bring him up here. One day I decided to come see it for myself." I shrug, looking out at the view. "Been coming here for years now."

"I'm sorry for how I acted when we got here earlier," Luis says. "I didn't get it, but I do now. This place is special."

"It's fine," I tell him, my voice as calm as the river below us. "From the outside, it doesn't look like much, but it's one of the best places there is." I sweep my hand across the horizon, trying to capture the grandness of it all in one gesture.

"I used to come up here sometimes with a basketball," I continue. I pretend to dribble, feeling the ghost of a ball bouncing against my palm. "I'd work on my handle, getting to know the feeling of the ball when I made certain moves, like I was trying to drive past a defender for a last-second shot." My eyes flicker up and down the Hudson. "And I would look down one way and see Manhattan, then turn the other way and see the suburbs. And I would tell myself, one day I was going to get to choose between them. I was going to get out of here. Out of Yonkers."

I pause, a lump forming in my throat. "I haven't really been up here since getting hurt, though," I admit, the words tasting like dust in my mouth. "But I felt like bringing y'all here." I turn to them, hoping they understand.

Luis steps closer, his eyes still holding the glint of the river's reflection. "I'm glad you did," he says, and I can tell he gets it. He has shared parts of himself with me, and now I'm sharing parts of myself with him.

We let the silence settle around us. It's clear to Naima and me that Luis is still grappling with what happened the other night. The quiet grows, each of us lost in our thoughts, until Luis decides to break it. "Can I share something with both of you?"

"Yeah, of course," Naima and I say at the same time. I assume he wants to fill us in on what he's been processing the past couple days, but when he pulls out his phone and scrolls through it, searching for something, I expect to see a photo. Instead, he starts reading.

"'Dear Mateo,'" he begins.

"There is a certain silence that haunts the air after words, like
the ghosts of things we are trying to forget have been slammed
against the walls of our hearts. This is the kind of silence that
held me in the aftermath of the Halloween party, where my
parents' bigotry attempted to reduce the wonderful person
you are into something less, something unworthy. And I am
ashamed to admit that I let them.

I am writing this to you not only because I am sorry but
also because I fear that the way I didn't defend you might make
you believe I don't love you. That is the furthest thing from
true. And so I wrote you this poem, which says all of the things
I should have said that night, all of the things that are truly in
my heart.

For My Butterfly

Here, under the burning sky, two boys
find their hands knotted into the secret
language of skin. Love, as old as the first light,
sprouts from the youthful spring of their heartbeats,
a wildflower wrestling free from its bud.

Each kiss, a new galaxy whispered into
the cosmos of their closeness, tender worlds
birthed in the hush of shared breaths.
Fear, once filling the corners of their eyes, fades,
now a shadow under the radiance of their touch.

This love, it is not a drizzle—abrupt and apologetic.
It is a river's patient erosion, carving canyons
into the fortress of their reluctance. It is the truth
of the setting sun, a symphony of oranges and purples,
whispering, 'It's okay, it's okay.'

In the mirror of the other's gaze, a young man
sees himself. Not something odd, not an outcast,
but a being created from the same soil
that nourishes the things older than words.

He learns he is no less human,
no less holy.

Love,

Luis"

Tears are rolling down my cheeks like raindrops down a window.
I'm staring at Luis, marveling at his words, at how I can feel so much of
him. Sadness and anger boil up inside me. That something so beautiful,
like what Luis has with Mateo, has to be hidden away, tucked in a closet
like it's something wrong—it makes me want to scream.

Naima throws her hands around Luis's neck, whispering words
meant for his ears alone. But I don't miss the shine of tears on her own
cheeks.

"Thank you for sharing that," Naima says when they're done hugging.

"That was your letter for Ms. Hunt's class?" I ask, awestruck at how vulnerable he made himself for a school assignment.

He nods and shrugs. "I actually turned in a letter to my younger self at first. But after what happened on Halloween, I wrote this to Mateo. Ms. Hunt agreed to review it instead of my other submission. I knew after she assigned us *The Prophets* that I could trust her to respect my whole self."

I think again about Matthew's hateful words, about how he refuses to see the significance that books like the ones Ms. Hunt has assigned can have for students—especially those of us who don't always see ourselves reflected in literature.

"I feel the same way," Naima says. She bites her lip like she's debating something. "Would it be cool if I share my letter with y'all, too? I don't want to step on your moment or anything, Luis."

He shakes his head quickly. "No, I'd love to hear it—share! If you really want to, I mean."

Naima nods slowly. "Yeah, I think I do."

She pulls out her phone, searches for what she needs, and then she, too, begins to read.

"Daddy,

I hope this letter finds you wrapped in warmth, in some place that shelters you from the storm outside. From a world that feels increasingly constricted, a world where breathing is a conscious effort, where each inhalation is laced with the toxins of a pervasive and persistent supremacy—the white supremacy that put you in that hospital bed.

Those images of you, beaten and bruised, they haunt me. I keep circling back to that moment, like a bird hovering over an inevitable ending. The police, those supposed guardians of peace, always let their batons do the talking, their blows articulating a language of hatred and power. It's a language that has become all too familiar, yelled in the streets, heard in the stories we whisper to each other, seen in the silent nods of understanding we exchange when we pass by one another.

The protest was meant to be a statement, a cry for justice in a world where the scales seem forever tipped against Black and brown people. The way your students looked up to you as you stood there shouting for the safety of Black lives, I was so proud. I still am.

And yet that voice was met with violence. The sound of the police descending upon you is the soundtrack to my personal hell. The unprovoked aggression that unfolded with a surreal sense of death coming. It was as if the very act of standing up, of asserting our humanity, was an insult too great for them to tolerate.

The blows they rained down, each one a new sentence in the story of systemic oppression, were not just physical. They were symbolic, a demonstration of the power structures that underpin our society. And as I stood there, watching helplessly, I felt something break inside me. It was more than the pain of seeing you hurt; it was the shattering of an illusion—the illusion of fairness, of justice.

And almost as bad as the beating itself was the fact that no one believed us. They forced you to walk out of that hospital and carry on with your life as if you had not just spent weeks in a bed fighting for it.

The trauma of that day has not healed. It will never heal. Because the events that caused it still happen every single day. And not just to you and me, Daddy, or to Mom and Jamal. It is all of ours, a shared burden that we carry as a community. It is a trauma that speaks of the vulnerability of our bodies, of the fragility of our rights, of the fight for our place in a world that seems all too willing to silence those of us who dare to speak out. I think somewhere inside us, each and every Black person has this same fear. That we, or someone we love, might be next. Another news story. Another statistic. Another hashtag.

It's a smothering thing, this trauma. It makes it hard to breathe, even in a place like Braxton, a place you and Mom send me in the hopes of giving me something better. There, I may not be beaten with batons or shot with rubber bullets. But the same white supremacy that empowers those police officers to act with impunity is in every classroom, standing at the front of the room or sitting at the desk right beside me, telling me I'm not good enough, whatever my grades may be; telling me that I don't belong, even though I pay the same tuition that they do. It's in every textbook, whitewashing our history, erasing our community. It is an invisible force, forever pressing down.

You've always taught me to stand tall, to look the world straight in the eye, no matter how it tries to bend us. But, Daddy, the fear, it's deep. It's like a shadow, trailing me, whispering in my ear when I least expect it. Telling me that one day, the police might finish what they started with you at that protest.

And if not you, then maybe Jamal. My little brother, with his wide smile and sparkling innocence. In a world where Black skin is seen as a threat, what chance does he stand? A little Black boy with Down syndrome, so eager to embrace the world—so unprepared for the arrows and slurs and bullets that might be the world's response. It terrifies me, Daddy, the ease with which our humanity is disregarded, our lives discarded.

How do you do it, Daddy? How do you move forward, suffering what you've suffered, knowing what you know? This question orbits around my mind, like the earth around the sun. How do you muster the strength to keep going, to keep placing one foot in front of the other, as you limp now and hold a cane because of them? How do you look in the mirror and see a whole person, and not just the scars they left on you?

Your strength reminds me of the roots of an old tree. Unseen, buried deep in the earth, holding firm even in the fiercest storm. I wish I had the same strong roots. But I'm more angry than strong. More afraid than brave. Because seeing everything I see, feeling everything I feel, it makes me realize that I cannot save you. I cannot save Jamal. I cannot save Mom. I don't know if I can even save myself.

And if the worst happens, will the world shrug and move on? Because it seems people are more interested in the performance of change than its reality. Their posts and slogans are everywhere, but when it comes down to it, will they stand with us? Will they actually risk anything alongside us? For us? For themselves?

I hope that they will—but I just don't know.

With all my love,

Naima"

I stare at Naima, my eyes glued to her face. "That was . . . I . . . I . . . wow." It's like she's put her heart on a platter, baring it all. The love, the fear, the fierce protectiveness for her father—it's all there, raw and real. It's so incredibly powerful, the kind of love that could move mountains or at least shake the roots of ignorance. She's incredible. A magician with words.

Finally, I clear my throat. "Would y'all be cool with me reading mine, too?"

"Of course," Naima says, her eyes warm and reassuring.

"Let's hear it," Luis says, settling against the low wall, giving me his full attention.

With trembling hands, I find my essay in my email app and begin to read. My voice shakes at first, but as I read on, it grows more confident—louder, steadier. Stronger. Even without looking at them, I can feel the love coming off Naima and Luis, feel the warmth of their support. Heard aloud, my words seem even more powerful than I remember them being.

It's quiet when I finish, like we're all just trying to catch our breath after diving too deep.

Luis shakes his head. Then he smiles. "Damn, Ms. Hunt wasn't lying. These shits were good."

We all laugh, the sound filling the sky and touching everything the eye can see. We find some old crates on the roof and drag them to the low wall. Side by side, we sit there as the sun starts its slow descent. The world below us keeps moving, but up here, on this roof, time seems to stand still.

Chapter Nineteen

The next few weeks are a whirlwind. I decided to do my creative writing project on the character of Claudia MacTeer, the primary narrator of *The Bluest Eye*, and the bulk of my time is spent reading the novel and taking notes, working on my short story, and working with Mrs. Wright on my college applications. Naima and Luis have applied early action to all their dream schools: NYU, Columbia, Cornell, and Princeton. Meanwhile, Mrs. Wright and I are still working our way through various scholarship forms. She assures me that there's still plenty of time, but as Thanksgiving comes and goes, I can't help feeling like I'm falling behind.

Grandma Alice outdid herself at Thanksgiving this year. Our table stretched longer than a Monday morning, piled with food and surrounded by nearly every face in the neighborhood. Even Big Teak, who's always on Grandma's "I'm disappointed with you" list, got an invite. Even though she spent most of the night scolding him over his hustler ways, there was a deep love to her scolding. A tough love, but love all the same.

As we were in the kitchen cleaning up the meal, I asked, "Grandma, what made you want to go so big with Thanksgiving this year?"

Without missing a beat or even looking up from the pot she was washing, she said, "I was sick for so long that I just felt like celebrating life, baby. Let the people I love know how much they mean to me." She glanced my way. "Now, I know you're not about to use that steel wool on my cast-iron pan!"

It was a great night, but my mom and I are still like two planets orbiting the same sun but never quite meeting. We haven't spoken much at all, even though she's not pulling those extra shifts at the store anymore. But she's spending most of that time at Grandma Alice's apartment. It's hard not to feel like she's doing it to get away from me.

As for Naima, things have been amazing. We've got this silly competition going to see who can plan the best cheap date. We're both creative, going all out trying to outdo each other, but honestly, it's not about winning. It's about the moments, the smiles, the memories we're stacking up like precious coins. I've never felt this way about someone.

Our feelings for each other are also a great distraction as basketball season gets rolling without me. The school is alive with excitement as the team wins its first three games. And while I'm genuinely happy for them, it's hard to hear my classmates and the media question whether the team really needed me in the first place. Maybe I'm questioning it a bit, too.

And maybe it's partly to prove that there are no hard feelings that I decide to text Tommy, since he was the first to reach out over the summer and I left him on read.

ME: Congrats on the team. Y'all are rollin

But Tommy doesn't respond. I suppose I deserve that. And should have expected it, since we don't bother speaking when we see each other.

By far the worst thing that happens in the weeks following us sharing our letters is that Matthew, Sydney, and Morgan are turning into these internet stars. Right-wing darlings, talking loud and saying nothing. Ever since they found out I wasn't expelled for that altercation with Matthew (you know—the altercation *he* started), they've been all over social media. Talking about how Braxton and schools across America are being taken over by "wokeness"—and millions of people are eating it up. It's like they're standing on a soapbox made of twisted words, bent truths, and ignorance, and the crowd just keeps getting bigger.

The day after Thanksgiving, I'm back at my desk working on my short story when my phone dings. It's Naima.

NAIMA: How's your short story going?

ME: Lol. How'd you know I was working on it?

NAIMA: I had a hunch :)

ME: Anyway it's going good. Hard. But good. Thinking a lot. Probably too much. What's the situation like on your end? Y'all have a good Thanksgiving?

NAIMA: It's been . . . interesting

ME: What do you mean? You good?

NAIMA: Yeah, yeah. It's nothing bad. Just, when my aunt and uncle were here for Thanksgiving, they started asking questions about us—how long we've been hanging out, how you treat me, stuff like that. Then my dad started asking questions

NAIMA: Then my mom realized she hadn't asked enough questions

ME: Lol uh oh. Like what?

NAIMA: Like are we official . . .

ME: Good question lol

ME: What did you say?

NAIMA: I said I have to ask you before I could answer

ME: Well

ME: I'd want to be

NAIMA: Me too

ME: I guess we are then lol

NAIMA: :)

My heart does this thing like it's skipping rope, double-dutching between beats. Naima. My girlfriend. The words taste like something sweet, something I've been craving but never knew how to name. It's wild, the way just thinking about her sets my pulse racing, like I'm standing at the free-throw line and winning the game comes down to this shot.

NAIMA: There's one more thing . . .

ME: . . .

NAIMA: My parents want to meet you

Reading Naima's text, I nearly vomit from nervousness. I spent plenty of time around Laura's parents, but meeting them was not the same as meeting Black parents. I mean, setting aside the fact that Laura's family was using me, there's just something different about meeting parents from your own community. They'll probably rate me on a different scale or something, especially since Naima is as pro-Black as she is, and a lot of her views come from her parents.

Not to say I'm not pro-Black, but I can picture the whole thing: *He doesn't know what Coretta Scott King's favorite ice cream was? NEXT!*

Even worse, they're *rich* Black parents: *His family wasn't invited to Obama's birthday party on Martha's Vineyard? NEXT!*

NAIMA: Hello . . .

NAIMA: You there??

ME: Yeah sorry

NAIMA: So . . . what's up? Is that a yes?

ME: Sure. When?

NAIMA: See that's the thing

ME: ?

NAIMA: My parents are going to see Alvin Ailey tomorrow night and I know you have your Sunday dinners at your grandma's, so . . .

ME: . . . ?

NAIMA: So they asked if you can come over tonight. NO PRESSURE! I know it's last minute

ME: TONIGHT tonight?!

NAIMA: Yeah. But if you can't make it . . . all good

I know she means it. But it's also clear that this is important to her. And maybe it's better to rip off the Band-Aid. I take the deepest breath I have taken in my entire life, then send the text.

ME: No it's OK. I'll come

ME: What should I wear? I don't own a tux . . .

NAIMA: Ha ha. Maybe wear a button up or something. But jeans are OK. And definitely no tie

NAIMA: Thanks so much for doing this, Ossie. It means a lot <3

Shit.

My Uber drops me off in front of Naima's house, nestled somewhere in Scarsdale, the same town Braxton is in. As soon as I see their home, I find my assumptions turned on their head.

The house is more modest than I expected—in the best of ways. It's a beautiful home, and probably extremely expensive. But it feels more like a place that was built for a family to make memories, versus a mansion made to be featured on social media and in magazines, like the Martinezes' house. This feels like a place constructed with the intention of wrapping itself around a family, where people come to laugh, where children play, and family members, not a staff, make the meals.

It looks like some of my favorite houses I would see watching HGTV reruns while I was hiding out in my room after my injury. I gave that network more hours of my time than most people would ever believe—which is why I know some of the terminology to describe what I'm seeing.

The house's exterior is brick, punctuated by crisp white window trim and shutters painted a shade of forest green so deep they're nearly swallowed by shadows. A similar green covers the front door, tying the quaint aesthetics together. The lawn in front of the house is sculpted with such precision, it feels like a piece of art, not a blade of grass outta place. A short cobblestone walkway cuts through the beautiful lawn, its edges adorned with petunias still vibrant in spite of the growing fall chill. Mrs. Johnson must have a great green thumb.

A gruff voice interrupts my thoughts.

"Hey." It's the Uber driver. "This the right spot or what?"

He's probably wondering why I'm standing like a mannequin instead of going up to the door, an old shopping bag tightly gripped in my fist, a crinkly testament to my last-minute dash for gifts.

"Yeah, this is it," I confirm, my voice echoing strangely in the quiet street. Our eyes lock awkwardly, then, seemingly satisfied, or perhaps just fed up, he revs the engine and rolls away.

I take a deep, steadying breath, attempting to squash the butterflies wreaking havoc in my gut. It feels like I'm standing at the edge of a high dive, peering into the deep end.

Waiting for my ACL results didn't shake my nerves half this bad.

Come on, you got this!

As I stride to the front door, I hype myself up the way I used to before a big game. The musical chime of the doorbell is still floating through the air when a woman's voice carries from inside the house. "I'm sure you look fine, Nai! Come greet your guest!"

My mind kicks into overdrive, rehearsing greeting lines, mentally arranging and rearranging words like jigsaw pieces. *How's it going?* Too casual. *I'm honored to meet you.* Too formal. *Pleasure to be in the Johnson residence.* Too—I don't know what that is.

Before I can settle on a fitting greeting, the front door swings open, revealing the woman behind the voice.

Despite my attempts to catch a preview through social media, I have no idea what Naima's family looks like. Her page is just a curation of Black art, fresh kicks, and personal music reviews, no images of her family. Which is why I'm so surprised that standing in front of me is a near carbon copy of Naima. Same warm ebony glow, same sparkling brown eyes. Give Naima a pixie cut and a few extra years, and they could pass for twins. Even the brown romper she's wearing is straight out of Naima's style playbook.

"Hi! You must be Ossie." Her voice is warm, her smile inviting, instantly putting me at ease.

Flustered, and still without a greeting ready, I quickly reach into my bag and present her with a small pot of violas. "This is for you," I manage to say.

"Thank you, Ossie." She smiles politely, but I can't help feeling that I missed the mark somehow. Considering the well-maintained garden outside, I thought she'd be more enthusiastic about my gift.

You can't date a young man who doesn't know the Black history of why you shouldn't give violas to a person after Labor Day! I imagine her saying to Naima tonight after I'm gone.

"Come on in." She steps aside, sweeping an inviting hand toward the warm glow of the interior.

I gulp in a lungful of the crisp fall air, straighten myself upright, and pull my shoulders back.

All right, Ossie. You've got this.

The Johnsons' home is filled with the scent of crackling wood from their fireplace, evoking distant memories of campfires and marshmallows. Candles are lit in little nooks and corners, filling the air with the warmth of their flickering glow and the scents of vanilla and lavender. From somewhere in the house, jazz notes are softly finding their way to every room.

The interior of the Johnsons' house is just as beautiful as the exterior. The furniture looks like it's begging for you to sink into it and lose track of time. And the walls are like a gallery, filled with paintings and photographs: portraits of people who share the same warm smiles as Naima and Mrs. Johnson, including a young boy who must be Jamal, and pictures of sunsets, landscapes, and city skylines that bring the world right into this living room. There are also sculptures scattered around the room, some small and delicate, others bold and imposing. They've all got a sort of vibe to them, like they're by Black or brown artists. They've got that touch, that spirit.

Grandma Alice would be in heaven here.

"Your home is amazing, Mrs. Johnson," I say, my voice echoing a little in the high-ceilinged room.

"Oh, thank you, Ossie," she replies. "But I can't take most of the credit, you know."

Just as the last word leaves her lips, a man appears at the top of the stairs, holding on to a cane. He's got a bald head with a large scar on the side of it, a well-lined beard, and a rich chestnut complexion that glows in the warm light. He's dressed in a chocolate-brown turtleneck that molds to his muscular frame, well-tailored light-gray slacks, and a pair of shiny loafers that mirror the color of his shirt. His glasses sit perfectly on his face, adding an academic touch to his sophisticated look.

He walks down the stairs slowly, one hand on the rail, the other on his cane. He moves like a person much older than his age.

"The great Ossie Brown! Diggin' the shirt, big fella! I love a good short-sleeve dress shirt!" he calls out in a deep, hearty rumble that fills the room.

"It's an honor to meet you, Mr. Johnson," I say, extending my hand, butterflies doing backflips in my stomach.

"Call me Malik," he says as his hand takes mine and he pulls me in for what feels more like a dap than a formal handshake. It's a gesture so friendly, so unexpected, that I can't help but smile.

His stature isn't intimidating, but there's a strength to him, an aura of someone who's seen the world. But behind his eyes, there seems to be pain also. I can't help but think of Naima's letter and how perfectly she captured her father.

"Nai's been going on about you—all good stuff, thankfully," Malik says, releasing me from our embrace, his eyes twinkling and inviting.

"That's good to hear," I say. "I brought you something, Mr. Johnson."

I feel my heart racing as I pull out a bakery box, all fancy with a neat little bow on top, and hand it over to him. "It's an apple pie. From the best bakery in my neighborhood."

Malik grins like a kid on Christmas, but there's a hint of regret in his eyes as he says, "Again, just call me Malik. And I appreciate the gift, young brother, but I'm afraid I can't eat it. I've gotta watch my sugar these days."

"I'm sorry, Mr.—Malik. I didn't know," I respond, feeling my face heat up.

Before I can continue, Naima comes in, breezing down the stairs like she's floating. Somehow she's even more beautiful than she was the last time I saw her. "It's not your fault, Ossie," she says, her voice as sweet as the pie in the box. "If Daddy had been watching his sugar when Mom told him to years ago, he wouldn't be having health issues now."

Naima's wearing an oversize tie-dye sweatshirt with the image of Thundercat on the front and baggy tan cargo pants. Her hair, usually styled in faux locs, is in two large Afro puffs. Looking at her standing next to her parents, it's easy to see where she gets her eclectic fashion sense from.

She steps to me and gives me a tight hug as if she hasn't seen me in years. Then her eyes turn to examine the pot in her mother's hand, the vivid colors popping against the tones of the room.

"Where did you get those, Mom?"

"Ossie gave them to me," Mrs. Johnson answers, smiling at me.

"Violas! Been wanting to get more of these for the house!" Mr. Johnson exclaims, looking like he just hit the jackpot.

Naima grins at me. "Dad's *really* into plants and decorating. He dreams of being a full-time homemaker and gardener."

"Sometimes he spends more time with his plants than he does with his wife," Mrs. Johnson teases.

Mr. Johnson's eyes roll good-naturedly.

I'm barely paying attention to what's being said because I'm too taken aback by the fact that I gave Naima's father a pie that could kill him and her mother flowers, when her dad is the one who does the gardening.

"I'm sorry about the gifts. I shouldn't have assumed . . . I should have given you something else," I mumble to Mr. and Mrs. Johnson, aware of my mistake and the outdated gender roles it implied.

Naima walks over to me, her lips stretched in a mischievous grin. "You know what they say about making assumptions, right?"

"Nai!" Mrs. Johnson cuts in, her tone both playful and stern.

"Ossie knows I'm just teasing!" Naima's lips brush my cheek in a tender kiss.

I force a chuckle, nodding. "It's all good, Mrs. Johnson. I had that coming. Apologies again."

Mrs. Johnson shakes her head, a gracious smile spreading across her face. "Your heart was in the right place, even if you fell into the trap of gender stereotypes. These are beautiful."

At this, Mr. Johnson interjects, "I have an idea. What if we swap gifts?"

"Perfect," Mrs. Johnson replies, handing the pot of flowers to her husband. In return, he passes her the pie.

"Well, now that we've had a crash course in Feminism 101, why don't we move to the dining room and have dinner?" Mrs. Johnson suggests.

Mr. Johnson looks to Naima. "Did it seem like your brother's gonna make an appearance?" His tone implies that this is a regular occurrence the family understands.

"You know how Jamal is when it comes to strangers, Dad. He's nervous. Plus he's been kind of obsessed with Ossie lately, which is making him even more shy," Naima explains with a shrug.

"Yeah, I'll try to get him to come down at some point," Mr. Johnson responds, shaking his head and chuckling lightly. "He's a shy one, all right. But I know how much he wants to meet you, Ossie. The other night he was talking about how you're 'better than LeBron,' after watching some of your YouTube highlights. No offense, Ossie, but ain't no way."

"None taken," I respond with a chuckle. "Trust me, I agree with you!"

"I knew I liked you!" Mr. Johnson says, clapping me on the back affectionately.

Between their gracious reaction to my gendered gifts and their gentle teasing, I feel extremely comfortable being around Naima's parents. Now all I have to do is get through dinner without ruining the vibe!

Chapter Twenty

We trail into the dining room, the décor shifting into something distinctly more vibrant. The walls are fuchsia, with bold artwork in a style that reminds me of Basquiat. At the center of the room, a large glass table surrounded by plushly upholstered cream-colored chairs stands out. A contemporary glass chandelier with golden accents ties the room together, a clear nod to Mr. Johnson's design eye.

But what truly piques my interest is a sizable collection of vinyl records, proudly displayed on a shelf in the corner of the room, topped by a vintage record player.

"Wow," I murmur, captivated by the diverse collection.

"You like vinyls, Ossie?" Mrs. Johnson asks, her eyes gleaming with shared interest. "Nai told us you have a thing for music."

"Yeah, my grandmother has a record player. I've always loved that unique vinyl sound."

Mrs. Johnson promptly pauses the jazz soundtrack that has been softly playing in the background. "Okay, so let's dive into the vinyls and pick out a few records for tonight," she says with excitement. "Naima and her father can handle the dinner setup."

We delve into the extensive collection of records spanning genres from jazz and hip-hop to folk and even psychedelic rock. The range is wild. Mrs. Johnson tells me about how her and Mr. Johnson's shared passion for music has led them to visit countless yard sales in search of unique additions to their collection.

When Mrs. Johnson insists that I choose the music for the night, I gravitate toward albums by Joni Mitchell, Luther Vandross, Carole King, and D'Angelo.

"Wow, you have an eclectic taste in music, Ossie. Not many young people are aware of these artists."

"My grandmother loves soul and R&B, but my mom put me onto most other genres. I've been exploring music ever since," I explain.

She nods, a faraway look in her eyes. "Music has a way of bonding people. You must be close with your mom."

If only. I can't bring myself to be honest, but based on her sympathetic look, Mrs. Johnson seems to understand. Then, as Luther Vandross's voice fills the room, she closes her eyes and begins to sway to the rhythm.

Naima and Mr. Johnson reenter, their hands full of dishes. Between the aroma of home-cooked food, the uplifting vibe of the artwork, and the soulful melodies from the record player, the evening feels promising, like a unique blend of the unexpected and the familiar.

Once Naima and her father place the final dishes on the table, Mr. Johnson walks behind Mrs. Johnson and wraps his arms around her hips. She responds by tenderly laying her head on his chest as the two begin to sway together.

"Mmm. Luther Luther Luther," Mr. Johnson says. He's looking down at Mrs. Johnson like she invented the moon and the stars. "I swear, had it not been for Luther Vandross's music, our Naima might not even be here today."

"Luther and a whole lotta wine," Mrs. Johnson adds with a laugh.

Naima shakes her head at them. "Get a room, you two." But her voice is playful, her eyes soft. They all laugh, the sound traveling through the room, and I can't help but smile.

They dance a little more, just the two of them in their own little world, before the song fades out. Then we all pull up a chair at the table and dig into a feast: baked potatoes that make you beg for seconds, crisp green beans, juicy lamb chops, gooey mac and cheese, fresh dinner rolls still warm from the oven—and Mr. Johnson tells me he made everything himself.

We talk between mouthfuls. They ask about me, about my life, my writing, my family. They share their own stories, too, punctuating them with laughter. About halfway through the meal, Mr. Johnson disappears upstairs, only to come back a few minutes later with Jamal, Naima's little brother.

"Look who decided to join us!" Naima calls, breaking away from the table to give her brother a huge hug. Jamal is short for an eleven-year-old, which based on what I've read might be tied to his Down syndrome. But even if I hadn't just seen him in a bunch of photos, I would have no problem recognizing him, because he looks so much like their mom. He's got a short, curly Afro, and he's decked out in a colorful *Dragon Ball Z* shirt and matching sweatpants. Clutched in his hand is a stuffed bunny wearing a Knicks jersey.

"Jamal, do you and Hops wanna meet my friend Ossie?" Naima asks him, offering her hand. Jamal looks at me and nods, a shy smile playing at the corners of his mouth. He takes Naima's hand, and the two of them walk toward me. Jamal's eyes are wide with a mix of excitement and nervousness.

They get closer and closer, until Jamal's right in front of me. When he sees me stand up, his eyes go *really* wide. Suddenly, I'm this big, towering figure. He steps back, hides behind Naima. Naima tries to reassure him, tells him he knows me from the TV, from YouTube. But seeing me in person, well, that's a whole different thing.

"I'll be right back," I cut in. I leave the room, grab my bag from near the front door. When I come back, I've got a basketball with a world map printed on it. Jamal's face lights up at the sight.

"This is for you, Jamal," I tell him, kneeling so we're on the same level. "When I was your age, this was my favorite ball. All the places I dreamed of playing basketball one day, they're all right here."

He hands Hops to Naima and reaches out to take the ball from me, a shy "Thank you" slipping from his lips.

He begins dribbling, but Mrs. Johnson reminds him the ball is an outside toy. "Maybe after dinner you can play with your dad and Hops," she tells him.

"Can Ossie come, too?" Jamal asks with a hopeful expression.

I see Naima about to answer for me, about to protect me, knowing I haven't touched a ball since I got hurt. But there's something about the look in his eyes; it reminds me of how I felt when I would watch tapes of my father playing. The way the game used to heal and save me from the things that hurt.

"For sure, Jamal," I say, "I'd love to play with you."

That's all it takes to put a smile on his face. He hands off the ball to his dad, takes back Hops, and settles into his chair at the dinner table. We all follow suit, pulling up our chairs and continuing the meal.

Jamal is the first to finish his food. When he's done, he rushes over to the basketball. "Can we play now?"

"A promise is a promise," Naima responds.

As soon as we finish our food, Naima grabs Jamal's coat and hers. I grab mine as well, marching behind them out to the back of the house.

Their hoop stands in the cooling evening air, lowered just enough for Jamal to be able to make shots in it. Which he quickly begins doing. Watching him, I'm immediately brought back to the moment I got hurt. The sound of the footsteps running to me in panic. My doctor's voice when he said I would never play again . . .

Against the backdrop of night, the hoop, once like my best friend, suddenly reminds me of the monsters my mom used to protect me from.

My jitters are interrupted by Jamal, who is brimming with impatience, bouncing the world-covered ball toward me. "Let me see you shoot, Ossie!"

Jamal passes me the ball, and I turn it slowly in my hands. Looking at Africa, Italy, California—all the places I thought basketball would help me take my family one day. Places far from Yonkers. This basketball scorches like lava while somehow also being as cold as a block of ice.

"Come on, Ossie!" Jamal yells again. I look at Naima, whose face is telling me I don't have to do this. Then I turn to Jamal again, his eyes glowing with a fire I used to know well.

I launch a shot. It's rusty and crooked, and as the ball sails way off the mark, a jolt of pain shoots up from my left knee—though it's nothing compared to the hurt to my pride. Naima throws me another concerned glance, while Jamal's face falls with disappointment. This isn't the Ossie Brown he's seen on TV and YouTube.

Jamal's interest in playing with me dwindles after my missed shot, and he focuses on his own game. Tough crowd.

Watching him, I'm transported back to my younger self, exerting every ounce of my strength to hurl the ball toward the basket. Those were the days when basketball wasn't about the expectations of being Braxton's basketball savior, about one day making it to the NBA; it was just about mirroring a passion for something my dad cherished. Being a part of something my father loved.

"Can I try again, Jamal?" I ask, a tinge of something in my voice I haven't heard in months.

"Why don't we play later instead, Jamal?" Naima suggests, no doubt worried I might shatter after another missed shot. But I don't want an out; I want to confront my reality. I'm not the same Ossie Brown from before my injury, but maybe that's okay. Maybe it doesn't have to be all or nothing.

"It's all good," I respond. "I promise."

Jamal looks at Naima for approval. She studies me for a second to see whether I'm sure. I nod at her, and she then nods at Jamal. He passes me the ball.

I spin the ball in my hands, trying to rekindle my relationship with the contours and leather. I remember how I used to place my feet. How I used to see the rim.

Maybe it's all in my head, but my knee is suddenly pain-free. I take a deep breath, adjust my stance for the height of the rim, and the ball leaves my hands, cutting through the backyard light. And when it sails through the hoop, a sense of familiarity washes over me. It's like finding my way back home. *Swish.*

The successful shot injects Jamal with a fresh dose of enthusiasm. He passes the ball back to me again and again, each shot followed by the satisfying sound of the ball passing through the net. *Swish. Swish. Swish.*

Naima looks at me as if she's watching a child open birthday gifts.

I pass the ball to Jamal. "Watch this, Ossie!" he shouts. He takes a couple of steps back, dribbles a bit too aggressively, then launches the ball toward the hoop with all the strength his little frame can muster. It's a wild shot, completely off-target, but the joy in his attempt is what counts.

"Nice try, little man!" I say encouragingly, tossing him the ball again. "You'll get it next time."

220

Naima steps in, showing Jamal how to position his hands. "Remember what you learned at school, Jamal. Put your hands on the ball like this," she says, her voice tender. She demonstrates a perfect shot, the ball swishing through the net effortlessly.

"Okay!" I shout, impressed.

She laughs. "Just a little something! I used to play a lot with my friend Gigi when I was younger. Her dad used to play in the league, so she was a beast."

Jamal tries again, and this time the ball bounces off the rim. "So close!" he exclaims, undeterred.

We keep playing, the cool air filling our lungs, the song of laughter filling the night. I feel a lightness I haven't felt in forever, like I'm shedding layers of expectations and pressure with every shot. There's something about this, something healing in the simplicity of playing just to play.

Jamal's grinning from ear to ear, his eyes sparkling under the backyard light. And even in the darkness, Naima's glowing like she's lit from within. I can't help but think how lucky I am to be here at this moment.

The stars are twinkling overhead when Mrs. Johnson calls to us. "Time to come inside. Naima, Ossie—I need you two to see something."

Her tone sounds off, a solemn contrast to the warmth of the house when we follow her inside. Jamal's still bouncing from the fun of the game, but Mrs. Johnson gently nudges him. "Go help your father in the kitchen with cleaning up, Jamal," she says, more softly now. Jamal does as he's told.

Mrs. Johnson sits down at the dining table, her face illuminated by the soft glow of her laptop screen. She's got this look, this really serious look, like she's about to drop a bomb on us. She turns her laptop around, and there's a video paused on the screen, from the *Tradition Times*, a right-wing news outlet. My heart starts racing. I don't know what to expect—but I know it's not going to be good.

"Your dad and I received an email about this a little while ago," Mrs. Johnson says, her cursor hovering over the play button. "Apparently, the interview aired last night."

She hits play, and the screen fills with the faces of Matthew, Sydney, Morgan, and a middle-aged white woman I don't recognize. The banner at the bottom of the video reads, "Students Pushing Back Against Woke Mob Leader."

Naima and I exchange a glance, our eyes wide with fear and disbelief.

The interviewer, a different white woman, starts questioning them. "So, tell us about the dynamics within this writing program," she begins, her voice dripping with a sort of feigned concern. "It seems there's a certain . . . favoritism at play? Tell us about the 'woke' agenda you three have been mentioning in your videos."

Matthew shifts in his seat, clearing his throat. "Well, it's more than just favoritism," he says, his eyes darting toward the camera. "For example, there's this one kid, whose name I'm not allowed to say—he was a star basketball player, and then he gets injured and can't play anymore, so suddenly he's in this prestigious writing program? I mean, come on! It's clear that his race played a role in his acceptance. It's affirmative action, which everybody knows is just another way of saying reverse racism."

The interviewer nods, her expression tightening. "Interesting. And what about the other students?"

Morgan chimes in, her voice laced with a bitterness that makes my skin crawl. "It's not just Os—the basketball player. There's also two other minority kids in the program. They receive special treatment from Ms. Hunt all the time. It's like she has a bias toward them because they're Black or whatever, and one of them is an immigrant."

"Luis was born in New York!" Naima yells at the screen.

The woman being interviewed with them is apparently from a

group called Parents for Freedom. She adds fuel to the fire, saying, "These children are being abused by that teacher, Tasha Hunt. The books she's forcing on them are not only racist, teaching the students that all white people are evil, but they're also full of lewd sex acts, including *homosexual* sex acts! How this racist, anti-Christian teacher ever got a job at a school like Braxton, which educates some of the brightest students in our country, is beyond me! She is a danger to these students, and she has to be stopped!"

It's all spin, all lies, but to those watching, it might as well be the gospel truth.

Naima's hand finds mine under the table, her grip tight, like she's trying to hold on to something solid in a world that's suddenly spinning out of control. I can feel my pulse in my ears, thudding loud and clear. This isn't just an attack on the writing program or Ms. Hunt. It's bigger than that. It's an attack on everything we've been working on, everything we stand for. On *who we are.*

The interview continues, everyone speaking their rehearsed lines, the woman from Parents for Freedom nodding along. My stomach is in knots, my mind racing with questions. How did it come to this? What can we do?

The video ends, and Mrs. Johnson closes her laptop, the room suddenly feeling ten times smaller. She looks at Naima and me, her eyes full of worry.

"Dean Blackburn sent the link to that video in an email," Mrs. Johnson starts, her voice steady but strained. "It went out to every parent on the school advisory board and the board of trustees."

I feel my stomach continue to twist. This is big. Real big.

"I'm afraid it gets worse." Mrs. Johnson takes a deep breath. "As of this coming Monday, Ms. Hunt is under investigation and suspended from her role at Braxton until further notice."

Chapter Twenty-One

The next day, I spend hours with Luis and Naima at Naima's soul food spot, trying to figure out what we can do to support Ms. Hunt—and to get the books she was teaching back in the school. Because it turns out that not only is Ms. Hunt suspended, but the school board also voted to ban the books she'd been teaching in the writing program and in all of her English classes, and to remove these books from the library.

"We start a petition," Luis finally blurts out. "Get students from the writing program, Ms. Hunt's regular classes, anyone who knows what's really up to help us get her and the books back!"

I nod, feeling a glimmer of hope. "Yeah, yeah, that could work." It's something, anyway. A start.

Naima's already on her laptop, fingers flying over the keys, setting up an online petition.

But even though we spend most of the day on Monday hustling, trying to get people to sign, only fifteen people add their names out of the dozens of Ms. Hunt's current and former students. And only one person in the writing program signs—this quiet kid named Adam. Most say they want to but they're scared of the backlash, especially online. The few who do sign seem to do so with a look over their shoulder, like they're expecting to be jumped. It's heartbreaking, seeing how fear can silence people, how it can turn them away from doing what's right.

As we sit in the cafeteria during lunch on Tuesday, Naima's frustration is obvious, her usually bright eyes clouded with anger and worry. "Seventeen signatures! This is ridiculous," she says, slamming her laptop shut. "How can our classmates be so . . . so cowardly?"

Luis leans back, his face a mask of helplessness. "It's not just cowardice, Nai. It's self-preservation. They're scared of becoming targets. Some of those people online are dangerous."

I can't help but feel a surge of anger, but it's mixed with understanding. I get it. Matthew, Morgan, and Sydney have become a three-headed monster, gaining huge social media followings almost overnight. Acting as if anyone who says anything to challenge them will receive the same treatment Ms. Hunt did. Matthew is by far the worst of the three. He's been strutting around the school, gloating about what they did to Ms. Hunt. It's like watching a villain in a movie, except this is real life, and the good guys are losing.

The backlash is real, and it's terrifying. But that doesn't make it any less frustrating that so few people are standing up.

As the cafeteria buzzes with chatter and laughter, Naima's tapping her fingers on the closed lid of her laptop, a rhythm of frustration. Luis stares at his half-eaten sandwich, lost in thought. Then, out of nowhere, Laura appears. She's got this hesitant look on her face, like she's walking a tightrope. I don't miss the way Naima's eyes narrow, the way Luis looks her up and down.

"Ossie, can we talk?" Laura asks, her voice barely above a whisper.

I lean back, crossing my arms. "What do you want?" It comes out harsh, as intended.

"Can we just walk for a second?" Something in Laura's expression makes me soften. I glance at Naima, who's got a storm brewing in her eyes, but she shrugs, like she's saying "Go ahead but be careful."

I push back my chair and follow Laura out of the cafeteria. The noise fades behind us, replaced by the sound of our footsteps echoing through the halls. We step outside, the cool air hitting my face like a slap. We're walking toward the student parking lot, and I can't help but wonder what she wants to say.

We stop by a car, and Laura turns to face me. Her eyes are searching, like she's looking for the right words in a sea of chaos. "Ossie, I just . . . I wanted to apologize." Her voice cracks a little.

"For what?" I ask, even though a part of me already knows.

Laura's eyes are swollen and red. She takes a deep breath, steadying herself before she speaks. "I didn't know Matt was going to take it this far," she begins. "I didn't agree with the things he was saying or doing right from the start, but this . . . this is just too much. What he did to Ms. Hunt, it's so wrong."

I stare at her, my arms folded across my chest, feeling a mix of skepticism and irritation. "Okay, and why are you telling me this?"

"Because it's important that you know," she says, her eyes searching for some semblance of empathy in my gaze.

"Look, I'ma be honest—I don't care," I reply sharply, unable to mask my dislike. "You've always known what he's like, and you still chose to be with him. *Remember?* The two of us met in the hallway that day because he was *already like this.*"

She shakes her head, a strand of hair falling across her face, which she quickly tucks behind her ear.

"He was never like that around me," she insists. "I thought . . . I thought it was for show, you know? Some stunt he would pull to get a rise out of people, to get attention. When it was just the two of us, and when he was with my family, he was different."

I can't suppress a bitter laugh. "So as long as his racism wasn't directed at you and your family, it was okay? Just some 'rich white boys will be rich white boys' nonsense? Wow."

Laura looks at me, her face a portrait of pain and vulnerability. "You're right," she whispers, her eyes glistening with unshed tears. "I should've spoken up sooner. I shouldn't have let it get this far." The tears spill down her cheeks now, but rather than moving me toward sympathy, they only fuel my fire.

"Save your tears and your lies, Laura. If you really care at all, about me, Ms. Hunt, or even yourself—you'd actually do something about Matthew. Sign the damn petition. Break up with him. Do something— anything—real."

She's silent as I walk away.

As the week drags on, our petition stalls. Fear has settled in the bones of the school. Even the teachers seem wary, their eyes darting around the hallways as if they are expecting to be the next target.

It's a heavy feeling, carrying the weight of injustice. And through it all, Ms. Hunt's absence is like a gaping hole, a reminder of what's at stake. Giving up isn't an option. Not on Ms. Hunt, not on what she stands for. So we keep pushing, keep asking for signatures, keep fighting against the tide.

We have no idea what's going to happen with the writing program, but then, like a curveball nobody's ready for, an email hits our inboxes on Thursday evening. My phone buzzes in my pocket, a vibration that feels like the first raindrop of a storm. I pull it out, the screen lighting up with the sender's name. Dean Blackburn. I can almost hear the thunder rolling.

Dear students,

I hope this email finds you well. As you are all aware, there has been some turmoil with the Mark Twain Creative Writing Program over the past few days. I want to assure you that we are doing everything we can to address the situation and move forward.

With that said, I would like to remind you that your next meeting will take place as scheduled tomorrow in the English Lab. This meeting is mandatory for those who wish to remain in the program. I understand that recent events may have caused some hesitation or concern, but I want to emphasize that we are committed to ensuring a safe and productive environment for all of our students.

During the meeting, we will provide an update on the future of the program. We are working diligently to address the concerns that have been raised and to continue providing a space for creativity and personal growth.

Sincerely,
Dean Blackburn

As I finish the email, my mind immediately goes to Ms. Hunt. *How are they going to continue the program without her?*

When the final bell rings the next day, Naima, Luis, and I head to the English Lab. I'm so nervous about what's next, I could probably row us there in my sweat. We enter the room and take our seats.

The room's buzzing, alive with whispers and questioning eyes shooting around. Suddenly, Matthew, Morgan, and Sydney arrive. They strut in, taking their seats like they own the place, like they haven't been out of the program for over a month. Matthew's got this grin plastered on his face like he's just scored the winning basket in overtime. Morgan and Sydney are right there with him, eyes all wide. There's this itch in my gut, this twist of anger and something else— something like sadness, maybe.

Luis leans over. "I want to smack that smug look off his face." He's glaring at Matthew, his hands balling into fists, knuckles going white.

Naima's eyes are like two lit matches. "Yeah, how dare they be here." Her words are like sparks, ready to ignite.

The door opens, and Dean Blackburn walks in. The room becomes silent. Trailing behind her is a short-haired, clean-shaven middle-aged white man. His sharp eyes examine the room, taking note of each student before settling on me, then Naima, and finally Luis. He walks to the back of the room and takes a seat, leaving Dean Blackburn to be the center of our attention.

Dean Blackburn clears her throat. "Thank you all for coming today," she says enthusiastically. "I know that the events of the past few days have been difficult for all of us. But we are here to move forward with a new direction for this program."

She pauses, looking around the room. "First, I want to address the elephant in the room. Ms. Hunt will no longer be leading this program, and we are reconsidering her role as a full-time teacher here at Braxton Academy."

The words feel like a punch in the mouth.

"However," Dean Blackburn continues, her voice once again enthusiastic, "we have found a replacement for Ms. Hunt. Someone who is equally, if not more, qualified and actually passionate about teaching *all* of our students."

She introduces Mr. Richmond, the new chair of Braxton's English Language Arts Department and head of the writing program, making sure to emphasize the importance of him being here.

"Getting Mr. Richmond to come to Braxton is a gift we should all deeply appreciate. Not only is he a best-selling author; he's also a former Braxton student himself, meaning he knows what it takes to succeed in an elite program such as this one."

"Thank you, Dean Blackburn." Mr. Richmond strides to the front of the room. "Your words are as gracious as ever, and I am deeply honored to be back at Braxton. It will be a pleasure to walk the halls once again, to remember the old days when I used to dream of the future with Morgan's father. Now look at us."

Matthew, Sydney, and Morgan begin to clap lightly in approval. No one else joins in.

Hearing that Mr. Richmond is friends with Morgan's father makes me feel like I've just uncovered a plot. My blood begins to boil.

Mr. Richmond nods, a shallow dip of his head, engaging all of us. "Good afternoon, everyone," he says, his voice low and rumbling. "Please don't think of me as someone here to replace my predecessor. I'm here to take us on a new journey. One that will focus on America's literary icons, like the man this program was named after—the great writer Mark Twain—in the hopes of helping you potentially join their ranks."

The room is still as Mr. Richmond's words linger.

No one says anything. And then Adam, the only kid in the program who signed the petition besides me, Luis, and Naima, raises his hand.

"Will we still be reading some of the authors Ms. Hunt assigned?" he asks, speaking without waiting for Mr. Richmond to call on him.

Mr. Richmond's eyes narrow for a moment before he responds.

"We will be reading works from America's literary greats. My goal is to expose you to a diverse range of voices and perspectives, those seemingly overlooked and undervalued by Ms. Hunt: Hemingway, Whitman, Steinbeck. Writers who can help your understanding of what it means to be a voice in this country."

Adam's disappointment is obvious. "Sure, but we've already read most of those authors. Ms. Hunt was introducing us to writers who were less familiar to us, and a lot of us learned a great deal from their styles and perspectives."

Most students nod in agreement, but Matthew, Sydney, and Morgan scowl.

Mr. Richmond inhales and then exhales slowly. "Adam, isn't it? I hear everyone in this program is supposed to be bright. If you are all as bright as they say, you will understand that now is the time for listening. Otherwise, you can find yourself on the other side of the door."

Adam is clearly taken aback, but he doesn't respond.

The rest of the meeting is filled with Mr. Richmond outlining his vision for the program. As he speaks, I can't help but feel a sense of defeat. Ms. Hunt's work introducing us to books that made many of us feel seen and heard is being quickly replaced by typical white literary elitism.

As the meeting ends, Dean Blackburn leaves the room first, followed by Mr. Richmond, who is flanked by Morgan, Matthew, and Sydney.

All five of them look as if they've just won a war.

Over the weekend, Luis has plans with Mateo, and Naima has plans with her family, so I'm left to marinate in my thoughts. The weekend stretches out like a long, empty highway, each hour ticking by slower than the last. I'm in my room, surrounded by the familiar but feeling worlds away. I know I'm in a funk, so I decide to skip Sunday dinner. Grandma Alice will understand. She always does.

Late Sunday night, when the house is quiet and my thoughts are loud, my mom knocks on my bedroom door. It's surprising, almost startling; it's been months since she's knocked on my door, months since we've had a real conversation. She looks tired, the kind of tired that sleep won't fix, and there's a sadness in her eyes that seems to have gotten worse.

"Hi," I say, keeping it simple.

"Hey," she responds. We stand there, a silent standoff, each waiting for the other to break.

Finally, she speaks. "You missed dinner again at your grandmother's place." Her tone is both soft and reprimanding.

I try to explain, to let her into my world just a bit. "Yeah, I've been dealing with a lot of—"

But she cuts me off. "Just make sure you spend time with your grandmother. You know it means a lot to her."

Her words sting, like a slap to the face. I shoot back, frustrated. "You don't even care what I have going on."

For a second, just a second, our eyes lock, and I see something flicker in hers. Pain, maybe. Regret, possibly. But there's no anger. Then her gaze drifts to my father's jersey hanging on the wall. She stares at it as if she's having a silent conversation with the past.

"Just spend time with her, Ossie," she says, softer now. "She misses you."

I miss her, too. But I know I'd be poor company right now—and Mom would know that, too, if she'd show any interest in how I'm doing.

"Got it. I have mad homework, but I'll be there next Sunday for sure."

She walks away, leaving me standing alone in the doorway. The jersey on the wall seems to stare back at me, judging the two of us and how far we've fallen. I close the door, and the sound of the quiet room speaks loudly, saying all the things my mom and I never do.

Chapter Twenty-Two

"Nah. I'm not gonna just trash the short story Ms. Hunt had us working on. We've spent weeks on them! This isn't right," Naima says, her eyes locked onto Mr. Richmond's. There's a fire in her, and it's burning bright, refusing to be snuffed out by the wet blanket of his authority.

Mr. Richmond leans back. "'Nah'? 'Not gonna'?" he echoes. "Obviously, Ms. Hunt and rap music have done a great job with your command of the English language."

The room stiffens. It's like the air got sucked out, and everyone's holding their breath, waiting, watching. Matthew and his clan love it, though.

I feel my fists clench under the table, my nails digging into my palms. But Naima doesn't seem shaken. "I have *plenty* of command over the English language," she responds, her eyes blazing. "I just refuse to code-switch for you. I earned my place in this program, and my parents pay tuition just like everyone else's."

Mr. Richmond's eyes narrow. "Sure," he replies, his tone patronizing. "But as long as you're in this program, you will read the books I tell you to and do the assignments I give you to do." He leans forward.

"And if you continue to insist on disrespecting the English language, then I will have you removed from the program. So save the 'Nah's for the street."

Naima's jaw tightens, but she doesn't continue arguing with him.

That moment was like the first drop of rain in a storm. It doesn't take long for all of us to realize this is our new reality. Mr. Richmond's reign over the writing program feels like a choke hold, squeezing out everything Ms. Hunt worked to build. He's an elitist jerk, no two ways about it. He doesn't care about making anyone feel seen, not unless they are straight and white.

December ends up being a hard month. Like, kicked-in-the-chest hard. The writing program's turned into a battleground while we try desperately to think of a way we can help Ms. Hunt, and I'm juggling other stressors, too. Sending out my first batch of college applications to any good school that might offer me a scholarship has my stomach doing backflips. It's like shooting free throws with the game on the line. The pressure's real. And the basketball team has lost their last three games after winning their first three. Which, somehow, the media and other students are blaming me for—even though when the team was winning, the narrative was that they never really needed me.

Despite everything I've got going on, I've been keeping my promise to my mom, not missing any Sunday dinners. But each time I see Grandma Alice, she seems to be shrinking, like a flower wilting in fast-forward. She's always been petite, but this is something else. Her clothes hang loose, and there's this tiredness in her eyes that wasn't there before. When I asked her about it, though, she brushed it off. "That cold I had a few months back really did a number on me. Don't you worry, though; I feel a lot better than I look!"

Her spirits *do* seem higher than ever, so I try not to worry. Besides,

I know if it was anything serious, she or my mom would tell me. Still, I don't like seeing her looking so frail.

With so much going on, the arrival of the winter holiday break feels like the most necessary breather in history.

The last day of school before break, Naima, Luis, and I walk out of Braxton with a collective sigh that feels like it's been building up since September. It's lightly snowing. The air's crisp, biting at my cheeks, but I don't mind. It's refreshing, like it's clearing out all the clutter in my head.

"So, when we exchanging gifts?" Luis asks, his eyes going back and forth between me and Naima.

My heart skips, like when you miss a step going downstairs. Gifts? Shit. With everything that's been happening, I completely forgot.

Naima smiles. "Let's do it the day before Christmas Eve, maybe? Monday? Before we get swept up in everything with our families and stuff."

"Yeah, that works for me," Luis agrees, pulling his beanie down over his ears. "You good, Ossie?"

I nod along, but inside, I'm freaking out. What am I gonna do? I gotta get gifts, and fast. But what? From where? With what money?

We say our good-byes, and I break into a half-jog, half-walk toward the bus. My mind's racing, trying to come up with something, anything. I gotta get this right. Luis and Naima, they've been there for me through all this madness. And it's me and Naima's first holiday. I can't just show up with some last-minute corny gift. Nah, it's gotta be something special. Something that says, *I see you. I care about you.*

On my way home, I spot Big Teak and his crew chillin' by their flashy cars, having a few drinks. He sees me and grins wide.

"What's good, superstar!" he bellows, sitting all casual-like on his glossy black Mercedes coupe.

"Don't usually see you around on a Friday night. Everything good with your shorty?"

I laugh and dap him up. "Me and her are good. I just need to get some Christmas shopping done," I reply, calm and casual.

"Word, good luck with that." Teak chuckles, his voice smooth like the coat on his car. "Christmas shopping ain't cheap. You good on cash?"

It's like he can see straight through my front, straight through to my empty pockets. "Yeah, I'm fine," I say, putting on my best cool face, like I got it all under control.

He nods, his eyes still holding that knowing look. "Glad to hear it." Then he extends his hand, offering me a sip from the bottle of cognac he's cradling like a newborn. I see the amber liquid dancing, but I shake my head. "Nah. I don't be drinking like that."

Teak just shrugs, his face as calm as the night sky. "Aight," he says. Then, as per usual, he drops the line that's become as familiar as a favorite song. "If you ever need anything, you let me know."

I appreciate it, I really do. But deep down, I know I can't and won't take him up on it. Even though right now, with Christmas around the corner and my pockets hurting from emptiness, I really want to.

I dap everyone up, then turn and head toward my building, my mind a whirlwind of what-ifs and maybes, of gifts and wishes.

Before I can get far, Teak shouts after me, "Yo, superstar!" I turn, one foot in the doorway of my building. He's grinning, pointing at my feet and my fresh pair of cement Jordan 3s. "When you gonna let me buy some of them Js off you that those schools used to send? I see you still got some fire on the low."

I look down at the pair I'm wearing, and an idea to make Christmas money clicks.

I'm hurrying to Grandma Alice's, heart thumping like a drumline with excitement. I've got a mini gold mine of kicks at Grandma Alice's place that schools used to send when they were trying to recruit me. Technically, it was against NCAA rules to be accepting gifts, but Grandma Alice let me keep a few pairs at her place, under wraps, without my mom knowing.

She always said that athletes like me deserved something for all the money we were bringing into these schools without being compensated.

I get to her apartment and knock, and almost instantly the door swings open. Grandma Alice stands there, her smile wide, her eyes lighting up like stars.

"Ossie! What brings you here, baby?"

I step in, the apartment as warm as the hug she gives me.

"Hey, Grandma. I just came to take a look at some of the sneakers I got here. Thinking of selling a few online, you know, to make money for Christmas gifts."

She frowns. "Sell your sneakers? But you love those shoes, baby."

I sigh. "I know, Grandma. But I don't have much of a choice; I need money for Christmas gifts, and I'm broke."

She nods toward the couch. "Come sit with me. Let's talk."

I follow her into the living room, the familiar creaks of the floorboards sounding like an old tune. We sit on her plush couch, the one that always feels like it's begging you to lie down.

Grandma Alice eyes me, her gaze full of that wisdom she's been stacking up for decades. "Ossie, I know you're thinking I can't afford to help you out, but, baby, you'd be surprised."

I shake my head. "Grandma, you don't need to be giving me money. I know things aren't easy around here. Besides, I've got those shoes . . ."

Ignoring my protests, she pushes herself up from the couch and walks over to the corner of the room where her old record player sits. She reaches down, her fingers dancing over the player like she's a magician about to pull a rabbit out of a hat. With a swift movement, she detaches a piece of it, revealing a hidden compartment. My eyes go wide as she pulls out a roll of cash, wrapped tight with a rubber band, like it's been waiting there for just this kind of moment.

I'm speechless, my mouth hanging open. "Grandma, where . . . ? How . . . ?"

She chuckles, her eyes twinkling with a hint of mischief. "I've built a few little nest eggs for myself over the years, Ossie. And at this point, I don't have much to spend them on."

Carefully, she peels off a few hundred-dollar bills, the crisp notes looking almost out of place in her living room. She extends them toward me, her hand steady.

"I'll give this to you, baby, but you gotta promise me something."

I'm still trying to wrap my head around this unexpected turn, but I nod. "Sure, Grandma. What's up?"

"You gotta buy your mother something nice, too. She's always loved Christmas, and I think it will go a long way if you get her something special," she insists, her eyes locking onto mine.

I swallow, the significance of her generosity settling on my shoulders. "Okay, Grandma. But are you sure? I mean, this is a lot of money."

She smiles, a smile that's seen years of storms and sunshine. "Yes, Ossie, I'm sure. Just make this Christmas one worth remembering."

On Monday evening, it feels like the whole world is holding its breath, waiting for Christmas to exhale its magic. I'm standing outside, the cold nibbling at my fingertips, when I see Luis and Naima pull up in Luis's Range Rover. It's sleek and silent, like some sort of steel beast cruising through the concrete jungle.

Luis leans out the window, grinning. "Ready for some holiday cheer, young man?" he asks in a deep tone mimicking Santa Claus.

I laugh, his excitement contagious. "Yeah, man. Let's do this."

Naima suddenly turns to Luis, a sly smile on her face. "Hey, Luis, mind if I drive? There's someplace I want to take us."

Luis raises an eyebrow, but his grin doesn't fade. "Sure, why not. Take the wheel, Nai."

So Naima slides into the driver's seat. She drives us into the city, the streets alive with the sights and sounds of holiday hustle and joy.

Then she steers us into Dyker Heights in Brooklyn. And that's when we see them: the Christmas lights. They're everywhere—twinkling, dancing, turning night into a carnival of colors. It's like we've slipped into a fairy tale.

"Damn!" Luis breathes out. "This is wild."

The houses are lit up like they're competing for the sun's job, and the streets are alive with people, all of them caught up in the holiday spirit.

Naima smiles when she sees the looks on our faces. "I saw a post about this place on social media a few years back, and I've always wanted to come."

We park and hop out of the car, joining the flow of people. Luis whips out his camera, snapping photos like he's trying to capture each and every light. Naima's eyes are wide, her smile brighter than any of the decorations. And me? I'm just soaking it all in, feeling like a kid again.

We stroll around, our breath puffing out clouds of warmth in the chilly air. The houses are like castles, each one trying to outdo the next with lights and decorations. Some have got Santa's sleigh on the roof, others have whole Nativity scenes in the front yard. It's like walking through a living storybook.

We grab hot chocolate from one of the many food trucks lining the street. It's rich and sweet, the warmth seeping into our bones, fighting off the chill. We sip and walk, the laughter and chatter around us like the perfect soundtrack. It's exactly what we need to take our minds off of everything at Braxton.

After a while, we head back to Luis's Range Rover to exchange our gifts. Naima thrusts glittering gift bags toward both Luis and me, her excitement obvious. Luis, in turn, hands me and Naima neatly wrapped gifts, the paper crisp and shiny. As for me, my lack of wrapping skills is clear in the clumsily covered gift I give Luis and the plain envelope I hand Naima.

Luis, being the most eager of us all, dives into Naima's bag first. He pulls out a large cardboard tube. His eyebrows crinkle in confusion. "What's this? Something isn't going to jump out at me, is it?" he asks, holding it at a distance.

Naima rolls her eyes. "There's only one way to find out," she teases.

Pretending to be nervous, he uncaps the tube and pulls out several large laminated posters. He unrolls one, revealing an image of an elderly Latinx couple dancing, a moment I recognize from Luis's room. It's a photo he took last summer at a festival in Washington Heights. "What is this?" he asks again, his tone now full of wonder.

Naima answers with a triumphant grin. "You're always talking about wanting to sell prints of your photos, so I set up an online shop for them. These posters are to promote it."

Luis pulls her into an intense hug. His gratitude seeps into the silence. "I love you, too, Luis," Naima whispers.

As they pull away, Luis shakes his head, trying to brush off his overwhelming emotions. Then he rips into my gift. His voice is low and reverent as he reads the words printed on the cover aloud: "'your hands humming hurricanes of beauty.'" His fingers trace the letters like they're something sacred.

I lean back, watching his face. "I know how you've mentioned loving Sonia Sanchez's poetry," I say, hoping I got this right.

He nods, his eyes still locked on the quote, then flips open the album. On the first page, there's a photo of him and Mateo, side by side like two parts of the same heart. Next to it is the poem he wrote to Mateo for the writing program, the words singing off the page.

"How did you . . . ?"

"Mateo helped. He sent me some pictures and also the text of your poem."

Luis flips through the book. There are empty slots, spaces waiting for his photos, pages eager for his poems. It's like an unfinished story, his story, waiting for him to fill in the blanks.

His eyes glisten, and his throat bobs like he's trying to swallow something big. Then he reaches toward the back seat and hugs me, his arms strong and warm. "Thank you for seeing me," he whispers.

I hug him back, tight. "Always, man. Always."

Luis exhales to gather himself. "All right, enough with the mushy stuff," he says. "Open my gifts."

Almost as quickly as Luis finishes his sentence, Naima's shriek of joy fills the car as she unwraps a pair of Travis Scott Air Jordan 1s. "How the hell did you get these? Do you know how bad I've wanted these for years?" she cries out, holding the shoes to the light as if they are made of diamonds.

"I know people." Luis grins, pleased with Naima's reaction.

Now it's my turn. I peel back the wrapping paper to reveal a hardcover edition of one of the Toni Morrison books I've read this year and loved. A book that helped me become a better writer: *Beloved*. Luis tells me to open it. When I do, I can't help the gasp that escapes me. The book is an autographed first edition.

"This is too much, man," I say, barely able to contain my awe. After a moment, I extend a hand toward Luis, pulling him into another brotherly hug.

Next, I open Naima's gift.

"Where did you get this?" I manage to ask as I hold up a custom letterman jacket in Braxton's school colors. Instead of the jacket being covered in sports imagery, it has a quill and inkwell on the back, with *Wordsmith* and my dad's number 45 on the front left side.

"Is it corny?" Naima asks, biting her lip nervously.

"Nah . . . it's perfect," I whisper, feeling a wave of emotions wash over me.

"Good," Naima responds cheerfully. "I want you to wear that and remember that you have a natural gift."

A moment later, Naima begins squealing with joy as she holds up the two tickets to the Thundercat concert in June.

I grin. "I peeped your Thundercat sweatshirt when I came to meet your parents."

"Uh, I only see two tickets there," Luis teases.

Naima, ignoring him, pulls me into a passionate kiss. "I can't wait!"

We spend the rest of the night wrapped up in the joy of our bond and the holiday spirit. It's like for a moment, we forget the world outside this car, the Range Rover turning into our own little sanctuary of happiness and friendship.

The next morning, I'm up with the sunrise, my mind buzzing with plans. I've got work to do, finishing touches to put on the gift I came up with for Grandma Alice and my mom. Grandma Alice's request rings in my ears. So I put my heart into the gift, piecing together something I hope will bridge the gap, mend some fences.

On Christmas Day, the three of us gather in Grandma Alice's apartment, the smell of her famous sweet potato pie filling the air. My mom hands me a couple of neatly wrapped gifts, and I can tell from the shapes that they're clothes. It's always clothes.

Grandma Alice hands a package to my mom. It's a coat my mother apparently saw someone wearing on TV and mentioned how much she loved in front of Grandma Alice. She then surprises me with a pair of Jordans that just dropped. She must have asked around the neighborhood to know what's hot. It's ironic, considering that I was about to sell my sneaker collection just days ago.

"You shouldn't have spent this type of money!" I tell her, knowing how much a fresh pair of Jordans costs—knowing that she's down a couple hundred dollars already, helping me out with the gifts I bought.

My mom's expression says she agrees with me. She looks about ready to yank the shoebox right out of my hands and get Grandma Alice her money back. But Grandma Alice waves away our concern.

"I wanted to spoil you both this year. Now, stop your fussing and let the moment be sweet."

My mom saves one gift for last. "I know you've been reading and writing a lot," she says, and I can hear something deep in her voice, like she's reaching across a distance. I unwrap it carefully. It's a used copy of *Their Eyes Were Watching God* by Zora Neale Hurston. "It was your father's favorite book," she says softly. "This was his copy. He used to reread it all the time."

My breath catches. The book in my hands feels like more than just paper and ink. It's like I'm holding a piece of my dad, a piece of history. I feel my eyes get wet, knowing she could have kept this piece of him for herself, and I manage a choked "Thank you."

Finally, it's my turn. "This is for both of you," I say, holding out my gift. Grandma Alice tells my mom to unwrap it. She does, and for the first time in what seems like forever, her smile reaches her eyes.

"I remember this day," she says with a mix of nostalgia and wonder. Then she turns the gift around, reading the back. "Wow."

Grandma Alice leans in. "What is it, Denise?" she asks, squinting to get a better look.

My mom holds the gift closer to Grandma Alice so she can see better. It's a custom vinyl album, a mix of some of the songs my mom and Grandma Alice usually listen to when they're cooking. She flips it to the front and shows Grandma Alice the cover. It's a picture of the three of us, from back when I was about nine years old. We're in the kitchen, as they're showing me how to bake a cake. It's one of the last days I can remember the world feeling perfect. Before I started playing basketball and reminding my mother of losing the love of her life.

The title on the album reads *This Thing of Ours*.

My mom stares at it like she's trying to soak in every detail, like she's afraid it might disappear if she looks away. Like she's recalling what we all used to be. As she does, Grandma Alice looks up at me, her eyes all shiny, and she smiles. It's one of those smiles that doesn't need words, one of those smiles that says everything it needs to.

Chapter Twenty-Three

The day after Christmas, I'm chilling in my room when my phone buzzes. It's Luis. "Ossie, you and Naima gotta come to this New Year's Eve party at NYU," he says, excitement crackling in his voice. "Mateo and his friends are throwing it. It's gonna be wild!"

I pause. The idea is tempting. But there's a hitch, a big one. "Man, you know I can't just ask my mom to let me go to some college party," I reply, already feeling the plan slipping away. And I know Naima will be in the same boat. No chance of getting a yes.

But Luis isn't having it. "We need this. You already know life is going to be super stressful when we get back to school. Plus I've got an idea," he says. "We all go to my parents' New Year's Eve party first at my place. It's this fancy thing where everyone dresses up and gets so drunk that they won't know if we're there or at NYU. Perfect alibi. Plus I already booked an Airbnb for us to stay in after."

The plan's slick, I gotta give him that. But there's another snag. "I don't exactly have New Year's Eve mansion clothes," I say, looking at my closet, feeling the lightness of my wallet.

"Don't even stress," Luis assures me, his voice smooth like he's got it all figured out. "I'll come pick you up Saturday morning and we'll hit some of my spots in the city. You can pay me back by doing most of the talking at my parents' party." He laughs.

I'm not one to lean on friends for stuff like this, but I trust Luis; he won't throw it in my face. It means a lot for a person who's poor to trust that a rich person won't hold money over their head.

On Saturday, Luis comes and scoops me so we can head into Manhattan. Naima's tied up getting her hair braided, so it's just a guys' day.

"Know what's weird?" Luis asks as we rip down the West Side Highway.

"The fact that you drive even more reckless in the city than you do at home?" I counter, gripping the door as his Range Rover weaves between cars.

"I'm not even going that fast. But if it makes you feel better, I'll slow down," he says, the speedometer falling.

"Thanks." I sigh, letting go of the door. "So, what's weird?"

"That it took this long for us to hang out one-on-one," Luis responds.

"Damn, that's valid. Guess we are long overdue for a guys' night!" I say, whipping out my phone and cranking up the tunes.

Luis smiles wide. "Guys' night!" He turns the volume up even higher and begins speeding again.

We spend the day hitting Luis's top SoHo boutiques, hunting down my New Year's look. I can barely afford the socks in these spots. But eventually, with the help of a cool Black stylist we meet at one of the more affordable boutiques, I find a fit at a price that doesn't make me feel too weird about Luis paying.

"I see you, GQ!" Luis applauds as I step out in cream chinos, navy turtleneck, gray tweed blazer, and brown loafers. I hardly recognize myself in the mirror. I never thought I was a turtleneck guy, but it's growing on me.

"Just one more thing . . ." The stylist tucks a matching pocket square into my blazer. "Perfect."

Once we're done, we swing by another boutique to grab Luis's fit.

"Let me see your outfit!" I plead. But Luis isn't having it.

"Nope. I'm superstitious about people seeing me get my fits off until I'm actually wearing them. This one is extra special." He grins, making his purchase and heading out.

I'm even more intrigued now. "Really? What makes it 'extra special'?"

"Well, let's just say your Christmas gift meant a lot to me—and my outfit."

"Hmm, fine. I'll wait and see," I respond. "So, are you tryna head back now?"

"Hell, no! Let's live it up. You've got no idea what you signed up for, Ossie."

Luis is right about that. Because the next thing I know, we're dining at some of the swankiest places in New York City. Instead of one restaurant, we hit three. (Luis pays the bills for all of them—thank God.)

We start with appetizers at the Polo Bar—Ralph Lauren's restaurant. Then it's off to COTE Korean Steakhouse for dinner. I let Luis do the ordering because there's no way I'm gonna ask someone to serve me fries that cost twenty-five bucks. And Wagyu steak? That's a first for me. But I can't lie. I could get used to it for sure.

By the end of our dinner, I'm stuffed. What could possibly top this? But Luis has one more card to play.

"Dessert?" he asks, settling the bill at COTE.

"Man, I appreciate the day. I'll be honest, though—I don't feel comfortable with you paying for everything. But the way my pockets work—I don't think I can afford to put in," I confess.

"Well, you should get comfortable. It's not my money; it's my parents'. Think of it as what you're owed for their problematic bullshit every time you've been around them. And for them telling all of their friends how their son is friends with this huge basketball star 'from the hood' as a bragging point."

"And to make their son seem more macho . . ." I add soberly, shaking my head.

"Exactly," Luis says. Then he smiles sheepishly. "Though I'll be honest, when I first invited you over to chill, it was mainly so my parents would get off my back."

I nod. "Yeah, I figured that after you came out to me."

Luis seems surprised that I put that together. "I'm sorry. I should have said something."

"It's all good. Trust me: I get it," I say gently, letting him know I don't feel a way. "Now, what were you saying about dessert?"

We both begin to chuckle.

The last spot Luis takes me to is called Westlight, in Williamsburg. This place isn't just a restaurant; it's a rooftop bar with a breathtaking panorama of the New York City skyline—the shimmering high-rises, the twinkling lights, the highways snaking their way through the city. It's the most amazing view I've ever seen. We weren't even supposed to be there because they don't let underage people in after a certain time. But Luis made a call to someone and they were able to get us in.

We order enough desserts to feed a small army. I didn't even know half this stuff existed. When we're done, Luis stands and walks outside to the edge of the roof. He looks out into the night. I follow.

"You good?" I ask.

"Yeah."

"You sure?"

"I'm all right. I just . . . I can't wait to get down here—or anywhere that isn't home—after high school."

He's scanning the skyline like he's searching for a place to escape to. "I'm sick of that house, being around my parents, always feeling like I gotta be someone I'm not."

"I hear you. I'm sorry, Luis," I reply, wishing I could say more.

"You know what they got me for Christmas?" he begins, shaking his head. "Money, boxing lessons, an airsoft gun, and ringside seats to some big boxing match coming up. What better way to say 'I will die if my son's gay' than the most cliché dude-bro gifts ever?"

He exhales, as if wishing he could let out every single thing he's holding in and toss it into the blackness of the sky.

"You'll be out of there soon." I drop an arm on his shoulder, trying to let him know I'm here. "And if it counts for anything, I love who you are, Luis."

"You ain't so bad yourself."

We give each other a tight hug. It's the kind of embrace that seems to squeeze out all the worries and just leave room for brotherhood. In this moment, the city lights twinkle a little brighter, the night feels a little warmer. Maybe it's the magic of New York, or maybe it's just the magic of us.

A few days later, the night of the party, I pull up in an Uber to the Martinezes' house, and I can hear the music blasting from blocks away. As the front gate swings open, and we roll up the driveway, the driver's eyes widen at the display of wealth all around. Luxury and exotic cars parked all along the driveway. These aren't the Benzes and Beamers I've seen at Braxton—this is *money* money—I'm talking about Lambos and Aston Martins. Next-level stuff.

"You sure you're all right here, kid?" The driver peers at me from the rearview mirror, concern written all over his face. I appreciate it, knowing he's probably thinking I'm about to be an Illuminati sacrifice or something.

"Yeah, I'm good," I assure him, laughing.

I walk in, and there's gotta be at least 150 people in there, and, as I thought, it looks like something straight outta *The Great Gatsby*.

"Ossie!" Mrs. Martinez hollers from across the room. She's draped in a gold backless gown, cutouts showing off her obliques and a leg slit that would turn heads—if they're not too busy staring at the diamond necklace she's got on, which looks like it costs the same amount as about a thousand of the guys' night Luis and I had.

"Come here, Ossie!" She beckons me toward the crowd she's standing with.

The group is made up of two middle-aged white guys, one blond and the other a black-haired dude. It's obvious, even with the fancy tuxedos they're wearing, that they're both muscular as hell. Old NFL buddies of Mr. Martinez, I'm thinking. Two Asian women stand next to them, both with large flashy wedding rings. They look like they're only a few years older than me.

The second I step into their circle, Mr. Martinez slides in, too, trailed by a waiter with a tray full of fancy glasses.

"You clean up nice, Ossie!" Mr. Martinez says, grabbing drinks off the tray and handing them around. "I told you guys: he's a really good kid!"

I'm not sure why Mr. Martinez and his friends have been having conversations about whether I'm a "good kid" or not, so I don't respond.

"Good to meet you, dog." The blond-haired guy reaches out for a fist bump.

"It's Ossie . . ." I correct him, extending for a handshake instead of a fist bump.

"All right, then," he acknowledges, eyebrows shooting up a notch. Like he's surprised but respects it. He returns my handshake.

The greetings pass around the circle, and then it's back to Mr. Martinez. "Seeing you walk in without a limp, looks like your knee is doing much better. Maybe a setup for a comeback?" He nudges me with his elbow.

"Yeah, I'm in less pain and moving a lot better. But the doctors already told me I can't play again based on the extent of my injury. So no comeback for me," I respond, somewhat annoyed at having to say all this to a bunch of former pro athletes.

"Same thing happened to Pat here—he had a torn ACL, and they also told him it was supposed to be career ending. But then we went on to win two Super Bowls together." Mr. Martinez shows off his championship rings, bumping fists and matching rings with the two guys.

"I wish that was the case, but it's over for me." I shrug, wanting to move on.

"Watching you walk over here, didn't look like 'over' to me," the blond guy—Pat—counters.

Before I can respond, one of the wives is gasping, looking toward the door. "Wow! Who is *that*?"

I turn to find Naima striding in. She's just stepped through the door and is already the star of the show.

She's got on this perfectly fitted light-gray pantsuit, a matching blouse, and heels that are amazing. Her box braids are all done up in a bun, looking like a crown on her head.

"Excuse me," I tell the group, already halfway across the room.

"You look amazing," we say at the same time, laughing together as well.

"Just trying to match your fly, beautiful," I say, trying to be smooth.

"Well, I think you look good in Js and sweatshirts, too. But this whole James Bond thing you got going tonight—I'm into it."

"Oh word?" I start striking poses like I'm in a fashion show.

"Word." She takes my hand and lands a soft kiss on my cheek.

Suddenly, Naima's eyes widen, and a huge smile lights up her face. I swivel, following her gaze to Luis. He's draped in black—fitted slacks hugging his legs, dressy high silver boots stamping the floor, and a sequin jacket cropped just enough to reveal a hint of his abdomen. No shirt to cover him. Around his wrist and neck, pearls are gleaming.

Luis is a *Vogue* magazine cover come to life, the bright lights seeming as if they were made just for him.

"You like?" Luis's voice rings out as he twirls toward Naima and me, each sequin on his jacket catching the light and throwing it back.

"I love it," Naima says, her fingers tracing the sparkly pattern on Luis's jacket. "But what will your parents say?"

Luis shrugs as if he doesn't have a care in the world. "I'm tired, Nai. Tired of pretending I'm someone I'm not for them. I was thinking about the gift you got me, Ossie. How I felt honest writing that poem—courageous. I want to always be like that. I want to always feel true to myself."

Naima is about to respond when Mr. Martinez bulldozes into our conversation and grabs the end of Luis's jacket. His voice is harsh; his words are like razors. "What is this you're wearing, Luis?"

Luis tries to brush it off. "It's just a jacket, Papi."

"Don't play stupid with me," Mr. Martinez says, still clutching Luis's jacket like it personally offends him and pointing at his pearls. "¿Y qué es esto?" The words are so charged.

Mrs. Martinez, sensing the tension, steps in, trying to douse the flames. "Hector, ¡cálmate! Calm down. People are starting to stare."

"I don't care, Yaribel. No self-respecting man would wear something like this. . . . Look at the pearls—"

"They were Abuela's pearls; she left them to me." Luis, obviously nervous, tries to sound calm.

Mr. Martinez roars back, "TO REMEMBER HER! NOT TO—" But he subdues himself, looking around at the array of white faces turned in our direction. "Not to *wear*. You are not a girl. You are my *son*."

Naima chimes in to defend Luis. "It's not a girl's outfit, Mr. Martinez. It's a jacket and pearls. Luis is no more a girl for wearing that than I am a boy for wearing this pantsuit."

Mr. Martinez furiously turns to Naima. "This doesn't involve you, Naima. Be quiet."

I step in front of Mr. Martinez, knowing he could break me in half. "Watch how you speak to her!"

Mrs. Martinez places a hand on her husband's chest. "¡Para! People are watching, Hector. ¡Cálmate!"

"I will calm down when he goes upstairs, takes that off, and puts on one of his tuxedos!" Mr. Martinez declares, his eyes casting molten-iron stares in Luis's direction.

Luis's jaw is tensely pulsating like he's holding himself back from attacking his father.

Mrs. Martinez, her voice low, attempts to smooth the moment again. "Luis, just go upstairs and change. I know you like this whole fashion thing, but this outfit . . . it's too much for your father. It looks like something a maricón would wear." Her words are like jagged shards of glass, sharp and hurtful.

But Luis, he doesn't crumble. Instead, he stands firm, the contours of his face shaped with fierce determination instead of pain.

His voice, when he finally speaks, blasts through the tension like a cannon. "No, Mami. I'm not changing. You don't want me to embarrass you in front of your friends? Fine. Let's go, y'all." He turns on his heels and strides toward the door, grabbing his coat on the way. Naima and I follow closely.

Suddenly, the music goes quiet. "Sorry about that, everyone!" Mr. Martinez's voice booms. "I'm sure you all know how much of a headache this generation can be! And what is an evening hosted by Latinos without a little spice!" He laughs, twisting the knife further.

Everyone else begins laughing, too, and the music starts playing again. Luis shakes his head and walks out the door. We follow.

As the door closes behind us, sealing off the hostility inside, we find ourselves swallowed by the still night. Luis stands there, a silhouette against the brightly lit front of the house, grappling with his decision, weighing his emotions. Naima wraps him in a hug, a safe place to land after falling from a sky of nightmares.

"Let's go be around some real love," Luis says, and leads us toward his car.

We pile in his SUV, and with a flick of the knob, he fills the car with music, loud and defiant, drowning out the remnants of his parents as we peel off into the night. The city lights drawing us in as we head to Mateo's party at NYU.

Chapter Twenty-Four

The buildings zoom past as Luis drives us through Manhattan, belting out Beyoncé's "Church Girl" like his life depends on it. "'Nobody can judge me but me! I was born free!'"

He's pretending to be okay, just like after the Halloween party. And also just like then, we go along with his charade, nodding our heads to the music, pretending his parents didn't just verbally destroy their own son because of their homophobia. Trusting he'll open up to us when he feels ready to do so.

When we pull up to the NYU dorms, we are surprised to find that entire resident floors have been turned into party zones. It's like nothing I've ever seen. Hallways filled with music blasting, red cups bobbing, people laughing, dancing, living.

"This is wild. College students get to just do whatever they want?"

"Well, Mateo is an RA and so are most of his friends who are throwing this. So I guess the answer is yes?" Luis responds playfully.

Passing through the sea of partygoers wearing jeans and T-shirts, I can't help but feel overdressed, standing out like a neon sign in a dark alley.

Suddenly, Mateo's voice cuts through the noise. He walks up, gives Luis a kiss, and leads us into his room down the hall. The space is a nice escape from the raging party, though the air still pulsates gently with the muffled bass coming from the other side of the door.

The walls of the room are a collage of posters from movies along with portraits of prominent human rights activists from history—Che Guevara, Assata Shakur, Ho Chi Minh, and other figures I've learned about. Scattered all around are books, some stacked on the floor, others sitting on shelves, and more sprawled across desks. Their authors are a mix of familiar names and some I've never heard of.

The room feels like a space for intellectuals, more like a professor's office than a college student's room.

As we stroll in, there's an intense debate going on in the room. Two guys, one Latino, one Black, are sitting on a futon folded into a couch. Two young women, one white and one Black, are leaning in from the edges of the small bed in the room. They're too wrapped up in their fiery discussion to notice the four of us.

"The people in Belgium have it right!" the white woman declares, ending her statement with a sip from her red party cup.

"But it won't happen here. Too many people are just trying to keep their heads above water, trying to maintain the status quo," the Black guy counters.

"I don't agree," the Black woman challenges.

"Same here." The Latino guy backs her up. "What about the civil rights movement? Or the summer of 2020?"

"Or that *tiny* women's suffrage movement," the white woman tosses in.

The Black guy swivels around to face them. "Those times, those needs, they were clear as day. But look at Belgium right now, folks rising up because their government is approving 3-D-printed food that could be dangerous for citizens. Here we eat far worse, and nobody even bats an eye. And that 'racial awakening' of 2020? What'd it get us? 'Black Lives Matter' painted on a couple of streets and streaming services curating lists of old Black movies?"

"Okay, time-out!" Mateo raises his voice, halting the debate. "Before we start tearing apart performative activism, let's meet Naima and Ossie."

"You three look amazing!" the Black woman says as everyone gets up to greet us.

"Mateo, you might need to step up your game before you lose your man," the Latino guy teases, enveloping Luis in a hug.

"That's enough!" Mateo says, jokingly pulling them apart.

Mateo's friends introduce themselves, then Mateo offers us all a drink. I decide to join in, seeing Naima and Luis go for it. The drink of the night is whiskey. I've never had it—or anything other than a sip of champagne once with Grandma Alice. But I don't want them to know that.

"Here's to the ones who paved the way so we can continue the work!" Mateo says. The entire room toasts aloud, other than me, Naima, and Luis.

Naima and I shoot each other a quick look, trying hard not to laugh. The moment is extremely cringey. Luis catches us.

"They're all in the Human Rights Student Union together," he whispers.

"That's right: you defend your man," Naima whispers back, giggling into her cup. I laugh, too, and raise my cup in agreement. Then I take a sip of my drink.

Immediately, I spit the liquor back into my cup. Naima notices. She gives me a sweet nonjudging smile before whispering, "Pro tip: If you keep your lips closed, it looks like you're actually drinking it." She takes a "sip" to demonstrate.

I look down at my cup of poison, wanting to keep it as far from my lips as possible.

The room is alive with conversation and laughter, another round already being poured. More chairs are brought into the already crowded room for us to settle in. The more time passes, the more the scents of stale pizza and sweat cling to the air. Nobody else seems to notice, though— probably because they're all pretty saucy by this point.

The conversation eventually dives back into the deep end of the pool, where it was when we walked in. The refugee crisis, prison reform. When policing comes up, it's a hurricane of thoughts and opinions, each one colliding with the next.

"I just don't feel like every cop is inherently bad," Felipe, the Latino guy, says.

"Well, I think you're wrong," Sam, the white woman, argues. "We've seen it time and time again. Even if one cop means well, the institution itself is the issue. If the garden is rotten, so is all the fruit it produces."

Kevin, the Black guy, turns to me. "Mateo told us what happened to you and Naima a few months ago at the gas station. That was terrible, bro. You must have strong feelings about the police."

His words slam into me like a freight train, the memory of that night, the fear crashing over me in waves. I know it was never a secret. But to have it brought up like this, by someone we've just met, in the middle of a party—it feels like a sucker punch.

"Nah . . . I don't really have anything new to add to the conversation," I respond simply, hoping to deflect the heat.

Luis backs me up. "Maybe Ossie and Nai aren't comfortable talking about such a traumatic moment." He glares at Mateo in frustration. In the creases of his forehead and the clenching of his jaw, I see a mirror of my own feelings. He gets it. He understands that Mateo, with his loose lips, has basically dropped us out of a plane into the middle of a minefield.

Mateo straightens. "Luis is right. Sorry, Ossie, you don't have to say—"

"It's not really about adding something new, though," interrupts the Black woman, whose name is Janet. "You have millions of followers and the attention of the media, right?"

All eyes are on me, the glare of attention making my skin prickle. "The media's attention? I'm not sure about that. But, yeah, I have a lot of followers. Why does that matter?"

"Maybe you should be writing about what happened. There are a lot of people who would listen to you. People who think the rest of us are exaggerating. You could be making a lot of change," Janet persists.

"People don't follow me for that. They follow me for ball. They don't care about my thoughts on social justice," I respond, my face ablaze.

"So make them care," Janet quickly responds, clearly frustrated.

"She has a point," Felipe says, adding fuel to the fire. "And don't all of you go to school with those social media kids who got the Black teacher suspended—why haven't you used your platform like they did?"

"Yeah. I mean. We started a petition . . . But, I mean . . ." I try to stumble through a response, but Luis and Naima bulldoze right in.

"You don't owe anyone an explanation, Ossie. If you don't want to talk to the world about what's wrong with the world, that's your call." Luis's words are like a cool rag on a feverish forehead.

"Exactly!" Naima echoes Luis. "And he isn't the only one who went through it. I haven't said anything about the police or Ms. Hunt in public, either."

"You posting to a thousand people or whatever isn't the same as him posting to millions!" Janet chimes in, nearly yelling.

"That's the issue with today's world. People with the megaphones and platforms don't have anything real to say. Just trying to keep everyone happy instead of being honest about what's going on." Kevin holds up his phone screen, which is illuminated with my profile. "I'm sorry, but Ossie's got nearly three million followers. He's got an obligation to use that sort of influence for some good!"

"You don't know what he's going through in his personal life." Naima's voice is filled with fury on my behalf. "Just because he has a platform doesn't mean he's obligated to do anyth—"

"It's all good," I interrupt, my voice a low rumble. "I get it. Things need to change. But it's easy to tell someone else to turn their scars into lessons. You're not the ones who have to relive the way the cops pushed Naima onto her car, remember how that flashlight in the window could have just as easily been a gun, think about the times it *was* a gun pulled on someone in your neighborhood, someone who could've just as easily been you. You don't have to live with the knowledge that the only teacher in high school who ever cared about you is gone, pushed out by a bunch of bigots who are looking for any excuse to get *you* gone from their rarefied world, too."

I'm so wrapped up in the conversation, so caught up in my own world, that I don't realize I'm crying until I feel Naima's sleeve gently wiping away my tears.

"Believe me, I want change as much as all y'all," I continue. "I *need* change. But change isn't just about arguments at college parties—one of y'all gonna come protect my neighborhood when cops start harassing us if I post something about what they did? Have *y'all* said anything about the Black teacher who was suspended, since you obviously have so many opinions about it? No. All y'all do is point fingers, expecting someone else to put themselves in the line of fire while you can stand a safe distance behind them and pretend to be just as brave."

Mateo's friends are frozen, their eyes wide, their faces filled with shock and guilt. Finally, Mateo tries to smooth over the awkwardness.

"I'm sorry, Ossie," he murmurs, turning his eyes to his phone. "Look, we've got about an hour and a half until the new year rings in. Why don't we cool down and go see what's happening at the rest of the party?"

"That's a good plan," Luis agrees, trying to be a voice of reason. He turns to me and Naima, his eyebrows raised in question. "Y'all down?"

Naima stands. "Nah—I think I'm beat. Maybe we should dip. Is that okay, Ossie?"

Her suggestion feels like the release of a pressure valve.

"Yeah. Sounds good," I respond, fighting to bring my tone back to casual.

"Sure, we can head to the Airbnb I booked," Luis offers before looking at Mateo. "You want to come with?"

"I'd love to, but I still got to play the responsible card. Need to make sure things don't spiral out of control here," Mateo replies with a note of regret.

"No worries—we'll catch up tomorrow." Luis rises from his seat with a sigh of disappointment.

Naima eases him back into his seat. "Stay and have fun! We're good."

"You sure?" Luis's eyes are questioning.

"Yeah. Just text us the address and the code to the Airbnb," Naima says.

"You *sure*?" Luis asks again.

"YES. Have fun," Naima insists. "We'll see you later."

We say our good-byes and leave the party behind. The moment we step outside, the night air is a welcome change from the suffocating atmosphere we just escaped. The streets are nearly deserted, the world holding its breath in anticipation of the new year. Snowflakes swirl down, blanketing the city in white, muffling the distant sounds of celebration.

The wind is snapping at us, scraping its icy teeth against our faces. Swirling snowflakes batter us like a storm of frozen confetti.

"I'm sorry we had to leave!" I yell.

"Huh?" Naima hollers back, her eyebrows furrowed against the flurries.

"The party!" I bellow, cupping my hands around my mouth, a makeshift megaphone. "I'm sorry we had to go because of me!"

She leans closer and rolls her eyes. "Oh, whatever! They were mad pretentious anyway! It's all good!"

"Maybe they were right! Maybe I'm a coward for not speaking up!" My shoes plant themselves on the crisp snow-blanketed ground.

Naima stops, too, the wind knocking her braids out of her bun and laying them against her cheeks. She looks at me for a second. A deep, meaningful look that makes the wind feel less chilly, the regret feel less biting. She guides me under a nearby scaffolding, away from the snow, where we can hear each other better. Her hands find mine, her grip strong but tender.

"Many of the things you've been through are hell," she says softly against the wind's roar. "But you don't have to do anything except be alive. Not unless you want to. It doesn't matter what anyone else says; you know where your heart is. And Luis and I know it, too."

My tongue's lost, tangled up somewhere in my mouth. I just nod. Grateful for her, for her presence in this storm.

We carry on, plowing through the wintry blast toward the Airbnb. The apartment building towers above us like a glass-and-steel giant. We step in, shake off the cold, and head for the elevator. After we punch in the code Luis tossed us, we're whisked up, right to the top floor. The elevator doors open, revealing a posh penthouse. It's like stepping into a magazine spread—all polished hardwood, glimmering art, and panoramic windows. The New York City skyline is immediately before us, the lights flickering under a soft blanket of snow.

Naima and I find our groove, settling into the lavish apartment.

"So what's the plan?" She's got an eye on the clock, not wanting to miss the countdown to midnight.

"I'm usually in my room watching game tape or kickin' it with my family for New Year's Eve," I admit, the simplicity of those things feeling miles away.

"I'm always with my family, toasting with hot chocolate. You think they have the stuff to make it here?" Naima asks.

"Let me check."

The kitchen is a gourmet wonderland. I discover a treasure trove of cocoa, sugar, mugs, and even marshmallows. As I turn on the faucet, about to douse the mugs of cocoa and sugar with water, Naima steps in.

"Nah . . . You about to make my hot cocoa with tap water?" she asks, shock dancing across her face.

"Yeah, what's wrong with that?" I reply, genuinely baffled.

"Nah, that's not how it's done. Let me show you." She swoops in like a hot-chocolate superhero. She finds a saucepan and pours in some milk, then heats it on the stove. Once it's simmering, she adds it to the mugs and shakes a dash of cinnamon on top. She moves like she's been doing this forever.

"Damn, this is next level," I confess when I take my first sip, my taste buds doing cartwheels.

"You can add that to your 'Thank you, Naima' list." She grins, looking mighty pleased with herself.

"Sure. You got that," I say, smiling and staring into her eyes. "But I still know one thing I'm good at."

Naima raises an eyebrow. "What's that?"

I stride over to the stereo. My fingers graze its surface, feeling for the right button. *Click.* The speakers come to life, a gentle vibration that promises something soulful, something smooth. I shuffle through my playlists, my heart already matching the song I'm about to put on.

"Say So" by PJ Morton and JoJo begins to play, the first notes like a call to something deeper, something that's been waiting for just the right moment to surface. As soon as the song starts, Naima begins to sway to the music.

"I love this song," she says, offering me a smile that makes me tingle.

After watching her for a second, I take a deep breath to gather my courage, then walk over and gently take her free hand and begin dancing with her. The two of us dance and sing along, not realizing the clock has struck twelve until the sky begins to pop and crackle. It's midnight. The new year's here.

We rush to the balcony, eyes wide as the night sky bursts with light. It's just us and the fireworks. We look on, and as each second passes, I keep telling myself I should kiss her. But I know the moment probably slipped away already.

The two of us stay silent as the sounds of vivid explosions echo around us.

Naima looks up at me and grins. "You make me so happy."

Before I can process her words, her lips are on mine. The fireworks' glow casts a surreal haze around us. Time stops, or maybe it's racing forward. Either way, it doesn't matter. The world narrows down to her lips. A moment to bring in the new year, and to exist in a world where there is only the two of us.

Chapter Twenty-Five

Hours later, my eyes flick open, and Naima's still out cold, nestled up in the tangled mess of sheets. Quietly, I slip out of the room, letting the door close with the softest click. I breathe in deep, stepping up to the balcony window. I put on the Bali playlist and just stare at Manhattan laid out below, streets softly humming, the world barely awake after its wild night. I'm grinning so hard, my cheeks ache.

I can't shake the feeling of last night. Naima. The way our lips met at midnight.

The hurt from what the cops did to us, so fresh after last night's conversation in the dorm, isn't so heavy today. Laura's leaving isn't a brick on my chest. Losing the court, the thrill of the game, it's not a boulder I'm pushing uphill. Even the emptiness of my dad's absence doesn't leave the same lump in my throat.

But even with so much going right, there's still a nagging thought, like a pebble in my shoe, bothering me.

Last night. Mateo's friends. Their words. They're echoing in my head, bouncing around like a basketball in an empty gym. They called me out for sitting on a mountain of followers and staying quiet. Silent. They said I'm a coward for not using my platform. And maybe they're right.

I pull out my phone, swiping through the apps until I find Matthew's page. There he is, nearly three hundred thousand followers. And with every post, every word, he's stirring up a storm, doing so much damage. And here I am, nearly ten times his reach, and I'm as quiet as a library.

I think about Ms. Hunt, all the work she had us do, all the things she taught us. How wrong they did her. I think about Naima, the kinda noise she would make if she had my platform. How she wants to be a journalist. How even then, she might not have the reach I do.

Then it hits me. What if I use my platform not just to speak but to amplify? Our petition isn't working at all. But I can shine the spotlight on someone whose voice is even more powerful than mine. Naima's voice. But she hasn't wanted to speak out publicly, either. So how can I give her words a mic without thrusting *her* into the middle of all this?

I'm so locked in on my idea that I don't even realize Naima's standing behind me.

"What are you doing?" she asks, a bit of playful interrogation sneaking into her voice.

"Nothing. Just thinking," I respond, planting a comforting kiss on her forehead. I make a move to share an actual kiss with her but stop midway. "Damn. Nah, I'll take that kiss later."

Naima claps a hand over her mouth in shock. "Deadass?"

"As deadass as someone can be." I chuckle. "That breath is kicking."

Naima rushes to the bathroom, leaving me laughing when she's gone.

We make breakfast from the well-stocked kitchen, then spend the rest of the morning relaxing on the couch and watching movies.

Eventually we pack up and head downstairs to meet Luis. As soon as he pulls up in his Range Rover, he's apologetic.

"Man, I'm so sorry about what went down at the party. Mateo's been beating himself up about it."

I nod, gazing out the window, the buildings smearing together like wet paint. "It's cool, Luis." But my voice betrays the churn in my gut. It's not all cool. Not really.

I catch Luis's eyes in the rearview, a whole conversation in that glance. "He shouldn't have told them about what happened to you two."

I let out a slow breath, watching it fog up the window. "Yeah. But honestly, they gave me a lot to think about. A whole lot." And it's true. My head's been a beehive since.

Luis nods in understanding. "Just wanted to make sure you're good, Ossie. That's all."

"I'm good," I say, giving him a small smile.

After the traumatic incident with his parents, Luis isn't ready to go back to his house. Naima's parents extend an invitation for him to stay at theirs for as long as he needs. The two of them decide the first day of the year is the perfect time to do some shopping. I'm sure Naima knows it might help Luis feel a bit better.

I decide to jump on the train and head home to finish my last few college applications, knowing that Naima and Luis finished theirs weeks ago. Being home will also give me a chance to start planning out how I'm going to use my platform to help Ms. Hunt and amplify Naima's words. I also want to check in on Grandma Alice since I haven't seen her since Christmas.

The train is packed, bodies pressed against each other like sardines in a can. Everyone's bundled up in their winter gear, breath fogging up the windows. I find a spot near the door, standing because all the seats are taken.

My phone buzzes in my pocket, a message from Naima with a picture of Luis wearing a shirt that's way too small for him. I chuckle, shaking my head. My mind goes to how much love Naima has for the people in her life and how beautifully she captures that in her writing.

And then it hits me: Naima's letter to her father. It's the perfect example of the sort of writing Ms. Hunt pushed us toward. How she was working to get the best out of us and make us consider the experiences of other people.

I text Naima.

> ME: Hey. Can you send me the letter you wrote to your dad, the one you read to me and Luis?

NAIMA: . . . Uh, why?

> ME: I want to study it, if that's cool. I think it'll help me be a stronger writer

It's not really a lie—I *do* think studying her letter will make me a better writer. But right now, it's not *my* writing I'm thinking about.

NAIMA: OK weirdo. But only if you send me the
letter you wrote to your mom. That's some
powerful stuff, Ossie <3

A few minutes later, an attachment comes through to my email. When I get home, I head straight to my room and put my plan to amplify Naima's work into action. I take a few screenshots of her letter and black out her and her family's names and any other identifying details so no one will know who wrote it—just that it's written by one of Ms. Hunt's former students. ("Former" to further obscure Naima's identity; I don't want her to deal with any blowback.) Next, I create an email address where anyone interested in Naima's writing can reach out and Naima can connect with them if she's interested. The quality of her writing will show the impact Ms. Hunt has had on countless students who have been lucky enough to have her as a teacher.

The plan is set, so I get to writing my caption, which includes background about what Matthew and them did to Ms. Hunt. The caption reads:

Hey, everyone,

Today, I want to talk about something deeply important. A few weeks ago, an incredible teacher of ours, Ms. Hunt, was unjustly suspended due to some manipulative actions by racist students at my school. They went on TV and lied about what's happening at our school and silenced a voice that has helped many of us not only become better writers but also grow in our understanding of the world.

Ms. Hunt was more than a teacher; she was a mentor who pushed us to think critically, empathize, and strive for excellence. She was suspended for just trying to help us consider experiences beyond our own.

To show the impact she had on us, to show the kind of writing that we produced under her guidance, I want to share a powerful letter written a few years back by a friend of mine for an assignment Ms. Hunt gave.

I'm sharing this not just to showcase this student's talent but to stand up against the injustice faced by Ms. Hunt. It's time we use our platforms not just for ourselves but to amplify the voices that matter and make a difference. Let's not let racists silence teachers like Ms. Hunt!

Swipe to read the letter and see for yourself the impact of a great teacher. If you want to reach out to my friend, click the link in my bio to email them.

#JusticeForMsHunt #BlackTeachersMatter #EducationMatters

I read over Naima's letter one last time, making sure there's no way for anyone to identify her. Satisfied, I hit save. I'll post this tomorrow night, right before I see Naima at school. That way I can tell her about it in person.

I reach for my phone and send her a text.

ME: Hey

NAIMA: Hey :) How's your night going?

ME: I'm chillin . . . I have a big surprise for you when I see you on Friday at school

NAIMA: A surprise? Ooo what is it?

ME: Something that will earn me boyfriend of the year

NAIMA: I'll be the judge of that :)

Before bed, I can't help the smile on my face as I think about sharing Naima's words with the world. I'm excited for people to see how great a writer Naima is and for more people to support Ms. Hunt. And, I'm not gonna lie: I'm also excited to see the look on Matthew's face when people start coming for him.

I wake up the next morning feeling much better than I have in weeks. I throw on the letterman jacket Naima gave me, grab my laptop, and head to Grandma Alice's apartment.

I push open the door to Grandma Alice's, and immediately the scent of her home hits me. It's a mix of fresh baked goods, lavender, and something else that's always been uniquely her.

"Grandma?" I call out, taking off my jacket and hanging it by the door.

"In here, baby," she calls back from her room.

I find her wrapped up in a thick blanket on her bed, a steaming cup of tea on the nightstand beside her. I can't help but notice that the mattress seems to swallow her up. She's still looking frail.

"You feeling okay, Grandma?" I ask, trying to keep the concern out of my voice.

She chuckles, her laughter light and raspy. "Oh, I'm doing just fine. But when you get to be my age, you don't bounce back from things overnight."

I nod, not entirely convinced, but she swiftly changes the subject. "So, how was New Year's Eve at Luis's house?"

I hesitate for a moment. The party, the confrontation, NYU, the night with Naima. "It was . . . good," I say, not meeting her eyes.

Grandma Alice gives me that all-knowing smile, the one that says she's seen more years than I have and can spot a lie a mile away. "Mm-hmm. I won't push. Just know you can always talk to me."

I nod, grateful for her understanding. "Thanks, Grandma."

She takes a sip of tea. "Well, I had quite the New Year's Eve myself. Mrs. Collins, Ms. Peters, and the rest of them were over here. You'd think they were still young the way they were carrying on!"

I chuckle, imagining the scene. "Really? They were partying hard?"

Grandma Alice lets out a cough, which worries me a little, but then she continues. "Oh, they were drinking like they were in their twenties! I think Mrs. Collins even tried to dance on the table at one point. Your mother was here, too. She was smiling the whole night. I think your Christmas gift really helped."

I laugh, shaking my head. "Sounds like a good night."

She smiles, her eyes crinkling at the corners. "It was everything I could have wanted."

We chat a little more, and then I ask her if she minds if I pull out my laptop and do a bit of work on my college applications.

"Of course I don't mind, baby!" Grandma Alice looks at me with the kind of pride only a grandparent can muster: love and wisdom and a profound perspective on the world.

"Look at you," she says softly. "I always knew you were bigger than any basketball court. This is what your father would want to see—you applying to schools like NYU and Columbia."

"Well, I don't get to just pick. The schools gotta want me, too," I point out, trying to temper her high hopes.

"If any school can't see what having you would add, they don't deserve you anyway," Grandma Alice declares, motioning me closer so she can lay a kiss on my cheek.

Her spirit keeps mine soaring. Truth be told, the thought of college, the potential rejection, it scares me. College was such a definite thing when it came to basketball; people were *begging* me to come. To now have the tables turned, wondering if the same schools that were offering me full-ride scholarships for basketball would give me a shot for my academics, it's frightening.

When a Black kid's future is filled with essays and textbooks instead of jumpers and dunks—does his future still matter?

Another thing that has been on my mind about college is Naima and Luis. We all know what schools we're trying to get into, but we haven't really talked about what happens next to us. I'm nervous about the truth that we'll no longer see each other every day and what that might do to our relationships. Beyond my feelings for Naima, the two of them are my first real friends since I was a kid.

Grandma Alice and I spend the day finishing applications and curating a long list of more scholarships for me and Mrs. Wright to discuss. After that, I head home, getting my mind ready for the second half of senior year at Braxton—and the fight to get Ms. Hunt back.

As soon as I'm in my bedroom, I pull out my phone and reread the draft of my post. Excitement sparks through me as I read over Naima's anonymous letter. Pride swells within me. It's so damn good! There's no way anyone could read this and not see the value in what Ms. Hunt does, or see the promising future of this anonymous writer. This is gonna be huge—for Naima *and* for Ms. Hunt.

I take a deep breath and hit share.

Less than an hour later, as I'm getting ready for bed, I check my phone to find that my post has blown up. It's already racked up over 150,000 likes, and thousands of folks are sharing it. My messages are filled up, too—hundreds of people praising Naima's words, applauding her love for her father, and asking how they can help get Ms. Hunt reinstated.

One of the best things, though? A handful of newspapers, blogs, and magazines have reached out, interested in spotlighting Naima's writing and working with her—or rather, with the "anonymous student."

When Naima calls me to fill me in on her day with Luis and ask about my day, I'm itching to tell her about the post. But I hold off. I want to see her reaction when I tell her in person.

"You're gonna flip when you see this surprise tomorrow," I assure her.

"You've been hyping this surprise up so much, it better be fire," Naima responds, laughing.

"It is—it's a game changer," I say, brimming with excitement.

A few hours later, I'm jolted awake by a series of texts. I groggily reach for my phone. It's Luis at 12:25 a.m.

LUIS: Why would you post this?!

LUIS: Does Naima know? She's gonna be so mad!

LUIS: The news just had her letter up. They're saying she's calling Braxton racist. Parents are going crazy in the social media groups and there's a petition to end the writing program . . .

I have to squint at Luis's texts one time, two times, just to make sure I'm not dreaming or something. But, no, this isn't a dream, more like the type of nightmare you wish you could wake up from.

ME: But they're not saying who wrote it, right? They don't know it's her

Luis doesn't respond. Gripping my phone like it's a floatation device in an ocean, I start scrolling, fingers tapping and sliding over the screen. Searching, hunting for answers in the chaos of the internet. My fingers are jittery as I type in the search "Braxton Academy + Naima Johnson," prayers trickling from my lips that this isn't as bad as Luis is making it out to be.

But as soon as the flood of posts and stories fill my screen, I know—this isn't just bad. This is *apocalyptic*. One particular article grabs my attention, a large snapshot of Ms. Hunt front and center.

The headline is like a declaration of war, yelling out of the screen: "BRAXTON ACADEMY STUDENT SPARKS CONTROVERSY WITH LETTER."

I take in each word of the article, every sentence like a punch, the impact vibrating through me. Apparently, this journalist did some digging into protests that could match the one mentioned in the letter and figured out that it was Mr. Johnson who was attacked and therefore that it was Naima who wrote the letter.

Not only is the article calling Naima out by name, but the journalist is also saying horrible things about her father.

> It seems the apple never falls too far from the tree. After claiming a false attack at the hands of the NYPD, Fordham University professor Malik Johnson attempted to sue the police force and the city of New York. Though he failed miserably, his daughter is obviously picking up where he left off, playing victim and stirring up chaos for the radical left against white people.

They're twisting Naima's letter—acting like she is making her experience up. The article goes on to say many parents and students have anonymously been bringing complaints to the administration about Ms. Hunt and the writing program. They're painting her as some sort of radical revolutionary for daring to let us read and write about diverse perspectives.

The sick churning in my gut deepens as I reach the end of the piece. It turns a whole lot worse when I dive into the comments section. People have all sorts of things to say about Naima, her father, her letter, me, Ms. Hunt, Braxton, Blackness, racism, even Down syndrome. Seems like every ignorant person with a keyboard has added their own fuel to the fire.

I scroll through the comments on other articles as well—they don't seem to stop:

> It's time for parents to wake up and realize the dangerous agenda being pushed by schools like Braxton Academy. This teacher is promoting toxic ideas that all white people are oppressors and all people of color are victims. This kind of thinking has no place in our society and certainly not in our schools.

This is why teaching woke books has no place in our schools. That hateful essay is because of the books that teacher was assigning. I'm considering pulling my child out unless Braxton agrees to remove that garbage from the curriculum.

When did being white become a crime?

I'm a student at Braxton Academy and ever since the BLM crap, all people like Naima do is talk about how hard they have it. YOU DRIVE A MERCEDES! I wish I could get some affirmative action, too.

I'm stuck. Lost. Not sure what to do. I think about calling Naima, but it's late. She hasn't sent me a message, so I'm guessing she's asleep or doesn't know what's going on. She'll hear soon, though. It's probably better if I break it to her face-to-face at school. Which gives me some time to think, to plan, to figure out how to navigate this disaster.

I shoot another text to Luis.

> **ME:** I had no idea this would happen! I wanted to amplify her voice, to give her a platform. I left her name and her family's name off of everything. I even changed details about the protest and said she's a FORMER student of Ms. Hunt's. I didn't think anything like this would happen!

LUIS: Sounds to me like you didn't THINK at all.

I don't bother trying to argue. The situation is so horrible that there's truly nothing I can say in my own defense. I know that I should text her before she finds out some other way, but she deserves to hear the news in person, needs to know how sorry I am for how this has all gone down.

ME: I need a favor . . .

LUIS: No, you need a miracle right now

ME: Listen, can you not tell Naima what's going on and try to keep her off social media until I can see her at school this morning and talk to her? I just feel like the news should come from me

Three minutes pass after I send my text to Luis, and he doesn't answer.

ME: ???

I become so nervous I decide to call him . . . twice.

ME: ???????

LUIS: Stop calling. If I answer she might hear me talking to you. I'm thinking about it

ME: Come on. PLEASE

LUIS: DO NOT tell her I knew and didn't say anything

ME: Say less. Silence

LUIS: Ugh. Fine. I got u

When the sun is finally up, I know I have to get to school fast so I can beat Naima there. Instead of taking the bus, I call an Uber, hoping the ride will also give me some time to gather my thoughts and prepare myself for the storm that's coming.

On my way, a text pops up on my screen from Naima.

NAIMA: Good morning. Can't wait to see my surprise!

I can't bring myself to respond. I'm drenched in cold sweat, mind racing, heart pounding. All I can think about is how my attempt to help spiraled out of control into this nightmare. I hope she understands when I tell her I only had the best intentions in mind.

When I get to school, I rush to Naima's parking spot. Time seems to slow, each second stretching out into an eternity as I wait for her to arrive. I rehearse what I'm going to say, how I'm going to break the news, how I'm going to comfort her if she already knows, and how I'm going to apologize for this mess.

As soon as she finally arrives, Luis hops out of the car, says something to her, and hightails it toward the school. Then her gaze lands on me. I can tell she sees it—the worry carved into every line of my face, the regret shining in my eyes.

She looks confused and then concerned.

I take a deep breath and go to meet her.

Chapter Twenty-Six

"Ossie." Naima's worried voice ripples through the morning air. "Where you been? I texted and called you."

A lump of unformed words sticks in my throat. "Yeah, I know," I mumble, my voice trembling like a tightrope dancer in the wind. "I was waiting for you to pull up."

"Yeah, I can see that," Naima responds. "What's going on?"

I swallow hard, a desperate attempt to anchor my restless nerves. "Your letter to your father," I begin, tasting the bitter truth on my tongue.

"What about it?" she asks, confusion written all over her face.

"I thought it would be a good idea if I . . ." The words begin pressing against the sandcastle of courage inside my mind. "I wanted the world to see what you're capable of. How talented you are. And what a great teacher Ms. Hunt is. So I . . . I posted your letter online and . . ."

"*You did what?*" Naima steps back, her surprise a violent wave crashing against me.

"I thought . . . after our talk . . . I could help you *and* Ms. Hunt by sharing your words, and . . ."

As I'm trying to get the words out, Dean Blackburn's assistant,

Mr. Boebert, walks up to us in the parking lot. He is one of the snakiest-looking people I've ever met.

I feel a prickling sense of unease faced with his beady gaze, and each second the feeling intensifies to an almost unbearable degree.

"Dean Blackburn would like to see you both in her office, *right now*," he finally says, like a judge delivering a sentence. His narrowed eyes and thin lips give off a smugness that tells me he's happy about whatever situation I've put us in.

Our walk into the school and down the hallway feels like a march to the gates of hell, every step echoing the weight of the trouble I've caused. When we finally reach Dean Blackburn's office, we sit in the waiting chairs outside, an intimidating wood door separating us from what feels like our impending doom. Mr. Boebert heads to the other side of the room and sits at a desk in a corner, likely plotting how to ruin someone else's day.

As we sink into the uncomfortable silence, an unexpected sound starts from the other side of the door: a heated argument between Dean Blackburn and Ms. Hunt. Their words, although muffled by the door, paint a clear picture of tension.

"You had no right to bring these kinds of issues into our school," Dean Blackburn snaps, the sound of her fist banging on the desk punctuating her words. "We have a reputation to maintain, and you've put it in jeopardy."

"It wasn't my goal to cause trouble." Ms. Hunt remains calm and collected as she responds to Dean Blackburn's accusations. "I just tried to give my students a broader perspective on the world they live in. I believe it's important for them to read books and write about things that don't only center cis heterosexual white people."

The tension's a living thing now, pushing down on my chest like a lion ready to swallow me whole.

I did this.

Dean Blackburn scoffs. "We have invested a great deal in diversity here. Most people understand that," she says. "You're the reason she wrote that letter and the reason he posted it online, and I won't stand for it."

"Naima chose to write that letter because she wanted to; it's her truth. As for Ossie, I'm sure he was simply trying to help," Ms. Hunt says, her tone taking on a hint of frustration. "I was doing my job. And I don't think it's fair for you to chastise me for that."

There's a pause; the pressure is like a storm cloud ready to bust.

"I'm not *chastising* you, Tasha," Dean Blackburn says as if she's more offended than she's ever been. "I'm trying to explain that I can't have this kind of controversy in my school. Despite what the board said . . . I took a shot on you. And have tried to help you keep your job."

"First of all, you didn't *take a shot* on me." Ms. Hunt's response is measured, but I can hear the anger behind her words. "I'm more qualified than just about anyone at this school. I *earned* my spot here, just like Ossie earned his spot in the writing program. Don't think for a *second* that I've forgotten the nonsense you tried to pull to ensure that Matthew Astor got a spot in that program—a spot that rightfully belonged to Ossie. His being a young Black man doesn't mean you did him a favor by letting him into the program; he was voted in unanimously. And my being a young Black woman doesn't mean any favors were given when I got the job here. So save your white saviorism, Carol. The board suspended me because white children complained about reading books by and about nonwhite people, and you're too much of a coward to stand up to them."

Naima and I trade glances as Ms. Hunt finishes speaking. The silence is like the calm before a typhoon hits.

Then Ms. Hunt's voice pierces the calm. "Are you *crying*, Carol?" she says, her voice laced with disbelief. "You can't be serious!"

"Am I not allowed to have emotions when someone has just accused me of such awful things?" Dean Blackburn fires back, her voice quavering.

"I'm getting death threats to my home! YOU ARE NOT THE VICTIM HERE!" Ms. Hunt hollers back. "You've called me in here to chastise me like a child because of an honest letter that was written in a program I oversaw. You've already suspended me to coddle racist parents! What's next?"

"That's it! First I'm a 'white savior' and now I'm coddling racists?" I can tell Dean Blackburn is furious now. "I've had enough. You're done, Tasha! You're fired!"

Naima's look of shock drills into me. "Ossie, what the hell did you do?"

The weight of my guilt makes it hard for me to breathe. Ms. Hunt leaves the room with her head held high and her shoulders back, though her face is tense with frustration.

I stand up, my legs barely holding me. "Ms. Hunt . . ." I say, and then my voice quits on me.

"Ossie, Naima," she says, looking at us. "I'm sorry this is happening. But listen to me: neither of you is to blame for this. Naima, you spoke your truth—in a hell of a strong letter, might I add. And Ossie, you tried to support that truth." She sighs. "Some people find the truth too threatening, and other people refuse to hear it. But I'm proud of you both for trying to make a difference. I have to go, but reach out if you need *anything*."

I want to tell Ms. Hunt it was all a mistake, that I never meant for any of this to happen, but the apology is stuck.

Ms. Hunt places a hand on my shoulder, and I can feel the weight of her compassion. "It's okay," she says, her voice tinged with sadness. "I know you were just trying to help. I just hope you learn to think more critically about *how* you try to help."

I nod, tears welling in my eyes. I watch her go, feeling a sense of disappointment in myself that I can't put words to.

The door creaks open as Dean Blackburn waves us into her office, her lips pressed into a thin line of disapproval. We shuffle into the room and sit in the two chairs positioned across from her large mahogany desk.

The walls are a testament to Dean Blackburn's time at Braxton, plastered with photographs of smiling former students who've had successful careers in various fields. Yet a glance reveals an uncomfortable truth—not a single face looks like Naima's or mine. So much for that diversity she mentioned to Ms. Hunt.

Her gaze seems to drill into us. Then she comes out swinging.

"Your actions have jeopardized this school," Dean Blackburn begins, her icy gaze bouncing between Naima and me. "You've drawn negative public attention that seeks to undermine everything we stand for."

My stomach's a knot, twisted and tight with dread and bitterness. Are we going to be expelled? Have I ruined Naima's future? I want to respond, to say something to challenge Dean Blackburn's claims, but I know it's pointless.

"We'll be contacting your parents so you and your families can work with our communications team on a public statement," she continues, her voice dripping with self-righteousness. "We need you to make sure everyone knows that Braxton Academy is not racist or bigoted in any way, that mentioning that sort of treatment was—misguided."

I can see the rage emitting from Naima's body as we listen to the lie Dean Blackburn wants us to tell.

I have to say something.

"But Naima had nothing to do with it," I say. "She shouldn't be punished for something that wasn't her fault!"

Dean Blackburn reclines in her chair, sighing heavily. "Look, I'm trying to help you. I understand young love and loyalty. And you've both obviously been swayed by Ms. Hunt's radicalism. But we can't have students going around—"

Naima cuts her off: "I refuse to make a statement I know to be false."

The room stills. I can see the anger reddening Dean Blackburn's face.

"You *will not* undermine my efforts to protect this school," she hisses. "You *will* make the statement—or face the consequences."

The threat hangs in the room like the blade of a guillotine. I have no clue what she's capable of, but I don't want to find out.

Naima remains focused, her eyes blazing with determination. "That's fine. Like I said, I refuse to make a statement," she repeats. "Do what you gotta do."

Dean Blackburn's anger spills over. "Get out! Both of you—get out before I say something I regret!"

As we shuffle out of her office, the weight of my mistake hits me even harder.

"Naima, I'm sorr—"

But she doesn't let me finish. "Don't. Just don't," she spits out. "I can't even look at you right now."

I watch Naima walk away, regret stabbing me in the chest.

I text Luis, needing to update him on what's just happened.

ME: Ms. Hunt just got fired

LUIS: What!!!!

ME: Yeah. This whole thing is wilder than I thought. Naima is pissed. You here yet?

LUIS: Just pulled up. Come outside so everyone isn't in our biz

The cold air outside gives me a deserving slap in the face. It brings a clarity, a sharpness that I need right now. I slide into Luis's car, and he doesn't waste any time.

"So what's going on?" he asks.

I sigh, deep and heavy. "I messed up, Luis," I manage to get out. "My post got Ms. Hunt fired, and now they want Naima and me to lie about our experiences at Braxton—to deny we've ever experienced anything racist."

Luis's eyes widen. "What did Nai say?"

"She's not doing it," I tell him.

Luis nods. "Yeah, she would never do something like that. So what's next?"

I bang my head lightly against the headrest. "They're talking about getting our parents involved."

As I sink further into my seat, I feel as though I'm going to vomit. I have no way to get us out of this mess.

The grip of Luis's hand on my shoulder feels like an island in the raging sea of my emotions. "We'll figure it out," he says firmly, like we've already won this battle we're about to fight. "Nai will forgive you eventually. But we need a game plan before this gets worse."

His words wash over me gently, their comfort seeping into my skin. I don't want a cure for my guilt, and it isn't that. It's a reminder that maybe I can fix things. Having Luis here with me, in my corner, ready to help me mend what I've torn apart—it means everything.

The rest of the day progresses in slow motion. The clock ticks, each second turning into minutes, each minute stretching into hours. It's like being stuck in quicksand, my apologies left unanswered on Naima's phone. I try to catch her after class, a face-to-face apology, but she spots me through the window in the door and sends Luis to talk to me.

"She wants you to leave her alone right now," he says, his voice dragging across the burning desert of my regret. "Just give her some time."

I respect her wishes, avoiding our usual hangout spots and calming my text messages to her. Whatever it takes to show her I understand the magnitude of what I've done.

When the school bell rings, I head home. Because of the uproar over my post, we received an email letting us know that the writing program was canceled this week. I think about going to see Grandma Alice, but I need to work this out alone. On the bus ride home, the events of the day loop like a broken film reel, the scene of Naima's betrayed expression burned into my memory.

I didn't mean for this to happen.

The silence that greets me in our empty apartment feels like my familiar lows from last spring and summer. My mom is still at work, and the sound of my footsteps seems to amplify my loneliness. I shut myself in my room, unable to eat, read, watch TV, or listen to music. All I can do is sit with the painful regret.

As the evening melts into night, my mind refuses to latch on to anything but Naima. I know I need to give her space, but my anxiety gets the better of me. Maybe Luis can tell me how she's doing.

ME: Hey, how is Naima?

ME: Hey

ME: What's good? You there?

ME: Everything okay?

The gaping hole of silence leaves me nervous. Luis, usually quick to answer texts, is nowhere to be found. The silence amplifies my unease, twisting my worry into a fearful knot.

ME: Luis?

ME: Luis . . .

I try calling him, but there's no answer. Just the lifeless sound of his voicemail.

My mind starts playing a terrible game of "What if," with me trapped in a maze of worst-case scenarios. Did something happen to Luis? Is Naima okay? In the midst of my frantic thoughts, a knock on my bedroom door cuts through, followed by my mother's voice.

"Ossie, come out here so we can talk."

I walk to the living room and have a seat on the couch. "Hey," I say, trying to play it cool.

"The school called today. About Naima's letter you posted," she begins, her tone soft, gentle, as if it's holding a carton of eggs. "Did she know before you posted it?"

My heart sinks, and I shake my head. "No. I thought she could be anonymous, Ma," I say, the words pouring out of me—words I never got to say to Naima. "I didn't include her name or her family's. I even changed the details about the protest where her dad was injured. I just wanted to amplify her voice and show the world what Ms. Hunt was helping us to become. I didn't realize—" My voice breaks. "I thought it would be okay. I thought I was doing a *good* thing."

Her sigh resonates with disappointment and understanding. "I figured it was like that," she says, then takes a second. "I'm guessing by now I don't need to give you some speech about why that was wrong."

"No." It's nearly a whisper.

"Good," she says, soft yet stern. "Well, I'm sure you were in your room trying to figure out what you should do to make things right. So I'll let you get back to that."

Her quick dismissal leaves me feeling disappointed and even more alone. No motherly wisdom, no guidance, nothing. So much for my Christmas gift being some sort of bridge between us.

As I drift toward my room, my mother adds, "And don't worry: I didn't read your letter or any of the other stuff they sent over."

"Huh? What are you talking about?" I ask, the hairs on the back of my neck immediately standing up.

She looks at me with surprise.

"The writing. The letters and stuff y'all worked on in the program," she explains, suddenly realizing she is sharing new information. "Some parents were worried about what students might have been working on in the writing program, so the administration emailed a link where we can access our children's writing. I feel bad for Ms. Hunt—they always do us like this."

My mother has my letter? Every parent has their kid's letter? Oh, my God . . .

And then an even more horrifying thought hits: *What if the links get into the wrong hands?*

I rush to my room and scramble for my phone. I find my social media overflowing with comments, posts, reactions. Among them, Luis's name stands out like a blazing fire in the night. His poem to Mateo, along with everyone else's words, is splashed across the screen for everyone to see. There's no way to know who shared it—who violated Luis's privacy or the other students' privacy. Or how they got access to the links. Maybe it was Matthew, or him and Morgan and Sydney working together. Maybe it was someone else, someone who was sent the links in private but decided to blast them to the world. But it doesn't really matter who did it or how; the damage has been done.

I'm horrified as I read what people have to say about Luis's raw vulnerability, his painfully honest love for Mateo, his insecurities about himself, his struggles with his identity. Most of the comments are filled with bigotry.

> How can he think that's okay to write about? Yuck.

> People like this should be ashamed of themselves. Sinners. All of them.

> I used to change near him in the locker room and thought he was looking at me funny. Probably had a crush on me.

There's a sickening rage burning in me. But the worst part is—I'm sure his parents know now, too. Know that Luis is gay. Know that he's in love with another boy.

I did this. My actions led to all of this.

I call him again, but just like before, his phone rings unanswered, then dumps me into the void of voicemail. Then I call again, and again. Eventually it doesn't ring at all.

I've been blocked.

The guilt eats my throat. I can't breathe.

I know the whole situation is my fault, but I can't understand why anyone would take it to this level. Why would someone be trying to hurt us? Destroying what has been a lifeline for us, a way to process the world and connect?

My eyes land on my dad's jersey hanging on my wall. I run a hand over the fabric, feeling the faint pulse of the memories it holds.

"I could really use you right now," I whisper to the empty room.

Chapter Twenty-Seven

When Monday comes, the world is gray and cold. I thought about skipping school, but that's cowardly. I'm gonna face this head-on.

I take the early bus. I want to make sure I get to Luis before first period. This time of morning, the streets look like a ghost town. Stores, apartments all quiet, tucked in, making me feel even more alone with the loud sound of the chaos I've caused.

Riding the bus, taking in the city as it wakes up, I can't stop thinking of Luis's parents. Wondering how they took it. When the bus groans to a halt, I hurry off.

"You're looking good, kid!" the driver calls after me. "That leg's healing up nice. Can't wait to see you back on the court."

"Appreciate it," I reply, the words slipping out in surprise. I've only met this driver a few times, since he drives way before I usually catch the bus, but he's right. I haven't even realized how well I've been moving recently.

I bolt off, my steps quick, heading up to the school. I'm so early that the school is all empty hallways and hushed classrooms. I sit on the floor right outside Luis's first class and cross my fingers that he will show up—and listen.

The bell rings; kids start pouring in. I'm scanning every face, but no sign of Luis.

Then I spot them. Luis and Naima, walking in from an unusual direction. Likely trying to avoid me. Luis's shoulders are sagged, and his eyes are as hollow as I've ever seen them; it's an obvious sadness that tugs at my soul. Naima has her arm around him, a silent gesture of love.

Seeing them approach, I jump to my feet. Their startled expressions tell me they didn't know I was sitting here.

I can feel Naima's eyes piercing through me like icicles. She exchanges some hushed words with Luis, their conversation drowned in the distance. Luis doesn't react as Naima hoped. She huffs, waves her arms in frustration, gives Luis a tight hug, then marches off. Disappearing back the way they came.

Naima's chilliness stings, but I know I earned it. I owe her space, and more. Still, it hurts.

Luis approaches. The heat of his emotions seems to radiate from his body, and even though I tower over him, it feels as if he's looking down on me. The silence grows, opening a crater beneath me.

"Luis, I . . ." My voice is a shaky whisper, echoing in the empty hallway. "I messed up. I didn't mean for this to happen."

"Messed up? *Messed up?* You've ruined my life, Ossie," he lashes back, each word a shard of glass.

"Listen, Luis," I plead. "I know I can't take back what people have said. But I swear to God, I'll go around and personally shut up every single person in this school if that helps."

His fierce gaze locks onto me, burning like embers in a raging fire. I try to meet his eyes, but it's like staring into the sun.

"My parents . . . they won't even talk to me," Luis says, his voice heavy with pain. "My mom texted me and called my sexuality a 'disgusting nightmare.'"

I'm desperate to find words that might soothe his pain, but I find none. "I . . . I wish I knew what else to say."

"'A disgusting nightmare,'" he repeats, his voice trembling.

"Luis . . . I'm so sorry," I say, reaching out to rest my hand on his shoulder. But he recoils, swatting my hand away as if it's a snake.

"Don't touch me!" he explodes. "You outed me, Ossie!"

"Luis, I didn't—" I begin, but he cuts me off.

"You *outed* me!" His words hit me like a tidal wave, made up of the tears now flowing down his cheeks. "Don't you ever speak to me again!"

And with that, he turns away, disappearing into his classroom, leaving me standing in the deserted hallway.

I spend the next few days giving Naima and Luis space at school. Knowing they are so physically close yet emotionally far is one of the most painful things I've ever been through.

Every time I see Naima, she shoots me a look that could turn ice into steam. Warning me to stay away at all costs. Luis, on the other hand, avoids my gaze completely. As if I don't even exist. If we were to bump into each other, I'm not sure he wouldn't pass right through me.

As the days drag by, the whole school seems to be buzzing more with gossip about the things people wrote in the program and what happened between me, Naima, and Luis. The rumors twist and turn, taking on a life of their own. Some people say that Luis's parents have disowned him; others say that the school is expelling me and Naima.

Being at Braxton feels like I am stuck in a fog, and outside isn't much better.

Grandma Alice has been calling me daily, but I don't pick up. I'm sure my mother has told her about what's going on. Which means she'll ask questions I don't have the answers to or tell me things about myself I'm pretty sure I already know. So I avoid seeing her, or anyone, even skipping out on Sunday dinners—which my mom has not been impressed by.

"You know what?" she said in my doorway one evening a few nights ago. "You're selfish. Hiding out like this again, when you know your grandmother wants to see you. Just selfish." She hasn't said anything to me since.

I spend most of my free time reading the terrible things people are saying on social media and in the news about everything happening. The words that spill from everyone's mouths and keyboards are like poison flowing into my brain. It is as if the world has turned against me, even more than it did after I got injured. But reading their horrible words, feeling this deep pain—it seems like atonement, the least I can do, since I'm to blame for all of it.

Fridays at the writing program meetings have become my own form of torture. It's like I'm stuck in a room full of mirrors, each one reflecting the mess I've made. I want to drop out of the program, vanish like a ghost, but I know I probably won't get into the schools I applied to if I do. The promise I made to Grandma Alice to try my best rings in my head. I can't add her to the list of people I've disappointed and hurt. So I just sit in the back, tucked away, as Mr. Richmond rambles on about all of the old dead white authors we have to read. Authors who would probably roll in their graves if they knew Black folks like me were even allowed to read.

In another part of the room sit Naima and Luis. They've formed an island away from me. They act as if I don't exist, as if I'm just a breeze that occasionally rustles their leaves. It's a silent punishment, one I can't argue against. I deserve it, but it doesn't make it any less painful.

And then there's Matthew, with his little smirk that he tosses over his shoulder at me every chance he gets. It's like he's got a ticker tape parade in his head, celebrating his victory over me. He knows he's got the upper hand, and he ain't afraid to show it.

The program, once a place of refuge and creativity, now feels like a prison. The words of the authors we study feel distant, irrelevant to the chaos of my life. The beauty of diverse literature, once so vivid and alive, now feels like a distant memory, a song played under water.

Days turn into weeks, spilling through my fingers like sand, as I'm anchored to a state of loneliness. Most days, I feel like a stranger in my own life, drifting through Braxton's hallways or hiding out in the four corners of my room, a hostage to my regret. Occasionally I stop by Grandma Alice's apartment, but when I do, I barely say anything. She seems to understand. She just puts on music and lets me do my homework or reading in peace.

I try to bury myself in the pages of Mr. Richmond's books, but it's so difficult. They feel as though they don't want me reading them. *A Farewell to Arms*, *The Catcher in the Rye*, *On the Road*. As I turn each page, there's an expected pattern. The words, the stories they tell, the voices they carry, are all rooted in the same places, the same perspectives. Stories of white people, by white people, for white people.

It's obvious that Mr. Richmond and the Braxton administration feel literature should only reflect their specific world. A world that they want to bleed into the rest of ours, muting all of our vibrance, our color.

Having these books replace what Ms. Hunt assigned is like Mr. Richmond whispering in my ears, telling me that I am not enough, that our voices are not important, that our stories are not worth telling. Even outside of all the other things I'm going through, these assignments make it almost impossible for me to have the same passion for writing that I had before.

And I'm not the only one in the program having an issue.

During the last meeting of January, the air in the room is thick with tension as multiple students, led by Naima and Luis, speak out against Mr. Richmond's lack of diversity in his book selections for Black History Month.

Naima's voice is the loudest. "Why are we only reading books by white men during the one month that's supposed to celebrate Blackness? Where are the books that reflect our experiences?"

Luis's voice is no less direct. "Yeah, I'm struggling with the assigned books because they all feel the same. How are we supposed to be great writers if we don't broaden our horizons and learn from various types of authors?"

At first, Mr. Richmond sits silently at his desk, his face a mask of indifference. But when others nod in agreement, Mr. Richmond breaks.

"The focus of this program is not on performing for some kind of liberal approval because it's a specific time of year," he snaps. "My job is to make better writers, and it's obvious by how you continue carrying on that that goal will be impossible for some of you!"

We're stunned into silence. I feel as if I should speak up.

"Mr. Richmond, Naima's right. I think it's unfair—" I begin, but Naima stops me.

"I don't need your help, Ossie!"

She turns her sights back to Mr. Richmond. "Assigning books like *Catcher in the Rye* during Black History Month feels racist."

Mr. Richmond's eyes narrow. "Watch yourself, Naima!"

"It's the truth!"

"Here we go!" Matthew chimes in. "The school is racist, the books are racist, hell, I'm sure the cafeteria food is racist in Naima's opinion! Everything is racist."

Anger surges within me. I want to respond to Matthew, but I also want to respect Naima's wishes. Thankfully, Luis steps in.

"Why don't you shut the hell up, Matthew?" Luis yells, springing from his seat.

Matthew trembles with rage as he jumps up. "What exactly are you going to do? Kiss me to death, you f—t?"

As soon as the words leave Matthew's mouth, Luis lunges at him. I jump out of my seat and hold Luis back.

"He's not worth it!" I yell, trying to calm Luis down. "He's not worth it!"

The room is a frenzy of commotion, as Matthew now tries to lunge at Luis while I'm holding him back. As we struggle, Morgan stands up and points a shaking finger at Luis.

"Mr. Richmond, do something! He's going to kill him!"

"Luis, sit down before I call security on you!" Mr. Richmond's voice booms like an explosion.

Naima stands up as well. "See! You're threatening to call security on Luis but not Matthew, the one who started this! That's the exact kind of racism I've been talking about!"

Mr. Richmond's eyes are sharp, like those of an animal about to pounce, glaring at Naima.

"Enough with your accusations!" he bellows. "Sit down, Naima, or you'll be the one dragged out of here by security!"

"Call them! Get them both out of here!" Morgan yells.

Naima turns to her. "If you don't shut up, I'll give him a *real* reason to call them!"

Morgan is taken aback. "Are you threatening to hurt me?"

"No. I'm promising you," Naima says, her jaw clenched. "Say another word and I'm going to drag you down these RACIST halls by that stringy mop you call hair!"

Morgan's eyes widen in response to Naima's words, which shake the classroom like an earthquake.

"You will not threaten to be violent with anyone in this program!" Mr. Richmond is stern and uncompromising. "Get out!"

"Gladly."

The rest of us watch in stunned silence as Naima gathers her things and makes her way toward the door. Luis begins to grab his bag and coat as well.

"I'm good, Luis. Trust me, it's better if you stay," Naima says.

Luis looks at her, searching for any sign of hesitation or doubt. "Are you sure?"

Naima meets his gaze with a calm and steady one of her own. "Yeah, I'm sure."

She walks to the door, places her hand on the knob, then turns back to Mr. Richmond.

"You aren't half the person or educator Ms. Hunt is," she says. "And this is definitely not over."

Then she walks out the room, the door slamming shut behind her.

The next week, Dean Blackburn begins an investigation into what happened, reiterating numerous times over email that she "won't let this program or our school devolve into chaos because of a few bad apples." I figure the "bad apples" are me, Naima, and Luis. Regardless, as much as she wants to avoid chaos, it's exactly what everything has turned into.

At the next writing program meeting, Dean Blackburn shows up.

Her eyes are on me and Luis, scanning our faces like we're prey. The room is quiet and tense when she begins speaking.

"I've had a discussion with Mr. Richmond about what happened last Friday," she says. "But before I make any decisions—"

"What sorts of decisions will you be making?" Sydney asks, interrupting Dean Blackburn. Though she doesn't seem to mind.

Dean Blackburn takes a moment, as if she wants to make sure we all truly understand the gravity of what she is about to say. "I'll be making the decision as to who will be permanently removed from the Mark Twain Writing Program and potentially suspended from school because of last week's incident."

Matthew, Sydney, and Morgan exchange a gleeful look, as if their master plan is working. My stomach clenches with fear for Luis and Naima.

"As I was saying," Dean Blackburn continues, shooting a quelling look at the celebrating Three Musketeers, "before any decisions are made, I want to hear from all of you. I want to know how and why this happened, from each of your vantage points. I'll be calling each of you into my office to discuss the matter next Wednesday."

In the days leading up to the interviews, the hallways hum with rumors about what's going to happen. But there is one thing that seems consistent: everyone is sure that Naima and Luis are going to be kicked out of the program and suspended. As if the context of the moment doesn't matter. As if Matthew being homophobic is irrelevant.

Thankfully, those rumors apparently made their way to Naima and her parents as well. Her parents and their attorney sent an email to Dean Blackburn, the school board, and every parent with a student in the writing program, demanding that Mrs. Wright is present to help oversee each of the interviews. They also mentioned that the attorney would be joining Naima and Luis during their interviews.

When the day of reckoning arrives, the air everywhere in the school is thick with anticipation. I feel my heart thumping against my chest as I near the door to Dean Blackburn's office. I'm one of the last people to be interviewed, and I can't help but wonder what everyone else has said.

As I enter the room, I spot Luis. He's walking out with the attorney Naima's parents hired. Our gazes lock for a brief moment, and when they do, I nod at him so he knows I've got his back. Surprisingly, he nods back.

The moment is brief and may seem small, but for me it's like a lifeline.

The room feels smaller than usual, even though it's only me, Dean Blackburn, and Mrs. Wright. I give Mrs. Wright a slight smile to acknowledge her, but she doesn't reciprocate.

Dean Blackburn clears her throat. "I must say, Ossie, I'm deeply disappointed about this whole situation. Especially after you and Naima refused to make the public statement I asked for. I could have punished you both then, but instead I chose to smooth things over," she says, her eyes latched on me.

"I don't think we should have been asked to make a statement in the first place," I reply, trying to keep my voice even. "Everything Naima wrote about Braxton is true, even if you don't want to believe it." As soon as I finish responding, Mrs. Wright types something in her laptop.

"And everything that happened the other day was Matthew's fault," I continue.

"Matthew's fault? And how is that?" Dean Blackburn asks, arching an eyebrow in confusion. Though I'm sure Naima and Luis have already told her the same thing.

"He called Luis a homophobic slur," I respond, my voice unflinching. "Luis was just defending himself, and then Naima was standing up for him, pointing out how problematic it was that Mr. Richmond was threatening to call security on Luis but not on Matthew, even though he started it all."

Mrs. Wright interjects, her fingers pausing on her keyboard. "Can you tell us more about what sparked the confrontation? What led to Matthew calling Luis—"

"*Allegedly* calling Luis," Dean Blackburn interrupts.

"Allegedly calling Luis a slur?" Mrs. Wright finishes.

I pause, considering my words carefully. "Well, I guess it started when Naima asked Mr. Richmond why we aren't reading any Black books during Black History Month. Though I'd like to add that when Ms. Hunt was here, it didn't have to be a special month to read work by Black people."

Mrs. Wright doesn't respond but begins to take notes again.

"But didn't Mr. Richmond explain that the books he has assigned are the ones best positioned to help you all succeed?" Dean Blackburn asks, her tone sharp. "I've seen his reading list—he's exposing you to American literary icons."

I can't help but feel like a criminal on trial, my every word scrutinized and dissected, the prosecution waiting for me to slip up.

"Well, that's subjective," I respond, shifting in my seat.

"Excuse me?" Dean Blackburn says, obviously surprised.

"What makes someone like Hemingway more of an American icon than someone like Baldwin? And what makes Steinbeck more iconic than Morrison—who has a Pulitzer and a Nobel Prize?"

"Are you saying that you shouldn't have to read authors who are widely considered American heroes?" Dean Blackburn asks.

"I'm saying the books we were reading with Ms. Hunt *were* by American heroes and that they *were* positioning us for success, and we should still be reading them. Especially during Black History Month. And that was all Naima was saying, too."

From the corner of my eye, I catch Mrs. Wright subtly nodding her head while typing.

"Even so," Dean Blackburn says in a tone that makes it clear she's done trying to argue that point with me, "Braxton Academy is not a place where we use threats of violence instead of discourse. If Naima or Luis felt strongly about their convictions, they should have found an amicable solution."

"Okay, so what about the time Matthew pushed me in the hall-way but security only approached *me*? And what about the fact that Matthew called Luis a horrible slur, yet Mr. Richmond was threatening to call security on *Luis*? Why does Braxton only consider something a threat of violence when it comes from Black or brown students?" I say, wondering if my words are going to get me kicked out of the program and suspended, too—but knowing I have to say them.

"What about the emotional and mental violence that *actually* happens to many students here?" I say, knowing that at this point I might as well say it all. "Receiving homophobic slurs isn't violence? Erasing Black and brown experiences isn't violence? Firing one of the few Black teachers right before Black History Month because she taught Black authors isn't violence?"

"Mm-hmm." Mrs. Wright lifts her head from her laptop screen, realizing from our expressions that she was louder than she thought. Dean Blackburn shoots her a look of disapproval.

I can feel Dean Blackburn's irritation bearing down on me, but whatever comes of it, I'm happy I held my ground.

"Thank you for your time today, Ossie," Dean Blackburn says, unable to hide her annoyance. "You can head to your next class."

After the interview, I'm extremely nervous. Not sure whether what I said was helpful or harmful for Naima and Luis or what's going to happen to any of us. But the next morning, Dean Blackburn sends a surprising email that says in light of a massive disparity in students' opinions of what took place, no one will be removed from the program or suspended from school.

I'm both relieved that nothing will happen to Naima or Luis and frustrated that nothing will happen to Matthew for his homophobia. But of course, what should I have expected?

That night, all I can think about is how the next day is going to be me and Naima's first Valentine's Day together. For weeks I've wondered how Naima would react if I got her something for the holiday, but I don't test the question. Instead, I do the one thing I can think to let her and Luis know how I feel: I spend the evening adding songs to the Bali playlist, which they seem to have forgotten to kick me off of, hoping the songs say all the things I can't.

"Thinkin Bout You" by Frank Ocean

"How I Feel" by Thundercat

"Come Home" by Anderson .Paak (feat. André 3000)

"Put on a Smile" by Silk Sonic

"Distance" by Yebba

"Are We Still Friends?" by Tyler, the Creator

Chapter Twenty-Eight

The next day, when the final bell rings, I walk to the English Lab for the writing program meeting. Naima is standing in front of the door to the room holding a cardboard sign with bright letters that reads STILL I WILL RISE.

"We matter, too!" she proclaims. "Bring back Ms. Hunt! Bring back our books! We matter, too! Bring back Ms. Hunt! Bring back our books!"

Naima's chant meets the ears of everyone in the packed hallway, bouncing off the lockers in rhythmic pulses. She's holding the sign high above her head.

Luis walks up and whispers something to her. But she responds in a volume everyone can hear, "I don't care, Luis. I'm done with the program. I have to do this."

He sighs deeply. "Fine. I hear you, Nai." They share a tight embrace before Luis heads into the room.

Naima obviously has no interest in letting Braxton pretend like everything that has happened is fine.

As I'm walking past her and into the room, I keep my head low, trying to avoid eye contact that might frustrate her. But then I hear the sweetest four words.

"Ossie. Can we talk?"

Naima pulls me to the side of the hallway, away from the other students trickling into the room. Her eyes are locked on mine, intense, like she's reading all my thoughts. I feel my heart pounding in my ears as she starts talking.

"I saw the songs you added," she says. "Luis and I listened to them last night."

I nod, finding it hard to speak. "I'm glad you heard them." There's this pause hanging heavy between us, and I don't know if I should fill it with words or let it be.

Eventually, Naima breaks the silence. "You really hurt me, Ossie. I didn't tell you about my father or let you read my letter so you could share it with other people. Now my father has to deal with the media calling him a liar all over again. You reopened a wound that had barely healed."

I swallow, feeling like I have a boulder in my throat. "I know," I say. "I'm sorry for hurting you, and putting your dad through that. I never wanted to. I was just trying to help you and Ms. Hunt. I thought I was trying to amplify your writing and let people know what an amazing teacher she is and how unfair what happened to her was."

"I know," she says, soft but firm. "But you were also trying to make yourself feel better about the things Mateo's friends were saying."

I'll be honest: my instinct is to deny it. To tell her *and* myself that that had nothing to do with it. But I force myself to confront the truth of her words. I owe her that much. "You're right," I admit. Because as much as I wanted to amplify her words and support Ms. Hunt, I also wanted to feel like I was doing something that made me feel good.

Made me feel like I wasn't on the sidelines of change, like Mateo's friends accused me of being.

Naima takes a deep breath, then says, "And that's what's hard. Because even though I don't think you wanted to hurt me, the fact is you *did* hurt me. And you hurt my father. If you hadn't been so focused on making this Big Thing about supporting me, trying to get activism clout or whatever—if you had just *talked* to me before posting anything—none of this would have happened. And I'm only having this conversation because I have these feelings for you and as much as I want them to—they won't go away."

My heart skips a beat, a flicker of hope sparking inside me. Until she continues speaking.

"But I can't trust you, Ossie. And I don't know what to do with a person I care about so deeply but trust so little."

I'm desperate now, grasping at straws. "I can fix this—I can fix us."

Naima shakes her head. "There is no us anymore. That can't be fixed. But I wanted to thank you for the songs—and ask you not to add any more."

There are so many words sitting in my throat like stones at the bottom of a lake. But I don't know how to grasp them—or if it would change anything if I did.

She gives me this sad smile, like a true good-bye, then she walks away to continue her protest. I stand there, feeling worse than ever, like I'm watching some beautiful flower wilt into nothingness. And I can't do anything to stop it.

"We matter, too! Bring back Ms. Hunt! Bring back our books! We matter, too! Bring back Ms. Hunt! Bring back our books!"

I walk into the English Lab and take a seat. The mood in the room is a mix of awkwardness and animosity. Mr. Richmond clears his throat. "We are going to ignore Naima's distraction—unless some of you want to go out there and also become former students of this program."

No one moves. So Mr. Richmond continues with the program as Naima's chants act as a soundtrack playing in the distance for the entire meeting.

As we leave the room, Naima's still going. Mr. Richmond walks out and shakes his head in disbelief. "This is not productive, Naima," he says, his tone laced with anger.

"Nah," Naima responds. "I think it's *mad* productive, *homie*."

Mr. Richmond huffs, then walks away.

Naima begins protesting in front of the English Lab every Friday. Each week with the same chant, new signs, and insider information from Luis about what books we are reading so she can make points about the focus on whiteness.

"This book has the n-word in it over two hundred times!" Naima waves a copy of *The Adventures of Huckleberry Finn* at passing students. The book we are currently reading. "Why do students of color have to read books that might make us uncomfortable because of racism, but white students don't have to read books that might make them uncomfortable because they *confront* racism?"

Even though Naima's not in the class to hear it, Mr. Richmond addresses the topic of authors using racial slurs in their writing, and it's like he's thrown a match into gasoline.

Luis and I, for the first time in what feels like forever, find ourselves on the same side of the argument. On the opposite end are—no surprise—Matthew, Morgan, Sydney, and Mr. Richmond, defending the use of these slurs as "literary tools" or "historical accuracy."

"It's about the context," Matthew argues condescendingly. "You can't just censor history."

"But it's not just history, is it?" Luis fires back. "It's about the here and now. How those words make people feel today."

"Exactly!" I chime in. "There are plenty of other books that capture this time in American history without degrading Black people."

Mr. Richmond shakes his head. "It's not about degradation; it's about authenticity and courage."

The debate rages on, words clashing like swords, but no ground is gained.

Meanwhile, Naima continues to protest outside the English Lab.

Her energy is contagious, and with each passing week, more and more people begin to listen. Some even ask what books she would recommend in solidarity. Others watch from the sidelines but post videos and photos of her online, which helps influence people to join her.

By the first writing program meeting of March, Naima and about ten other students are outside the English Lab, holding up signs, chanting, and handing out free books by authors who are Black, brown, queer, or disabled and any other examples of what Mr. Richmond is refusing to assign. Taped on the wall behind them is a sign that reads:

CHANGING THE THINGS I CANNOT ACCEPT

—*ANGELA DAVIS*

After the meeting, Laura is in the hallway meeting Matthew. He's standing across from Naima and the others, looking like he wants to spit on them. Laura looks uncomfortable, listening to their chants.

"Matthew, can we please go? We have dinner with my parents," she pleads.

Matthew, red-faced and furious, snaps, "No. These snowflakes think they should be able to control everyone's free speech. They're trying to cancel *Mark Twain*, one of the greatest writers in American history!

You're a minority, too, Laura. What do you think? Does it hurt your feelings when Mark Twain uses a word that was used all the time in his day?"

Laura scans the faces around her. Then her eyes land on me, and there's a flicker of understanding.

"I think if people are telling you that something hurts them, it's not okay to ignore those people."

Matthew looks like he's been slapped. "You're agreeing with *him*?" he asks, glaring at me.

All I can do is smile, feeling like I finally got a win on him. And then, surprisingly, Luis makes eye contact with me and smiles, too. It's a small moment, but it feels like a bridge being rebuilt.

Matthew, unable to contain his fury, just says, "Fine," and storms off. Laura rushes after him. I'm going to replay that moment in my mind for a long time.

Over the weekend, as I'm in my room trying to make my way through various homework assignments, I notice I've been tagged on social media in posts about an opinion piece in a huge media outlet that's gone viral. It's titled "Is Wokeness Destroying Education?"

The piece is almost all about Naima and her protest. The writer of the article spouts nothing but lies, suggesting that students like Naima have been indoctrinated by anti-white curriculum and books taught by people such as Ms. Hunt. He says that the books we were reading are nothing more than propaganda, designed to build a "victim mentality" in "minority communities."

The end of the piece says:

America's great institutions, such as Braxton Academy, are in danger of being scorched to nothingness by the wildfires of wokeness if the blaze is not put out immediately. True patriots need to work just as hard as the woke mob to end the unfounded protests in favor of hatred-focused teachings. All you have to do is read the viral letter she wrote to see that people such as Naima Johnson not only hate America; they also hate the police who are risking their lives daily to protect it. To protect her. This isn't about one school—this is about our nation's legacy.

My blood is boiling as soon as I finish reading the article, but not as much as it is when I see who wrote it:

Ronald Henley, PhD
Professor of American Literature
Columbia University

My grip tightens with so much rage, I'm surprised my phone doesn't turn to dust.

THIS SHIT WAS WRITTEN BY MR. RICHMOND'S FRIEND! MORGAN'S FATHER!

Naima has probably read this garbage, too, and she's probably hurting. I want to reach out, to tell her that I am here for her, to say again how sorry I am for having pushed over the first domino of all this. But I think about the boundary she has put up. If I really care about her, I have to respect the walls she has built between us.

I put my phone down.

When I arrive at Braxton the next day, there are reporters huddled outside the school. The article has turned the place into a zoo.

"Hey, Ossie! This way! Would you answer a few questions about claims of a woke agenda here at Braxton?"

"How does it feel to be on people's minds again after your injury?"

"Looks like your leg is healing well. Any chance of stepping away from writing and back onto a court?"

"You haven't joined Naima Johnson's protest or said anything about it publicly. Is that your way of making a point that you disagree with her stance? Are you on the side of the other student activists saying that your old teacher was anti-white?"

As I ignore the reporters' questions and the clicking of cameras on my way to the front doors, I'm worried about Naima. And then when half the day passes and I haven't seen her or Luis at all, I'm even more worried.

I decide to walk to Luis's locker in hopes of seeing him. Thankfully, he's there. He looks up as I approach him. I can see the tension in his jaw, the way his shoulders are hunched up by his ears. Something's definitely wrong. Besides the fact that he hates me.

"Hey," I say, trying to sound casual. "Is Naima okay? I haven't seen her all day . . ."

Luis shakes his head slowly. "No, she's not," he says. "Her parents kept her out of school today."

"Why?" I ask, my heart sinking. "What's going on?"

Luis sighs. "Like an hour after Morgan's father's article came out, Naima started getting death threats on social media. And then yesterday someone threw a brick through her living room window."

"What?" I ask in a panic. "Is everyone okay?"

"No one got hurt, if that's what you mean," Luis begins, shaking his head in frustration. "But even though they called the cops, no one came. Her parents think the cops are refusing to protect them because of what she wrote in the letter about them."

"Shit. Is there anything I can do?"

"I think you've done enough."

I don't respond. What can I even say?

"Look, I've been with her all day and just came in because I can't miss calculus," he says, closing his locker. "I'd appreciate it if you'd leave me alone." He walks off.

I feel powerless—useless.

When I walk through my bedroom door after school, I plop onto my bed and stare at the ceiling. My mind races with all of the things people are saying about Naima, the danger I've put her family in. I become more and more angry.

I stand up and look around my room, the walls lined with glimmers of a past that feels like a distant dream. Trophies, medals, certificates — they all stare back at me, mocking reminders of a time when things were simpler. My chest heaves, my breaths broken, and without a second thought, I sweep the trophies off the shelf. The sound of metal and glass clattering against the floor echoes through the room like a hailstorm. Each crash a release, each shatter a tiny bit of the anger inside me bleeding out.

I walk from one shelf to the next, my movements mechanical, robotic. Awards that once meant the world to me now just feel like anchors, pulling me down into an abyss of frustration and guilt. The walls, once a museum of my achievements, now look like a battlefield, littered with debris of a life I'm not sure I even recognize anymore.

Then my eyes land on it. Dad's jersey. For a moment, my hand hovers, the urge to tear it down almost overwhelming. But I can't. Instead, I just stand there, staring at it.

Tears blur my vision, warm and relentless. I don't bother wiping them away. I'm wrecked, lost in a sea of emotions with no land in sight. The weight of everything — the article, Naima, the protest, the threats — it all feels like too much.

I sink to the floor, my back against the wall, knees drawn up to my chest. The sobs come in heaves, each one a physical ache. Time slips away like the evening sun. Eventually, exhaustion takes over and I sleep, right on the floor amid the ruin of my past glory.

I'm not sure how long I've been asleep, but the ring of my phone cuts through the haze. I jolt awake, disoriented, the remnants of tears still sticky on my cheeks. I fumble for the phone, my heart pounding, hoping, praying it's Naima. But when I see the caller ID, my heart sinks.

"Hello?" My voice is hoarse, tired.

"Hey," Laura responds tentatively. She's clearly nervous.

"What do you want, Laura?" She's the last person on earth I want to be speaking to.

"I don't want to keep you," she says. "But I think Matthew's up to something."

I sit up, shaking off the remnants of sleep. "What do you mean?"

Laura hesitates, the silence stretching like a tightrope. "I don't know exactly, but he's been angry. Especially since Friday. You know, when I agreed with you."

I nod, even though she can't see me. "Yeah, I remember."

"I saw him on some encrypted messaging app, talking about an event at Braxton this Friday. Like a protest or something. I don't know what's going on."

I rub my face, trying to wake up fully. "Protesting what? He already won."

"I don't know," she says. "He seems *off* recently. Anyway, I just thought you should know."

I take a deep breath, feeling the gears in my head start to turn. "Cool, thanks for the heads-up."

There's a quiet, as if she's expecting me to say something else. But I have nothing more to say. She finally gets the hint.

"Okay, then. Bye, Ossie," she says, and the line goes dead.

I sleep on the information Laura gave me, wondering whether I should say something to Naima at school, but for the second day in a row, she's not there. Eventually, I decide Luis is probably my best bet.

> ME: Hey Luis. If you're at school today . . . can we talk?

A few seconds after I send the text, I see an ellipsis pop up in our chat, showing that Luis is typing a response. But then it disappears. I give him a few minutes to see if he'll respond, but when he doesn't, I follow up.

> ME: I know you hate me. But I REALLY need to talk to you

Twenty minutes after that text, he still doesn't respond.

> ME: I'm not going to stop texting you. Because like Eragon said "There is always hope"

I wait for a few minutes before getting ready to send my next text, but before I do, Luis finally responds.

LUIS: It's Aragorn* . . . and it's cheating to use LOTR quotes

> ME: Whatever it takes, my precious

LUIS: *eye roll emoji*

LUIS: What do you want?

> ME: I need to fill you in on something. It might be nothing, but . . .

> ME: Are you here today? It will just take a few minutes

LUIS: Fine. If it will get you to stop butchering things from my favorite movies

LUIS: Meet me at the football field after my sixth-period gym class

ME: I'll be there

Chapter Twenty-Nine

I arrive at the football field and sit on the bleachers just as Luis is finishing a game of flag football. I've never seen Luis play sports before, and I'm surprised by how good he is. It makes it more impressive that he's just choosing to tap into other things instead—though I can imagine it's a source of frustration for his father.

As the game finishes, he spots me and makes his way over, his eyes narrow and his face firm. When he arrives, he stands at the bottom of the bleachers and looks up at me. The sun is beaming down on us, creating shadows across the yard lines on the field.

"So what did you want to talk to me about?" he asks, his voice distant and sharp.

I hesitate for a moment in the face of his indifference before I gather my courage and fill him in on what Laura said.

"I just think someone ought to warn Naima," I say. "And since she doesn't want to hear from me . . ."

"I'll tell her, but she's still gonna keep goin'," Luis says finally.

"Should I—?" I stop, not sure if it's fair to ask him the question. But when he snaps an annoyed "What?" I feel like I have to continue.

"Should I tell someone? Like Mrs. Wright or someone else in the administration? I mean, it could be nothing, but what if—?"

"Sure, go ahead and tell them. But they probably won't do anything, since all you know is that some people *might* protest. And realistically, Matthew's nonsense isn't going to make Naima back down."

He turns and begins walking away, leaving me sitting there, feeling the chill of his coldness covering me as if it's not a sunny afternoon.

Suddenly, my feet start moving, almost on their own. My knee is feeling surprisingly okay as I jump down from the bleachers and run after him. "Luis, wait!"

He stops and turns around, his eyes fixed on me. "What?"

"I wish I could take it all back," I begin, desperation creeping into my voice. "If I could take all the pain I've caused you and hold all of it for you—I would. In a heartbeat. You mean so much to me, and it kills me knowing I hurt you, that I caused others to hurt you, too. Knowing that I caused you to hate me."

There is a long pause between us, the only sound the distant chatter of students on the other side of the field. Finally, Luis speaks.

"I don't hate you, Ossie," he says, his voice softening. "I'm hurt—and angry. But I don't hate you."

"I know how hurt you are, and I—" I begin, before Luis interrupts.

"No. *No, you don't,*" he says, shaking his head in irritation and sadness. "You could never know how this feels. The whole school and half the country know I'm gay. And it wasn't my choice. My parents don't speak to me anymore. And I've been sleeping in Naima's parents' guest room for weeks. You don't know how hurt I am."

The truth is as loud as thunder in my mind—there's nothing I can say or do to fix the hurt I've caused him. There's no way for me to feel the depth of his suffering. But there's something I can give him—if he'll accept it.

"I love you, Luis. And I'm sorry," I say, soft and tender.

"I don't care." He scowls at me. "I'm so mad at you, Ossie!"

I nod but stand firm. "I love you, Luis. And I'm sorry."

He fights to keep his scowl in place, but slowly his expression crumples. "It hurts so bad, Ossie."

"I love you, Luis. And I'm sorry," I whisper.

"It hurts so bad," he says again, and the pain in his voice cracks my heart in two.

And I say it again, my apology now a promise: "I love you, Luis—and I am so, *so* sorry."

Tears stream down Luis's cheeks, and I step forward, my arms as wide open as my heart. The world seems to hold its breath, waiting to see what Luis will do, and then—he embraces me. I hold him tight, hoping he can feel how much I mean every word. We linger like that, somewhere between the hurt I've caused him and the opportunity for a stronger brotherhood going forward.

Luis eventually pulls away gently, shakes his head, and looks up at me. "Fine. I guess I love you, too," he mutters as he wipes his tears.

"What was that?" I ask jokingly.

He rolls his eyes. "You heard me, Ossie."

"Nope, I don't think I heard you, *my precious*!" I say, doing a terrible impression of Gollum from *The Lord of the Rings*.

"Please stop," Luis says as he begins walking away—slowly enough to be an invitation.

"Stop what, *my precious*?" I continue as I walk beside him.

"Seriously, Ossie! You suck at that!"

"Oh, do I? What about this one?" I say in my best Gandalf voice.

"Okay . . . That's not bad." Luis laughs. The sound is the sweetest music.

. . .

Now that we're talking again, Luis finds time to fill me in on what Naima and her parents have been going through since that article went viral. He says her parents want to keep her out of school for the next few weeks at least, to make sure she's safe.

"It's bad, Ossie."

"What happened now?" I ask, fearing what he's about to say.

"Me and her dad spent all night trying to get paint off her mom's car." Luis sighs. "Her father was able to get private security for the house, but someone found her mom's car parked at the hospital where she works and spray-painted the n-word on it."

How can people be so horrible? How can people want to hurt Naima and her family just for speaking up about the racism they've faced? I can't explain how angry I am knowing that Morgan's father didn't care about what could happen to Naima after he wrote that piece, calling out a seventeen-year-old by name, basically inviting people to threaten her, intimidate her. Maybe even hurt her.

The one consolation is that since Naima is staying home, I don't have to worry about whatever nonsense Matthew might be planning. Luis and I each search online for information about a protest on Friday, but we can't find anything. Still, I let Mrs. Wright know what Laura told me, and she promises to alert Dean Blackburn. Luis tells Naima about what Laura said, too, just in case. But we're both breathing easier knowing she's safely at home.

When Friday afternoon comes around, Luis and I head to the English Lab together.

"Do you think Naima would be mad, knowing you're talking to me again?"

"Oh, she knows," Luis says. "I told her I was going to try and give you a chance."

"What did she say?"

He shrugs. "Not much. With everything going on, her mind is on a lot of things. But I do know she's confused about her feelings for you. She—"

His words cut off abruptly. There's a voice, a familiar one, floating down the hallway, weaving its way around the corner from the direction of the English Lab. We exchange a look, then break into a half-jog, half-run.

As we round the corner, we see her: Naima, standing alone with one of her signs.

"We matter, too! Bring back Ms. Hunt! Bring back our books! We matter, too! Bring back Ms. Hunt! Bring back our books!"

Luis steps forward. "Nai, what are you doing here? You're supposed to be at home to stay safe."

"I'm not scared of those people. If I stop protesting, they win," Naima says, glaring at Mr. Richmond through the window of the English Lab door.

"Nai, please. It's not safe. You gotta leave."

But Naima is immovable, her eyes fiery and determined. "No, Luis. I won't run. I won't hide. This is bigger than me."

I can see the conflict in Luis's expression, the battle between his concern for her safety and his respect for her courage. He wants to protect her, but how do you shield a fire that refuses to be contained?

Students begin streaming into the room, their eyes landing on Naima, her sign, her unyielding stance. Some stop, some whisper, some just keep walking. But they can clearly all feel it—the electricity in the air, the kind that raises hairs and wakes up minds.

Naima's voice rises above the murmurs, her chant steady and strong: "We matter, too! Bring back Ms. Hunt! Bring back our books!"

Suddenly, Morgan walks up, flanked by Matthew and Sydney.

As soon as Naima spots her, she lowers her sign and fixes Morgan with a stare that could cut glass. All the hurt, all the anger, all the dislike Naima is feeling about what Morgan's father wrote in the article is contained in that gaze.

Morgan tries to pretend like everything's normal, but the tension can't be ignored. I'm holding my breath, waiting to see what Naima will do. Will she lash out? Will she confront Morgan?

But Naima doesn't say anything. She just stands there, her eyes locked on Morgan, until the trio quickly heads into the room—each of them trying to act nonchalant, as if they can't feel the heat radiating from Naima's smoldering glare. Cowards.

Luis and I don't want to leave Naima, but the meeting is about to start. So the two of us reluctantly walk in behind them. The room is filled with murmurs, the clatter of chairs, the rustling of papers. But all that background noise seems to fade when we step inside. Maybe it's the tension from outside still lingering around us, or maybe it's just everything that's gone down in the past week.

As soon as Luis and I take our seats, Matthew stands up. "Can I run to the bathroom?"

Mr. Richmond nods. "Fine, but be quick about it. We've got a lot to discuss."

Matthew hurries out, and Mr. Richmond clears his throat. "All right, everyone, let's get started. As I said, we have a lot to discuss today."

As the meeting kicks off, I notice the other students checking their phones, then exchanging nervous glances with one another. Adam looks up from his phone, his eyes darting between me and Luis.

Adam makes a face as if he's thinking. Considering. Then he gets up and heads our way.

Mr. Richmond sees him. "Take your seat, Adam."

"Mr. Richmond, Ossie and Luis have to see this."

"Whatever it is, it can wait," Mr. Richmond responds sternly.

Adam insists, "No, you don't understand. This is important. I think something is about to happen to Naima."

Mr. Richmond's eyebrows furrow in frustration. "I have heard all about the empty internet threats Miss Johnson has received. She will be fine. Either sit down or you can find yourself outside with her, chanting nonsense."

As if on cue, we hear Naima's chants echoing in the background: "We matter, too! Bring back Ms. Hunt! Bring back our books! We matter, too! Bring back Ms. Hunt! Bring back our books!"

That seems to settle it for Adam. He hurries over to me and Luis, holding up his phone.

"GET OUT, ADAM!" Mr. Richmond bellows.

"Just a sec, Mr. Richmond!" Adam places the phone in front of us. On the screen, there's a flyer:

STAND AGAINST WOKENESS
IN OUR SCHOOLS
— FRIDAY, MARCH 14 —
—-- 3:45 P.M. --—
Braxton Academy
152 Larimey St.
Scarsdale, NY 10583

Join us as we come together to advocate for maintaining American traditions in light of the woke agenda taking over Braxton Academy and our great nation.

I look up from the phone and see the fear in Adam's eyes. "My brother is on the baseball team and got this from a teammate. It started being shared in a few secret online chats last period. Supposedly, some students are sneaking these guys into the school."

Guys? What guys?

A cold realization washes over me.

This is today.

I look up at the clock on the wall.

This is NOW.

Suddenly, Naima's chants outside stop, replaced by a distant, unfamiliar sound. It's low, but it makes the hairs on the back of my neck stand tall, like soldiers called to attention. The room falls quiet.

No . . .

Naima!

I'm up and out of my seat. Luis, too. Before we can get to the door, the sound has grown closer. The walls begin to shake. A new chant—louder, angrier—fills the hallway.

"This is our nation! Don't tread on us! This is our nation! Don't tread on us!"

The voices boom through my bones, striking a sort of fear in me I've never felt before.

I yank open the door, desperate to make sure Naima is safe—and what I see stops me dead in my tracks, eyes wide with horror.

At least forty chanting white men—their faces hidden behind bandannas, masks, hats, and dark glasses—are walking down the hall toward Naima, who stands alone, like a wooden shack in the way of a tornado. They march, a sea of yellow and black clothing, American flags waving in their fists, their rage terrifying. Here and there, DON'T TREAD ON ME flags snap in the air, and some hold signs reading WOKE STOPS NOW!

"That's her right there!" one man cries, his finger jabbing at the air like a knife.

Then I finally see it: the fear in Naima's eyes, telling the truth about the invisible tremors running through her body.

The three of us stand there, frozen.

Mr. Richmond bursts out the door, the other students spilling behind him, their faces full of shock. None of us can believe this is happening.

Five security guards come pounding down the stairs, the sound like a stampede of wild horses. They form a line between us and the oncoming horde and demand the men leave. Their voices are firm but with notable undertones of fear. But the men don't back down. It's as if their rage and sheer numbers make them a force of nature—destined to wash us away.

"We're not going anywhere!" one man bellows, like a battle cry.

"Make us!" another snarls at the security guards, his face twisted in defiance.

A third man points at Naima and spits out, "Get that Black bitch!"

Three of the guards advance toward the mob while the other two stay close to Naima and the rest of us. One of the guards holds up a palm. "Stop or we will call the police!"

One of the men lunges forward, his fist connecting with the guard's jaw. "The cops ain't coming!"

My body is flooded with panic. They aren't going to stop until they turn Naima into an example.

My hand finds Naima's arm, my grip firm. "Run!" I yell, and I pull her with me as I begin sprinting away from the mob. Luis is right next to us. The rest of the students follow suit, along with Mr. Richmond.

Behind us, the mob surges forward, roaring like an animal in a frenzy. As we run from them, the two security guards rush to join the others. But I don't look back, because I know what the result will be.

There's not enough security.

We tear toward the exit at the end of the hallway, joined by other students and teachers who are in other after-school activities—all of us running in search of safety.

As we near the door, I glance back and see some of the men crashing like waves against the fleeing students and teachers.

"Hurry up! Let's go!" Luis hollers, making it to the door first. He pushes it open, and students begin pouring out.

Naima's arm is still locked in my grip, and we are both gasping from fear and sprinting as hard as we can. When we finally reach the exit, the sunlight feels like a safe haven, a chance to wake up from this nightmare.

But before we can step outside, one of the men reaches us and grabs at Naima, pulling her from my grasp.

He's a hulking white man, his body a mass of muscle. His eyes above the bandanna covering his face are cold and devoid of care. He's shorter than me, but wider and full of rage. He holds Naima with his left hand, and I can see his broad shoulders begin to tense, his right hand forming a fist. In that instant I know that he is about to hit her.

As he cocks back his fist, every ounce of me ignites, and with a primal scream, I hurl myself at him. My fist connects with his eye, a sickening crunch ringing in the air—though whether it's from his face or my fist, I can't be sure. He lets go of Naima and staggers back—and then someone grabs me and drags me to the ground. More men begin to surround me as I cover my head.

Sharp pain erupts through my body as I'm kicked and punched, the blows raining down like hail.

Naima's screams slice through the chaos. I just want her to run. I just want her to be okay. I try to choke out the word *Run!* but I can't draw a full breath. I wrap my arms around my head, trying to shield myself from the worst of it, but it's like trying to stop a hurricane with a paper bag. My breaths come in ragged gasps, each one feeling like my last.

As the pain in my body reaches new heights, the turmoil around me begins to fade. I wonder if this is the moment before I get to be with my dad.

Then, just as suddenly as the blows began, the abuse stops.

One of the men who was beating me crumples to the floor beside me. A familiar voice yells, "Get off him!"

I look up and see Tommy, his jaw clenched, standing shoulder to shoulder with Luis. Naima pulls me up, steadying me on my feet. My body aches, but her touch helps. As does the sight of almost the entire basketball team, and other athletes, standing beside us, united against the mob. Suddenly, there's a blur of motion. It's Laura. She jumps on a white dude wearing a hat, mask, and sunglasses who was creeping up behind Luis. Her arms flail as she tries to beat him away. It's like watching a lioness defend her pride.

Another man—this one wearing a DON'T TREAD ON ME bandanna around the bottom half of his face—sees her and pulls her off his friend, tossing her aside like she's nothing. She hits the ground with a loud thud. The man looms over Laura, ready to attack.

"No! Not her!" The words rip from the masked man's throat.

The other man's confused, angry. "What are you talking about?"

"She's not supposed to be here! Not her!" the masked man commands. The voice is familiar, but it's muffled by the mask and I can't quite place it. "Get the other ones! Get *him*!" The man points directly at me.

The man in the bandanna ignores him, tightens his fist, and swings at Laura.

"No!" the man in the mask yells as he grabs the other man's arm, trying to hold him back. But the other man is stronger.

He shakes free of the masked man's grip. "You're protecting this Chinese bitch? You damn race traitor!" he yells.

He punches the man in the mask. Once, twice, a sickening barrage of flesh against flesh. The man in the mask raises his arms to defend himself, but he soon crumples under the onslaught of blows.

Suddenly, a wail echoes from outside, sirens slicing through the chaos. Everyone's head turns as the reality of what's happening sinks in.

The men begin to scatter like roaches when the lights flick on. Their shouts and chants fade into the distance, leaving behind a mess of fear and fury. But one of them doesn't get up. One of them lies beaten and unconscious on the ground.

I step over to him, my legs heavy, my body aching with every move. The adrenaline's fading now, and I finally feel the stinging pain of cuts and the deep ache of bruises. But I gotta see. I gotta know who's under that mask.

I kneel next to him, my knees hitting the ground with a thud. Slowly, I reach out, my fingers trembling, and pull off his bloody hat. Then his dark glasses, which are cracked and bent. And finally, I peel away his mask, revealing the face underneath.

Matthew.

Laura's scream rattles everyone, tormented and broken. "Matt, no! Please, no!" She runs to him, tears streaming down her face like rain. She falls to her knees, her hands hovering over Matthew like she's afraid to touch him, afraid to hurt him.

"What did you do?" she cries out, her voice cracking with pain. "No! No! What did you do, Matthew? No! What did you do? What did you *do*?"

Chapter Thirty

The following morning arrives, but the sunlight peeking through my window hardly feels like enough to cast away the darkness I'm feeling. It's like that light is just a weak whisper trying to talk sense to a storm. I drag myself to the window and look out. Just as I thought, there are reporters outside my building, swarming like flies. Even more than when I came home last night, after my mother picked me up from the police station. They wanted student statements about what happened.

The sight of them makes my stomach churn. So I crawl back into bed, tucking myself under the covers as if maybe they can shield me from the world, from the memories. But no such luck.

Before I know it, the afternoon comes, sneaking in like it's afraid of bothering me. My body is still aching, every muscle screaming a reminder of yesterday's chaos. And my mind is like a broken record. It can't help but replay Naima being grabbed by that man, watching my friends fight for their lives, seeing Matthew rushed to the hospital.

Every time I close my eyes, the images, the sounds, they just keep coming. The sight of the reporters only makes it worse.

Later in the afternoon, there's a soft knock on my door. It creaks open, and my mom steps in. She's wide-eyed as she takes in the empty shelves and the trash bag filled with broken basketball awards. She doesn't comment, though.

"Just checking on you," she says softly. "How are you doing?"

"Fine," I reply. The word is a lie, even to my own ears.

"You sure?" she presses, seeing right through my facade.

"Yeah, thanks," I say, trying to infuse a bit more conviction into my voice.

She's about to leave and give me my space, but then her eyes land on Dad's jersey. The last remnant of basketball that is still safely hanging on my wall.

"I don't think you're fine," she says, turning back to face me. Her tone is gentle, but there's a firmness there, a resolve that surprises me.

"Get dressed and head to your grandmother's place," she instructs me. "I'll go outside and get rid of the reporters — tell them you're going to speak with them near the basketball court or something. You can go the opposite way. They won't know you're there."

The surprise must be clear on my face. It's like she's seeing me for the first time in a long time.

"Your grandmother has been worried sick about you," she continues. "But she hasn't wanted to bother you. Go on and see her. It will be good for both of you."

"Yeah, okay, sure," I agree. "Thanks, Ma." My gratitude is genuine.

I make my way to Grandma Alice's apartment without incident. I knock on the door, once, twice, three times, but there's no answer. With a sigh, I fish out the key and let myself in.

The door swings open to reveal Grandma Alice wrapped in a large throw blanket, sitting on the couch. She's cradling a cup of tea, the steam dancing up to meet her face, while the soft strains of jazz fill the room. The sight is like a still-life painting. There's a faraway look in her eyes, like she's somewhere else, somewhere distant.

"Is everything okay, Grandma?" I ask, barely above a whisper. "I was knocking on the door."

She turns, her face lighting up with surprise. "Hey, baby! I'm sorry, I couldn't hear the door over the music, I guess. Take your coat off and come over here and sit with me. Let me have a look at you, make sure you're okay."

I do as she says, shrugging off my coat and taking a seat beside her. The couch feels like a place of calm in a world falling apart.

Grandma Alice leans in, her eyes scanning my face, her fingers gentle as they trace the bruises that paint my skin in shades of purple and blue. Her touch is featherlight, but I can feel the gravity of her worry, the depth of her care.

"Mmm. I'm so sorry, baby," she murmurs, soft as a lullaby amid the jazz notes. "I can't even imagine what you and those other kids are feeling. I'm so glad you're safe."

"Yeah, I guess," I mutter. I feel like a deflated basketball, all the air and fight squeezed out of me.

"Sounds like that Matthew boy who let them in is lucky to be alive," she says.

I don't respond. I'm not sure where I stand on Matthew at the moment. He's in bad shape, and I don't wish that on anyone. But . . . he could have gotten us killed. The way he yelled for them to go after me . . . Maybe he wanted me dead.

Grandma Alice's eyes are usually like two pools of wisdom, deep and knowing. But right now, they're searching, looking for the right words, the right way to piece me back together. It's this more than anything that makes me realize how *horrible* everything that happened really was—how frightening and serious. How life-changing.

Her lips part, and she's about to speak when suddenly she's seized by a coughing fit. It shakes her body, each cough like a clap of thunder in the quiet room.

In an instant, my hand is on her back, patting gently, hoping to ease the storm. The coughs finally subside, and she takes a slow sip of her tea, the steam swirling around her face.

"Grandma, you shouldn't still be coughing like this. Are you sure you're okay?" I ask, my concern for her overshadowing my own turmoil at the moment.

"I told you I'm fine, baby," she insists. "Your old girl is getting up there, is all. Age conquers everything. Plus that damn cold threw my system all off. But I'm fine."

She pauses, takes another sip of her tea, and then continues. "Anyway, like I was saying, the news said Matthew is still in critical condition but should make it. Senator Astor said he's going to have a rally at your school next week, protesting the 'abhorrent violence of the woke mob' that led to his nephew's beating—as if Matthew and them are the real victims. They never stop pointing the finger."

The senator's words sit in my stomach like stones. How can they twist it like that? How can they turn the world upside down and inside out until the wrong seems right and the right seems forgotten?

Grandma Alice sets her tea on the coffee table next to a crumpled newspaper. "What's that, Grandma?" I ask.

She glances at it, a flicker of annoyance in her eyes. "Oh, nothing. Just some nonsense in the paper Mrs. Collins brought by earlier."

I reach for the paper, my fingers brushing against the wrinkled newsprint. The headline jumps out at me, bold and accusing: "THIS IS WHAT WOKENESS LEADS TO."

It's another piece by Morgan's father. I'm not sure if there are heights of my anger that can surpass what I feel at the moment. The words rage like fire in front of me, swaying as if to mock everything we went through.

> The advocates of this movement, with their relentless pursuit of representation and inclusion, are knowingly playing a dangerous game to make money and gain acclaim—nothing more. People like Naima Johnson, Ossie Brown, and their ringleader, Tasha Hunt. Each of them no different from any other grifters we've seen throughout history: Black Lives Matter, the Black Panthers, and others. By insisting on dismantling institutions that are far from broken, they are placing the backs of patriots against the wall, inciting fear and resentment among those of us whose way of life is under attack.
>
> The result of this? What happened yesterday afternoon at Braxton Academy. A group of men fearing the erasure of their way of life tried their best to demonstrate before being attacked—leaving Matthew Astor clinging to life after a barbaric assault by a fellow student. And no one is being held accountable for his grievous injuries.
>
> I suggest you stand with me and with Matthew's uncle, Senator Patrick Astor, this coming Friday at Braxton Academy, my beloved alma mater, as we put an end to the woke agenda there once and for all. Let's set an example for the entire nation.

The lines crawl into my consciousness, stinging my senses. I can't help but think of the generations before me who fought to stop people like him. Then I look at Grandma Alice, knowing what she's been through in her life. Knowing how much hasn't changed.

My anger swells up and bursts into a stream of tears.

The walls of the apartment feel as if they are closing in on me, like I'm suffocating. I can't help but think that I'm the cause of it all, the root of everyone's suffering. Grandma Alice tries to reach for my hand, her eyes filled with love and concern.

"Don't, Grandma," I whisper, choked up. "This is all my fault."

She shakes her head. "No, baby, you ain't at fault for nothing. Bad people took advantage of the good you tried to do."

I clench my fists, my heart aching with a sadness I can't contain. "No. I'm always messing up. Ms. Hunt. Naima. Luis. Basketball."

The tears begin to blur my vision.

"Baby, listen to me," Grandma Alice says. "I've seen darkness—and that ain't you. You're a light in this world."

"If you say so," I say, my voice cracking, as I stand up. "I'm gonna go, Grandma."

"Baby, please sit down," she says tenderly.

But I'm already halfway to my coat. I've gotta get out of here, go be alone with my thoughts and my fears and my self-pity.

"I said sit your ass down, boy!" Her voice is sharp now, a crack of thunder that startles me into obedience.

She looks at me, her expression softening. "You know, I wish you and your mother could see how alike you two are. Both of you so stubborn. Trying to do everything by yourself when you don't have to."

"Grandma, you don't get it—" I start, but she cuts me off.

"I don't get it? Child, I've seen more than you can imagine. Been through things I hope you never face. Please don't tell me what I don't understand."

Her words stop me cold. In her eyes, I see the power of years, the depth of experiences. For a moment, I feel small, like a child lost in a mall too big, too complex to navigate alone.

Grandma Alice leans back against the couch, the cushions swallowing her small frame. She looks at me with a gentleness I can always count on, even when the world outside her door is anything but gentle.

"Do you know why I have Sunday dinners?" she asks.

I shrug. "Because you like cooking and watching Ms. Peters and Mrs. Collins argue over spades?"

She chuckles. "Yeah, I do enjoy those things. But there's more to it, baby." Her hand reaches out, resting softly on mine. "Sundays are about more than food or cards. They're about community, about connection. They're about bringing people together, sharing our stories, our struggles, our joys."

Her hands gesture in the air like she's painting a picture only she can see. "When the world outside is too much, when it tries to tell you who you are, who you should be, who you *can't* be, you need a place where you can just be yourself. Where you can find the strength to keep telling the world it's wrong about you. That's what Sundays are for."

Her words settle on me like a blanket. "I never thought about it like that."

She nods, her eyes never leaving mine. "Sunday dinners have held me together, kept me rooted. Because my community, the people who love me—y'all are my foundation. My center."

A silence stretches between us as the jazz continues to play softly, a soothing backdrop to the suffocating thoughts swirling in my mind.

"But, Grandma," I start, "what do you do when your center seems to be falling apart?"

Her gaze is even softer now. "Oh, that's simple. You do what my daddy used to tell me: 'Put one foot in front of the other and look forward.' That's the only way you can see what direction you should be heading in. The direction of the places and people invested in helping you be whole."

I hang my head, not sure how to take those steps forward. Not sure I deserve to.

Grandma Alice squeezes my hand, her grip firm. Her eyes are turbulent with emotion, and her voice trembles. It's like there's a fragile thread connecting her heart to mine. "You know, baby, this whole life thing is sort of like a shooting star. It's beautiful. Humbling. And so breathtakingly brief. It's hard to really understand how short it is until you get to the final stretch of it. But when you're looking back, you'll realize, we're all bound to stumble, to make mistakes. No one, not a single soul, can claim to be perfect."

Tears gather at the corners of her eyes like dew on morning leaves, but she holds them back. "But here's the thing," she continues, her voice gaining strength. "It's not about the mistakes you make. No, it's about how you try to fix them. How you learn, grow, and move forward. That's what will truly define you, especially when people look back at your life."

Her hand, now shaking slightly, cups my cheek. "The people who genuinely matter, the community you build and hold dear, they will see beyond your flaws. They will see your heart, your efforts."

Her voice cracks. She looks at me like she misses me, though I'm right here. "You weren't a great basketball player because you were perfect. You were great because you learned from your mistakes, adapted, and improved. If you apply that same effort to life, to learn and keep growing, you'll have lived a life worth living. A life of meaning, of purpose. Growing is the reason we do this life thing in the first place."

I lean forward, giving her a tight hug, the kind that says everything without a single word. As I pull back, I catch sight of the crumpled newspaper again. That headline. That rally. Matthew's uncle and Morgan's father, they think they've won. A bitter taste floods my mouth.

But then something comes to me.

"Grandma, I have an idea," I say. The words come out like a whisper, but there's a spark in them, a flicker of something I haven't felt in a while. Hope, maybe. Determination, definitely.

Her face lights up with curiosity. "What's on your mind, baby?"

I chew on my lip, thinking. "Would you be open to me having a few extra people over tomorrow for Sunday dinner?"

She hesitates, a cloud of concern passing over her face. "Well, you know, I haven't been feeling too well lately. Haven't cooked much. And I don't know how many people Mrs. Collins and Ms. Peters can handle."

"That's not a problem," I assure her, feeling a plan taking shape in my mind. "I'll ask Mom if she can show me a few things. So I can help, too."

Her smile returns, warm like sunlight. "Well, then, of course. That sounds amazing." Then she tilts her head. "Who's coming over?"

I stand up, feeling like I'm stepping onto a new path. "I'm going to try and get my community together. To help me fix things."

Chapter Thirty-One

I spend the rest of Saturday and most of Sunday morning hitting up everyone who might listen, who might care enough to come through. Texts, calls, door knocks. My phone's battery is bleeding out from the effort, and my knuckles are raw from rapping on every door that might open up to the idea of change, of standing up.

Some folks give me a nod, a maybe, a "We'll see," which I know is code for "Probably not." But it's all good. I keep it moving, keep the hope. Because even a few is better than none. And with so much on the line—Ms. Hunt's job, books that tell our stories, Braxton's future, and the potential of this happening in other places—even a one-man army is better than silence.

Back at Grandma Alice's place, the kitchen is a storm of scents and sounds. Mom's working the stove like a DJ on the decks, her hands mixing, flipping, stirring up magic. Ms. Peters and Mrs. Collins are the backup dancers, their laughter and bickering a familiar tune to the rhythm of chopping and seasoning. And I'm running around doing whatever they tell me to. We're preparing enough food to feed a small country.

Getting them to help me with my plan was easier than expected, especially my mother. I told her what I was planning to do, and she said she was happy to help. Between this and the way she took care of those reporters yesterday, I feel like maybe she's ready to really try this time.

As we cook, Grandma Alice is in the living room, listening to music and relaxing. I'm happy she's resting, but I can't wait until she's in here with us again soon.

I steal a taste of the mac and cheese when no one's looking, and it's like a whisper of *You got this* from the ancestors. We're gonna need that energy, that spirit, because tonight, we're going to be brainstorming ways to stand up against more than just a rally. We're going to be standing up against a mindset, a history, a whole system that's been trying to silence us since forever.

The food is done. The sweet smell is like a welcome mat, inviting the neighborhood in as it does every Sunday. The usuals come through the door—Mrs. Jackson with her hands full of homemade rolls, Mr. Edwards with banana pudding. They slide into the living room like this is just another Sunday.

I'm nibbling on a corner of cornbread, watching the door, waiting for the faces of the folks I reached out to, the ones who gave me that "maybe" look. But time is ticking away, and I'm starting to think they ain't gonna show. My stomach is in knots, and it isn't from hunger.

Then, just when I'm about to write it off as a failed mission, there's a knock at the door. I open up.

Big Teak fills the doorway first. His boys stack up behind him like a human fortress. No smiles other than Teak's, but they're here. That's what counts.

Before the door even closes, another knock, a bit lighter this time. It's some of the Woodcrest kids. They always got a joke ready, but today their grins seem genuine. They nod at me like we share a secret and walk in.

Then a few minutes later, the sound comes again, firm and purposeful. Tommy stands there with a couple other guys from the Braxton team.

"What up, Tommy. Happy you came, man," I say, my words loaded with more gratitude than they can carry.

"That's what friends are for," he says as he daps me up, then he steps inside. He smirks. "Plus I wouldn't miss the chance to see if you can actually cook."

I chuckle. "You'll see."

One by one, they all come in, taking seats, filling up spaces on couches and chairs, some leaning against walls or sitting on the floor. The room is getting full, not just with bodies but with something bigger—purpose, maybe. Or hope.

Plates piled with food pass from hand to hand. A mosaic of mouths moving, the sounds of a soul food symphony mixed with jazz. And as the first round of satisfied sighs begins to fade, I finally stand up.

"Hey, everybody," I start, my voice shaky but forceful. Heads turn. Eyes lock on me. The room goes quiet except for the music. "This Friday," I say, "I'm gonna be at that rally at Braxton. And I'm hoping you and others will be there with me. Because if they get away with this now, they'll just keep doing it until they erase all of us."

A few nods from around the room. I see it in their eyes—some are with me, some are just curious, and some . . . some are scared. And I get it. I'm scared, too. But not as scared as I am of people like Mr. Henley getting what he wants.

"I'm not gonna let them control our story like they know it, like they wrote it," I say, my voice growing stronger. "They act like they are victims. But Ms. Hunt is a victim. Naima is a victim. Everybody that stands in their way is an actual victim."

I look around, hoping they feel what I'm saying, hoping they see what I see—a chance for us to write our own headlines.

Then, in the midst of people considering what I'm saying, there's a knock. A pause button pressed on the moment. I make my way to the door, pulling it open to find Luis. His hair's a mess, like he's been running his fingers through it all day, probably wrestling with the same shit we all are.

"Sorry I'm late," he says, his eyes darting past me to the crowd. "Had a few things to handle."

I can't help but smile, relief washing over me like a warm wave. "It's all good, man. There's still plenty of food left."

He steps in, and I'm about to swing the door shut when a familiar voice halts me. "So you're not gonna let me see if your grandmother's sweet potato pie is as good as you say?"

I turn back, and there she is, standing in the hallway, the dim light catching the edges of her smile. Naima.

"You came," I say.

"I wasn't sure if I was going to . . ." Her voice trails off, a river of uncertainty that's been running since everything turned upside down.

"So what made you?" The question is out before I can corral it, wild and wanting.

Naima shifts, her gaze lifting. "I don't know. Maybe it was just what happened the other day . . . and realizing how short life is. And really thinking about who's to blame for everything. Because even though I still don't approve of what you did, I know you were trying to help." She takes a breath, each word measured like she's been practicing them. "But that knight-in-shining-armor bullshit . . . I don't need it. And I don't need your assumptions about what I do need or want.

I think you're starting to learn that. I see you trying to fix what you messed up, and also fix the stuff that wasn't your fault at all. . . . It means something. Especially since you're asking for help, not trying to handle it all on your own, prove some sort of point."

The words hang between us, heavy and hopeful. "So what does that mean for us?" I'm treading on thin ice, but I gotta know.

"Like I said the other day, my feelings . . . I can't shake them." Her eyes don't waver. "But right now, I'm only focused on seeing if I can be your friend. Nothing more."

I nod. I get it.

"I can respect that," I say. My words are honest, no frills, no fluff. Just the simple truth, because that's what she deserves. That's what *we* deserve.

Naima smiles, the kind that seems to light up the dim hallway. Then her expression shifts to something that looks a lot like pride. "And besides coming over for your grandmother's pie, I also had to come flex."

"Flex about what?"

"You remember that writing competition Ms. Hunt told us about months ago? To be in her friend's anthology book?"

"Yeah, I forgot all about that," I say, thinking about how much has happened since then.

Naima nods. "Well, the editor reached out after reading the letter to my father, and since Ms. Hunt is no longer having a competition, she gave me the spot." Her words are modest, but I can hear the triumph in them.

"Oh, shit, congrats!" I can't keep the smile off my face or the volume out of my voice. This is big, and she deserves it.

She grins. "Yeah, Luis is a bit salty about it, saying there should've still been a competition, but I would've smoked him anyway." Her eyes sparkle with mischief. "Just don't tell him that."

We laugh. The sound is full of relief, hope, and life. It's the kind of laugh that feels like it could push back the darkness for a minute or two. And as we walk into the apartment, I think maybe, just maybe, we've got a shot at turning this thing around—the rally, the mess I made. All of it.

As Naima and I step into the apartment, the laughter and chatter are like a warm hug. We're stepping into a place that feels like the world should—full of life, full of color, full of people just being people. And there on the couch is Luis, leaning back like he's been part of the furniture for years, chopping it up with Grandma Alice and my mom. They're laughing, and it's a good sound, a sound that fills the room like a melody.

Grandma Alice's eyes snap to us as Naima and I enter, her smile widening in a way that makes her whole face glow. "Ossie, why don't you bring that beautiful young lady over here to sit with us," she calls out, and it's not a suggestion. I take Naima's coat slowly, like it's something precious. Because it is. Everything about her is. We make our way to the couch.

Naima sits down next to Luis, a little cautious, a little curious. "Nice to meet you both," she says, and her voice is like a song that's just beginning.

"You're quite a force, young lady," Grandma Alice says.

She smiles wide. "Thank you, Ms. Brown."

Grandma Alice smiles. "Oh, no, my daughter and I are Fords. It's our family name," she corrects gently.

My mother nods. "I never had the opportunity to become a Brown."

Naima gulps slightly. "Oh, I'm so sorry," she says.

"No need to be sorry," my mom says, like she's at peace with many things. "I'm just as lucky to be a Ford as I would have been to be a Brown." She looks at Grandma Alice and smiles.

Grandma Alice places her hand on my mom's hand and squeezes it.

"I'm happy y'all came," Grandma Alice says to Naima and Luis. "I've been wanting to meet you both for some time." She leans in like she's sharing a secret. "And just so you know, 'Ms. Ford' is too stuffy for me anyway. Call me Grandma Alice."

Naima's smile breaks free, and it's like sunshine. "Okay, then, Grandma Alice."

I'm just standing there, watching this exchange, feeling like I'm witnessing something special. Then Grandma Alice gives me a look, a look that says *Move your feet, boy*.

"Ossie, why don't you get in there and make these two a plate?" she says, sounding like her usual self.

"Sure, Grandma," I reply, turning toward the kitchen.

Walking away, I sneak a glance back, just in time to catch Naima tucking a loose braid back into her bun, looking comfortable next to Grandma Alice and my mom. Luis catches my eye and gives me a nod, like he's reading my mind. And for the first time in a long time, I feel like I'm exactly where I'm supposed to be—in the middle of this wild, beautiful storm of people I call family.

We spend the rest of Sunday buzzing with the kind of energy that could jump-start a car. Talking, planning, each idea bouncing around the room like a basketball during warm-ups. We're trying to figure out how our counterprotest can make a statement loud enough to be felt. We know we won't be able to match their numbers, so we're counting on being able to surprise them so they're thrown off—for them and the media to expect a few dozen people at most and to grab some headlines when a hundred or more folks pull up. Word of mouth becomes our strategy, the old-school kind of social media where you look someone in the eye and they pass it on the same way.

As we're hashing out the nitty-gritty—who's gonna make signs and shirts, who can order the megaphones—I notice Grandma Alice's eyes watching us. There's a look in them I've never seen before, almost like she's happy and sad at the same time.

"Are you okay, Grandma?" I ask after threading my way through the packed living room to her side.

She blinks, and for a second, I see the years in her gaze, like rings in a tree trunk. "I'm fine, baby," she says. Her tone is a soft song that could lull the moon to sleep.

I'm not convinced. "Are you sure?"

Grandma Alice nods, her hand reaching out to pat mine, the same way she used to when I was little and had a scrape or bruise from playing ball. "I'm sure." Her eyes drift across the room, touching on each of my friends' faces like a painter adding the final strokes. "Seeing everyone here, meeting your friends, it's good to know you have people who care about you. And y'all are going to keep fighting."

Then she pauses, and the walls seem to breathe deep with her. "Reminds me of us back in the sixties and seventies." She chuckles, the sound sort of bittersweet. "I've been fighting for a long time. And I guess I'm just . . . at peace."

Before I can respond, Naima walks over with a slice of half-eaten pie in her hand. "Ossie, you weren't kidding; Grandma Alice's pie is *amazing.*"

I blink. "Nah, that's not Grandma Alice's. She didn't cook today. Someone else must've brought the pie."

Grandma Alice smiles at me, that all-knowing smile that says she's five steps ahead, always. "I found some time yesterday to make that one thing. I had a feeling somebody might want some."

Then she looks over at Naima and adds, "But Ossie and his

mother have the recipe, too. I wouldn't mind them sharing it with you one day."

A smile blooms on Naima's face.

"I'd love that."

When Sunday ends, it's like the night before a big game. We've got the play drawn up, know our positions, and have our marching orders leading to Friday. There's a game plan, a strategy, with each of us knowing what we gotta do.

Monday morning at Braxton feels like stepping into a parallel universe. These are the same halls I've always walked, but now they're lined with security guards. Their eyes follow us like we're pages in a book they're trying to read real quick. I didn't think it could get more difficult to be here.

But we're on a mission, and that's the focus. Can't let the new metal detectors or the extra badges and walkie-talkies throw us off. I've got flyers in my backpack, whispers on my lips, spreading the word about our counterprotest. I slide the flyers across tables in the cafeteria to the few people we can trust, tuck them into textbooks in class, even slip a couple into lockers. It's all about Friday.

It's obvious everyone's on edge, but they're also on the fence. Some give me that nod, like, "I got you." Others slide their eyes away, and I can almost hear their brains clicking like they're calculating the cost. No judgment; standing up can be heavy. Too heavy for some.

Come Wednesday afternoon, our numbers seem nowhere close to what we need. I start thinking maybe we're about to stand up and find out we're standing alone. As I'm in my room about to let that sink into my bones, my phone buzzes. An email.

Dear Ossie,

I hope this message finds you in good spirits despite the challenging circumstances. My name is Randall Houston, and I am president of the NAACP.

We have been informed by Ms. Tasha Hunt about the counterprotest you are organizing for Friday. Please know that we have been monitoring the situation at Braxton closely and are deeply concerned about the developments there.

In response to the courageous efforts of you and your friends, I want you to know that we stand with you in solidarity. The NAACP is currently reaching out to our partner organizations and local community leaders to gather support for your group. It is our belief that when we come together as a community to raise our voices against injustice, we embody the strength and resilience that drives meaningful change.

We commend your initiative and the peaceful stance you are taking to make your voices heard.

See you Friday.

Warm regards,
Randall Houston
President
NAACP Westchester County

 I can't believe it. I'm staring at the glowing screen of my phone, at words that seem like they're written in some kind of holy light. The NAACP. With us.

I call Luis and Naima. They're both just as excited, relieved, and determined as I am. Then I dial Grandma Alice. It rings and rings. Voicemail. I hang up, call again. Still no answer. She's probably napping, got her jazz turned up too loud, or lost in some book. But I gotta tell her what's going on.

I'm out the door before I even realize I've put my sneakers on. The air outside is crisp, feels good, feels right. Like it's carrying me to her apartment. I knock, wait, then knock again. *She never hears the door.*

Suddenly, the door opens. It's my mother. And her face, it's a river. Tears. So many tears.

"I was just about to come home and tell you," she says, her voice cracking.

"Tell me what?" My heart, it's pounding. I look past her into the apartment. It's too quiet. "Where's Grandma Alice?"

My mom looks at me with eyes that are saying what she barely can.

"She's gone, Ossie." The words are heavy, pulling the air right out of the room. Gone? No. *No*, not Grandma Alice.

The world stops. Stops. Like someone hit the pause button on life, on everything. My mother's standing there, a statue with eyes like oceans, and I can't—I won't—believe what she's trying to tell me.

"Grandma?" I call out, my voice a stranger in this too-still apartment. It's bouncing off walls, off family photos, off the vinyl records, off the throw blanket she was wrapped in days ago.

I don't even realize I'm moving. My feet have their own plans, their own need to find her, to prove the truth is a lie. I rush to her bedroom. Her bed is made up neatly, like she's coming right back. Just stepped out to the store for some sugar or something.

"Grandma Alice!" Louder now, a demand, a plea. I hurry into the kitchen. She's got to be here, mixing up something sweet, something that smells like cinnamon and history.

The pots are still, the oven's cold, and there's the rest of that pie sitting there, hurting me with its stillness.

"Grandma!" I shout, louder, back to the living room. The couch and its worn cushion still hold the shape of her. But no answer. Just the silence. A silence so loud it's screaming.

"Grandma Alice, please . . ." My voice breaks, shatters into a thousand pieces of hopelessness.

My mother just watches me, tears streaming down her face. Then her mouth opens for a moment, as if she can't get the words out, but eventually she does.

"She's gone, Ossie," she says softly, like anything louder might snap me in half. But I'm already broken.

And then it hits. The truth. Like a wrecking ball to the chest.

I slide down the wall, the wall that's been a witness to so many of her stories, her laughs. I hit the floor. The rug is rough against my palms, but I barely feel it. I can't feel anything but the void, the emptiness that's swallowing me.

Tears come. Like they've been waiting behind my eyes for permission to fall. And now they're free, running down my cheeks in rivers, in lakes, in seas, in oceans, in floods. These tears are loud. They're violent. They're all the words I can't say.

I cry. For her. For my mom. For the neighborhood. For me. And I think I might cry forever.

Chapter Thirty-Two

Wednesday night fades into Friday morning like a bruise going from purple to black. My phone has been somewhere in the darkness of my room, lighting up again and again. Luis. Naima. A bunch of numbers texting messages I don't have the energy to read. They're all sorry about Grandma Alice. The messages are supposed to be soothing, but they sting. The truth hurts. I don't want to accept it.

My mom must've told someone from the school. Mrs. Wright, maybe. Doesn't matter. I can't talk. Can't form words over the pain.

I couldn't do school yesterday. Can't do school today. Can't do responding to people.

Can't do the protest.

Yesterday, I found myself in bed all day, drowning in tears. Today, I find myself at the old warehouse on the Hudson River, the one that used to be a castle in my daydreams. The one where I'd make plans to pull us out of the grind, away from the too-tight spaces of the projects. It's quiet here. The kind of quiet that lets you hear your heart breaking.

I climb up to the roof, the metal staircase railing cold and unforgiving under my palms. I sit on one of the large crates I dragged over months before with Naima and Luis, looking out where the water meets the sky. The horizon's just a line. Simple. Not like life. Not like death. The water doesn't know or care about what happened. It just keeps flowing.

I feel lost. Floating. The world is still moving beneath me, around me, in front of me. How? Doesn't the universe realize what's gone? I'm angry that everything is still going.

As I stare out at the horizon, it's all blurred. It must be hours now that I've been sitting here. Numb. Trying to make sense of a world that still spins even though my center, Grandma Alice, is gone.

It turns out Grandma Alice had breast cancer. And everyone knew but me. It was Grandma Alice's decision to keep it from me. She didn't want the rest of our time together to be clouded by grief. But I can't help feeling angry at all the time I wasted, all the days I stayed away, too caught up in my own little dramas. I would give *anything* to redo one of those days, to make different choices.

To have more time with Grandma Alice.

There's a sound. Footsteps. Soft but steady. Someone's coming, just behind me. I have no energy to be startled or even turn around to check who it is. Then a figure sits down on the crate beside me. I turn slowly to see who it is.

My mom.

She doesn't say anything. Just sits, looking out at the same nothing and everything I've been looking at. Her presence is like a slight breeze. There's a quiet understanding, a shared silence that doesn't need words. Not yet.

After a while, the wind picks up. It's playing with the edges of my jacket, and drying the wet spots on my cheeks.

I finally ask, "How'd you know I'd be here?"

She doesn't look at me, just keeps her eyes on the water, the sky, the distance. "I've known that you've been coming here to get away since you were younger. After I told you I used to bring your father here."

I turn to her, and my face must be twisted in surprise because she gives me this little smile. "I know a lot more about you than you'd expect."

I turn back to the water.

She sighs. "But it would be fair if you didn't expect me to know anything. I haven't been great at this whole mom thing for a while now."

"That's not true," I say. But it's more a reflex than my honest feelings.

She smiles, sad-like, and shakes her head. "That's nice of you, but, yes, it is."

And in that moment, it's like we're seeing each other for the first time in a long time.

"When you were little, I used to take you to the playground and push you on the swings. You would reach your arms out as far as they could stretch. For a while, I thought you were reaching for a cloud, trying to grab a fistful of white fluff to bring back down. But as you got older, I realized what you were really reaching for—your father."

My heart gives a painful lurch, a reminder of what's been lost. I risk a look at her. She's staring into the sky as if she's looking to see if he's up there watching.

I want to say something, to reach out, to bridge the crater that's keeping us apart. But I can't grasp the words.

"Ossie," she begins, soft, tentative. "I haven't been there for you like I should have for some time now. And I knew it. But I wasn't really honest with myself about it until I got that call last Friday saying someone almost took you from me. I should have been there for you long before that."

I watch the horizon, too, knowing she's not done saying what she needs to say. Knowing the best thing I can do for her right now is to listen. And so I listen.

"When all the writing y'all did was posted online, your grandmother read most of it. It was irresistible for someone who is nosy and loves to read." She chuckles. "Then, when you started growing distant from her, she told me I should read your letter. I didn't want to—but eventually I knew I needed to."

My heart feels like it's going to catapult out of my mouth.

"That was just for an assignment. I didn't mean for you to ever read it," I say, wishing I could erase the essay from her memory. Knowing I probably hurt her deeply.

But instead of pain, I see . . . relief on her face. And understanding. "It's okay, Ossie. I'm glad you wrote it—and I'm glad I read it, too. Sometimes we need a mirror turned on us to show what's wrong."

The understanding in her voice cradles me, beginning to heal things I thought I would continue carrying alone. I look into her eyes, deep pools of pain and love swirling together, and confess what I believe is true.

"I haven't been a great son, either." As I speak, the tears begin to rush harder. But my mother wipes them away from my cheeks.

She shakes her head.

"That isn't true. We all have our issues, but you've been a *wonderful* son," she says with fierce conviction. "And besides, I'm *your* parent. You're not mine. You're still a child, and it's my job to help you learn and grow. The only job you have is to be open to how you can be an even more amazing and beautiful soul."

And then, as if the floodgates have opened, tears stream down her cheeks. She's choking on emotions she can no longer contain.

"You . . . you were right in that letter, Ossie. When you got to a certain age, you started reminding me so much of your father, and I . . . I didn't know how to handle being so close to you anymore. Not without thinking about losing him. I was so scared of sitting in that pain . . . I distanced myself. Then, when I found out about your grandmother's cancer, I hid myself in the lie that I was working all of those extra hours to pay for her treatments that insurance wasn't covering. But the truth is, when she told me she wanted to stop treatment, I was angry with her. Not just because I was going to lose her sooner than I might. But because I had to pull my head out of the sand sooner than I wanted to and accept the things that were happening. Losing her, losing your father, hurting you."

Her honesty slices through years of silence and misunderstandings. I see a vulnerability in her I've never witnessed before. It's one of those rare moments where we realize our parents are only human—just like us.

I reach out to her, my hand shaking slightly, and brush away the tears from her cheeks, just as she did for me moments ago. Her eyes meet mine, baring her soul in a way I've never seen.

"Ossie, I'm so sorry. But I don't want us to each sit alone in the pain of losing your grandmother. I want us to deal with it together," she whispers, her voice cracking under the weight of emotions she's been carrying.

I nod, my heart swelling with understanding and love we've both been yearning for.

"It's okay, Mom. Life is about how we fix our mistakes."

She holds my gaze, her eyes watery, and smiles as if she knows where I've heard that before. "Your father and your grandmother, they're both so proud of you."

My chest heaves with sobs. "I wish I could have said good-bye to her."

"Oh, Ossie," my mom says. "You did say good-bye to her. I saw the look on her face last Sunday. You helped her be ready to go home." The wind picks up, carrying her words over the Hudson, scattering them like ashes.

"But I wish . . ." My voice cracks, breaks like a twig underfoot. "I wish she could have known how much she meant to me."

"Trust me: she knew." My mom's hand finds mine, holds it like it's sacred. "Your grandmother was so proud of you. For everything you've overcome, for the beautiful writer you are, for the beautiful *person* you are, for organizing what's happening today . . ."

I sniff, wipe my nose with the back of my hand. "I guess she would be disappointed I'm not there, then."

My mom shakes her head. "She would want you to do whatever is best for you." She holds my gaze, then glances at her watch. "You know, if you're having second thoughts about what that might be, it's not too late. You can still make it. If that's what you want."

I look at the water, its surface a mirror of the sky, just as troubled and stirred up as I am. Then I lift my eyes to the clouds, searching, like they might have an answer. I look back at my mom, her face open, her hand still holding mine.

I nod once, decisively.

"Let's go make Grandma Alice proud."

When we arrive at Braxton, the air is thick with tension. It's a circus, but there isn't anything funny about it. Cameras flashing, reporters shuffling, trying to catch the spectacle of pain and protest on their screens. The shouts are loud, clashing against one another, a level of noise that could rival Madison Square Garden. My mom's hand finds mine, her grip tight, telling me she's here, really here, for the first time in a long time.

We push through the crowd, a sea of anger and hope, barricades like lines drawn in the sand. Hundreds of people on both sides, screaming their truths, their fears, their demands. And there, in the midst of it all, a podium stands like a throne.

My eyes scan the crowd on the left, flicking over faces, some who promised to be here, others I never expected. Almost everyone from the writing program is here, as well as current and former English students of Ms. Hunt's. Coach Ryan, Tommy, and most of the basketball team are here. Then I see them, my people, my pillars in the pouring rain of this storm—Naima and Luis, standing strong with Mateo and his crew from NYU. They see us, and their surprise is a wave that washes over their faces. Naima's parents are here, too. Her mother smiles at me, and her father gives me a nod. It's more than I have a right to expect from them—especially her father.

I spy people from my neighborhood—Big Teak and his boys, the Woodcrest crew, and Grandma Alice's Sunday dinner regulars: Mrs. Collins and Ms. Peters, Mr. Edwards and Mrs. Jackson.

Then I see her: Ms. Hunt. She's standing with Mrs. Wright and a few other Braxton teachers. My heart aches as I imagine how she must feel to be at the center of all of this.

My mom walks over to Mrs. Collins and Ms. Peters as I head over to Ms. Hunt. My steps are measured, like I'm walking through a minefield of emotions that's been laid out in the last couple of months.

"I'm sorry to hear about Ms. Alice," she says. "She was a remarkable woman. I know she must have been so proud of you for planning this. Thank you for doing it," she says. "It means a lot."

I shuffle my feet, hands jammed in my pockets. "It's the least I can do after everything that happened. You believed in me, and I made things worse."

Ms. Hunt's smile is a sliver of light. "As I told you before, you are not to blame for all of it. You went about trying to make change in the wrong way—that is all you're guilty of. And you learned your lesson. And now look at what you've done today." She gestures, an arc that takes in the sea of people on our side, the banners, the raw determination. "Look at these faces; listen to these people. We wouldn't be here challenging things that need to change if it wasn't for you. And there is no place I would rather be right now."

Her words are healing the wounds on my conscience. I allow myself a smile.

She smiles back, and for a second, it's just the two of us—a student and a teacher who've been through the wringer and maybe aren't on the other side yet but will get there together.

Mrs. Wright steps up, her hands gripping a sign like it's a baton in a relay race we've all been running. She hands it to Ms. Hunt, who then turns and offers it to me like a torch.

I take it and read the bold black letters screaming their message. It feels heavy, not with weight but with purpose. I square my shoulders, lift the sign, and join my voice to the chorus of the crowd chanting for change, for justice, for the future.

"KEEP YOUR HANDS OFF OUR TRUTH!" I roar.

The rumbles of the opposing crowds carry on for the next fifteen minutes or so, until the hosts of the rally—Mr. Henley and Senator Astor—make their way to the podium. Everyone dies down to a murmur, then to silence. We all want to hear what's about to be said.

Matthew's uncle stands stiff and polished. Meanwhile, Morgan's dad looks like the kind of man who chews iron nails for breakfast, his face all hard lines and anger. Morgan, Sydney, Mr. Richmond, and Dean Blackburn file up to join them behind the podium.

Senator Astor clears his throat, and his voice cuts through the hush like a bell at a boxing match. He begins by giving a speech about American values, talking about how his Matthew was just trying to uphold them. And I can't help but wonder what values he's talking about. The kind that don't mind putting a knee on the neck of anyone who looks like me? He talks like he's weaving a spell, words designed to tug at heartstrings and maybe even make you forget that those same values have been choking us out for centuries.

When he's done, Morgan's father, Mr. Henley, steps up, and he's all fire and brimstone, painting Matthew like some kind of martyr. He says the violence that got Matthew is waiting in the wings for all white people if they keep letting their children's brains be fed with what he calls "divisive" books and history. Divisive. Like the truth about who's been doing what to who in this country is something we just made up to cause trouble.

Our side isn't having it. Boos rain down loud and fierce.

Then Dr. Henley drops his bomb. "We're crafting something transformative," he declares, leaning in with a mix of determination and arrogance. "It's called Matthew's Law. Senator Astor and I are forming a national oversight committee. And I'm at the helm."

His eyes light up with an excitement that's unsettling. "This committee will help decide what's safe to be taught in our schools. We're going to make sure the curriculum reflects a more . . . honest version of America's history. One that fits our values, our goals."

With a casual wave of his hand, as if brushing away any possible objections, he continues. "Any teacher who dares defy our guidelines, who insists on teaching narratives that challenge the direction of this nation, they're out. Just like that. It's high time we took control back from the woke mob." His smile sends a chill down my spine; it's cold, self-assured, as if he's already seen this future unfold and is relishing it.

As soon as he's finished, the boos from our side are a wave, a storm surge, a tsunami of sound washing over us. But then, like a record scratch in the middle of our rage, Mr. Henley ups the ante. He's got a last card to play, and he lays it down with a smugness that sticks to my skin like humidity.

"Ladies and gentlemen," he begins with a flourish of his hand that feels more like a magician's trick than a genuine gesture. "You've heard from Senator Astor, you've heard from me, but it's time we hear from one last voice."

The murmurs in the crowd are filled with intrigue.

"Because it's about more than race; it's about more than them hating us for being white. It's about the values that are being eroded in the classrooms where our children spend their days," he continues, his voice a false alarm. "It's also about the so-called progressive agendas, the normalization of lifestyles that fly in the face of traditional American values. These agendas are being forced upon our unsuspecting students, corrupting our youth, turning child against parent, turning boy into girl, *he* into *she* or even *they*—whatever *that* means."

The other side begins hooting and shouting in agreement.

"And so," Mr. Henley declares with satisfaction, "I have invited a brave pair of parents to speak on this matter. Parents who stand with us in ensuring the sanctity of our children's education. Please welcome Mr. and Mrs. Martinez to the podium."

The other side roars in approval. Beside me, Naima gasps and Luis stiffens. Then the crowd parts as Luis's mother and father step forward, moving with determination toward the microphone.

"Hector, Yaribel, the mic is all yours, amigos," Mr. Henley says.

Mateo reaches for one of Luis's hands and Naima reaches for the other. His eyes are filled with hurt, with betrayal. His folks are about to speak words he's never gonna be able to unhear, to put weight behind a hate that he's gonna have to carry for the rest of his life.

Mr. Martinez clears his throat.

Chapter Thirty-Three

"I have thought long and hard about what I would say here today," Mr. Martinez begins. He glances down at his trembling hands before searching the crowd. When he finds Luis, he locks eyes with him. "I was angry when I found out my son was gay. I felt like I had lost my little boy."

A hush blankets the crowd, the tension obvious. I feel Luis's hurt vibrating through the space between us.

"But a few days ago, my wife and I read the poem he wrote to his boyfriend, Mateo," he continues, and there's a softness in his voice now. "This was something he wrote for the writing program back when Ms. Hunt was teaching it. We read it when we were first sent the link, but we didn't *really* read it. We were too focused on the truth that our son has a boyfriend. We were too upset . . . and, if I am being honest, we were disgusted."

A strangled sound escapes from Luis, and even though there's no way his parents could hear it, they both turn and look at him, almost as if they could *feel* it.

"And then last week, after what happened at the school—and what *could* have happened to our son—we read his poem again. And it was beautiful. It was *beautiful*, Luis," he says, speaking directly to his son now. "And do you know what your mother said after we read it? She said, 'He's probably never written anything this beautiful about us.'" He pauses, looking down at the podium. "I sat with that for a few days, mijo, and came to realize that maybe I don't deserve for you to write a poem about me. Maybe I haven't earned that level of your love yet. But I want to. And so does your mother."

The other side begins booing loudly, but Mr. Martinez seems unfazed.

"Which is why," he begins, raising his voice and squaring his shoulders like a man stepping into a new skin, "I have asked Braxton Academy's board of trustees and its president to come here today so they can see for themselves who is really causing the divisiveness Dr. Henley and Senator Astor spoke of."

The opposing crowd shouts in response, a tornado of anger and racial slurs. And then I see them, the board members, stiff in their suits, their faces unreadable. Standing to the side with a police escort. The looks on Senator Astor's, Dr. Henley's, Dean Blackburn's, and Mr. Richmond's faces tell me they had no clue.

"They have requested to hear from Naima Johnson, the student who has been at the center of the issues raised over the past few months." Mr. Martinez turns slightly, nodding toward the crowd. "Naima, would you come up and say a few words?"

My heart leaps as hundreds of heads turn toward Naima.

Her eyes are wide, the weight of the moment written all over her face.

"You should be the one to go up there," she says to me. "This whole thing is happening because of you."

I shake my head, a small smile playing on my lips. "This *event* might be because of me. But this movement? That's all you. You have been the backbone of this whole thing, standing tall and speaking loud even when you stood alone, even when your world was crumbling. So many voices have controlled the narrative . . . but you're the voice everyone actually needs to hear."

I can feel the heat from the two crowds, the energy. It's like electricity buzzing around us, ready to spark. Naima's eyes search mine, looking for doubt, for hesitation. But she finds none. "You think I can do this?" There's a tremble in her voice, a crack of vulnerability.

I nod, resolute. "I know you can. I only set up this rally because you showed me what courage looks like. You inspired me to be better, the same way you'll inspire this whole place."

She smiles, then takes a deep breath—the kind that stretches the chest, that prepares the soul. "Aight."

There's this shuffle, then Naima steps toward the podium, her head held high, her eyes alight with the fire that lives in her soul. She moves like she's walking onto a stage, her stage, where she's always belonged.

Naima looks around, as if taking in the magnitude of the moment before continuing. She reaches into her pocket, taps her phone a few times, and places it on the podium facing her.

"Hello, my name is Naima Johnson, and I really didn't expect to be up here today. But since I am, I have set up my phone to live stream this to anyone online who wants to watch, because I'm tired of the media and powerful people getting to control my narrative—*our* narrative." A few people laugh gently. The faces on the other side remain stony.

"Many of you probably know me from the letter I wrote to my dad, a letter that a good friend shared with the world"—her eyes find mine, and they are filled with surprising affection—"because he wanted to help. He wanted to give me a platform, the kind of reach that's afforded to the types of people we idolize in this country: celebrities, athletes, performers, influencers. He believed in what I had to say, and he believed in how I said it. He wanted to shine a spotlight not just on me and my voice, not just on our amazing teacher, Ms. Hunt, but also on my experience and on the experience of countless other people who look like me or sound like me or have names like mine."

She gives me a slight knowing smile, as if to let me know she understands.

"Because the reality is, people like me don't usually get to tell our truths. And when we do, people are beaten for their truth, called liars for their truth, imprisoned for their truth, fired from their jobs for their truth, and even killed for their truth. My friend couldn't have known what would happen when he shared my letter. He couldn't have known how his gesture of love and support would blow up, would be twisted by some into a weapon—a weapon used to abuse the very people my letter was trying to help. People like Ms. Hunt, who remains one of the best teachers I have ever had the pleasure of learning from. People like Luis Martinez, whose sexuality was splashed across the internet like gossip rather than like the sacred thing it is. People like my family, who've been the victims of hate crimes ever since my words went out into the world.

"Maybe my friend should have anticipated what would happen. I found myself thinking that in the days after the letter went viral. How could he not know the hate that's in this world? How could he not realize how threatened so many people are by a young Black woman's words—by a young Black woman's existence?

"How could he not know?"

Her eyes lock on mine. "But I've come to understand that his not knowing is one of the most beautiful things about him. He has more faith in humanity than I do. More trust that good will prevail. That the world will ultimately tilt toward justice. How could I ever be mad at him for being so foolishly in love with humanity?"

Tears are streaming down both our faces, but Naima doesn't seem to notice she's crying. She turns back toward the crowd, seeming to have grown taller. "Many of you may also know me from the protests I've been leading at Braxton over the past few weeks. Thanks to Dr. Henley, this peaceful demonstration, which at its height included a whopping ten students, has been well publicized. But less well-known is why I've been protesting. The real reason why.

"Activist and scholar Angela Davis once said, 'I am no longer accepting the things I cannot change. I am changing the things I cannot accept.' I saw that quote for the first time when I was just seven years old and accidentally watched protests on TV for Sandra Bland. I didn't know what those words meant at the time, but somehow I knew I would never be the same again.

"A few years later, I watched my father be beaten nearly to death by the police for carrying the same spirit as those words. For daring to push for change in a world that needs it desperately. And the media and our justice system said he was lying. That the blood rushing from his head, spilling out on the sidewalk, was a lie. That the weeks he spent in the hospital were a lie. Since then, I have tried to play an active part in standing up for things I believe in. Things like history, truth, and equality. Which is why I began my protest—because I saw things happening that I cannot accept.

"One of the greatest gifts of the human experience is our ability to learn from one another, to grow and evolve from perspectives different from our own. It's through this exchange of ideas that we become better neighbors, classmates, co-workers, friends, and family. It's this kind of learning that Ms. Hunt and her books were fostering. I saw it in myself and other members of the Mark Twain Creative Writing Program.

"Through those books, we navigated the troubles of our world, created new friendships based on our previously unknown similarities, and grew as individuals. Firing Ms. Hunt and banning those books were actions that denied this school and its students the opportunity to become something more—something better.

"But this school doesn't just have a responsibility to be better for some of its students—it has a duty to be better for all of us. As a student of Braxton Academy, I'm aware that my parents' money matters, since the school is glad to take it. But *I* should matter. My *voice* should matter. My *experiences* should matter. The same goes for my fellow marginalized classmates. Our education should reflect the diversity of our experiences, offering us a chance to see the world through each other's eyes. Anything less than that is a failure.

"Not just a failure for students who happen to be Black, brown, queer, or disabled. But for students like Matthew. Because his uncle and Dr. Henley are right; he is a victim. A victim of the hatred they taught him. Just as they are victims of the hatred *they* were taught. That's how hatred works; it's a fire that doesn't stop burning until it consumes everything—even the people who started it.

"Matthew will thankfully survive, and maybe he'll be arrested for his actions that day or maybe he won't. But either way, he'll never be the same. Neither will this school. Neither will I.

"But in some ways, that's a good thing. Because we need to not be the same anymore. It shouldn't take horrific acts of violence, or the firing of talented teachers, or the banning of books to make us realize we need to change.

"My hope is that the board members won't hide from the power of literature and honest dialogue that will help us change. That will help put out the fires of hatred. Thank you."

The applause after Naima's speech isn't just loud—it's a thunderous affirmation that rattles the podium and shakes the leaves on the trees. It's a sound that feels like truth finally punching its way through a wall of stubborn lies. Even a few of the people who came here waving signs for the other side are clapping now.

Naima, her eyes glistening with the determination of a warrior, walks back to us, to our little island of change. She slides in next to me, her smile finding mine.

As the commotion settles like dust after a storm, an older white lady separates from the group of trustees and takes the stage. Her hair is silver, her back straight, and her eyes are clear as she surveys us all.

"Hello, everyone. My name is Michelle Stanton. Some of you may know my niece Laura Wong-Stanton. She couldn't be here tonight, as her ex-boyfriend Matthew is currently in the hospital and she is with him. Anyway, I have the honor of serving as the president of the board of trustees for Braxton Academy."

She pauses, letting her gaze sweep over the crowd, making sure she has the attention of every last person. I knew Laura's aunt went here, but I didn't know she was on the board, let alone the president.

"I'd like to start by thanking Miss Johnson for her brave and powerful words. Naima, you are a true credit to this school."

I reach for Naima's hand—then start to draw back, afraid it's too much too soon. But she grabs my fingers and doesn't let go.

"My mother was the first woman to be allowed to attend Braxton, in 1941," Ms. Stanton continues, her voice tinged with pride. "A time when this institution stood on the precipice of change, much as it does today. The impassioned speech by Miss Johnson and the turnout of voices we have witnessed this afternoon have reminded me not only of Braxton's historic desire to stand on the right side of history but also of its duty to point generations in that direction."

She takes a moment to let that all sink in.

"Thus it is clear to me and to the rest of the board that we must amend this school's recent failings. Though the road will be a long one, it is a road we are committed to traveling. We must try our best to do right by Ms. Hunt and by the marginalized members of our student body . . . if they will allow us."

The crowd here for the other side has been thinning out since Mr. Martinez's speech, so what was once a hurricane of shouts is now a sprinkle of disapproval and murmurs. But everyone still here is anxious with anticipation about what comes next.

"That making of amends starts today, with the immediate termination of Dean Carol Blackburn and newly appointed English chair, Kyle Richmond," Ms. Stanton declares. "Their actions, which have stoked the fires that led to the violent attack at Braxton, cannot and will not be tolerated."

I can't believe what I'm hearing. And if the expressions on Naima's and Luis's faces are any indication, neither can they.

"We will take additional steps to address our shortcomings and to ensure that the voices of *all* students are heard and valued. This is our promise. This is our commitment to change."

With that, she steps back from the podium, her statement hanging in the air, signaling a new beginning for Braxton Academy.

And then, as if the reality of Ms. Stanton's words finally sinks in, the crowd around us explodes with euphoria. People whoop and cheer and laugh and hug. The news cameras circle, trying to capture the joy. It's the kind of moment that clings to memory, carving a piece of time that seems as if it will live forever.

I feel my heart beating in my chest, a drum, a signal, calling my community to me. Luis, Naima and her parents, my mom, Ms. Hunt, Mrs. Wright, Big Teak, Tommy, and so many others all reach me, and without a word our arms open wide, and we wrap one another. Our bodies tremble with the warmth of a battle fought and a victory hard earned. Our hug is a fortress, a temple, a promise.

My cheeks glisten with tears that can only come from a well deep inside, a well of pure, unrivaled joy. My tears are contagious. They feed the fire that Naima sparked within everyone, a fire in our bellies that thrives on hope and love and growth. Our eyes are damp, our cheeks wet. Our tears tell a story, a story of nights spent worrying, of days spent fighting, of a love so deep — for craft, for progress, for the words and worlds that are so often erased. Our tears are a language, telling us we've done something right, telling us that sometimes the world cracks open, and through those cracks, light pours in.

There are so many unknowns looming ahead of us. Will Braxton sustain a commitment to real change, or will this be just another short-lived trend, another empty promise to those of us whose ancestors' ears rang with similar promises? What does the future hold for me and Naima, for me and Luis? Will I get into a good school — or be able to afford it? Will I ever play ball again, even if it's not at the same level? Will my mom and I continue leaning in to becoming better, stronger, developing a relationship we can both be proud of?

Will this all one day seem like a distant, hazy dream?

I can't predict the future. What I do know is that the heartbeat of progress is the ability to embrace your victories, the moments that remind you to keep pushing. Which is why I'll live fully in the now. Standing here, in the middle of what feels like a battlefield turned into a garden, letting myself feel it all: the surprise, the relief, the old ache of losing my dad, the inevitability of tomorrow's hurt over losing Grandma Alice, and the absolute beauty of being here with these people. *My* people.

And as they hold me, and I hold them, it's enough. We have everything we need right here.

Acknowledgments

For Grandmommy, who gave me my first pen and paper. You showed me how *love* is a verb, something lived out loud and in the margins. Every word I write is just another way of trying to be better, the way you taught me.

To my mother, whose laughter I carry in my bones, whose stubbornness I carry in my breath, and who calls to me in the quiet moments between chaos. We may walk different paths, but I can never deny how much of me is you.

To Kaylan: thank you for being not just an editor but also a copilot on journeys neither of us could have foreseen. There are destinations I never would have reached without you—each page, each line, a new shore we discovered together.

To Black literature: I owe a debt too vast to name. You have been the keeper of our stories, the architect of our dreams, the record of our survival. Baldwin, Morrison, Hughes, and Hurston—you spoke with tongues dipped in the ink of struggle and triumph, your words carving paths where none existed. You stretched the skin of our history over pages, made every syllable a pulse, a rhythm, a heartbeat.

* * *

To the young people who are forced to move like whispers through the halls, who have perfected the art of smallness so no one notices their joy, their ache—I see you. I know how love can feel like an impossible thing, like something only other people deserve but not you. Not in this body, not in this life. You think there's a code to crack, a better version of yourself you need to become, so maybe someone will finally hold you right. But listen to me: You don't need to be fixed, bent, or unbent. You don't need to shrink or soften your edges.

The world might tell you that you are too Black, too queer, too disabled, too immigrant, too strange, too loud, too hurt, too much for its liking, but I'm here to remind you: The way you exist, every glittering facet of your being, is beautiful. You, just as you are, are loved beyond the limits of this moment, beyond the sting of rejection, beyond the lonely places you've been told to hide.

You are a poem, meant not to be deciphered but felt. Let the world catch up to you.

I see you, and I love you.